FLYKILLER

FLYKILLER

J. ROBERT JANES

ORION

First published in Great Britain in 2002 by Orion Books
an imprint of The Orion Publishing Group
Orion House, 5 Upper St Martin's Lane, London WC2H 9EA

A CIP catalogue record for this book
is available from the British Library

ISBN (hardback) 0 57507 211 3
ISBN (trade paperback) 0 57507 212 1

Typeset in Minion by
Deltatype Ltd, Birkenhead, Merseyside

Printed and bound in Great Britain by
Clays Ltd, St Ives plc

This is for Frances Hanna, of Acacia House, my agent of a good many years, who has persevered in spite of all my uncertainties. It is also for her husband, Bill, whom I first met nearly thirty years ago and who later became my editor on *The Alice Factor*. Both are very dedicated people in an age when such an attribute is often so hard to find.

To each a moment, let time alone decide.

Acknowledgements

All of the novels in the St-Cyr–Kohler series incorporate a few words and brief passages of French or German. Dr Dennis Essar of Brock University very kindly assisted with the French, as did the artist Pierrette Laroche, while Professor Don MacRae, of Germanic and Slavic Studies at Brock, helped with the German.

A very special thanks must also be extended to Joel and Laurence Sherman, of Nat Sherman Tobacconists, 500 Fifth Avenue, New York, for their very kind and patient answers to my queries about cigars and for permission to use some of the Sherman brand names in a historical sense.

Should there be any errors, however, they are my own. For these I apologize but hope there are none.

Author's Note

Flykiller is a work of fiction in which actual places and times are used but altered as appropriate. As with the other St–Cyr–Kohler novels, the names of real persons appear for historical authenticity, though all are deceased and the story makes of them what it demands. I do not condone what happened during these times, I abhor it. But during the Occupation of France the everyday crimes of murder and arson continued to be committed, and I merely ask by whom and how were they solved.

1

Ruefully the line, which stretched alongside the waiting train, advanced one footstep: bundled-up, grey travellers in all but complete darkness, colds, coughs – sneezes – and, under a dim blue wash of light, two railed walkways below a distant signboard that read in heavy black letters on white: HALT! DEMARKATIONS-LINIE, and in very polite but much smaller French, *Êtes-vous en règle?* Are your papers in order?

Hermann, as usual, thought it a great joke. His partner would be scrutinized, accosted, searched, perhaps even roughed up, simply because he was French and the boys on duty hated *Schweinebullen* more than anything else but dared not touch their own cops!

'Relax. It'll go easy this time. I can tell,' confided Kohler. 'Just act normal and *don't* get hot under the collar.'

'It's too cold for that. It's snowing heavily, or hadn't you noticed?'

Emptied out of the train from Paris, Louis wasn't happy. It was Thursday, 4 February 1943 – 2.47 a.m. Berlin Time, 1.47 the old time. Ever since 11 November last, when the Wehrmacht had moved into the South in response to massive Allied landings in North Africa, the whole of France had been occupied, yet still there was this wait, this frontier between what had since June 1940 been the *zone occupée* and the *zone libre*. Here, too, at Moulins, some fifty-five kilometres by road to the north of Vichy, the international spa that had become the capital.

'Did you bring your vaccination certificates?'

'*And* my Great War military demobilization, my ration card

and tickets, residence card, *carte d'identité*, Sûreté ID, the letter from Gestapo Boemelburg – from your chief, not mine – authorizing the visit. My *Ausweis* – my *laissez-passer* – my last tax declaration, and yes a thousand times, my letter exempting me from three years of forced labour in your glorious Third Reich because I work in a reserved job and am considered necessary, though I cannot for the life of me understand this since no one among the higher-ups cares a fig about common crime or that hardened criminals freely walk the streets because the SS and Gestapo employ them and have given them guns!'

'*Gut.* I'm glad you've finally got that off your chest. Now be quiet. Leave it all to me. This one won't understand a word of French, so don't even try it.'

'*Name?*' demanded the portly Feldwebel, a grey blob with sickly blue-washed bristles under a pulled-down cap, the greatcoat collar up and a scarf knotted tightly around the throat. Leather gloves – real leather! – thumbed the crushed fistful of carefully cared-for papers.

'St-Cyr. Sûreté.'

'*Mein Herr*, that is not complete,' grunted the staff sergeant, his eyes straying from the torchlit identity card.

Nom de Jésus-Christ, must God prolong the torture? 'Jean-Louis St-Cyr, Oberdetektiv der Sûreté Nationale.'

'Age?'

'We've a murder investigation in Vichy. It's urgent we get there.'

'It can wait.'

'Murder never does!'

'Easy, Louis. Just go easy.'

'Hermann, the humiliation I am suffering after two and a half years of this sort of thing has at last frayed my nerves!'

'*Dummkopf*, just give him your age.'

'Fifty-two.'

'Hair?' asked the Feldwebel, still studying the card.

'Brown.'

'Eyes?'

2

'Brown. Nose normal. Look, *mein lieber* General, would I attempt to legally cross the Demarcation Line between two now fully occupied zones if my nose were that of a communist, a Gypsy, a *résistant* – a *terrorist* – or even some other *Rassenverfolgte*, some racially undesirable person, and I knew exactly what would happen to me if caught?'

'Nose?'

'Normal, but broken twice – no, three times, though years ago.'

'He was a boxer at the police academy.'

'Hermann, who the hell asked you to interfere?'

'*Bitte*, Herr Oberdetektiv St-Cyr. *Diese Papiere sind nicht gültig.*'

Not good ... '*Ach! was sagen sie?*' What are you saying? 'They're perfectly in order,' shrilled St-Cyr.

'Argue if you wish.'

Two corporals with unslung Schmeissers leaped to assist.

'Hermann ...'

Kohler was let through with a crash of heels, a curt salute and a, 'Pass, Herr Detektiv Aufsichtsbeamter. This one must, unfortunately, be detained.'

'Louis, I'll wait in the barracks.'

'You do that. Enjoy the stove, the coffee and outlawed croissants but ask for real jam not that crap we French have had to become accustomed to!'

Oh-oh. 'Louis, I'll go with you. I think that's what he wants.'

'*Gut! Mein Partner* finally realizes what is required of him!'

'I knew it all the time.'

'You didn't. You were simply enjoying my predicament!'

'Then you tell me who those three are who've been waiting all this time for a quiet word?'

They were standing outside the barracks, standing side by side like a little row of increasingly broad-shouldered, overcoated and fedora-ed set of steps. 'Bousquet is the middle one. The others I don't recognize.'

3

'The shorter, thinner one will reluctantly tell us who he is; the taller, bigger one will wish to remain nameless.'

French, then, and Gestapo. Occupied and Occupier, with the Préfet of France as the cement between them.

'Things must be serious,' confided Kohler.

'Aren't they always?'

Hermann had never met René Bousquet, but then the partnership didn't move in exactly the same circles. 'Monsieur le Secrétaire Général,' said St-Cyr, convivially swallowing pride and extending a hand, but with a crushing lump in the throat, for this one had already become a legend.

'Chief Inspector, and Detektiv Aufsichtsbeamter Kohler, it's good of you to have come on such short notice.'

'And of you to have waited out here half the night,' countered Kohler in French.

These two had a reputation. 'We've been warm and you haven't,' chuckled Bousquet. 'But, please, we must still stamp the feet until your suitcases have been cleared through customs. No currency you've agreed to pass on for friends in the north, eh?' he quipped. 'No letters to post?'

The pre-printed postcards, with their word gaps to fill in and words to cross out or use, were still mandatory.

'Not even a train novel,' snorted Kohler. 'No British detective novels or spy thrillers. Not even any chicory. No time to get them, eh, Louis?'

A huge, illicit trade in Belgian chicory existed on the *marché noir*, the black market. The number one coffee substitute and better than cash! 'Just a kilo of dried horse chestnuts,' offered St-Cyr drolly. 'For personal use – it's an old Russian remedy for aching joints, Secrétaire. You boil them until soft, then mash them up before spreading the poultice on a towel and wrapping the inflicted joint. My left knee. An old wound from the Great War.'

Horse chestnuts! St-Cyr was known to have a White Russian girlfriend in Paris, a very popular chanteuse, Gabrielle Arcuri, hence the remedy! 'Then perhaps you'll have time for the thermal baths.'

'Are they still open?'

'A select few.'

Cigarettes were offered and accepted and why not, wondered Kohler, with tobacco in such short supply, and certainly Bousquet didn't know it wasn't Louis's left knee but that of his partner! Only when the flame of a decently fuelled lighter was extended did the Secrétaire confide, 'Monsieur de Fleury, Inspecteur des Finances, felt it might be useful for him to join us, since the latest victim was his mistress.'

The gloved hand was cold and stiffly formal. 'Inspectors,' muttered de Fleury uncomfortably, 'whatever you wish to know from me I will gladly confide but please, you must be discreet. My wife and family . . . My mother . . .'

'Of course,' said St-Cyr with a dismissive wave of his cigarette. 'Please don't give it another thought.'

The third man, the taller one, had still not said a thing or come forward, in any way. Darkness clung to him like a second overcoat. Beneath the pulled-down snap-brim, a watchful gaze took in everything from behind rimless glasses.

Kohler shuddered inwardly. He knew that look only too well, as would Louis. It was one of ruthless assessment chilled by a total lack of conscience, and it said, Don't even wonder who I am. Just understand that I am here.

'Ah!' exclaimed Bousquet. 'Your bags have been cleared. Gentlemen, the car. We can talk en route and I will fill you in as best I can.'

'Céline Dupuis née Armand,' mused Louis, pausing as he always did over the victim's name. Kohler knew his partner would be thinking of the girl's family and of her past – he'd be letting his imagination run free, the cinematographer within him probing that name for everything he could dredge, savouring it, too, as a connoisseur would.

'Married, but a widow as of June 1940 and three days before

the Maréchal's radio broadcast to the nation on the 17th,' said Bousquet, who was sitting in the back of the car next to Louis, with the nameless one on his left.

' "It is with a heavy heart, I tell you today that it is necessary to stop the fighting," ' said St-Cyr, quoting the Maréchal and remembering the tears he, himself, had shed at the news. 'And then on the 20th, "We shall learn our lesson from the lost battles." What lesson, I wonder? Any children?' he demanded harshly.

'A daughter, age four and a half, domiciled with the victim's parents,' answered Bousquet – this one had had it all memorized, thought Kohler. Préfets weren't normally good at such things. They were friends of friends in high places and had been chosen so as to keep the existing hierarchy in power, and were either reasonable or abysmal at police work and the same at what they were supposed to do.

But not René Bousquet, age thirty-three and the youngest secrétaire général, probably, in the past two hundred years. 'Brilliant,' some said; 'Exceptional,' others. 'A man we can trust,' Himmler, head of the SS and Gestapo, had enthused. 'Our precious collaborator.'

'Age: twenty-eight, therefore pregnant at twenty-three,' Louis went on, knowing exactly what his partner had been thinking. 'Was it love? I ask simply so as to know the victim better.'

'Love,' grunted Bousquet. 'When word came through that her husband had been killed, she tried to join him and very nearly succeeded. Aspirins, I believe, but now they are in such short supply one never hears of similar attempts.'

'And since then?' asked Louis, using his sternest Sûreté voice.

'Back to dancing. A contract to work in Vichy at the Théâtre du Casino and other places and to teach part-time at the ballet school.'

Teaching the offspring of the elite? wondered Kohler, mentally making a note of it. Everyone was smoking Gitanes, the tobacco black and strong. De Fleury was squeezed between himself and the driver, chain-smoking and nervous as hell. The road ahead wasn't good. Visibility was down to thirty metres, if that. Snow everywhere and *Ach!* a Schmeisser on the floor at his feet. Had they been expecting trouble? The son of a bitch behind the wheel had half his gaze on the road and the other half on the woods and fields. 'Want me to drive?' he asked, implying, Would it help?

'Georges is good at his job, Inspector,' chuckled Bousquet knowingly. 'When a man is so skilled, we like to leave him there but increase his wages.'

Thermoses of coffee, laced with marc, had been provided, sandwiches too, but the Delahaye was so crowded it was hard to manoeuvre.

'Nationality: French,' went on Louis, scanning the *carte d'identité* under blue-blinkered torchlight, having lowered it to his knees to help hide the light. 'Born: 10 April 1915, Paris, Hermann. Monsieur l'Inspecteur des Finances, how old are you, please?'

The cigarette de Fleury had been smoking fell to his overcoat lap and was hastily brushed to the floor with a muted *'Merde!* Fifty-six.'

'And twice her age, Louis,' snorted Kohler. 'Do all of Pétain's top-ranking civil servants go for girls half their ages?'

Hermann, who was the same age as de Fleury, lived with two women, one of whom was twenty-two, but no matter. The Maréchal Pétain had a lifelong history of just such affairs, having married one of the women in 1920 when she was forty-three and divorced, and he had reached the less-than-tender age of sixty-four, but having also bounced her on his knee in 1881 when she'd been four years old. *Un homme,* then, with a long memory and utter patience. Thirty-nine years of it!

'Inspector, could we not stick to the matter at hand?' muttered Bousquet testily.

It's coming now, thought Kohler, and smiled inwardly as Louis said the inevitable: 'All things are of interest in murder, Secrétaire. The victim's family and little daughter live at 60 rue Lhomond. That is almost halfway between the Jardin du Luxembourg and Jardin des Plantes. The house will overlook place Lucien-Herr which divides the upmarket neighbourhood of the Panthéon from that of the little shopkeepers and working-class people to the east along the rue Mouffetard and other such streets, and it implies our Madame Dupuis was well educated. Was she a good conversationalist, Monsieur de Fleury?'

'*Jésus, merde alors,* Jean-Louis, can you not let me fill you in? Me, *mon ami*! Your secrétaire général.'

'Please, first his answer. We need everything. It's best my partner and I get it clear right away. The coffee is excellent, by the way, and most appreciated. *Merci*.'

Ah damn, thought Honoré de Fleury. 'Céline was a very quick-witted girl – marvellously so, at times, and knowledgeable about many things. Birds – pheasants, guinea ... Ah! I go on. Music ...'

'Operettas?'

'Jean-Louis ...'

'Please, another moment.' Birds ... why had de Fleury cut himself off like that? 'Monsieur ...?'

'Musicals, Inspector,' snapped de Fleury. 'Cabaret things and yes, operettas, but much, much more. Chopin, Debussy – she played the piano beautifully.'

'At private dinner parties?'

'Yes,' came the defeated reply as Hermann found the Inspector of Finances another cigarette and lit it for him at a bend in the road, a tunnel through tall plane trees whose mottled bark caught the blue, slit-eyed light from the headlamps, momentarily distracting their driver.

'Place of residence: Hôtel d'Allier, on the rue des Primevères in Vichy,' went on Louis. 'That's just upstream of the Boutiron Bridge, is it not, Secrétaire?'

'If you know, why ask?'

'Was the ID found on her person, or was she so well known no one had to ask who she was and it was only later taken from her room or handbag, or both?'

'In short, tell us who found her, where she was found, how she was killed, and particularly,' demanded Kohler, 'why the hell her body was where it was.'

'The Hall des Sources,' grated Bousquet with an exasperated sigh. 'Early yesterday morning.'

'Naked?' demanded Hermann, not waiting for the other answers.

'Clothed in a nightgown I had bought her, Inspector,' confessed de Fleury. 'White silk with a delicate décolletage of Auvergne lace.'

'It's winter,' grumbled Louis. 'You've not mentioned an overcoat, a warm dress, boots, or a scarf and gloves. Therefore she was either taken to this place as found, or went there freely and then put the nightgown on, after first undressing.'

'Inspectors ... Inspectors, *mon Dieu*, that is why we wished to speak to you in private,' sighed Bousquet. 'The Hall des Sources is all but adjacent to the Hôtel du Parc. Footprints in the snow – a set clearly from her boots – suggest that Céline Dupuis was taken from the Hôtel du Parc by at least one other person. Jean-Louis, you've had experience at this sort of thing. In 1938, as an associate of the IKPK, you worked closely with Gestapo Boemelburg on the visit to France of King George VI and his Queen.'

'The Blum Government were worried about an assassination, yes,' conceded St-Cyr. 'The Internationalen Kriminalpolizeilichen Kommission's* Vienna office were all aflutter and no doubt the Gestapo used the visit to gain further insight into the workings of our Sûreté. But ... but, Secrétaire, are you suggesting there is a plot to assassinate the Maréchal?'

Who has a bedroom and adjoining office in the Hôtel du Parc and loves the ladies! snorted Kohler inwardly. 'And if so, please tell us why the mistress of this one was in her nightgown and knocking on that one's door?'

'And, please, where were the guards that normally patrol those corridors?'

* The forerunner of Interpol.

9

These two ... Why the hell had the Premier had to ask for them, why not others who would be tractable? demanded Bousquet silently. He would ignore St-Cyr's question and tell them as little as possible. Yes, that would be best! 'We French are no innocents when it comes to assassinations, are we? Admiral Darlan, only last Christmas Eve in Algiers. Marx Dormoy, the Popular Front's ex-minister, on 26 July 1941, and exactly one month later, an attempt was made on Monsieur Laval himself.'

'On 27 August,' muttered Louis. 'If I understand the matter correctly, Secrétaire, though out of office but still fulfilling some state functions, Monsieur Laval had felt there might be trouble and hadn't really wanted to present the flag to the first contingent of the Légion des Volontaires Français contre le Bolchévisme.'

French volunteers who willingly joined the Wehrmacht on the Russian Front! 'Both he and Marcel Déat were wounded,' said Kohler, picking up the thread. 'Laval so seriously that a weaker man would have died.'

'The bullet in the shoulder was removed without complications,' confided Bousquet, 'but the other one had lodged so closely to the heart that the chief surgeon felt it necessary to leave it and only repair what damage he could.' This information was not well known.

'A 6.35 millimetre and lodged an equal distance,' said St-Cyr. 'Pneumonia set in, and for days Monsieur Laval's temperature hovered at around 40 degrees Celsius (104 degrees Fahrenheit).'

These two had done their homework, so good, yes, good! thought Bousquet. 'Our Premier and Marcel Déat revealed considerable understanding of the nation's psyche when they begged the Maréchal to show clemency and keep the boy's head from the breadbasket.'

The guillotine ... 'Paul Collette, age twenty-one and a former seaman from Caen who would otherwise have made a beautiful martyr,' said Kohler flatly. 'And now you're telling us there's a plot to assassinate the Maréchal Pétain.'

Out of the darkness of his little corner, the nameless one

tonelessly said, 'Our Government does not want this to happen, Kohler, and you are to see that it doesn't.'

Scheisse! 'Or else?'

'Just make certain you understand that we are all treading on broken glass these days,' grunted Bousquet. 'The hills of the Auvergne may well be a haven to terrorists.'

'But ... but if what little you've told us so far is true, Secrétaire, these terrorists, on being interrupted during an attempt on the Maréchal's life, took the girl from outside his door to silence her for fear of their being identified.'

'That is correct – at least, it is what I suspect must have happened, and that is why Monsieur Laval has asked for you both.'

' "Flykiller slays mistress of high-ranking Government employee," ' quoted Kohler, remembering the telex Laval had sent to Gestapo Boemelburg in Paris. 'Why "flies"?'

'An assassin!' swore Bousquet angrily. 'Can you not listen?'

'But ... but a conclusion, Secrétaire, for which you have as yet offered no proof,' countered Louis, deliberately baiting him.

'Only three corpses, idiot! The first two are being kept at the morgue in spite of the pleas of relatives for their release; the latest one is just as she was found and nothing – I repeat, nothing – has been touched. Not in her room at the Hôtel d'Allier, except for her *carte d'identité* which I myself removed, and not at the crime scene.'

'Good, that's as it should be,' said Louis. 'But, then, perhaps before we view the victim, Monsieur de Fleury would enlighten us as to why, since she was his mistress, Madame Dupuis was knocking at the great one's door? And on what day and at what time, please?'

'Céline didn't want to do it but ... but I begged her to, Inspector. The Maréchal, he has a passion for beautiful young women. He's old – oh *bien sûr* – but age does not necessarily make a glacier of the urges.'

'And you were pimping for him?' blurted Kohler, startled by the admission.

11

'A small favour,' muttered Bousquet acidly.

'One I felt I could no longer refuse,' de Fleury added.

'And at what time, then, Monsieur de Fleury, was he to have had his little moment?' asked Louis.

'Tuesday night, at ... at 9.40. I ... I dropped her off outside the hotel. She ... she was wearing her overcoat, scarf and beret, her gloves too. These things, they ... they have not as yet been found.'

Not found. 'Height: 170 centimetres, Hermann (five feet seven inches); hair: blonde; eyes: blue; particular signs: none; nose: straight and average – normal, if you wish. Face: oval but the side profile doesn't really do her justice. A very handsome young woman, Monsieur de Fleury. Stunning, I should think – you do like the pretty ones, don't you? Complexion: pale.'

St-Cyr tapped his partner on the shoulder and passed both torch and identity card to him. 'A young widow, *mon vieux*. A working girl with a child to support who is no older than the one the Maréchal once bounced on his knee. Madame Pétain is known to be a very jealous and spiteful woman.'

'Idiot, Madame Pétain is well aware of the Maréchal's *infidélités!*' spat Bousquet.

'And you are angry with me, Secrétaire, when calmness is called for.'

'Truncheon! Just stick to what you've been told to do and leave Madame Pétain out of things. The fewer who know of this the better!'

Just before St-Germain-des-Fossés they stopped at the side of the road for a piss. Kohler stood upwind of de Fleury. 'Was she good in bed?' he asked companionably.

'Inspector, you're splashing my trousers.'

'Oh, sorry. Did she enjoy sex, seeing as she'd tried to kill herself at the loss of her husband?'

'*Salaud!* How dare you?'

'Calm down and tell me exactly how faithful a mistress was she?'

'We were going to get married. I was going to divorce my wife when . . . when it became possible.'

Divorce had all but been outlawed by Vichy. 'Yet you asked her to service another?'

'I had to! I didn't know she'd be killed! How could I have?'

'Just who else knew what you were up to?'

'*Merde alors*, do you not take the hint Monsieur le Secrétaire has given? Dr Ménétrel, the Maréchal's personal physician and confidant. His personal secretary.'

'And Ménétrel okayed the session?'

'Céline was not some cheap *putain*, damn you!' Tears fell and were agitatedly wiped away with the fingers. 'He gave his blessing. He said it was exactly what the Maréchal needed to restore faith in himself during such a difficult time and that . . . that Céline would be handsomely rewarded as would . . . as would I myself.'

'Then you were pimping and that's an indictable offence, unless you followed Vichy's latest ordinance on it to the letter. Oh don't worry, *mon fin*, we'll be discreet but if you've lied to me and not told us everything, you'd better watch out.'

'She was a dancer. You must know what such women are like!'

'And that bit about your marrying her?'

Would this Gestapo find out everything? 'It . . . it wasn't possible. I couldn't have done so and she must have been well aware of this yet we spoke of it as if there was no impediment. A little game we played.'

How nice of him, but one must hold the door open so as to grab a breath of air. It took all types, thought Kohler, and the arrogance of top civil servants, though well known the world over, was legendary in France.

Had all of what had been felt necessary been said? wondered St-Cyr. The engine throbbed, the road climbed. Frost clung closely, snow was everywhere and darkness lay deep among the trunks and bracken.

For some time now each of them had withdrawn into private thoughts. Hermann, never one to keep still or silent unless

13

necessary, had taken to staring out his side window but hadn't bothered to clear the frost from it. Was he thinking of his little Giselle and his Oona, was he worrying, as he often did these days, that when the Allies invaded, as they surely must, his lady-loves would be caught up in things and blamed for sleeping with the enemy, with himself? Was he still trying to figure out a way to get them false papers and to safety in Spain or Portugal?

René Bousquet would also be on Hermann's mind, for here, beside his partner, was the man who had met with Reinhard Heydrich and others of the SS at the Ritz in Paris, on 5 May of last year. Here was the one who had convinced Karl Albrecht Oberg, the 'Butcher of Poland' and Höherer SS und Polizeiführer of France, not to take over the French police but to let him handle things.

'The Marseillais has a reputation as a practical joker, Secrétaire. He calls a tender shower of rain a tempest, a lost shirt from the laundry line an armed robbery in which the wife and daughters were strip-searched and their virtue plundered. But he has an even more significant reputation, one for vengeance. Has your suggestion of an attempted assassination been prompted at all by fear of repercussions over what the first *arrondissement* suffered? I ask simply because I must.'

The Vieux Port de Marseille had been a rat's nest of steep and narrow streets, the home of prostitutes, pimps and gangsters! 'We did what we had to do.'

A month ago, on 3 January, German security forces had raided a *maison de passe*, one of those seedy, walk-in hotels where prostitutes took their clients for a little moment or an hour or two and then left. Suspecting to find *résistants* and Wehrmacht deserters hiding out and fast asleep, there had been an exchange of fire in which several on both sides had been killed or wounded. Hitler, in a rage on hearing of it, and having at that time all but suffered the final loss of the 6th Army at Stalingrad, had demanded the levelling of the whole of the first *arrondissement* and deportation of 50,000 of its citizens to camps in the east. Bousquet and Lemoine, the regional préfet, had managed to convince Oberg that French police should do the job, and at 3 a.m. on the night of the 13th–14th, 30,000 residents, having been told they had but a few hours to vacate their homes, had moved out. Their papers were all checked, but far fewer *résistants* and deserters than anticipated had been arrested and the homeless citizens, for want of anything better, had been shunted off to camps at Fréjus and Compiègne, where they still resided and would for as long as it took to free the country. Then on 15 January, Wehrmacht engineers had begun to dynamite every building – tenement houses, warehouses, churches, loading docks and port machinery – and had, by the 24th, even sent 173 vessels to the bottom thus unintentionally blocking the harbour for months.

'The Führer was appeased,' exhaled Bousquet exasperatedly. 'Twenty thousand were saved and the other thirty thousand kept in France and not deported.'

'But has this event anything to do with the suspected attempt on the Maréchal's life?'

'Has the *Grande Rafle* also anything to do with it, eh? Come, come, Jean-Louis, let us get things out in the open.'

'That, too, then.'

'I had no choice. Too much would have been lost. We gained. In all such things there are the pluses and minuses. Be glad you don't have to make such decisions.'

'I am.'

Doucement, Louis, go easy, thought Kohler, alarmed at the exchange. On 16–17 July of last year Bousquet and the préfet of Paris had convinced Oberg and Heydrich that French police, under French direction, could handle things. Nine thousand Paris police had surrounded five *arrondissements* in the dead of night during what had since come to be known as the Great Roundup. They had then arrested 12,000 terrified men, women and children and had locked them up in the Vélodrome d'Hiver, the cycling arena, for eight days without sufficient water, food or toilet facilities – Jews that had then been deported by rail in cattle trucks; the children kept in France for a little longer and then sent on as well, but not knowing where to or why they had been taken from their parents or whether they would ever see them again.

Louis and he had been away from the city at the time, thank God, but since then Louis had pieced together a record of the tragedy that he intended to pass on to the Résistance for the day of reckoning that would surely come.

'Just do as you've been told, Jean-Louis,' grunted Bousquet. 'Don't let your brand of patriotism interfere.'

Only one of those Paris *flics* had resigned and refused to take part. Only one, Kohler told himself, but, to be fair, a good many of them would have been too afraid to object. And orders were orders especially in a police force of 15,000, for that's what Paris had. But if the Résistance had wanted a target, then why not Bousquet himself?

On the outskirts of Vichy the car was stopped at a control by armed Wehrmacht sentries, no longer by members of the Garde Mobile de Resérve, Vichy's small paramilitary force. The latest password was demanded, as one had been since 1 July 1940 at all entrances to the town, and never mind that it was still the curfew, thought Kohler wryly. Assassination had been on the Government's mind right from the beginning!

'Spring brings the new growth; autumn the harvest,' said their driver – the only words he had spoken on the whole damned trip. Had Pétain written the thing?

With a wave, they were released, and drove into the heart of the town.

Out of the cold, the damp, the blackout and the silence, and from the deeper darkness of the covered promenade that ringed the Parc des Sources, Hermann's voice came gruffly. 'Louis, was it right of you to have told them to leave us?'

'*Merde*, Hermann. We are greeted in the small hours by a secrétaire who doesn't appreciate our little visit, but brings along the victim's supposed lover, yet fails to brief us completely and tucks in a Gestapo for good measure. Does this not make you concerned?'

16

They had been dropped off about mid-park and on the rue Président Wilson, some distance from the Hall des Sources and the Hôtel du Parc, and not at all the route the victim would have had to take. Acetylene lanterns had been provided but were, as yet, unlit.

'All right, it smells.'

No collabo and no Pétainiste either, Louis had once been a *poilu*, a soldier in the Great War at Verdun and other such places, and had, like ninety-eight per cent of his fellows and most of the nation, thought fondly of the Victor of Verdun, hailing Pétain's offer of leadership in June 1940 as a godsend to a nation in despair.

Some leader. Very quickly Louis had lost whatever respect he'd had for the Maréchal.

'Come on,' breathed Kohler. 'I guess it's this way.'

'It is, and we walk as the *curistes* – those seeking the cure – walked beneath Émile Robert's marvellous thistledown of wrought iron, which graced the Great Universal Exposition of 1890 in Paris and was moved here in 1900.'

'I can't see a hell of a lot of it. Too dark, I guess.'

'Yes! But I'm trying to remember it as I first saw it when a boy of eleven going on twelve, Hermann. In the summer of 1902 Grand-mère thought she had a load of gravel in her guts and made me accompany her. My father urged me to do it, and I could not bear having him suffer her tongue any more. Of just such things are heroes made, but look at me now. *Sacré*! My left shoe has come apart again.'

'I'll reglue it for you later.'

'That glue you bought on the *marché noir* won't be worth the lies that budding *horizontale* told you. Just because she was young and pretty and headed for a life on the streets was no reason for you to have trusted her!'

And still bitchy about Bousquet! Glue was all but impossible to find these days; shoes only more so, unless one bought the hinged, wooden-soled ones with their cloth or ersatz leather uppers. Twenty-four million pairs of the things had been sold to date in a nation of forty million, which only showed how lousy they were!

'Think of La Belle Époque,' muttered Louis, mollified somewhat by his own outbursts and wanting to be calm. 'Think of high society from 1880 until we all bid adieu to such splendour in 1914. Think of the grand hotels that were built here with their covered terraces and art nouveau ironwork and interiors, their verandas, dining rooms and atriums delicately graced by Kentia palms and other exotics. Of silk or satin gowns, jewels and sensuous perfumes, of princes, duchesses, lords and ladies – marquises, courtesans and counts.

'Then think of the hordes who followed them, especially in the twenties and thirties, Hermann. Old maids and war widows, shopkeepers, postal clerks and accountants, lawyers too, and judges and young girls of easy virtue. Gamblers also.'

'Think of a swollen liver, an attack of gout, an enlarged prostate or constant dose of the clap. And then think of guzzling or gargling that *Quatsch*, that crap! An international spa, eh?'

'But, Inspector, opera singers did it, actors and actresses too, and artists. All such believers came here for the *cocktail thérapeutique* and the baths.'

'And other things, so don't get pious. *Nom de Dieu*, Louis, will you look at that!'

They had finally reached the Hall des Sources. Under torchlight, great daggers of discoloured ice hung from the rusting, green-painted frieze. Sheets of that same ice coated the tall, arched windows as a frozen signboard above the entrance spelled it out for them: FERMÉ POUR LA SAISON.

It had been left here in July 1940, and no one in the Government had seen fit to have the sign removed!

'None of our politicals have a sense of humour, Hermann. This, too, we'd best remember.'

In addition to the Government of France, thirty-two embassies and legations had moved to Vichy in those first few months of the Occupation. Now, of course, there would be far fewer of them – cold and empty villas as of last November, but still there

18

would be the Italians and Japanese, the Hungarians and Rumanians, the Finns too, and neutrals like the Spanish, Portuguese and Swedish, thought Kohler. Could *Ausweise* for Giselle and Oona be prised out of the Swiss?

'Don't even consider it,' mused St-Cyr, having easily read his partner's mind after the two and a half years they'd spent constantly in each other's company. 'It's far too expensive a country for you. Concentrate on the murder. All things in their proper place and time. Besides, the Swiss are turning them back.'

Freeing the tall iron-and-glass doors brought only grunts and curses and then, at a sudden yank, the pungent smell of hydrogen sulphide and that of warm, wet mould.

Water dripped. Effervescing carbon dioxide hissed as it escaped, but from where? wondered Kohler. Pipes banged in protest as if throttled.

Through the pitch darkness of the hall, the beams of their torches began to pick things out. Pollarded lime trees that were dead – those palms Louis had mentioned were coated with so much ice their blade-like foliage had collapsed about the glazed jardinières of another time.

The hall must be huge and would have held five hundred or a thousand at a time. Breath billowed, and as they looked at each other and then shone their torches around and upwards, they found that the beams of light would penetrate only so far. The air was filled with vapour, grey and layered, especially when not stirred by footsteps.

'Four sources have their *buvettes* here, Hermann. Their pump kiosks. La Grande Grille, which issues at a temperature of 42.4 degrees Celsius (108.3 degrees Fahrenheit); Chomel, at 43 degrees Celsius; Lucas, at 28.1 degrees Celsius; and Parc, at 22.5 degrees Celsius (72.5 degrees Fahrenheit). Although Grand-mère should have warned me, she said, "Why not try them all, *mon petit*?" I foolishly did and spent the next twenty-four hours locating the toilets, something she probably had had in mind for me to do in any case.'

By just such little exchanges do we keep ourselves sane,

thought Kohler, dreading what they'd find. The throat probably hacked open but not before the breasts had been slashed, the womb repeatedly stabbed, the buttocks and . . . *Jésus, Jésus,* how much more of this could he stand? 'Chomel, Louis. There it is. Bousquet said we'd find her behind that counter.'

Though seen under the scanning beams of their torches, the Buvette du Chomel was much as St-Cyr first remembered it. A marvellously curved and ample art nouveau, glass-topped table, perhaps five metres by three, whose ringed ridges, atop the glass, had given the image of water flowing outwards from its source in a curved, eight-sided, glass-and-gilded, beehived dome with interlaced crown. Both the table and its source had been suffused with the soft glow of electric lights, as if shining upwards from deep underground.

Wicker-clad bottles, vacuum flasks, jugs and measured glass cups with handles were still much in evidence. Had those in their hundreds who had come to take the waters, and those who had served them from behind the enclosing counter, simply departed in haste?

'Take a little stroll, Hermann. Look for things Bousquet and whoever first found her will not have seen.'

'I'm okay. Really I am.'

'You're not and you know it!' Hermann had seen too much of death – at Verdun on 21 February 1916 when 850 German artillery pieces had suddenly opened up at dawn in a sheet of flame, his battery among them, and the flash of thunder had been heard 150 kilometres away. Death then, and later. Death, too, as a detective in the back alleys and streets of Munich, then Berlin, then Paris. Ah yes, Paris.

Céline Dupuis was but a short distance from one of the gaps in the counter. She was lying on her back, but the hips and legs were turned towards her left and that arm was stretched well above her head, as though, in her final spasm, she had sought to pull herself away from her assailant.

The coat of the nightgown was unfastened, the bloodstained

20

décolletage of antique lace clasped instinctively by a right hand that had then flattened itself and now hid the wound.

The blue eyes, their lashes long and false, were wide open and she was staring up into the light of the lantern Hermann now stubbornly held over her.

A black velvet choker encircled the slender neck; the face was not the classic oval but long and thin, the cheeks pinched even in repose, the painted lips parted, the blonde hair askew and of more than shoulder length.

'Caught between the dispensing bar and the table, Louis, but did someone pin her arms from behind as the bastard knifed her? That is a knifing. I'm certain of it.'

'But why, then, does she reach that way?'

Louis saw so much more than he did. Always he was better at it. Well, nearly so. And always one had to tone oneself up when working with him. He demanded that, but silently.

Beneath the nightgown she wore a teddy of black lace, black garters too, and black lisle stockings that reached to mid-thigh from the tops of tightly fitting, well-polished black riding boots.

'Greasepaint, heavy lipstick, mascara and the eyelashes,' grunted Kohler. 'Did she come straight from the club or theatre? If so, that "lover" of hers forgot to tell us.'

'Was she told by de Fleury to throw the nightgown on over her costume because they were late, or is this what was wanted?'

Two costumes. The first revealing the bad girl, the second for bed. 'Did he have the nightgown with him, or did she have it in her dressing room, wherever that is?'

Questions ... there were always those. 'Leave me with her now, Hermann. Please. I'll be sure to tell you what you need to know.'

'Okay, Chief, she's all yours.'

Hermann could be heard vomiting. He'd be thinking of the victim's daughter, an orphan now. He'd be wondering if he'd have to be the one to tell her what had happened.

He'd be thinking of the grandparents, too. Would they put the child into a convent school as a boarder or do the proper thing and watch over her day and night?

He'd be wondering if Giselle and Oona could help out. He was like that.

'Dead certainly for more than twenty-four hours,' sang out St-Cyr. 'Probably at about 10 p.m. Tuesday evening but the coroner can, perhaps, elaborate. A knife, I think, but must . . .'

'That goddamned tap above her feet is dripping, idiot! It's the only one in this *buvette* that is, so her killer must have cracked it open to wash off his hands and the knife.'

Looking like death itself in a greatcoat, Hermann held up the spluttering lantern. A Fritz-haired* giant under a battered grey fedora, with sagging pouches beneath pale blue eyes that seldom revealed emotion but were now filled with tears – those of rage at what he had to face; those, too, of loss. 'Easy, *mon vieux*,' breathed St-Cyr, deeply concerned about him. Too much Benzedrine to keep him going, too little sleep, alcohol whenever he could get it *and* tobacco!

The stormtrooper-like lower jaw and cheeks that needed a shave carried shrapnel scars from that other war, the brow the fresh scar of a recent bullet graze, and, from the left eye to the chin, the duelling scar of a rawhide whip the SS had used on him early last December for his insisting on the truth. Another case.

'Here, have one of these,' said St-Cyr. 'Our secrétaire was so worried he forgot to take the packet back.'

The big, raw-boned hands that had defused booby-traps and 500-kilo bombs shook as the lighter was lit. Disloyal, a lousy Gestapo to his confrères and a lampooner of the Führer and of Nazi doctrines, Hermann had become a citizen of the world long before Paris had polished him.

'A cabaret dancer, Louis. Painted fingernails, good, nice legs – was she playing at being in the seedy nightclubs of Berlin in the twenties and about to do a striptease for the Maréchal?'

* World War One slang for a German soldier.

'Or was she first to have sung for him, since he's known to love operettas and other such simple pleasures?'

'"*Patrie. Suivez-moi! Gardez votre confiance en la France éternelle,*"' quoted Kohler, imitating the high, reedy voice of Pétain. Follow me. Keep your confidence in eternal France.

'"Think upon these maxims: Pleasure lowers, joy elevates; pleasure weakens, joy gives strength." But was she to have given him pleasure, Hermann, or joy?'

'We'll have to ask him.'

'Or Dr Ménétrel who, unless I'm mistaken, initiated the little visit and put our Inspecteur des Finances in such a spot that his pension was threatened and he found he couldn't refuse.'

Ménétrel vetted nearly everything the Maréchal did or said, and thus wielded enormous power. 'Or once did,' snorted Kohler, 'seeing as Vichy no longer has the *zone libre* to govern, no longer a navy, an Army of the Armistice, her African colonies or anything else but this town and the day-to-day civil service stuff.'

'And France is now united, those in the *zone occupée* no longer envying those in the *zone libre*.'

The north and the south. 'And no longer believing in the Maréchal. Her fingers really are those of a piano player, Louis. She even wears her wedding ring like a good girl should, even though a widow.'

'I'm going to have to move her hand, Hermann.'

'The lace of the nightgown will only hide the wound, that of the teddy too.'

'Bear with me. Turn away if need be.'

Overly loud in the imagination, the breaking of rigor's stiffness at the wrist and elbow would sicken Hermann. 'There,' sighed St-Cyr. 'Forgive me, madame, but it was necessary. Hermann, have a look at these.'

Two parallel scars marred the right wrist. 'Not aspirins, then,' grunted Kohler, 'and Bousquet must have known it. There are ashes, too, Louis, from a cigar, I think, though can't be sure. Spilled down her front either before she was stabbed or during the killing. Either at the theatre or club, then, or here.'

Good for Hermann. As they fell, cigar ashes tended to smear more than cigarette ashes. There was usually more of them, too, and they were softer, sootier and greyer, especially so these days when cigarettes could be made of almost anything and cigars were all but unheard of.

Taking tweezers from a jacket pocket, Louis teased away the bloodstained severed threads. Patiently the battered brown fedora was removed to let the light shine more fully on her, then he rocked back on his heels.

'A knife, of course,' he said. 'Straight in and upwards with maximum force, the haft then lifted hard to make certain of it.'

Skin was elastic; the wound must be wider at the top than a simple entry and retrieval would leave. But *merde*, how could he remain so calm? wondered Kohler. No feelings of revulsion and loss – that horrible gut-sick emptiness – only a totally absorbed curiosity. A need to know.

'The blade was probably no more than one and a half centimetres at its widest, Hermann. A single cutting edge. She can't have moved afterwards, must have been stopped by the shock of it. Our killer knew exactly what to do. Madame Dupuis could well have lived for hours had the haft not been lifted while the blade was still deeply in her.'

'There's not a lot of blood.'

'Precisely!'

'Therefore the sac that encloses the heart . . .'

'The pericardium has been flooded.'

'Putting her into shock and stopping the heart.'

'We'll want Laloux, Hermann. As an ardent socialist with an unbridled tongue, he'll have been dismissed, but you will tell Bousquet our Félix is the only one who can be trusted to be discreet.'

The coroner. She'd voided herself, poor thing, and would probably have been ashamed of it.

'Leave me with her now, Hermann. I can't be in two places at once and need your eyes elsewhere.'

Louis would 'talk' to her. That Sûreté with the pugilist's nose,

24

bushy brown moustache, brown ox-eyes and broad brow, that somewhat portly partner of his in the open, shabby brown overcoat would be gentle, so gentle.

'One earring is missing,' he muttered, not looking up but arching the thatch of his eyebrows.

Hermann had already gone in search of it.

Beyond the circular stand-up bar of white marble, with its geometric lines and patterns in black, the stonework of the Buvette de la Grande Grille climbed into the fog.

Kohler shone the torch upwards. Four cherubs, two facing outwards, two inwards, held a flowering platform on which stood and stretched the statue of a naked girl of eighteen or so. Beautiful, graceful – athletic – the absolute picture of health, the left arm crooked above her head, the right arm bent at the waist, the thighs slender, the buttocks perfect.

Stone faces – two male, two female and mature – gazed benevolently out from around the base of this heap of pulchritude.

He shone the torch behind the bar and over the floor. Had Céline Dupuis been able to break free? he wondered. Had she tried to hide where he was now standing? Was that when she had removed the earring or simply lost it? Her left lobe hadn't been torn, so robbery couldn't have been the motive, could it? Her killer would have taken the remaining one unless interrupted.

Again he looked towards the Buvette de Chomel. Louis had put the lantern on the bar and had taken off his overcoat and scarf, but was nowhere in sight, was distant across a floor whose bluntly triangular pieces of dark grey stone, each of about five centimetres in length by half that in width, provided thousands of shallow hollows. Enough and more to hide an earring if thrown.

But why thrown? Fear of being discovered wearing them? Then why have them on if visiting the Maréchal?

Round brilliants – Jagers, or had they been Top Cape or Cape? – but worth plenty in any case.

Two stones each, the one of about two and a half carats, the other much smaller – and linked to the larger diamond by a tiny loop of gold.

But why remove it? And where, exactly, had the Maréchal's bodyguards been when all of this was happening?

Finding each tap, he felt the subterranean warmth, saw one dripping here, too, and heard the escape of effervescing bicarbonate of soda and hydrogen sulphide: 42.4 degrees Celsius, Louis had said.

In a nation where warm water was rarely if ever seen, used or felt, Kohler longed for a good soak. It would ease that right shoulder he had failed to tell Louis about, it would ease the knee those 'horse chestnuts' had really been for.

'I should have told him about the shoulder. He depends on me. He says I'm his "alter ego", whatever that is.'

Ashes had fallen on the counter, grey and soft against the polished stone. When he touched them, they smeared and he knew the girl had hidden here and then had run.

To where? he asked. Her boots would have sounded harshly on a floor that was warm in places, due to the pipes that passed beneath it.

'Louis, she got away from him,' he called out, his voice muffled by the fog and the distance.

'Track her, Hermann. The other earring has been loosened. Its disc has almost been unscrewed.'

The right earlobe was cold, the skin soft. Having gone behind her, and now kneeling near her head, St-Cyr gingerly turned the disc through the last of the threads.

Gently pulling on the larger diamond, he felt the post slip free of her ear. 'There,' he said and sighed, asking, as he held the earring to the light, 'Were you greatly troubled by having worn them, madame?'

Cartier's were at 23 place Vendôme in Paris, Van Cleef and Arpels at number 22, Chaumet at number 12. 'But Boucheron has been at number 20 since 1893 and is the favourite of the *beau monde*, and these, I am all but certain, came from their house. They would easily fetch 350,000 francs, or about £1,750 at the official rate, or 7,000 American dollars, but at least twice those amounts on the Black Bourse. Were you wearing someone's freedom? I ask simply because I must. Several do try to buy their way to Switzerland and other such places.'

If she thought anything of it, she didn't let on and this made him sigh more heavily and chide, 'You must trust me, madame. My partner and I will see that your daughter receives them, have no fear.

'A young man?' he suddenly asked, gazing down at her, she staring up at him. 'Not Honoré de Fleury, madame, but someone in the Résistance. Were you thinking of making the Maréchal a present of them in return for allowing that young man to escape and is this why you felt it best to remove them when threatened?'

Moisture seemed to well up in her eyes, brightening their blue under the lantern light. Her lips seemed to draw in a breath, her wounded chest to rise.

He would have to tell her what he knew of the diamonds. '*Blancs exceptionnels*, madame. Dancers don't wear such things when on stage – they would only be lost, *n'est-ce pas?* – so you must have put them on before you left your dressing room and Monsieur de Fleury must have seen them.

'Unless, of course, you put them on after he had let you out of his car.

'After, I think, because that one, if he'd given them to you, would not have wanted us to find them on you. They're from the Belle Époque, aren't they, and were doubtless someone's mother's or grandmother's.'

She couldn't smile but would have wanted to softly, he felt, and when he took her by the left wrist, he knew she wouldn't have minded his running a thumb over its scars. So many young women had lost their men during the Defeat, either to the grave or to POW camps in the Reich where one and a half million of them still languished in spite of all promises to repatriate them.

The scars indicated the wounds had been deep and decisive. As with the other wrist, they'd been carefully stitched so as to lessen their visibility but still she'd camouflaged them with a thin smear of greasepaint and a dusting of powder. 'You wanted to die in 1940, but now wanted very much to live. Had you found another lover, and I don't mean de Fleury?'

Her hair had been deliberately stiffened so as to accentuate the scraggly look of a loose woman. Bending closely, St-Cyr smelled it. 'Inconclusive,' he said, leaning back but still fingering it. 'Was it Dr Ménétrel who set this whole thing up and excused the guards from their duty? Come, come, madame, Monsieur de Fleury was only the go-between, the procurer, the standby, the pimp.'

Would she really have gone to bed with the Maréchal? Pétain certainly did have a legendary reputation as a *tombeur de femmes*, a Casanova. While engaged to his present and only wife, that moralizing hypocrite had carried on a torrid affair with Germaine Lubin, aged twenty-nine and singer to the troops. Madame Lubin was to have been his 'war godmother' but, unlike so many of his lovers, had apparently been reluctant to leave her husband.

'"What I love best is infantry and making love,"' sighed St-Cyr, quoting him. 'And you, I think, madame, went to him under duress but hoping perhaps to exact a promise. A little something over and above the "reward" Dr Ménétrel had so generously promised you and Monsieur de Fleury? Or were you even aware of that little arrangement?'

Vichy was a nest of vipers – the whole nation knew of this, rumour building on rumour in an age rampant with them. Ménétrel, along with Premier Laval, was known as an *éminence grise*, a grey eminence who was responsible for many of the Maréchal's mistakes and for a lot of other things.

'But he would not have spoken to you directly about this liaison with Pétain. Everything would have been done through Monsieur de Fleury and if asked, I'm sure the doctor would disclaim all knowledge of you. After all, he's a family man with a wife and three children.'

There was perfume but far too much time had elapsed since it had been applied. 'Expensive, though,' he sighed, leaning back again to gaze at her, the cameras of the mind searching out each detail. The way the killer must have yanked her nightgown open – a broken tie-string – the way the black lace showed through the white but also revealed her skin. The grey smear of the cigar ashes, the left arm stretched out above her head.

It had to be asked. 'Why, really, did you have to die? Why here of all places? And please, madame, though my partner wants to be convinced that your killer was a man, I still require further information.

'*Hermann, have you found it yet?*' he called out from behind the bar.

'NO!'

No ... No ... came the echoes.

'He will, madame, if it's here. He's like that.'

Moving the right hand back to where it had covered the wound, St-Cyr again went over the corpse. She'd been trapped at the last but could have retreated, yet hadn't taken more than a backward step or two. The killer had come in through the gap in the bar, had grabbed her by the nightgown's coat and then an arm. There'd be bruises from the fingers, scratches perhaps. Something ... They had to have something definite. The cigar ashes? he asked, but these could have been left on purpose to mislead them. *Look*, damn you, he said to himself. Do as Hermann would.

The floor was bare. Going down on his hands and knees again, he gently lifted the looseness of the nightgown away and ran a hand as far in under her as possible. 'Nothing ... There is nothing.' He was certain of it.

Only when he got to her head did he find anything. It was buried well beneath her hair.

'Ah *grâce à Dieu*, madame,' he sighed but was surprised and disturbed to see it was the back of a small separable cufflink. Rather common. Not of silver or gold but of tin-plated steel. Punched, pressed, the diameter all but that of the larger diamond, the post shaped like an inverted eggcup so that the eyelet of the cuff would be kept easily open as the cufflink's head

29

was pressed into place. Mother-of-pearl, probably. Flat and cheap and like so many, many thousands.

It could simply have been lying on the floor and could well mean nothing. The girls and women who had once dispensed the waters here had all worn grey-blue maid's uniforms whose cufflinks, if not buttons, could well have been the same.

But had Céline Dupuis caught at a woman's arm and inadvertently freed the cufflink, and, if so, where was the other half?

And wouldn't that woman have worn an overcoat, which would have got in the way, unless ... unless, of course, this had also been left elsewhere as it would have been with ... Ah *merde*, had there been blood on that blouse, had it been dumped with her ...

'The victim's overcoat, Hermann. We have to find it. Please, there may not be time. It's urgent.'

'Then go!' sang out Kohler. 'I'll join you when I've finished.'

'I'll leave you my lantern.'

'You do that.'

'The Hôtel du Parc, third floor. Perhaps a maid's closet,' said St-Cyr.

'Don't forget Ménétrel's office is also on that floor.'

Floor ... Floor ... The echoes died and Louis was gone from him. Gone, thought Kohler. *Merde*, where would this affair lead them? Into the arms of the Gestapo, the Garde Mobile, the Milice or the Résistance?

Laval had wanted Louis and him to handle the investigation; Bousquet hadn't and had been upset enough at their arrival to meet them well outside Vichy.

The Buvette Lucas was near a far corner of the Hall and when he held his lantern high, Kohler saw its light reflecting from the tall, arched windows. A simple railing of art nouveau wrought iron had separated the grilled floor and sources from the *curistes*, the long oval of the *buvette* being perhaps seven metres by four across. Again there were the hanging cups, jugs and vacuum flasks, but here two eight-sided, carved stone fountains would spill the elixir into shallow basins that encircled them and above each of these basins there were taps.

Square holes made a complete cross-hatching over the floor, a grillework that brought only dismay, for if she'd thrown the earring in there, he had little hope of finding it.

Hanging the lantern from the railing, Kohler set to work. Distances were so hard to gauge here, sounds were too flat and muted. Had she really come this way? Had she even hidden behind either of those fountains?

Ivy had at one time spilled from them to trail to the basins. The leaves were brown, the basins dry. No taps dripped. Whitish encrustations of bicarbonate of soda caught the torchlight. Again there were cigar ashes, again that sense of her having knelt or crouched and then slipped away.

Absolutely terrified and yet concerned enough about her earrings to have tried to remove them both.

Through long use and much rinsing some of the glass cups had become frosted. Sip thirty cubic centimetres twice daily, monsieur. Morning and evening before eating. Gargle if you wish, but please use the gargle-atorium or whatever they called it!

'Come on,' breathed Kohler impatiently. 'Lead me to it, madame.'

The earring was in one of the hanging cups – not near any of the gaps in the railing but midway between two of them. She'd not quite had time to remove the other one but must have stood here in the pitch darkness feverishly trying to do so.

Outside the Hall, he found where Vichy's *flics* had encircled sets of footprints with marking string. A little snow had blown over them, but one set had probably been made by her boots. And, yes, the others were not nearly so clear but held suggestions of that hinged gap, the curse of all wooden-soled shoes, since it often trapped clay and small stones and the wearer then had constantly to tap them or flex the hinge. The snow, too, would build up in the gap, forming ice.

Those shoes made sounds that weren't at all like those of

31

leather-soled ones. A harsh clack, clack, which she would have heard very clearly from that floor in there.

A dancer, a singer and piano player – a good conversationalist at private dinner parties. Quite knowledgeable about many things. Birds, de Fleury had said, and then had cut himself off before revealing too much.

A working mother, a young widow. At least two sets of footprints but was the second set that of a man?

Getting down on his hands and knees – gasping in pain as his left knee objected – Kohler blew the soft snow from the prints. Only the forward halves of the wooden soles were clear, but they were larger than the toes of the boots. 'A man's,' he said and looked for the scratches and gouges all such soles would bear.

There was a ridge of snow that indicated a deep gouge in the right sole. The thing was about four centimetres in length and parallel with the long axis of the print, so at some time their owner must have struck that foot against something sharp and it had cut the gouge.

Sabots or leather boots would be worn on the farms and in the hills. These prints were from town shoes and, yes, they led from the Hôtel du Parc at a quick pace.

All the others that had been enclosed by the string were older, he felt – the day-to-day traffic probably and not involved. There'd been only the two of them, then, the killer and his victim.

Forcing himself to return to the body, Kohler shone the torch over the soles of her boots and then ran an explorative thumb over the scratches and cleats. At least the local gendarmes had got those prints right.

She hadn't begun to stink as corpses soon do – the cold weather had retarded that – but when he looked along the length of her, he saw so many other corpses that he, too, asked, 'Why you, why here, when the bloody place should have been locked?'

Louis wouldn't have run off like that had he not realized something significant. 'Urgent,' he had said. 'It's urgent.'

But had it really been an attempt to assassinate the Maréchal or had the killing been for some other and totally unrelated reason?

Crossing the rue du Parc at a run, St-Cyr made for the main entrance of the hotel, which faced on to that street. He was following in Céline Dupuis's footsteps, he told himself, but at least up until 11 November of last year neither she nor he or anyone else could ever have gotten so close to the hotel without having first passed through the iron-fisted cordon of the Garde Mobile.

Now they were, apparently, no longer in evidence. Perhaps Pétain and the Germans were still discussing whose responsibility it was. Perhaps the fifteen degrees of frost at this hour had simply kept them indoors. 'But had a window of opportunity been made available?' he demanded, not liking the thought as he pushed through and into the lobby, was challenged, shrieked at – *vos papiers!* – and hit, struck hard across the brow with the flat of a revolver.

Slumped against the wall, he found himself sitting on a cold stone floor. Blood had welled up above his left eye and was trickling down to blind it. Blinking, he gingerly explored the parted skin and rapidly swelling goose egg, tried to clear his head. The victim's overcoat . . . must find her coat, he warned himself. The killer may have left her blouse with it.

'Henri-Claude Ferbrave,' he said, tasting blood – his own blood! – and looking up at his assailant. 'Age thirty-two. Former altar boy of the Saint-Sulpice, and between June 1936 and the call-up of '39, a key member of the Parti Populaire Français's "riot guard". Accused of killing an obstreperous socialist with a wooden club during a noisy intercalation at the March 1937 gathering of the PPF when one hundred and thirty thousand of the faithful were crowded into the Vélodrome d'Hiver to hear your leader, but released for lack of reliable witnesses. Being one of Doriot's former toughs won't help you, *mon fin*, nor will being one of the Maréchal's bodyguards. You are under arrest for assaulting a police officer. Please put that gun down before I take it from you.'

'Why not relax, since we have to work together?'

'*Never!* Ahh ... my forehead, you *salaud!*'

'Some ice and a few stitches will help.'

'And there's a doctor in the house, isn't there?'

'It's only five-thirty. Ménétrel doesn't usually show up for breakfast until after seven.'

'And I'm to bleed to death for having reached only for those papers you demanded?' Hermann ... where the hell was Hermann? They had to find her overcoat, they had to ...

'Messieurs, I ... I have some sticking plasters in my case. Perhaps ...'

Again the detective blinked to clear his eye. She must try to smile softly and hope he wouldn't notice she'd been crying, thought Inès. She must forget everything else and put him at ease. 'My name is Mademoiselle Charpentier, Inspector. From Paris to ... to see the Maréchal.'

'She's from the Musée Grévin,' snorted Ferbrave, not bothering to look behind himself and across the lobby to where the girl sat in her overcoat, scarf and cloche on the edge of a chair. 'A sculptress whose train arrived last night.'

'I spent the intervening hours in the station,' confessed Inès, 'until ... until the curfew had ended.'

At 5 a.m. 'Your sticking plasters, please, Mademoiselle Charpentier. It's most kind of you to have offered them.'

Had the Inspector deliberately repeated her name to let her know he wouldn't forget it? she wondered. Four others of the Garde hung about, all with machine pistols – Bergmanns and Schmeissers. All in their disgusting black uniforms with brown shirts, black ties, black berets and black leather, three-quarter-length coats. Arrogant smart-asses all of them and cruel. Cruel!

The girl was gentle but unsettled, thought St-Cyr. Several tissues sopped up the excess blood. Some water was called for, a little brandy. More tissues were needed to quickly dry the cut, then there came the sting of the iodine she had taken from her case. 'It's necessary,' she said, the accent clearly from the *quartier* Sorbonne and the Panthéon but with suppressed overtones of the rue Mouffetard also.

On her knees beside him, and still wearing the fawn-coloured, camel's hair overcoat with the big lapels and deer-horn buttons of the thirties, she taped the parted skin as best she could, then lingered a moment to examine her workmanship. 'It will do for now,' she said with beautifully modulated tones, and gave a curt little nod more to herself than to anyone else. A girl with soft reddish hair and lovely but still smarting sea-green eyes under finely curving brows, the freckled nose turned up a little, the lips slightly parted, the chin and lower jaw delicately boned but determined.

'Guerlain,' he heard himself muttering. 'Absolute rose, bergamot and jasmine, mademoiselle. Oil of cloves and cinnamon, but with sandalwood, of course, and ambergris. You or your lover have exquisite taste. Though the scent is not a recent one, the memory of it haunts.'

Ah *Sainte Mère*, her perfume! '*Merci*,' she managed.

'My case of tools, Inspector,' he heard her quickly saying as she indicated a worn leather valise with a tray of many compartments. Spatulas, hooks, knives and other wooden-handled tools – the same essentially as a taxidermist would use – were there. Scissors, balls of knotted twine, rolls of surgical gauze . . . a small, tightly stoppered phial of some kind of oil, another of the perfume – could he manage to get a closer look at it? he wondered. Some drawing pins . . .

'All the rubbish of my humble trade, Inspector.'

'And the Maréchal is to sit for you?' She was still close to him, still on her knees . . .

'The Musée is always late when granting its commissions, but fortunately has decided Monsieur le Maréchal should have a head-and-shoulders done for posterity's sake. I am nervous, of course, but understandably so, even though experienced. Ten years, and with the medals to prove it.'

Pétain, like Charlemagne, would take his place in the

waxworks of history at 10 boulevard Montmartre. 'The Musée already has a life-sized statue of him, mademoiselle.'

'Yes. The Victor of Verdun and on the white horse he once rode in a parade, but that ... that was done long ago.'

'Not so long. Not even twenty-five years ago. I was among those who marched in that Bastille Day parade of 1919, the Treaty of Versailles having just been signed in June.'

A veteran, then, but one who was determined to let her know of it. The young these days ... Did he think them cowards? wondered Inès. 'You are correct, of course, Inspector. The bust is simply to show how the demands of state have superimposed themselves upon those left by that other terrible war. One in which the father I never knew was taken from me, and at Verdun as well.'

An ice pack arrived and she gently placed it against his forehead, guiding his hand to hold it. Closing the case, she retreated to her chair. A girl of twenty-eight or so, not too tall but above medium height and of good posture. Very correct. Calm, too, now that the introductions were over.

'You must rest a little, Inspector. There may be concussion. Please don't try to move. Just try to relax.' And let your dark brown, wounded eyes, now cleared, take in the swift-eyed little gangster who hit you. Please note the scar beneath the thinness of that black goatee he thinks so handsome. It's to the right of that chin which is so pronounced, and was caused, I assume, by the razor's edge of a broken lump of sugar* and a fight over some pimp's girl, but at the tender age of sixteen perhaps. Note, too, the insolent way he looks at you, the carefully trimmed moustache that extends to the turned-down corners of thin lips but is not so thick and bushy as your own. Note the forehead that is surprisingly free of wrinkles for one so bold. Note the nose, its sharpness, the clarity and paleness of the skin – he's no outdoors man, this Henri-Claude Ferbrave of the Garde Mobile, otherwise

* Before the war, sugar was often obtained in blocks or cones, and when broken as in a bar or club, was very sharp and a favourite weapon.

those beautifully chiselled and shaven upper cheeks would be ruddy, *n'est-ce pas?* The jet-black, carefully combed and parted hair glistens with a pomade that holds the scent of ersatz spices – cinnamon, I think, but it's doubtful. The deeply sunken dark brown eyes have late-night shadows that are caused, no doubt, by repeated visits to his favourite *maison de tolérance*. Note, too, the suspicion with which he now, under my scrutiny, gazes at me, Inspector. But please remember that I arrived late last night and can therefore have had absolutely nothing to do with this tragedy.

2

Having caught a glimpse of what was going on behind the blackout curtains of the foyer, Kohler found the Hôtel du Parc's side door that was off the rue Petit, between that hotel and the Majestic, and went quickly up its staircase. It was still early, not yet 5.45 a.m. Louis was keeping the troops busy. Louis was sitting on the floor of the foyer and bleeding, but there'd be time enough to settle that little matter. The Government of France stirred. From somewhere there was the sound of a cough, from elsewhere that of teeth being brushed. *Mein Gott*, were the walls that thin?

The Quai d'Orsay had taken the first and part of the second storey – Foreign Affairs – but Premier Laval also had his offices on the second. The Élysée Palace – Pétain and his retinue – were on the third. The main lift sounded. He paused, his heart hammering – those stairs; that Benzedrine he was taking; he'd have to watch himself.

The lift had stopped. The cage was being opened. Again sounds carried, again he heard them clearly but still couldn't see the lift. Was that the Maréchal snoring? Pétain was known to be an early riser. Whispers were heard, the lift-cage closed, as it descended to the ground floor . . .

Céline Dupuis would most probably have come in through the main entrance to cross the foyer and step into the lift. Had she been challenged, given clearance, or had there been no one on guard in the lobby? And why wouldn't the lift attendant have been on duty, or had he, too, been excused?

Questions . . . There were always questions. Presumably still wearing her overcoat, the girl had come up to this floor and then . . . then had walked towards the Maréchal's bedroom, had been seen or heard by her killer who must have been about to target that same door, had been taken from the hotel, forced down the stairs – which stairs? – and out into the street and the Hall des Sources.

'Without her overcoat,' he sighed, 'and in a white nightgown that would have been easily seen at night.'

Yet, in so far as Louis and he knew, no one had come forward to say they'd noticed her. And where, please, had she left her overcoat? And why, please, remove her if Pétain was to have been the intended target?

The corridor he was in was flanked by back-to-back pairs of tall wooden filing cabinets, with tiny makeshift desks between them and iron chairs that had been taken from the nearby park. Green-shaded lamps would give but a feeble light to the legions of clerks who worked here day in and day out. A duplicating machine leaked, a typewriter held an unfinished synopsis. Names . . . letters and postcards of denunciation – Pétain had received about 3,000 a day in 1940, now it was still about 1,800, and eighty per cent of them, like the thousands received by the Kommandantur in Paris and every other French city and town, were the poison-pen missiles of a nation that had all too willingly adopted the saying, 'I'm going to *les Allemands* with this!'

A bad neighbour, jealous wife, unfaithful husband or cheating shopkeeper were all fair game. Old scores were constantly being settled and, to the shame of everyone, the authorities still gave credence to such trash.

Perhaps thirty of these bulging mailbags, fresh in from the main PTT, the Poste, Télégraphe et Téléphone station, were all waiting to be opened and synopses made for the Maréchal. Yet when Kohler came to the corridor on to which the lift opened, it was like that of any other big hotel, though here there were no trays outside the doors for the maids to collect, no newspapers lying in wait to be read. Simply brass nameplates below the room numbers, and on his right, first that of Captain Bonhomme, the

Maréchal's orderly, then that of the Secrétariat, then that of its chief, Dr Ménétrel . . .

Stopping outside the Maréchal's bedroom, Kohler looked back along the corridor – tried to put his mind into that of the victim. She hadn't really wanted to do this, would have been nervous, worried, was wearing a pair of very expensive earrings – why, for God's sake?

Had been let out of de Fleury's car and had had to make this little journey all alone.

Ménétrel's private office, he knew, was connected to Pétain's bedroom. Rumour had it that there were two approaches to the Maréchal: the official one via the Secrétariat and then down the corridor to the reception room and office at the very end; and the unofficial one, through Ménétrel's office and into Pétain's bedroom and then to the reception room.

Had she stood outside the doctor's office and done her discreet knocking there? Was that where she'd taken off her coat, scarf, beret and gloves, and if so, had the killer seen her slip back into the corridor, or had she intended to use the unofficial route?

The snoring was sonorous. Across the corridor were the rooms, the offices of more of the Maréchal's immediate staff. Several of them not only worked here but lived, ate and slept here as well, but any of those doors could have been left unlocked; she could have left her things in any one of those rooms if told to do so, yet they hadn't been found.

Searching – taking in the lingering odours of boiled onions, garlic and dinner cabbage or the sweetness of fried rutabaga steaks that had emanated from the various rooms over the years of the Occupation – he went along the corridor to its very end, to where a small balcony opened off it. The french windows were on the latch, but when released to a blast of frigid air and the threat of arrest for breaking the blackout regulations, he could see her coat lying neatly folded next to the windows. Beret, scarf and gloves were on top of it, but no handbag of course, for that would have been stolen, wouldn't it?

She had been confronted by her killer – would have realized

the windows hadn't been on the latch but had been too worried about the Maréchal and her little visit to notice that someone was there.

Shining his torch across the snow-covered balcony with its frozen geraniums in terracotta pots, Kohler picked out the footprints, their hollows only partly hidden by the snow. There were lots of them, too, but when brushed clear, the prints weren't from wooden-soled shoes but from the hobnailed boots of the Auvergne. Worn ones, too, with cleats, just like thousands and thousands of others.

The bastard must have waited here for quite some time, had been damned cold and had stamped his feet to get warm, but had he known she'd come, or had her little visit been unexpected? And why, please, hadn't anyone with a grain of competence found her things and the prints yesterday, or had they all been far too worried about their own assassinations?

No signs of a struggle, though. None at all. The girl had simply gone with him quietly.

The toughs, *les durs*, were still hanging around the foyer, smoking their fag ends and looking as if they'd missed something. Pensive, the girl with the valise sat staring at her hands, avoiding Louis, not even glancing up at his partner who was carrying the victim's clothes, which he had obviously just found.

Kohler helped Louis to his feet. They'd speak privately as was their custom when in company that strained to listen.

'Hermann, was there a blouse?'

'A what?'

'The killer – a woman – was wearing one in the Hall des Sources and may have got bloodstains on it.'

'But ... but I found his footprints on the balcony.'

'A man's?'

'Yes!'

'Cigar ashes?'

'None.'

41

'Cigarette, then?'

'None again. He'd have flicked them into the wind. No struggle either.'

'Did she know him?'

'It's possible, but maybe he had a gun.'

A man and a woman. It would be best to let a sigh escape, thought St-Cyr, and then ... then to simply say for all to hear, '*Ah bon, mon vieux*, the *marmite perpétuelle* begins to look interesting.'

The perpetual pot of soup that was to be found at the back of every kitchen stove in rural France! 'It smells, and you know it,' hissed Kohler.

More couldn't be said, for they'd fresh company: dapper, of medium height and with newly shone black leather shoes – real leather – below dark blue serge trousers that were neatly pressed – no turn-ups these days, a concession to the shortages of fabric; the grey woollen overcoat was open and immaculate; the suit jacket double-breasted and with wide lapels, no shortages there; the grey fedora neatly blocked; the round, boyish cheeks of this thirty-seven-year-old freshly shaven, the aftershave still not dry; the dark brown eyes livid.

'*Pour l'amour du Ciel*, why can't people do as they say they will? Inspectors, why was I not taken to meet you at Moulins? The secrétaire général promised to include me.'

Doctor Bernard Ménétrel was clearly up early and in one hell of a huff. 'It was very late,' tried St-Cyr, giving him a shrug.

'Pah! That was nothing. *Nothing*, do you understand? It is I who am in charge of security. I who was left waiting at the train station here when I should have gone with them to meet you. Isn't the Maréchal my responsibility? Don't I look after his every need? An assassin? An abduction from our hotel? Another killing? Three ... it is *three* of them now!'

'And this?' asked Louis, indicating the goose egg and not bothering to ask who had got the doctor out of bed or why Bousquet had chosen not to include him in the welcoming party.

'Ferbrave?' demanded Ménétrel.

'The very one,' mused Louis.

'He will apologize. For myself, I regret the discomfort you have suffered, but you should have had clearance from me and I was not taken to meet you. Henri-Claude was just doing his duty. Surely a veteran such as yourself can understand the reflex of a defensive action?'

Oh my, oh my, thought Kohler. The nose was fleshy, the mouth not big, not small, the neck close down on the squared shoulders. A medium man all round, the voice cherubic but acidic, the chin narrow and recessed so that the nose led the way in emphasizing everything he said. 'Fix him, Doctor. Stitch him up. I need him.'

'And you?' demanded Ménétrel, stung by the intrusion and still incensed.

'Kohler, Kripo, Paris-Central.'

'Gestapo. You belong over on the boulevard National* with Herr Gessler. Have you checked in with him? Well, have you?'

'He sent me here,' lied Hermann. 'He told me to keep an eye on you.'

'*On me?* Well . . .'

The doctor gave a shrill laugh. Quick-tempered, jealous of his place in the scheme of things, this court jester to some set down his bag and, motioning to Ferbrave and the others, called for a chair. 'Sit,' he said to Louis. 'Let me have a look at that.'

In addition to an ample desk, propaganda posters of the Maréchal, designs for a new postage stamp and banknotes, children's books, school books, maps of France, directions to housewives on the baking of bread without flour or sufficient of it, to farmers on the need for their work, et cetera, Ménétrel's office held a made-up cot that, judging by the scattered items on it, hadn't been recently used.

The taint of moth crystals was mingled with those of disinfectant and aftershave; the doctor was clearly agitated. The

* Changed to the boulevard États-Unis after the Second World War.

needle went in. 'Don't move, Inspector!' he breathed. 'Five should do it and we still have four to go. In a few days they can be taken out and I'll be pleased to do this since it will give us another chance to speak in private, and speak we must. Is that understood? These walls have ears, though, so one must whisper, and I *don't* want the Maréchal upset any more than he already is. He knows nothing of Madame Dupuis's murder, was completely unaware that she was even to have paid him a visit.'

It had to be asked. 'Were there *billets doux*?'

Love letters ... 'If there were, you will see that I receive them immediately. Come, come, we can't have a scandal. We *don't* want to trouble the Maréchal with this business. He's far too busy with the affairs of state, is worried enough.'

'I'll try to keep that in mind, but my partner ...'

The needle went in, the gut was pulled, a gasp given by the patient. 'Such things are larger than any of us,' cautioned Ménétrel. 'Please don't be fooled into thinking that because the country is now fully occupied, power no longer rests in Vichy.'

'Then when did the Maréchal first notice her?'

'How long has the infatuation been going on – is this what you're after? Ah! you police. Always looking for dirt, always suspecting the worst even when you should be doing your duty and finding this ... this assassin before he strikes again – *again*, Inspector!'

'And the Maréchal has had his eye on others, has he?'

'Some.'

'What was she like?'

'On stage or in the drawing room and around the dinner table?'

The gut was being tugged! 'Both, please.'

Ménétrel's eyes lit up with mischief. 'She'd a way with her, that one. *Mon Dieu*, I must grant her that. Naughty, ribald, *voluptueuse, sensuelle* yet *diabolique* – it was all an act, when on stage; when not, why, well brought up, *très belle, très intelligente et différente*. The Maréchal recognized this last instantly and, yes, he had set his cap at having her.'

44

'Then there may well be love letters?'

'Find them, damn you! I haven't been able to!'

The patient winced, which was good and necessary, thought Ménétrel. St-Cyr had been a sergeant in a Signals Corps at Verdun. Wounded twice – the left thigh and left shoulder – he had managed to crawl back to the trenches. Unruly as a boy, he had been sent to the farm of distant relatives near Saarbrücken for the holidays each summer for three years; had then used the *Deutsch* he had learned to good effect in 1917; had managed to convince the Boches he was one of theirs in no-man's-land and had got away.

No medals, no awards, just memories he shared with that partner of his from the other side. Like brothers, those two, grated Ménétrel. Both honest, both insufferable seekers of the truth who couldn't be bought. And damn Laval for having asked that they be sent from Paris! Damn Bousquet for not having overruled that boss of his and found others who would listen! Damn him, too, for not having had the decency to have kept his word and included him, the Maréchal's *confident*, in the briefing!

'Where were you on the night of the murder, Doctor?'

The gut was yanked!

'Was I here, in my office, eh? Did I plan to let that woman into his room and then to watch over the evening's performance? Of course not. Have more sense. When privacy is called for, privacy is always guaranteed.'

'Then where, exactly, were you?'

'With my wife and children in the Hôtel Majestic which is but a few steps away. I've a suite there, as has the Maréchal for Madame Pétain, but can be here in a matter of minutes.'

The needle was inserted again and again, the gut drawn, the carefully manicured short and finely boned fingers deft and swift. Ménétrel concentrated even as he clipped the gut at last, then sighed.

'Now we will leave it bare, I think, so as to have it heal faster and better. Unfortunately you will look like a boxer who has just been punished, but that can't be helped.'

45

And you've found out as much about me as possible, noted St-Cyr, but asked, 'What rewards did you offer the victim and Monsieur de Fleury?'

The chin tightened. The doctor took a moment to answer.

'I see that our Inspector of Finances has been indiscreet, but such rewards as I offered are a private matter, Inspector. Find this assassin before he kills his intended target. Bring him to justice and I will see that you are awarded one of these.'

'The *Francisque*,' sighed St-Cyr. The medal for the faithful that the doctor had had a retired jeweller design. 'Modelled after the Victor of Verdun's swagger stick, the blades after those of' – Ah! one wanted so much to say Madame Pétain but must humbly substitute – 'a two-headed battle-axe.'

'Be the detective inspector I know you to be. Go where you wish, interview whomever you feel necessary, but be discreet. Leave the Maréchal and that wife of his totally out of it. Madame la Maréchale knows nothing of the matter and will only slow you down.'

And interfere? wondered St-Cyr. Ménétrel had been the one, it was said, who had arranged for the arrest of Premier Laval on 13 December 1940 when Pétain had dismissed the *Auvergnat* for assuming too much power. The Garde Mobile had locked up Laval in his château but had been stopped short of the requested assassination by an armed contingent of SS, under the leadership of Otto Abetz, the German Ambassador, who had arrived to whisk the former premier off to the safety of Paris.

Such were the state of things in Vichy then, and probably still.

'Who knew of this little visit she was to have made?'

The doctor waved an impatient hand. 'Ask de Fleury. He or Madame Dupuis must have let something slip. I didn't.'

'Yet you excused the Garde from their duties?'

The needle was put away, the excess gut dropped into an envelope for later sterilization.

'They were called away. A false alarm.'

'Not all of them, surely.'

Jésus, merde alors, must this *salaud* persist? 'All right, I did tell them things would be secure enough. The visit would be in the evening. It's the depths of winter ... How was I to have known an assassin would strike so closely and in our hotel, a hotel that is always guarded?'

'Then she wasn't challenged as she entered the foyer?'

The bag was closed, the catches secured.

'The lift attendant was also absent,' confessed Ménétrel, not looking at him. 'The Maréchal needed to have his self-confidence restored, Inspector. If I have erred, it was only for his sake, and I don't really know how anyone else could have learned of her visit but someone obviously did.'

'And were there any other such visits recently?'

'From her, no!'

'From others, then?'

Ah damn him! 'Bousquet had to be summoned late one evening last autumn. The woman's husband had got wind of the liaison and was pacing up and down outside the hotel in a fury. Fortunately our secrétaire général has the ability to pacify not only the Boches, but even a distraught cuckold whose wife is upstairs being penetrated by another.'

St-Cyr didn't smile and that was as expected. Early last December he had lost his wife and little son to a Résistance bomb that had been meant for him but had been purposely left in place by Gestapo Paris-Central's Watchers. She'd been coming home from a particularly torrid affair with the Hauptmann Steiner, nephew of the Kommandant von Gross-Paris, and yet St-Cyr was still missing her, still blaming himself for what had happened!

'Did you see the victim after she'd been found, Doctor?'

Such coldness of tone was commendable. 'I did. I was the one who pronounced her dead. That *imbécile* of a groundsman who found her was incoherent.'

'Then describe how she was. Leave nothing out.'

'Were things tidied? Is this what you're wondering?'

'I would not ask otherwise.'

The clearing of a throat next door indicated Pétain was waiting for his daily massage and the heat treatments Ménétrel would administer. 'A moment, Maréchal,' sang out the doctor. 'Let me just tie my shoelaces.'

'Breakfast, Bernard. I want to go down. The hotel is up.'

'Begin the exercises, please. The arms ...'

'Yes, yes,' came the reedy answer, heard as clearly as if there'd been no connecting door.

'Sometimes at night he drums his fingers on the wall above his bed,' confided Ménétrel. 'The older he gets, the less he sleeps. Now where were we? Oh yes ... She was lying on her back, the left arm extended well above the head, the legs parted slackly. One knee – the left – was bent a little.'

'And you're certain the legs weren't turned either to one side or the other?'

'How *did* you find her?'

'For now, Doctor, please just answer.'

'The legs were as I've described. One hand, the right, was flattened over the wound. She'd been knifed, I felt, but didn't move her hand to make certain of this. There was no sign of the weapon.'

Ménétrel took a moment, but it was impossible to tell what he was thinking.

'Anything else?'

'Her earrings. I had the feeling her killer must have taken one but had then panicked and left the other.'

'Which one?'

'The left. I'm certain of it.'

'*Blancs exceptionnels*, Doctor. Who gave them to her?'

How pleasant of this Sûreté. 'I only wish I knew.'

It seemed strange, stepping back into the Hall des Sources knowing what he now did, thought Kohler, carrying the victim's overcoat, scarf, gloves and beret, but not her handbag. The place was still pitch dark in its recesses even with the lanterns glowing – hell, the dawn wouldn't break until well past seven the old time and it wasn't quite seven yet.

She couldn't have cried out when confronted by the bastard on that balcony, hadn't struggled, nor had the curtains or windows been damaged.

A gun, then? he asked himself again. Had she recognized her assailant's voice? Had he been afraid of this? Had there really been two of them? The one here and waiting in an unlocked Hall – a woman with a knife and wearing no overcoat or woollen cardigan – the other bringing the victim to her at pistol point?

But the wrong victim.

'Then they hadn't wanted to kill Pétain in his bedroom for fear of awakening Captain Bonhomme, or someone else,' he sighed, longing for a cigarette and for time to think it all through with Louis.

She'd got away from the one who'd brought her here. He would have called out to the killer, would have told her what had happened and that they had no choice but to silence Céline . . .

'Madame Dupuis. I've got to think of her only that way,' he said.

'Inspector . . .' came a voice.

It was the 'iron man', the police photographer and fingerprint artist – nothing ever upset these guys. Tough . . . *Mein Gott*, they could photograph anything and then patiently dust all round for prints. Old men who'd had their brains blown out, *horizontales* who'd been carved up, kids, housewives, it didn't matter.

'Marcel Barbault, Inspector.'

Merde alors, the son of a bitch looked like a defrocked priest! The body was round, the face round, the precisely clipped and black-dyed Hitlerian moustache perfect, the cheeks smooth, the throat no doubt dry and regretting the sour red it had consumed last night.

'Ah *bon*,' said Kohler, offering fresh nourishment and a light, for it took all types to make this world. 'Give us shots of her and the *buvette* from all angles, Marcel, then one or two of the Buvette de la Grande Grille and another two of the Buvette Lucas, just for local atmosphere.'

Barbault grinned. 'The corpse?' he asked, eyebrows arching

beneath a fastidiously blocked black homburg, the overcoat collar of carefully brushed velour.

'Oh, sorry. She's behind the bar. I'll leave you to it, then, shall I?'

'A clean killing?'

'Tidy, I think.'

'You going to stick around in case there's anything else you want?'

'Of course. Prints on that dripping tap above her feet when you get to them.'

Barbault moved the lanterns so that they wouldn't cast his shadow on the corpse. Popping flashbulbs, he went to work. *Merde*, how could he be so calm? He didn't whistle like some, didn't sing or mutter things to himself like others. 'A good fuck,' he said, his voice gruff and echoing. 'A nice cunt for the old sausage to ram, eh, Inspector? They say he never wears a rubber, that he simply tells them to wash it out!'

'I'm going to get a breath of air.'

'Don't catch your death.'

Jésus, merde alors!

The skies were clear but dark. Always before dawn it got like this, and which cities and towns at home would be in ruins? Jurgen and Hans had been killed at Stalingrad – just kids, really, his sons, and why hadn't they gone to Argentina like he'd begged them to? Gerda, the ex-wife, was at home on her father's farm near Wasserburg but was now married to an indentured French farm labourer . . .

Giselle and Oona were at the flat on the rue Suger in Paris, just around the corner from the house of Madame Chabot and Giselle's old friends in the profession. Thank God Oona was there to keep an eye on her.

'I really do have to get them out of France before it's too late. Louis, too, and Gabrielle, his new love, though that definitely hasn't been consummated.' A chanteuse, a war-widow with a ten-year-old son, a beautiful lay who was keeping it only for Louis.

The Résistance would shoot that patriot simply because he

worked with one of the Occupier and in their need for vengeance they'd make lots of similar mistakes.

'Vichy can't last,' he muttered as, remembering the matter to hand, he hurried back inside the Hall. 'Marcel, make sure you get close-ups of those cigar ashes on her front and on the counter, those also at the Buvettes de la Grande Grille and Lucas. I'll show them to you when you're ready.'

'Cigars . . . ?' gasped a female voice. 'Ah *Sainte Mère*, I have brought some for the Maréchal, Inspector.'

'Just who the hell are you and what do you think you're doing in here?'

Here . . . Here . . . came the echoes on the damp, cold air.

'Inès Charpentier . . . Sculptress and patcher-up of injured detectives. Is it really true that there is a sadist who rapes and then murders only virgins? I ask simply because . . . because I may have to work late and return to my boarding house after dark and alone.'

Had there been a catch in her throat? 'Your information's a little off. She wasn't raped and wasn't a virgin.'

'Oh. The . . . the men who are clearing the snow have it wrong then. Are these really cigar ashes, Inspector? You see, the Maréchal detests cigarette smoke but apparently enjoys an occasional cigar, and my director, he . . . he has sent him a little gift of some Havanas, from Cuba by submarine, I think.'

Had the kid been crying? She was standing behind the bar, with her left hand wrapped tightly around that dripping tap and the other one flat on the counter, smudging the ashes. She couldn't stop herself from staring at the corpse, was sickened, no doubt, and likely to throw up.

'Come on,' said Kohler gently. 'You need what I need.'

'And the ashes?' asked Barbault, not turning from his work.

'Find the rest of them yourself and then have her moved to the morgue.'

The broom kept going. The man, the boy under torchlight, didn't look up but down at the snow he was clearing from the covered walk. The jacket of his *bleus de travail* was open, the coveralls well padded by two bulky pullovers, two flannel shirts and at least one pair of long johns.

A tricolour – a blue-, red- and white-banded scarf – trailed from its tight knotting about the all but absent throat. The face was wide and flat, the dark brown eyes closely spaced under a knitted woollen cap and inwardly grooved by fleshy folds of skin beneath frowning black, bushy brows.

'Albert,' said the father gently. 'The Chief Inspector St-Cyr has come all the way from Paris to speak to you. Surely you could spare him a moment?'

'I went round as I always do,' retorted the son. 'All the doors were locked except for that one!'

The broom flew up to fiercely point at the distant Hall des Sources, indistinct in the darkness.

'Albert, I know you did. Haven't I trusted you all these years we've worked together here? Inspector, my son is very intelligent, very diligent. No task is too big or too small. Each morning before I and the others arrive, Albert checks round the park to see if there is anything amiss. He found the padlock and chain in the snow beside the entrance to the Hall. The key was still in its lock, the door open.'

'*She was asleep, father! asleep!*'

'Now, now, let's not have tears in public, eh, Albert? God gave you too much heart, but I know you can be tough on yourself when necessary.'

The nose was wiped, the broom lowered, the sweeping petulantly taken up again.

'Ah, it's a little early for our mid-morning snack but when it's cold like this, a person needs something extra. Would you care to join us, Inspector?'

'Coffee ...' said Albert slyly. 'He thinks I'll be fooled by temptation. Bread ... is there any left, Father?'

The elder Grenier patted his jacket pocket but said only, 'Show the Chief Inspector where our nest is. I'll just let the others know we've gone below.'

The broom was carefully leaned against one of the wrought-iron uprights, the booted feet were stamped to remove their snow. Deep in the cellars beneath the Hôtel du Parc, the younger Grenier led him to the furnace room, to straight-backed wooden chairs, a warming pot of real coffee, a small glass jar of honey and one of milk ... Simple things most of the nation hadn't seen or tasted in years.

'We're lucky,' said Albert shyly. 'This is our very own place. Warm in winter, cool in summer.'

There were newspapers, well-read by others no doubt, before being gathered and smuggled down here. The *Völkischer Beobachter* – the People's Observer, in *Deutsch* that probably none of the caretakers could understand. *Die Woche*, too, the Nazis' weekly magazine with lots of pictures, and *Signal* – Hitler's own magazine. *Paris-Soir, Le Matin* and other Paris dailies were with them – all collaborationist, all thin and heavily censored, but among these, and more significantly, were copies of *L'Oeuvre Rassemblement National Populaire*, the paper of Marcel Déat's violently fanatical collaborationist and fascist party, and *Le Cri du Peuple*, that of Jacques Doriot and his PPF, the Parti Populaire Français, equally pro-fascist and violently collaborationist. The extreme far right of Paris, who reviled and ridiculed everything Vichy did and constantly plotted to take over.

'Those were the doctor's,' spat Albert, indicating *L'Oeuvre* and *Le Cri.* 'He doesn't like me and I don't like him either, but I prefer to read these.'

Stabs had been made at filling in the pictures of the colouring book but crayons were in such short supply only a few colours had been used.

'Read this one, Inspector. It's special.'

One had best say something. 'The pictures are lovely. Perhaps the ...'

'They're the nicest I've ever received as a present! That's what it says.'

So it did.

'This one is also my book.'

A fairy tale, an illustrated biography of the Maréchal who was pictured in a two-page spread as a fatherly figure sitting before a group of young children under a giant oak. Vichy flooded the country with its propaganda. Texts and books like this were in every school and at every reading level.

' "And as he spoke," ' said Albert reverently, ' "all the rats, the wasps and worms that had done so much damage to *la belle* France – the termites, too, and spiders – suddenly ran away." He promised he would make things better and he did, Inspector. He really did! He's a good man. A great man. He has even signed my book – see, that is his very own writing.'

A forefinger was stabbed at the inscription.

Patience ... I must have patience, said St-Cyr silently to himself. 'Dated 4 November 1941 ... Did the Maréchal also give you that ring?'

I'd better shake my head, thought Albert. I'd better not look at him. 'I found it.'

'In the Hall des Sources?'

The man, the boy, cringed. There was a nod, a further turning away and yanking off of the knitted cap. 'It's pretty. It's mine. Finders keepers, losers weepers!'

'Of course, but was it near her, Albert?'

'I'm not listening. I can't hear you.'

'Albert, you'd best tell the Inspector,' urged the father, pushing past them to warm his hands by clasping the coffee pot.

'Do I have to?'

'Ah *mon Dieu, mon vieux*, need you ask? Show him that you're good at cooperating with the police and that you know right from wrong.'

'He'll only want it for himself.'

'Just tell him, Albert.' But had the boy found something else? wondered Grenier. Something so dear he would yield the one to keep secret the other?

'It ... it was lying on the bar of the Buvette du Parc when my torch discovered it as if by magic. Real magic!'

'And then?' prompted the father.

'I . . . I found her in the Buvette du Chomel. *Chomel!*'

'Now have your coffee, Albert. Serve the Inspector first. Put a little honey in his and some milk. Inspector, let my son keep the ring. It can't be of any value.'

'It's too dangerous. Believe me, the fewer who know of it, the better.'

'But . . . but surely Albert is no threat to this . . . this assassin?'

'But the ring is, Monsieur Grenier. That band is from an El Rey del Mundo – the King of the World – cigar. A Choix Supreme or Corona Deluxe.'

'A Choix Supreme, but it could just as easily have been a Romeo y Julieta Corona or a Davidoff Grand Cru. The Maréchal occasionally enjoys a cigar and that band is not the first of such rings my son has worn until they are so torn they can't be mended. There are gold coins on it, and a gold coat of arms, but it's mainly because, with him, by wearing it he feels just a little bit closer to his hero.'

'Then tell him that if he values the Maréchal's life he'll let me have a piece of evidence that could well lead us to the killer.'

There *is* something else, thought Grenier. Albert is giving the ring up too easily. That sly and rapid glance he has just tossed the Inspector only confirms it. *Sacré nom de nom*, what am I to do? Stop him now, or wait to find out for myself?

I'd best wait. Yes, that's what I'll do. The boy's upset enough as it is, and we can't have that. Not with *les Allemands* and their Gestapo now here in force, not with the way they are known to treat such people.

Black coffee, hot, freshly baked croissants, real blackberry jam and a glass of brandy sat before the girl. Timidly Inès Charpentier reached for the napkin-draped wicker basket and brought it close.

'It's like a dream,' she said, exhaling softly. 'White sugar on the table. These,' she said, indicating the croissants. 'They've been banned in Paris and the rest of the *zone occupée* since the fall of 1940. And this? Oh for sure it's an *eau-de-vie de marc* from the

Auvergne and exactly what is needed to settle me down, but on a no-alcohol day? It is a Thursday. Aren't Tuesdays, Thursdays and Saturdays the *pas-d'alcools* days even here in Vichy? I wouldn't want to be arrested and you are, after all, a . . .' She wouldn't say Gestapo, said Inès to herself. 'A detective.'

The kid had really been shaken up by the murder, still was for that matter. 'Relax. Forget about the war and the Occupation. Tell me about yourself.'

Somehow she must try to keep her mind on things and try not to panic, thought Inès. 'There's not much to tell,' she said, but did Herr Kohler find wariness in such a modest reply? 'I sculpt and have done so since a child. Garden clay first, then plasticine – sketching things too. When one is driven by loneliness to such an urge one does not question it at first but only later sees that behind the desire there must have been escape. I'm happiest still when working and need little else.'

A simple soul, Louis would have said, that Sûreté head of his full of doubt simply because the kid, on viewing the corpse, had inadvertently destroyed whatever fingerprints had been on that dripping tap and had left her own in their place and elsewhere. Or had it been inadvertent? *Ach*, why must he always be expected to suspect the worst? Why must Louis constantly demand answers to everything? The kid was clean, no problem, but . . . 'Do you live at home?' he asked.

'Ah, no. I've a studio in Paris.'

Offer little, Louis would have said and impatiently clucked that tongue of his as he nodded, but everyone tried to offer little these days. 'That's a pretty big city, isn't it? My partner and I are seldom there.'

And you don't know it well – is this what you're trying to tell me, monsieur? wondered Inès, pleased that her resolve had stiffened. 'It's on the rue du Douanier* at . . . at number 5. One of several, and unheated these days or in the past, for that matter.'

* Now the rue Braque.

'Rent?'

'Two sixty-five a month.' Did he know Paris and its struggling artists well enough to see the truth of this reply?

'Salary?'

'Twelve hundred from the Musée and whatever else I can earn through part-time teaching and private commissions. It's not even that of a ticket-taker on the *métro*, but don't people always say that artists are doing what they like?'

'Family?'

'None.'

'That's too brief an answer, mademoiselle. Surely you've a past?'

And with croissants waiting! 'My father is buried near Verdun, my mother in the Cimetière du Montparnasse. Father's brother and sister-in-law took me in when I was two years old, Inspector. Both of them were much older than my parents and childless, and both have since sadly passed away.'

'But they let you sculpt?'

'Of course.'

'Their names, then?'

She was becoming flustered, must remain calm! 'Inspector, I thought I was to relax? Charpentier – what else? André-Émile, accountant for Le Printemps, one of the big department stores, and Odette née Marteau. I've some photos – a few even of the father and mother I never knew, but these, they are in a cardboard box in my studio.' Would he check this out? *Would he?* demanded Inès silently.

'Forgive me,' he said and grinned boyishly – a nice grin, *bien sûr*, but ... 'Sometimes I hate myself,' he said. 'You have to understand that my partner is always on about my letting the prettiest of girls take advantage of me. He'll ask what I've learned and I'll have to have something to tell him. You've no idea what he's like. A real pain in the ass!'

Was that definitely all there was to the inquisition? wondered Inès. 'You are forgiven and ... and the compliment is much appreciated though I fear I am far too thin these days.'

And can't get much to eat even on the black market, since about 600 francs a day was needed! 'Salut,' said Kohler, raising his glass to her. 'À votre santé.'

'Et à vous, monsieur.'

It was only in passing that he mentioned the quartier Petit-Montrouge, the Parc de Montsouris, and the École de Dressage, which was at the end of the street, thus letting her know that he knew Paris well enough but that she didn't have to worry.

But I will, said Inès to herself. There were deep circles around her eyes and he had noticed them, no doubt concluding that they weren't just from hunger but from too many late nights – particularly the one that had brought her here on the same train as he and that partner of his. The same! Would he check its passenger list? Would he?

More coffee came. The girl sat back with hands in her lap as the waiter poured.

'Merci,' whispered Inès, and then . . . then tried to smile across the table at this giant from the Kripo with the terrible scar down the left side of his face. 'The Chante Clair Restaurant of the Hôtel Majestic is lovely, isn't it?' she heard herself saying. 'Very fin de siècle – turn of the century. Very of another time. Ferns and fish-tail palms, Kentias and rubber plants – the smell of the orange and lemon trees in their glazed jardinières – tulip shades of soft amber glass on goose-necked lamps and, above the widows, stained-glass panels of ladies bathing or drinking the waters and taking the cure.'

The place was filling up. Ministers of this and that would arrive singly or with their wives; the respective assistants would wait patiently, then dash in to ask if anything was required of them, or they would divulge the latest little confidence. Often there were glances up and around, whispers about the two visitors – these two, thought Inès, only to see Herr Kohler grinning at her again and hear him saying, 'Don't worry so much. The Minister of Culture won't pester you while I'm here.'

Was this safer ground? 'They're all so serious,' she whispered, leaning across the table as he did towards her. 'No one smiles, all seem worried and not among friends.'

'Tall, thin, short, corpulent or otherwise, they're all wondering what the hell they should do. Leave the ship or stay until it goes down.'

Had Herr Kohler seen right through her? Had he *wanted* to test her yet another time? 'I . . . I know nothing of such things. For me, it's enough to have been chosen to do such an important commission, and my room and board is only one hundred francs in total, Inspector, for as long as it takes. A fabulous deal. Mind you, I doubt the family with whom I'm to board will be able to provide such luxuries.'

And where is it, exactly, that you're staying? She could see him wondering this but there was no time for him to ask.

'Inspector . . . *Mon Dieu*, you certainly don't waste time! Mademoiselle . . . ?'

It was the Secrétaire Général of Police. Incredibly young and handsome for one so powerful, thought Inès, his eyes alive with imagined mischief and loving the joke of what he'd come upon. The hair, neatly trimmed and well back from the forehead, was parted high and to the left; the white shirt and blue tie were immaculate and showed clearly through the open V of his overcoat because there was no scarf, the broad lambskin collar making him look like an immensely successful banker or investment broker.

A lighted cigarette was held between the thumb and forefinger of the right hand. There were nicotine stains on those fingers . . . 'Charpentier, monsieur,' she heard herself telling him. 'Inès.'

'The sculptress. Herr Kohler, I might have known! He has a reputation with the ladies, mademoiselle. I would watch it with him if I were you.'

Monsieur Bousquet sat down but continued to enjoy his little discovery. If he was upset about anything at all, he wasn't going to let the assembled even guess at it. Dashing, always impeccably dressed and self-confident, he was one of the most well-informed and well-connected men in the country and yet here she was sitting at a table with him.

The Maréchal arrived with Premier Laval. Dr Ménétrel was right behind them. Throughout the dining room, coffee cups were put down, croissants abandoned, napkins quickly used and set aside as everyone stood.

The Glacier and the Moroccan carpet dealer, the horse-trader, the shady operator – *le Maquignon* – headed across the room to where a screen hid the Maréchal's table from prying eyes.

Pétain said a brief good morning to everyone. Laval said nothing, Ménétrel ducking round behind the screen to join the conference, Bousquet . . . Bousquet saying, 'If you will excuse me, Herr Kohler, mademoiselle, I'd best see what's up.'

He, too, went behind the leaded glass panels on which bare-shouldered maidens, swathed in soft white towels, their curls pinned up, dabbled their pretty toes in the rushing waters of an imaginary stream.

The four of them are behind that screen, said Inès to herself, but to Herr Kohler, who was watching her reactions closely, she would have to say with a smile she knew would be weak and would utterly fail to mask her thoughts, 'There is Vichy, Inspector. If you had told me this morning that I would shortly see them gathered around one table like that, I would not have believed you. Now I must leave. Excuse me, please. My presence here will only cause you further embarrassment, and I would not want that.'

Seen in the reflection from the corridor's wall mirror and through a side entrance, the Chante Clair's clientele grew increasingly uneasy. Whispers here, others there, thought Inès as she straightened her cloche and tidied her scarf. Oh *bien sûr*, they were now worried. Rumours of an aborted assassination attempt must have circulated; a dancer had been murdered – slaughtered perhaps to protect the identity of the would-be assassin. A hurried, urgent conference had been convened with the Maréchal . . .

From either side of that privacy screen they came, the conference suddenly terminated, Bousquet swift and no longer looking so confident, Ménétrel and Premier Laval grim and to the left, the *Auvergnat* easily elbowing the doctor out of the way so that the closest of empty chairs could be grabbed.

One by one they sat down at Herr Kohler's table, leaving the Maréchal to dine alone but with thoughts of what? she asked herself. The nearness of death while having adulterous sex with a beautiful but lonely young woman whose child had had to be left in Paris, messieurs? Paris! The lack of guards? The affront of their not having been on duty?

'I'd best join my partner, hadn't I?'

Ah *Sainte Mère*, it was the Chief Inspector St-Cyr. For how long had he been watching her? From the moment she had sat down over coffee and croissants with his partner or simply now?

Doubt, suspicion and a too-evident interest filled the look he gave her, since she had pretended to tidy herself in the mirror . . .

He had seen right through her. Not waiting for a reply, the Sûreté departed. Fedora in hand and overcoat unbuttoned, he headed for that table and, seizing a free chair along the way, took it with him.

Then he, too, sat down but next to his partner so as to face the others and yet also see her still standing in this corridor.

Ducking her eyes, the girl turned away from the mirror, soon to cross the foyer and leave the hotel. A sculptress, said St-Cyr to himself. A patcher-up of battered detectives.

'Hermann, a moment. Let me begin.'

'No, you let me!' seethed Ménétrel. 'Which of you idiots told the lift operator that the Maréchal's life had been threatened? Come, come, messieurs. I told you to be discreet – I *warned* you!'

'Bernard . . . Bernard, go easy,' urged Laval, his olive-dark eyes glistening.

'Easy, when the Maréchal has learned the Garde Mobile were not on duty and is furious? He's . . . he's demanding a full inquiry!'

'But neither of these two would have released such information,' said Laval, shaking his head. 'These things simply have a way of getting out, Bernard.'

'And to his ears?'

'His good one, I trust. The Maréchal's stone deaf in the left one, Inspectors.'

'Messieurs, *please*,' cautioned Louis. 'This key was taken from the groundskeepers' board in the furnace room of the Hôtel du Parc. Whoever took it not only knew where to find it, but more importantly, since none of the keys was identified, exactly which one would be needed.'

'A town resident, an employee, perhaps,' said Ménétrel, not looking at them. 'One who has passed by that padlock every day and has seen it many times.'

The key looked as if suitable for any padlock of that vintage. 'Why the Hall des Sources?' asked Laval. 'Why plan to take the Maréchal there? Why not simply kill him in that bedroom of his?'

'The girl would almost certainly have screamed,' said Kohler. 'There would have been a scuffle. Others would have been awakened and, if not, the Maréchal is still surprisingly fit.'

'He exercises. I do the best I can,' muttered Ménétrel testily. 'If neither of you let it out, who did?'

It was Laval who, lighting another cigarette from the butt of the one he'd been smoking, calmly said, 'Why not ask the switchboard operator, Bernard? You know as well as I do that the Maréchal always rings downstairs first thing in the morning to ask if there have been any calls.'

'*Sacré*, that bitch! I'll see she's dismissed. Just let me get my hands on her. Passing classified information. Breaking our strict rules about secrecy . . .'

'See to it, Bernard. We can't have that happening, can we?' urged the Premier, as the doctor bolted from the table to make his way across the room. 'Red-faced and in a rage,' chuckled Laval, delighted by the result, but then, taking a deep drag and exhaling smoke through his nostrils, he returned to business. 'There's more to this, isn't there? Inspectors, you can and must speak freely. Secrétaire Général Bousquet and I are as one, and we both need to know.'

Bousquet remained watchfully silent, his cigarette still.

'A man and a woman,' said Louis levelly. 'The first to encounter the victim and then to take her to the Hall, the second to lie in wait there.'

'Two assailants . . . A team, is that it, eh?' demanded Bousquet, sickened by the thought.

'A vengeance killing?' asked Laval. 'Assuming, of course, that the Maréchal really was the intended victim and that this Madame Dupuis had simply to be silenced.'

'As of now the matter is still open to question,' confessed Louis and, finding that pipe of his and a too-thin tobacco pouch, frowned at necessity's need but decided it would have to be satisfied.

'He takes for ever to pack that thing,' quipped Kohler. 'It helps him think.'

And there is still more to this, isn't there? thought Laval. That is why this partner and friend of yours is so carefully giving me the once over. He sees the hank of straight jet-black hair that always seems to fall over the right half of my brow to all but touch that eye. He sees not so much the swiftness of my glance as the glint of constant suspicion. He notes my dark olive skin, bad teeth, the nicotine stains, the full and thick moustache, double chin, the squat and all but non-existent neck and the white tie that has been so much a part of me since my earliest days as a trade-union lawyer and socialist candidate in Aubervilliers. He says to himself that tie really does make me stand out for any would-be assassins but readily admits I will never be persuaded to change it.

But does he hate me too? Does he call me, as so many do, *le Maquignon*, or is his interest simply that of detachment, the detective in him a student of life out of necessity?

St-Cyr returned the questioning gaze. Tough . . . *mon Dieu*, this one was that and much more. Premier from January 1931 to February 1932, Foreign Minister from May of '32 until June '35,

Premier again until January '36, after which he'd been out of office until September '39 but always there behind the scenes, and back as Premier from July '40 until his arrest on 13 December of that first year of the Occupation and now, since April '42, Premier again.

'A self-made man, Inspector,' acknowledged Laval. 'The youngest son of a butcher, café owner, innkeeper and postman – Father had a lot of irons in the fire and a wife and four children to feed. Châteldon is less than twenty kilometres to the south and a tiny place, but it's home, you understand, and my house is the one on the hill.'

The château Laval had been bought in 1932 after that first term as Premier. He'd left the village when still a schoolboy, had insisted on taking his *baccalauréat*, then a degree in Zoology, then Law and, to finance himself, had taken a position as a *pion*, a supervisor of secondary schools in Lyons, Saint Étienne, Dijon . . .

He had bought into and then come to own several newspapers, Radio-Lyons and printing presses – the one in Clermont-Ferrand did all of Vichy's printing and had done so since July 1940, even after his arrest by the Garde Mobile. One of his companies bottled a mineral water – La Sergentale – which was reputed to be a cure for impotence and had been sold on railways and oceanic liners before the war (now only on the trains, of course). Farming, too, was among his business interests, wine also.

'A happy family man, eh, René?' he said, looking steadily at Bousquet. 'One who adores his only child and daughter and dearly loves his wife, so doesn't fool around with those of others. But if you are as well informed as I think you are, Inspectors, you will also be aware that my Jeanne often refers to the distinct possibility of Madame Pétain's having Jewish blood in her family, whereas that good woman constantly refers to me behind my back as "that Moroccan carpet dealer", or even "that *Jamaick*" – that Jamaican – she having dug that last one up from my days as a schoolboy more than fifty years ago.'

'An *éminence grise*,' said Louis guardedly, 'but one who,

whether I agree or not with your policies, causes me to realize that you are no ordinary man and that with you, things had best be up front.'

'Two assailants?' prompted Bousquet.

'The female, having gained access to the Hall, removed her overcoat and, most probably, also a woollen jersey. Then, after lighting a cigar, waited for her victim.'

'A cigar . . . ?' blurted Laval. 'Was it one of Pétain's?'

'There's a humidor in his office, Inspectors,' interjected Bousquet. 'People come and go all day long. Any of them could have helped themselves or been offered one they did not smoke at the time.'

Lost to the thought, Laval muttered, 'Someone so close, he, she or both can come and go as they please, with us none the wiser. Is this what you're suggesting, René?'

'It's possible.'

'But . . . but cigars are available elsewhere?' cautioned Laval. 'The Marquis de Bon Goût, on the boulevard du Casino at the other end of the park, has plenty, Inspectors. Ask the elder Paquet to go through his register. Take the old man into your confidence a little. He knows everything there is to know about this town, save what's left of the nation's government. Maybe even that too.' He glanced at his pocket watch and then turned again to Bousquet. 'René, make certain they tell you everything. Relay it to me but keep that little Florentine intriguer of a doctor in the dark, eh? Find out who among his overblown staff knew about this liaison he'd arranged and if that person or persons squeaked it to anyone else, including the members of his private army. Let us show that starchy Rasputin a thing or two and baste his goose with the sauce it deserves!'

'A moment, Premier,' cautioned Louis as Laval got up to leave. 'The killer knew enough about the heart muscle to know it would be best to enlarge the hole she was putting in it.'

'The haft of the knife was lifted hard before the blade was withdrawn,' offered Kohler blandly, 'so we're dealing with a professional and had best keep it in mind.'

'And is the Maréchal the only target,' snorted Laval, 'or is it that this double-barrelled assassin of ours wants us all to feel the *coup de grâce* before it arrives?'

The finishing stroke . . . 'We shall have to see,' said Louis.

'Premier, your use of the name Flykiller in the telex you sent Gestapo Boemelburg?' asked Kohler.

Laval threw Bousquet a silencing glance. 'Assassin would have been too harsh a word for the sensitive ears of our comrades and allies, Inspector. Surely as one of them, you would agree? Enjoy the coffee. René, a further word in private. Walk me to my office. Catch up with these two later.'

'Transport . . .' hazarded Hermann. Laval had left the table.

'I'll see what can be arranged,' shot Bousquet. 'For now, the morgue is within easy walking distance and she'll soon be moved. Wait there, and don't either of you go anywhere else until we've spoken. Please, I must insist. Have a look at those first two corpses and let us hope there won't be any more.'

Daylight had finally crept over the Allier Valley to expose the iron fist of a purplish-grey ice fog. Out on the rue Petit breath steamed. Bundled up, some of them with only their eyes uncovered, people hurried to work, mostly civil servants and cursing weather that was normal for the Auvergne at this time of year, so good, that was good, thought Kohler. They ought to suffer like the rest of us!

Vélo-taxis, those wretched bicycle-rickshaw things the Occupation's lack of petrol and automobiles had brought, waited in a line outside the Hôtels du Parc and Majestic. Blankets for the passengers and vacuum flasks of those equally wretched herbal teas, the tisanes Louis loved to drink. Anything for a few sous. There'd even be a 'little charge' for the rental of the blankets.

A horse-drawn cutter looked better. Whistling shrilly, Louis threw up a hand, startling the mare into going back on her hind legs. 'Sûreté and Gestapo,' he shouted before dropping his voice to all but a whisper. 'The Hôtel d'Allier, monsieur, and make it snappy unless you want this animal of yours to leave for the Russian Front.'

No patience whatsoever and still knows damn all about horses, snorted Kohler to himself. 'Idiot, don't speak like that in front of or behind her. She's sensitive. She'll . . .'

'She was volunteered for service and rejected seven times, monsieur,' said the driver, bitching silently too, and with a dead fag end glued to his lower lip and a moustache that was coated with frost.

'*Jésus, merde alors*,' shrilled Louis, 'must we have an argument?'

'Only if you insist,' countered Hippolyte Simard as the two from Paris clambered into the sleigh without permission.

'Then the eighth review will be her one-way ticket to adventure and your loss,' went on Louis. 'Now get this crap-heap moving.'

The stitched-up wound above the left eye was cruel, the goose-egg red and probably still swelling. A fight, then, chuckled Simard to himself, so good – yes, it was good to see a cop that had been taught a lesson, though this one had obviously not yet learned it!

'Paris . . . Must all those who come from the centre of the world lord it over us, Marguerite? Pay no attention to the acid, *mon ange*. Let us do as this *flic* asks and leave others to question his manners.'

Oh-oh, this wasn't going to end unless someone intervened. 'Louis, I thought we were to head for the morgue?'

'Certainly.'

'The morgue, messieurs? But it's at the other end of . . .'

'Just do as you've told the angel who's doing all the work unless you want to take her place. Repeat anything we've said and you'll be wearing two of what I've got on my forehead!'

'He's right. I wouldn't fool with him,' grinned Kohler. 'If you think this is cold, you ought to try Russia.'

Silence followed.

'There, that shut him up,' sighed Kohler, sitting back. 'You should always leave such things to me, Louis. No arguments. He simply hears authority in my voice and understands.'

'*Sacré*, you're sounding like the Occupier! If I were you, I'd be careful.'

They turned towards the river and were soon racing through the English Garden that Napoléon III had commissioned in 1861. Snow on the branches of the silver birches and tulip trees, last leaves still clinging ... More snow on the Lebanese cedars. A bandstand ... a rose arbour ... a lone woman carrying a thin burlap sack of sticks, a German officer on a dappled grey, others of the Occupier on skis and looking as if on holiday, still others on patrol – twenty in all and most of them boys no older than seventeen, wearing cut-down uniforms that were still far too big for them.

'They look ridiculous,' said Kohler sadly. 'But why couldn't my boys have had that chance? Paradise here; hell where they died.'

A large swastika flew above the entrance to one of the villas that had been built in those early days, the Turkish flag was next door, the tricolour still in the near distance atop the Hôtel du Parc.

'Maybe God thought He needed them in Russia, Hermann, just as He thinks we're needed here.'

Louis was always calling that God of his to account for being miserable to honest, hard-working detectives. 'You know Bousquet doesn't want us to go anywhere but the morgue.'

'And that, *mon enfant*, is exactly why we're going elsewhere!'

'You want to have a look at where he supposedly found the *carte d'identité* that should have been with our victim and in her handbag or pocket.'

'Why the earrings, Hermann? Why try to hide them? Was it simply fear of robbery or was there some other reason for that Florentine intriguer's saying to me with all sincerity that he "*wished* he knew who'd given them to her"?'

'Admit it, you were stopped cold in your tracks. Don't be bitter. The good doctor just wanted to make certain he was out of bed and at the hotel before we got there.'

'You leave Henri-Claude Ferbrave to me. I don't need my big Bavarian brother to take care of such things.'

'Flies, Louis? Why the hell did Laval throw Bousquet such a silencing glance when asked about that telex?'

Good for Hermann. 'High-ranking administrators, even those as gifted as our secrétaire général, must be cautioned from time to time. He also shouldn't have told us he had found the victim's ID in her room and has now realized the killer or someone else must have deliberately put it there, and so he is worried he might have missed something else.'

They had arrived at the Hôtel d'Allier. The mare was sucking air. 'Louis, what's a Florentine intriguer?'

'The Medici, the Renaissance, deceit, treachery, torture and court killings that time alone has not been able to erase the memory of. Their knives, dirks and especially their ghastly poisons. Stick around. I'm sure you'll have ample opportunity to find out!'

'And when I do?'

Must Hermann always have the last word even when they were in a hurry? 'Just make sure you're right behind me.'

They were running now, going up the steep and narrow staircases two and three steps at a time. At each landing, hips banged against waist-high wooden wainscoting, shoulders against wallpaper whose turn-of-the-century flowers were faded.

Gleaming, the banister's railing and darker spindles led the way, their steps hardly muffled by the thin carpet.

'One more floor,' managed Kohler. 'Right up under the eaves where the help used to sleep.'

A garret . . . In the spring of 1940 Vichy had had a population of 25,000, which had now almost doubled. The Hôtel d'Allier, never first or second class during the *fin de siècle* or at any time since, had been converted into a rooming house for the legions of secretaries and clerks that had been needed – dancers too, and singers.

'Number 3,' swore St-Cyr, catching a breath and vowing to smoke only certified tobacco, not the sometimes necessary experiments with dried, uncured beet tops, celery leaves and other things.

The doorknob was of white porcelain, the lock not difficult. Through the lace curtains of a grimy mansard window, daylight filtered to touch the terracotta pots of a tiny kitchen garden – herbs, chives, green onions, lettuces, geraniums too – and among these, as if it belonged there for ever, a plump white rabbit stirred in its little cage but otherwise ignored them.

She hadn't been able to bring herself to kill it, thought St-Cyr, parting the curtains. So many kept meat on the hoof in their flats and rooms these days. Guinea pigs, the latest Paris food fad, chickens, pigeons – cats that had been captured, kidnapped dogs too, if they could be silenced and were obedient.

The small glass pitcher she had used to water things had shattered with the frost but there was water in the rabbit's dish and even winter grass that must have been recently scavenged from one of the parks or country roadsides.

Beyond the roofs of houses that would some day surely be demolished, he could see the river and above its far bank the racecourse and stables. Upstream, a little to his left, was a narrow weir and footbridge, the Pont Barrage, and to his right and downstream, the much wider, larger Boutiron Bridge.

Though still well within the town, they were some distance from the Hôtel du Parc. 'The blackout curtains have been opened, Hermann.'

'Louis, Bousquet is already taking the lift.'

The sound of it came clearly through the walls. An iron four-poster, one of its brass knobs long gone, was unmade, but the pillows had been smoothed. A clutch of hairpins marked the place where Céline Dupuis had last sat.

There was a photograph of her daughter, another, in uniform, of the husband who'd been killed during the Blitzkrieg, a third of her parents and the house at 60 rue Lhomond.

The leather-clad alarm clock from the early thirties had stopped at 11.22. The alarm, though, had been set for 7 a.m.

'A rehearsal?' asked Kohler.

'She left in a hurry on Tuesday,' muttered St-Cyr. 'Flannelette pyjamas, heavy woollen socks, a cardigan, knitted gloves and a toque are in a heap on the carpet next to that wicker *fauteuil* she must have rescued from the hotel's garden. On that side table below the wall mirror whose gilding has long disappeared there are a tin basin and a large enamelled pitcher of water whose ice she would have had to break had she not been in such a hurry. The facecloth, towel and carefully rationed sliver of soap are neatly piled and were unused.'

'Louis, the lift. It's stopped.'

'Must you keep on about it? There are still two sets of stairs for him to climb. Just let me memorize the room.'

'You haven't time. Why not concentrate on the bed? Women who've been out working late at night and have to get up early invariably hug the pillows for a stolen moment after the alarm's been shut off. If I were you, *mein brillanter* Oberdetektiv, I'd be asking myself who the hell slipped in here to tidy up?'

'The same person who fed and watered the rabbit?'

'And opened the blackout curtains?'

'Or the one who . . .'

'*Nom de Jésus-Christ*, do you two not listen?' demanded Bousquet, fedora in hand as he stormed breathlessly into the room. 'I told you to go to the morgue I . . .'

'You felt it prudent to beat us here, Secrétaire,' said Louis, not backing off. 'You had, I think, to take another look in case whoever left her identity card but not her handbag had also left something you had missed.'

'Nothing . . . There was nothing else.'

'No ration tickets? No residence permit?' They were all but shouting.

'All right, all right! Those must have been in that overcoat you found, Kohler, and were taken from it, or were in her bag which has yet to be found, and yes, whoever killed her came back here afterwards to leave the card!'

'And these?' asked Louis, removing the first of the freshened pillows to expose a neat little pink-ribboned bundle of letters in their scented envelopes.

'Those weren't there when we found her *carte d'identité* on Wednesday morning,' managed Bousquet, sickened by what must have happened. 'We searched. *Mon Dieu*, but we did. Ménétrel insisted on accompanying me and at the time I realized those must have been what he was after, but they simply weren't there then.'

Not then. 'So this unknown visitor must have come back?' asked Louis.

'*Yes!*'

'And recently, too,' said Kohler, indicating the curtains. 'Had we not been here, Secrétaire, I wonder what might have happened to you? A big place like this and you here all on your own.'

'And waterers of rabbits are killers, are they?'

He had a point. 'Were no fingerprints taken after that visit?' demanded St-Cyr.

'Ah! don't be so difficult. It was a crisis.'

'And how, please, did you and the doctor find her *carte d'identité*?'

'Why should it matter?'

'Just answer, please,' said Louis, keeping up the pressure.

'On the bedside table, leaning up against that photograph of her husband.'

'As a warning?'

'As a reminder, perhaps, of our lost heroism. All right, it was deliberately left there for me, or so I felt at the time.'

'Why you, Secrétaire?'

'I ... I don't really know.'

'And Dr Ménétrel?'

'Felt the same, I'm certain.'

'A visit that was done after the killing and that anticipated your coming here,' said Louis. 'And then another, which anticipated our own and yours again. It's odd, is it not?'

'Look, people come and go in this place at all hours up to and

72

even beyond the curfew. Anyone could have slipped in and out if asked to – the killer too, of course. Old Rigaud, the concierge, was having a hell of a time keeping track of the residents and finally went on strike. They were driving him crazy simply for the fun of it, so we had to let him stay on.'

'Please wait downstairs or in your car, Secrétaire. Hermann and I won't be long.'

'Will there be fingerprints on those?' He indicated the letters.

'Other than the Maréchal's, Madame Dupuis's and those of any number of postal clerks, since the letters were mailed? Not likely, but they'll have to be dusted.'

'Then don't tell the doctor what you've found. Let him continue to worry about them. Learn that it's always best to keep him in the dark and distracted.'

'*Merde*, Louis, he's really edgy,' sighed Kohler when Bousquet had left them. 'Does he think he's the target?'

'He must, but does the killer or the one who took her to the Hall have a room here, Hermann, or do both of them? And is this what our secrétaire is now wondering since you so kindly pointed it out to him?'

'Someone so close to each of them, he, she or they can come and go at will and all are targets.'

'Pétain and his right hand; Laval and his. And why, please, did Monsieur Bousquet not drag along the local *flics*, eh? Look for little things, Hermann. Things that will tell us not only who our victim really was but why the Secrétaire Général de Police should have such a lapse of duty.'

'Things that may have been missed by our visitor or left on purpose, *Dummkopf*. Things we might never know the reason for their being here but others will.'

A Saint Louis crystal perfume bottle was still in its presentation box, tucked away at the back of her dressing table drawer. Right inside the lid, and probably never read by Pétain, there was a note: *Maréchal, please accept this small token for your dear wife in recognition of our esteem and devotion to you both.* It was signed M. Jean-Paul Brisset and Mme Marie-Louise of 32a *bis* rue

Dupanloup, Orléans. Though their numbers had dwindled, Pétain still regularly received such gifts from supporters all over the country. A bit of lacework from Normandy, a Sèvres soup tureen or vase, silver tea and coffee services, paintings too, signed and sent by their artists, books by their authors. All such things ended up in storage rooms at the stately home, the *maison de maître*, he had rented as a weekend retreat in the tiny village of Charmeil just six kilometres by road to the north-west of Vichy.

Céline Dupuis had obviously read the note and had carefully returned it to its place before shoving the box well out of sight.

Hermann was thumping a book he'd taken from the pile she'd been reading when time allowed ...

'*La Cuisinière Bourgeoise et Économique*, Louis. Well thumbed, somewhat tattered and probably published in 1890.'

The charming housewife on the cover wore a long, striped white and red dress, with white apron and frilly cap, but was holding a bloodied butcher's knife that was far more than needed to decapitate the chicken she'd just finished plucking for the steaming pot on the stove behind her.

'But why learn to cook, Louis, unless you plan to leave here or at least to leave the profession you're in?'

The wicker hamper at the woman's feet had spilled a rush of vegetables on to the floor. Pots hung in the background; pots that now would have been commandeered for scrap metals!

'Do you really need the reminder, eh? You know damned well people go to the films to watch the feasting, and that they read cookbooks that are centuries old just to taste the food they can only dream about.'

She hadn't heated the leftovers of some 'coffee' in a pot on the simple electric ring that served for all cooking. There were three carrots in the little larder, a thin slice of questionable cheese, a bit of bread – the grey 'National' everyone hated – two onions, a few cloves of garlic and some cubes of Viandox, a beef tea that was all but absent from the shops. Little else.

Her underwear, beyond a couple of pairs of pre-war silk, was nothing special, thought Kohler. Manufactured lace on the brassieres, a pair of black, meshed stockings she'd rolled up and had set aside to try to mend, a few slips and half-slips . . .

'Blouses, Hermann. Part of a costume, perhaps. The uniform of a troupe. Look for ones with cheap, mother-of-pearl cufflinks that may have been left in. Her killer might have been a colleague.'

Kohler went quickly through the contents of the armoire. Evening dresses, halter-necked and off-the-shoulder ones, a couple of suits with trousers, a few skirts . . .

The flat box of pre-war cardboard, a gift, was lined with tissue paper, the halter-necked dress of a soft, silvery silk over which were panels of see-through, vertically pleated strands, each about three millimetres apart and five centimetres long, separated by horizontal panels of scalloped, sequined lace. A long strand of blue sapphires lay atop the dress. A fortune.

'The earrings, Louis. Were they to have been worn with this?'

'The shoes . . . There are leather high heels to match.'

'She'd have looked fabulous in them.'

'No attempt has been made to steal the sapphires.'

'Then were these left for us to find along with the love letters?'

'The perfume, Hermann. Unless I'm mistaken, it's the same as our sculptress wore. It's Shalimar, one of Guerlain's, and was a smash hit in 1925. Sandalwood, bergamot and jasmine, absolute rose and iris, but vanilla also and that is what set it off to create the sensation it did at the International Exhibition in the Grand Palais. Our victim was wearing it when killed. This cheap little phial was on her dressing table.'

'And a hugely expensive dress from the twenties,' breathed Kohler. 'Did de Fleury give it to her, and if so, why the hell didn't he tell her to wear it?'

'You're forgetting the sapphires.'

'And that she must have put the earrings on after de Fleury had let her out at the hotel.'

'But were the necklace, the dress and the earrings all from the same person?'

'Blue eyes and fabulous blue stones, Louis. Nice and dark.'

The strand was dangled. 'Surely no *résistant* worth his salt would have left these when funds are so desperately needed by them?'

'And the ID, Chief?'

'Could well have been left by a *résistant*, yes.'

A tail feather from a male hen harrier had been used as a quill in an unsuccessful attempt at writing a postcard to the daughter. That of a pigeon had proved little better but the victim was, she had stated, 'planning next to use those of the quail, the merlin and guinea fowl or even one from a peacock'.

The postcard was a photo of the Maréchal in uniform with the words of the song every schoolchild in the country had to sing each day during opening exercises. Maréchal, *nous voilà! Devant toi, le saveur de la France.* Marshal, here we are before you, France's saviour. *Nous jurons, nous, les gars, De servir et de suivre tes pars.* We, your 'boys', swear to serve you and follow in your footsteps. For Pétain is France and France is Pétain!

And weren't they all now worried that the Résistance, the 'terrorists' or some other unknown would *bousiller les gars*? Smash the boys, bump them off?

3

The morgue was nowhere near the Hôtel du Parc, and certainly not within easy 'walking' distance, swore Kohler silently. Well to the south of the old town, it was near the river and above the marshy flats into which the town's septic bed drained. A cruel breeze, out of the west, stirred the frozen reeds, bringing a thin dusting of snow and the stench. Over the snow-covered hills beyond the river, the light was like gunmetal, the frost so hard that the branches of the trees would snap and creak – had it been like that at Stalingrad when his boys had died? he wondered. Of course it had. Woodsmoke would rise, marking the site of a camp fire – Jurgen and Hans would have known this only too well by then and would have agreed that, huddled over cold ashes, any *maquisards* out there would freeze to death rather than show themselves.

War was like that, like Christ on a platter in cold storage.

'Look, I know this won't sound right,' said Bousquet, cupping his hands as he lit the last of their cigarettes, the three of them standing but a few steps from the car whose engine idled, Georges, the driver, still behind the wheel and minding his own business because he'd been told to. 'The second victim ... Camille Lefèbvre. She and I ... An evening or two. Ah! it was nothing, I tell you. A chance meeting at a local inn well before last Christmas, a small gathering, a few friends. Who would have thought anything would have developed? Certainly I didn't.'

'Married?' snapped Kohler.

'The daughter of an officer, one of the recently disbanded Army of the Armistice.'

Demobilized 21 November of last year.

'I was careful. So very careful. One has to be in a little place like this and with a position such as mine.'

'We're waiting,' sighed Louis, impatiently flicking his cigarette away and not bothering even to save it for his little tin. 'You've not answered my partner's question.'

These two would think the worst but would have to be told. 'We had agreed to meet downriver at one of the cabins the open-air cafés let to people in summer. Swimming, boating, water-cycling and sunbathing, that sort of thing, but closed in winter.'

'Except that you've a year-long lease on this one,' muttered Kohler. It was just a shot in the dark but . . .

'I hardly ever have the time to go there. Friends use it, my wife and family in summer when they come for a little visit.'

'Hermann, ask him what he told those who needed to know where he'd be?'

'En route to Paris. There were three rooms. Not big, quite small. She got up during the night. Perhaps she had to take a pee, perhaps she heard a shutter banging – one was loose. I awoke when I heard her struggling. I reached under the pillows for my gun and called out that I was armed. There . . . there was still a good fire in the kitchen stove, light from its firebox and from her torch which had fallen. She . . . she was lying in a heap on the floor, twitching. Her robe was open, the back door swinging in towards me. I fired into the night. Twice, I think. Maybe three times.'

'The date and time?' grumbled Louis.

'7 January, a Thursday at . . . at about 2.45 a.m.'

'A Friday?'

'Yes . . . Yes, it was Friday by then.'

'Knifed, garrotted – what, exactly, Secrétaire?' demanded Louis, using that Sûreté voice of his.

'Garrotted, the wire still embedded in her throat.'

'And blood all over the place,' sighed Kohler. 'The jugular, the carotid artery . . .' They'd seen it all in Avignon ten days ago. One of a group of madrigal singers, the Palais des Papes . . .

'Her pessary had fallen out. I reached to pick it up but ... but hesitated because I felt whoever had killed her would come back to finish the job.'

'Footprints, Secrétaire? Two sets or one? A man and a woman or only...'

'Jean-Louis, that is all in the report but, yes, I think now that there could well have been two of them.'

Confusion, then, and doubt, the prints not clear. 'And were you the target or was she?'

'*Merde alors,* why would anyone have wanted to kill her? I was the target. *Me!* And now Georges is always kept near and always ready, and I am more than convinced of the danger, but at the time was far too concerned with...'

'With saving your own ass and buggering off,' sighed Kohler. *Mein Gott,* were they all the same? De Fleury and now Bousquet.

'Be reasonable, eh? I had to leave her. I had no other choice. Paris ... I had to be in Paris by four that afternoon.'

'To meet with Oberg and others of the SS, and Gestapo Boemelburg?' demanded Louis.

'Marseille ... Since you appear to think you know everything about the destruction of the Old Port, you will understand why I had to leave her.'

'Threw the pessary into the stove, did you?' quipped Hermann.

'Yes. I ... I gathered up all evidence of my having been with her. I'd often let others use the cabin. Sous-préfet Robert was well aware of this since he and his family had stayed there for a week this past summer. Camille had come on skis. There was really nothing to link me with her.'

'And Ménétrel, was he told in confidence?' demanded Louis.

'Don't be absurd! Of course, if I had felt for a moment they would make an attempt on the Maréchal, I'd have spoken up. That private army of the doctor's is supposed to keep our Head of State as secure as a termite's ass in a beehive but obviously didn't. And that, messieurs, is why you're here.'

Grey in the light, the river looked muddy where the ice had failed to form due to heat from the septic outfall. A lone hawk, a male hen harrier perhaps, thought St-Cyr only to mutter absently, 'They migrate don't they?'

'*What?*' yelped Bousquet, flinging his cigarette down.

The hawk was indicated.

'Idiot, it's searching for mice and voles.'

And waiting to have its tail feathers plucked for quills? wondered Kohler. *Merde*, what were they to do? 'Where was your driver, Secrétaire?'

'Downriver at a small hotel. He was to collect me well before dawn and did so. No one was to have known I'd be there. No one.'

'But someone obviously did,' grumbled Louis, giving that Sûreté nod his partner would understand only too well.

'And now you'll have to be charged with withholding evidence,' sighed Kohler. Oberg would hit the roof and threaten piano wire! Boemelburg would simply carry through his threat to send Louis to the salt mines of Silesia and himself to man a machine-gun on the Russian Front!

'But I haven't withheld it, have I?' said Bousquet. 'I've come clean.'

'Then join us in the morgue, Secrétaire,' said Louis with all the acid he could summon. 'Tell us who and where her husband is. Flesh out the little details while we examine the corpses.'

'Hermann, a quiet word.'

They drew away from the counter, Bousquet offering the attendant behind it a cigarette and trying to exchange pleasantries so as to cover his being here with two detectives from Paris.

'There's no need for you to see them,' said Louis, those big brown ox-eyes of his moist with concern. 'Get Georges to drop you off at the Hôtel du Parc. Pump him dry and find out what really went on the night of that little rendezvous, then talk to the switchboard operator that Ménétrel will probably have dismissed. Dry her tears. She may be a bank.'

'Bousquet won't tell you everything.'

'Of course not. None of them will, but Premier Laval would

most certainly have been aware of this and may well have sicked Ménétrel on to the switchboard girl not only to get rid of him but to let us know we ought to talk to her.'

The French ... *Mein Gott*, the wiliness of their peasants! Laval had grown up as one of them and was known to make much of it. 'Or to those at the PTT?'

The main exchange. Hermann was learning. 'Those too. Apart from the plentiful hotels, and the lack of a prominent politician who might not have agreed with them but would have demanded a powerful position, the Government came here because the town possessed a modern telephone exchange and calls could be made to New York, London or anywhere else, even Berlin.'

'Enjoy yourself.'

Stark under lights that must be far brighter than needed, the victims lay side by side. The white shrouds had been drawn fully back ... The skin of each was so pale and waxy-looking – blue and cold, especially in the lips and fingernails, livid elsewhere in blotches, the autopsy incision of the one crudely stitched up from her black-haired pubes to her throat ...

'That ... that is Marie-Jacqueline Mailloux, the first of them. Found in the *Grand établissement thermal*. Drowned,' managed Bousquet only to hear St-Cyr calmly saying, 'Take a moment, Secrétaire. Calm yourself.'

The thermal baths ...

'Unmarried – divorced when still quite young; nineteen, I think. A nurse with her own practice. Age thirty-two or three. Alain André Richard, our Minister of Supplies and Rationing, was quite infatuated with her.'

'And you, Secrétaire? Were you as "infatuated" with Madame Lefèbvre?'

Whose throat was greenish-yellow and tinged with coppery blue in places and still depressed on either side of where the wire had cut through, the flesh gaping ... Flecks of dark blood beneath the skin – showers of them, the smell of her ...

81

'*Don't!*' said St-Cyr. 'Come away, Secrétaire. *Away!* A brandy! A glass of water!' he called out to one of the attendants.

'Brandy?' came the echoing response. 'He asks for a marc, Hérnand.'

'Then get it from the safe, idiot. Hurry!' said Hérnand, the boss perhaps.

'*Merci*,' gasped Bousquet when it had arrived and been downed – three fingers at least and rough. 'Another. And another. Now leave us and close the door. This is a private matter. Speak of it to anyone and you'll be planting corpses in Russia for our friends.'

The door closed. '*Sacré nom de nom*, forgive me,' said Bousquet, looking at Camille's corpse whose nipples had collapsed and were tinged with bluish green and yellow, and whose breasts were slack and marred by livid blotches, no longer warmly being kissed or suckled as she cried out in ecstasy and begged, 'In, René. In and deep. I have to have you in me!'

'Tell me about her, Secrétaire. Tell me everything you know. Don't hold back. Hermann and I will only find out, and the sooner we have everything, the sooner we will have her killer or killers.'

The auburn hair was thick but because she'd been hosed down and it had been so cold in here, the hair was slicked and matted and had lost its permanent wave. 'Her eyes . . .'

'They've sunk a little into their sockets. A film of mucus and dead cells forms over the cornea – it's normal with exposure to air after a few hours. Dust collects on it and the surface of the cornea soon becomes brownish and wrinkled. Again, that is normal.'

'She had beautiful eyes.'

'Then imagine them as they once were and tell me about her. You loved her?'

'A little. I'd have been a fool not to have. She was a teacher – it's all in the report. Her husband, a captain, is a guest of our friends. She missed him terribly, this I know, for she'd often say his name when we made love. I think she needed to be held. The

82

old man, her father, was always bitching about his son-in-law's cowardice, always complaining that the boy had taken his daughter away from him and then had shirked his duty. Herr Gessler has his *gestapiste*'s eye on him. One can't go around this town continually griping about cowardice in the face of our friends. It doesn't do any of us any good.'

'A teacher,' said St-Cyr of the victim. One had to bring Bousquet back on track.

'Nervous – she greedily smoked cigarettes when she could get them, which lately was often enough because I always took her some and the old man was always asking her how she'd come by them.'

Women weren't allowed the tobacco ration which, if available, had been cut in half from two packets, each of twenty, and one of loose tobacco a month. Resented when caught smoking, they had to suffer the censure of most men and so tended to smoke in private or among trusted friends and relatives.

'That father of hers caught her often,' muttered Bousquet. ' "He thinks I'm selling myself for tobacco," she once said and laughed at the idiocy of it.'

The secrétaire was taking things harder than had been expected. 'Did she know either of the others?'

'Madame Dupuis taught ballet, but whether or not at Camille's school I simply don't know. But I will quietly make inquiries. They weren't friends. At least, Camille never mentioned her. Perhaps just casual acquaintances – the usual sort of thing one finds among the staff of such institutions. Madame Dupuis would only have been there part-time in any case, so it's possible but not probable they were friends.'

'And the other victim? A nurse, you said.'

'Mademoiselle Mailloux worked part-time at a private clinic, but I don't think any dancers went to its doctor simply because the cures he offers must be the usual for this place.'

Tired livers, flagging libidos, et cetera. 'But the school . . . ? Would she have done part-time nursing there?'

'Links . . . you look for links when the only one is that all were killed as another was about to die?'

'Yet all three of these attempted assassinations failed and you've yet to tell me how Mademoiselle Mailloux was drowned. Was she sharing a bath with the Minister of Supplies and Rationing? Did he, too, avoid the scandal and simply bugger off?'

'Don't. Please don't. It's painful enough that you've forced me to see them, Camille especially.'

A cigarette was found and, once lighted, was passed to Bousquet. The pipe was packed, the pouch emptied to its last grain.

'I'll tell Ministre Richard that he has to be completely open with you, Jean-Louis. That little affair of his had been going on for some time and he'd not been as discreet as one would have liked. Marie-Jacqueline would come to his office when she was out on a call and it was near to lunch or the *cinq à sept.* Everyone knew he was fucking her. One saw it in the looks they exchanged and in the lightness of her step, the mischief in her candid dark eyes, the toss of her head – ah! so many signals. That one was a real filly and didn't give a damn if everyone knew what was going on. Indeed, I think she revelled in it. After all, he's quite well off and powerful. A real catch.'

'They shared a bath?'

'They drank champagne.'

'The water was quite hot? A private cubicle, a "discreet" attendant, money in a palm and the couple left alone?' Five to seven were the usual hours for such little liaisons.

'The autopsy will show that she had consumed at least three-fifths of the bottle of Bollinger Cuvée Spéciale that was found with her. The lights went out. Richard went to see what was the matter – another of the power failures we're all plagued with these days. He called out to the attendant – at least, he will swear to this but isn't sure how far along the corridor he went. Then he felt his way back to the tub, thinking nothing more of her silence than that she must simply be wanting to relax. They touched hands. The toes of her right foot came between his thighs to play

84

with him. He was *certain* she was alive until the lights finally came on again.'

'But was he the target? Come, come, Secrétaire, if what you have just said is true, he wasn't.'

'But he must have been.'

Alone, St-Cyr replaced the shrouds, gently tucking each under a chin. 'Forgive me, please, for uncovering you all like that. I had to shock the secrétaire into yielding more than he wanted, but have failed. Now I need your hopes and desires, your strengths and weaknesses – everything including fast friends and enemies, and yet . . . and yet we have so little time.'

All had either just had sex before they'd been killed, or had been about to, and only in the case of Madame Dupuis would it not have been with a man she regularly kept company with. But had she really loved Honoré de Fleury?

Ménétrel had made the couple an offer they couldn't refuse.

She was blonde, blue-eyed, and had been born on 10 April 1915. 'And therefore a couple of months short of your twenty-eighth birthday. When asked how and when you first met Monsieur de Fleury, Secrétaire Général Bousquet could not recall his ever having enquired of such a thing. Nor could he say with any certainty how long the affair had been going on, only that de Fleury had been careful – "discreet" was the word he used.

'Camille Lefèbvre née Roux,' he said, turning to her and noting how her expression so vastly differed from that of the latest victim. 'Death by knifing brings sudden shock and disbelief, while that of garrotting brings panic and terror. Your identity card states you've brown hair and brown eyes, but really your hair is that lovely chestnut shade many men admire, and your eyes were of a soft, warm brown with flecks of green, or so our secrétaire maintains. But here, too, his memory is surprisingly unclear. Perhaps the two of you met at the races, or was it at the tennis or swimming club? Sunshine and long, hot days in any case, so last summer but late, he felt, in August. You introduced yourself to him – he *is* positive about this and says he wasn't looking for an affair and is quite happily married and content. You asked if he could possibly give you a lift home but he has no further recollection of that first meeting. Was it late at night and did he initiate things, as I suspect? You're beautiful and young – your husband has been locked up since the summer of 1940. Did René Bousquet consider you vulnerable? Remember, please, that he's incredibly handsome, outgoing and self-confident, is only thirty-three and parks his wife and family in Paris for the schooling of their children.

'You were born in Lyons on 18 February 1917 – that father of yours must have somehow got himself home on leave, or did he even partake of the Great War like so many, many of us?'

Those who hadn't – Premier Laval among them – had found their reasons, but one would have to hear what Major Roux had to say. Perhaps he would be able to reveal the date, time and place of his daughter's first meeting with Bousquet. It was a thought. And, yes, the Maréchal's closest friends and acquaintances, though few, were often military men, so the two could well know each other. One had best be careful.

Marie-Jacqueline Mailloux, the nurse, had jet-black hair and deep, dark blue eyes that were widely set in an angular face whose expression must often have appeared vital, for the brow was high and wide, the chin narrow, the nose sharp, and there had once been dimples in her apple cheeks.

'Not a tall woman, but "leggy", my partner would have said, had he seen you strutting out across a park or walking along some hospital corridor under the appreciative gazes of others like him. The card that everyone has to have filled out when they apply for a marriage licence, a divorce, a lease or house purchase, et cetera – that great bankroll of index cards the Gestapo inherited from the Sûreté and all *préfectures* – states emphatically that you gave birth at the age of nineteen in Tours to twins just as your divorce came through. There were mitigating circumstances in the application and it was granted because your husband, a much older man, was one of the shell-shocked and you couldn't possibly have been expected to cope any longer with his sudden fits of screaming in the night and at other times. The twins, two unnamed girls, were immediately given to the Carmelites, and as soon as you could, you moved to Paris.

'Born 30 June 1906 in Tours, you were not the thirty-two or -three Secrétaire Général Bousquet imagined, but thirty-seven and hiding it well, though surely he would have examined your papers and this card? The mistress of the Minister of Supplies and Rationing?

'And you were Bousquet's,' he said to Camille, 'and you, that of an inspector of finances. Food, Police, and Money. That's simpler than their long-winded titles, isn't it?'

Marie-Jacqueline would have laughed – he was certain of this; Camille would have watched to see where the thought was taking him.

'And Madame Dupuis?' he asked. 'Oh for sure, the Maréchal has exquisite taste, but you were completely unaware that someone was waiting on that little balcony. Once taken though, you did manage to slip away in the Hall des Sources – how was this possible? Did he call out to his associate? It was pitch dark – was he momentarily distracted?'

Her killer had also been waiting. The smell of cigar smoke must have permeated that of the damp and the hydrogen sulphide, especially since she had then to be hunted down.

'A long strand of blue sapphires and a pair of diamond earrings,' he said. 'The first in the style of the 1920s to go with the dress and shoes; the second in that of the Belle Époque and the *fin de siècle* but, really, the earrings could have been worn at any time since 1890 and beads were in vogue then too, so perhaps both came from the same source.'

There'd been no card or name in that gift box. There'd been two visits to her room, the first to leave her identity card, the second, the love letters, dress and jewellery.

'The letters were tied with a pink ribbon as though cherished when, if I understand your feelings for the Maréchal, you didn't want to have anything to do with him.'

Ménétrel had pronounced her dead at 7.32 a.m. on Wednesday

as the groundskeeper's son had babbled that she was only asleep. 'But then our killer or her assistant must have ducked into the Hall to reposition your legs while desperately searching for something. Not the earrings, but was it this?' he asked. 'The post from a cheap, snap-on cufflink whose mother-of-pearl button is as common as dust?'

Ménétrel had made no mention of rigor having set in – the degree of frost would have delayed its onset. There'd been no sign of the knife, and he had maintained that the legs hadn't been turned aside.

Then either whoever had searched had come in right after him and before rigor had made the legs so stiff that considerable force would have been necessary to change their position, or the doctor had lied and had moved them himself.

The garrotting of Camille Lefèbvre had been done with iron wire, very fine but easily obtained before the war, and not even fastened at its ends to short pins, simply wound around the hands perhaps. 'And carried coiled in a handbag or pocket, but apparently a professional killing all the same.'

Noted in the autopsy report, there was bruising on her back, where her killer's knee had been jammed against it as she'd gone down . . .

'You couldn't have cried out much or struggled for long.'

There were bruises on Marie-Jacqueline's throat and shoulders. She'd been held under, had struggled, had banged her left elbow on the stone steps of the bath. Strength would have been needed to hold her under even though she must have been light-headed and sleepy, yet the bruises were inconclusive as to the sex of her assailant. Older scratches and bruises, now all but healed, had also been noted. The arms and face, the breasts, knees and buttocks. A fight perhaps.

Céline Dupuis's right arm had been bruised by her killer. That knee and thigh had also been badly bruised but in a fall, the coroner had felt, that must have happened some weeks ago . . .

A throat was cleared, a breathless voice broke into his

thoughts. 'Jean-Louis, I came as soon as my hotel received Secrétaire Général Bousquet's summons.'

It was Félix Laloux, scruffy-bearded and looking grey and wasted in a shabby blue suit that was now far too big for him. Still blinking from behind wire-rimmed spectacles, the right lens of which was cracked, he was unaccustomed to the light.

'I've been a guest of the state.'

'Given free board and lodging?' That is, prison.

'Forgotten since the farce of the Riom trials.'

They'd been in the spring of 1941, when the Maréchal had tried to blame the Defeat of France on the ills of the Third Republic and the Blum Government, including its most vocal supporters of socialism and Freemasonry. 'Have you eaten?'

'Don't ask stupid questions of a man whose death sentence has just been commuted. Ask, Will I help you? The answer is yes, and I'm grateful you have remembered so fondly our working together in the past.'

'Then look closely. Tell no one but myself or my partner of what you find – Hermann is on our side, so please don't worry about him. He's not the usual by far. But see if all three here were killed by the same person or persons.'

'And yourself?'

'Will look for links elsewhere, but trust my partner will have turned up something.'

Kohler didn't hesitate but stepped into the telephone exchange at the Hôtel du Parc, the room no bigger than a large closet. There was constant clicking, constant motion. The operator, still with her shapely back to him, sat bolt upright on a high, wooden stool before the board on which eighty or so lines had connections. Headset strapped on over permanent wave, receiver clamped over the left ear, mouthpiece and transmitter dead in front of lovely lips, her left hand moving deftly to control the keys or yank out one of the cords with its brass plug-in, or flip back up one of the traps that fell open when a line was needed, the right hand putting the cords into the jacks on the board and jerking still others out, or writing up the day's log. Lights flashing, demands being made, and *ring . . . ring . . . ring!*

'*Allô . . . Allô . . . Ne quittez pas*, Monsieur Arnold. A moment. PTT, do you have Général Giradet for us yet? Please try his office again. Giradet? Ah! Monsieur le Général, Monsieur Arnold at the Hôtel du Parc wishes to speak with you. A moment, please. Monsieur Arnold, I have your connection. Go ahead now.'

Defence was in the Hôtel Thermal, Finance and Justice in the Carlton, the Diplomatic Corps in the Ambassadeurs, Education in the Plaza at 9 rue du Parc, Marine in the Helder, the Senate in the Salle des Sociétés Médicales over on the avenue Thermal, the Chamber of Deputies in the Grand Casino, and every outside call had to pass through here as well as those from room to room.

'A quiet word, mademoiselle.'

'*C'est impossible!* Something has set the hotel to buzzing. *Allô . . . Allô . . .*'

Kohler placed a hand over her left one and prised the receiver up a little from her ear. 'The girl you relieved,' he said.

'In the cellars, I think.'

She stopped then. Yanked off the headset and blurted tearfully, 'Lulu wouldn't have told anyone someone had tried to kill the Maréchal. We're all sworn to silence and each of us had to sign a paper that we understood a three-year prison sentence would be our reward if we broke our oath!'

'But you just did.'

The scar on his face was cruel, the look in his pale blue eyes utterly empty. 'You're Gestapo. I . . . I overheard this in one of the conversations – a word or two, that's all, Herr . . .'

'Kohler, Hermann,' he said and grinned like her son Paul, warmth and concern now entering his eyes. 'Look, please don't be upset. I'm here to help. Ménétrel's crazy and just on one of his rampages. Let me calm him down.'

'He . . . he threatened to feed her to the pigs or let the boul. National have her.'

Though officially here only since 11 November last, Herr Gessler had already made a name for himself. In Paris, just after the Defeat, people had soon come to speak in hushed tones of the rue des Saussaies – the Gestapo; the rue Lauriston also – the French Gestapo; and av. Foch, the SS. All were dreaded for equal reasons. Now here, the boul. National . . .

'Look, I hate what's been happening, but why the pigs?'

She shrugged and, dragging the receiver back over her ear, winced at further thoughts.

Lulu wasn't upstairs in the doctor's office, she was deep in the cellars, and even from a distance Kohler could hear them.

'*Salope!*' shrieked Ménétrel. '*Fuck with me and I'll let Hercules have you first before the sows dine.*'

'*Hercules?*' shouted the woman.

'*The boar, idiot!*'

'*Oh là là, docteur, I might even enjoy it, eh? after all, I've not had it since my husband fell to one of the Kaiser's bullets.*'

'*Putain, the boar's cock is a corkscrew,*' yelled Ménétrel. '*Those two pork chops you call labia will be torn to shreds if you don't give me answers!*'

Answers . . . Answers . . .

'*Maudit salaud, how can you treat a trusted employee like this?*'

'*We'll let Hercules have a ride in your little shanghai train first!*'

Jésus, merde alors, Ménétrel certainly did warrant his reputation for crudity! She was sitting on a wooden stool, jammed into the far corner of the freight lift, had seen this Kripo before the others, had seen the pistol in his hand. Ferbrave was with the doctor; two others blocked all escape.

'Then ask elsewhere,' she hissed, glaring up at Ménétrel. 'Ask Madame Pétain what she said to her *coiffeur* the day that girl was murdered. Find out what Monsieur Laurence then whispered to another, don't ask me. My lips have always been sealed. My husband worshipped the Maréchal and I would do nothing to discredit his good name or that of my own, and you know it. Now give me a cigarette and don't tell me you haven't any when I

91

damn well know you have plenty. Quit picking on a girl half your size and old enough to have been your mother, may God forgive her. You exhaust me, Docteur. And all this after a twelve-hour shift. *Merde, c'est scandaleux!* It's enough to make a saint want to piss during his final confession, and now I have to.'

She tossed her faded curls, Ferbrave swung his fist back. Plum-dark in the doughy pan of her face, her eyes leaped. 'Go ahead, *mon brave.* Beat a war-widow and grandmother to a pulp. That way my lips will be sealed and I won't ever be able to tell anyone how you get those cigarettes or the brandy and the cigars. Ah! I see that I've made you reconsider.'

The fist wasn't lowered.

'You hit her and I'll kill you,' breathed Kohler, pressing the muzzle of the Walther P38 to the back of the bastard's head. 'Maybe I will anyway. Now get out, all of you. Out, fast! RAUS! RAUS! SCHNELL!'

'Herr Kohler . . .'

'Silence! *Ach!* bugger off before I do it, Doctor. I'm Gestapo, eh? *Gestapo!* And don't any of you forget it!'

They weren't happy but they fled. Kohler found a broken cigarette and, putting the pistol away, tried to straighten the Gauloise bleue for her.

'*Merci,*' she said, 'but I really must take a piss.'

'She . . . she can use our pail.'

'Your name?' asked the Gestapo, looking over a shoulder.

'Al . . . bert. Groun . . . Groundkeeper.'

The boy, the young man, had wet himself. 'Don't be afraid any more, Albert,' said Kohler. 'Henri-Claude isn't going to hurt her while I'm around and he won't hurt you either. Just show Madame Lulu to your pail and then bring her back here for a chat.'

'It's . . . it's warm in the furnace room. We've a little nest there.'

'Then that's where we'd better go.'

Whenever she could, and too often, Lulu Beauclaire turned the conversation and his attention back to Albert Grenier. *Mein Gott*, she was tough but damned wary and scared, too, thought Kohler. Shrewd enough to know that Ferbrave or Ménétrel, or both of them, would be after her, yet willing to be made a fuss over here if it didn't necessitate breaking her vow of silence. Instead, using an innate curiosity mingled with motherly patience, she balanced the books by coaxing answers for him from the groundsman's son who could know nothing of the telephone calls she daily arranged.

'The keys . . . ?' she said as if they weren't staring at her from a board that was nailed to one of the furnace room's uprights.

'Three down, one over. Hall des Sources,' chimed in Albert as he opened the firebox door to bring an added blast of heat and let everyone see the glowing coals.

'Casino?' she said, taking it all in, the room with its gargantuan furnace and boiler, the pipes, the 'nest' with its coffee pot, broken chairs and lunch boxes, the newspapers . . .

'Five over, three down,' came the swift response, Albert's back still turned to her.

'*Toilette* number one?' she shot back. 'There are two of them in the park, Inspector.'

'One over, one down. I've got them all memorized. You won't catch me out!'

'Remarkable, isn't it, Inspector? And to think his mother had a terrible fall when he was eight months in the womb. Fifteen stone steps and then the wall of that old church. It broke her waters and harmed Albert, but not too much, I think. How is Yvette, Albert? You see, I know the family, Inspector. Yvette and I . . . Ah! the times we had as girls and she not getting in the family way until nearly forty. *Forty*, I say! Prayed constantly for it and finally the Virgin had to listen.'

'A miracle,' sighed Albert shyly. 'She's fine, Madame Lulu. She's going to bake me a *pavé de santé* just like her mother used to for her but it's . . . it's against the law.'

Gingerbread. The pavement or cobblestone of good health.

And there's no ginger or butter, no flour or sugar, or is there? wondered Kohler.

'All of us girls try to catch Albert out with the keys, Inspector,' hazarded Lulu quickly.

'Mademoiselle Trudel didn't. She just asked me which one was for the Hall des Sources. She couldn't remember,' said Albert.

'And has now gone away to visit her father who is ill.'

'She wanted a bottle of water for him. The Chomel, Madame Lulu. I ... I let her fill one.'

Ah, nom de Dieu ...

'You see, Inspector. Not an unkind bone in his body and so conscientious, he sometimes gets here two hours before any of us.'

'Five. She was waiting for me at just after five because she had to catch the morning train. Half frozen and shivering in that thin coat of hers. No mittens. No hat. I brought her here to get warm while I built up the fire and got the key.'

One had best go easy. 'When? What day, Albert?' he asked.

'Last Saturday. I know, because she said she wouldn't be seeing me at church and she didn't, Madame Lulu. She didn't!'

'Lucie is a shorthand typist with the Bank of France,' yielded Lulu, letting him have benefit of it with a curt nod. 'Mademoiselle Trudel is really needed these days, but it is odd, now I think of it, Albert, that she was able to arrange compassionate leave at such a time when everyone is so busy.'

Trying to govern a country someone else occupied.

'She's very fond of her job and lives in the same hotel as Madame Dupuis used to,' went on Lulu, butting out her fourth cigarette.

Oh-oh was written in the look the detective threw her, so now she had best give him another titbit. 'Albert, what's the name of that club by the bridge? You know, the place some of the girls go to after work? Chez Robinson, was it?'

'Chez Crusoe,' trumpeted Albert. 'It's by the Boutiron Bridge and not far from her hotel. They play records and dance. Sometimes when she comes to Vichy, Yvonne Printemps sings there after hours and there's a piano player, but usually it's ... it's only records or the wireless. Never the news from the BBC London. Never! That's ... that's against the law.'

'And the cigarettes, the brandy and cigars Henri-Claude Ferbrave gets?' asked Herr Kohler quietly.

'They come in a van,' said Albert eagerly. 'A van that has the Bank of France written on it. I know because I heard him saying so, and then saw it myself. I watched. Cartons and cartons of cigarettes from the Tabac National in Vannes, brandy from the Halle aux Vins in Paris – heaps of white flour, too, and coffee, this coff—'

The bloody Bank of France!

'It's all right, Albert. Don't worry,' soothed Lulu. 'The Inspector's a friend. You heard what he said to that one when he had me trapped in the lift. "You hit her and I'll kill you. Maybe I will anyway." '

'I ... I borrowed our coffee from the van,' confessed Albert, not looking at either of them. 'The driver and his helper were too busy to notice. It was cold and dark. I hid it but then ... then I made the coffee, real coffee, for the boys and ... and told them the sack had fallen off a German lorry. They all patted me on the back, my father especially.'

'A bank,' Louis had said of the woman. A full safe with extra strongboxes just waiting to be opened if one could find the keys!

'Madame Pétain ...' he attempted, only to hear Lulu cluck her tongue and tartly say, 'Is not a friend of Albert's.'

'She doesn't like idiots,' whispered Albert, ducking his eyes down at the floor. 'She and the doctor think I should be sent away.'

'But she did say something to her *coiffeur* on the day Madame Dupuis fell asleep ...' hazarded Herr Kohler, a slow learner perhaps, thought Lulu, but a learner all the same.

'Asleep – there, you see, Madame Lulu. I was right!'

'Of course you were. Of course. Inspector, I did not listen in as Dr Ménétrel supposes, nor do I tell anyone what I may or may

not have overheard. Monsieur Laurence Davioud is *coiffeur* to
many of the wives of important ministers and government
officials, those of the foreign ambassadors, too, and even those of
inspectors of finances, I believe.'

A treasure . . . 'And Ferbrave?'

'Is a very dangerous man, so Albert and myself, we will
appreciate your continued protection.'

'He knows things,' said Albert darkly. 'Secret things. I'll bet if
he knew what I'd found, he'd want to take it from me, but I'm
not going to tell him my special secret, Madame Lulu. I'm not!
I'm going to keep it *all* for myself.'

Ah *Sainte Mère*, why must the boy always be picking things up?
'What, Albert? Show me what you found?' she coaxed. 'You know
I won't tell anyone, not even your mother, if you don't want me
to, and as for the inspector, why he's here to help us.'

'I hid it. I can't tell.'

'Now, Albert . . . One good turn deserves another.'

'I can't hear you. I've got to stoke the fire.'

'Albert, I must insist. Yvette will only ask me and I want to be
able to tell her how helpful you've been.'

'The other one took my ring. He said it would be dangerous
for me if I kept it.'

'Yes, yes, but this . . . this assassin they're looking for will know
you found something else. Nothing is ever secret for long in this
place. Nothing.'

The firebox was stoked, the coals rabbled for clinkers. Sparks
flew up, mesmerizing Albert. Madame Dupuis had been asleep.
She had!

'Son, give it to him,' said the elder Grenier, coming into the
furnace room. 'You must, Albert.' His hand went out to caution
the others. 'My son knows how important it is, Inspector. Albert
was just waiting for the right moment to turn it over to you or
your partner.'

The hiding place, no doubt one of several, thought Kohler, was
behind the access plate at the bottom of the chimney. Dusted

with soot, some of this sprinkled away as the folded rag was opened.

Brass at its ends, rosewood along its gently curved and palm-fitting haft, the folded-in blade silvery, the pocket knife gleamed.

Herr Kohler was humbled, thought Lulu. 'I'll see you get another just like it,' he said, so gently for such a big man. 'Now tell me where you found it.'

'In the toilet. On . . . on top of the shit.'

'The drains to our outdoor toilets become frozen in winter, Inspector,' interjected the elder Grenier. 'Since we have so many visitors these days, the Government decided to install two portable toilets next to the permanent ones in the park. Among my son's tasks is the job of checking these twice each day, just to see there is paper if needed.'

Paper was in such short supply it was a wonder it wasn't repeatedly stolen, unless, of course, Albert kept his eye on those two portables more than twice a day . . . 'And the knife was lying there as if dropped?'

'Albert washed and oiled it.'

'I polished it. I shined it up. It's brand-new and hasn't . . .' His voice trailed off. 'Ever been used, I guess.'

'Had the person who dropped it been sick?' asked Kohler.

Albert gave an eager nod, then frowned and said, 'It . . . it must have slipped and fallen. Yes . . . yes, that's what it did!'

'Open or closed? The blade, that is.'

'Open. Straight up, and in like a dagger!'

'Blood . . . was there blood?'

'Frozen. It had been washed,' grumbled Albert, gritting his teeth. 'There wasn't any blood. Why should there have been?'

'When . . . when did you find it?'

'In . . . in the morning, after the . . . the vomiting.'

'A cigar? Did you find one?'

'No.'

'The key . . . ?' prompted Lulu, meaning the one to the Hall where the murder had taken place. *Merde*, the tension was terrible, but had Albert lied to protect the killer?

97

'Those portable toilets are never locked, Inspector, only the permanent ones,' said the elder Grenier.

The kid, the boy, the man, deserved a medal, but would Louis still be at the morgue?

'A tisane of lime flowers with apple skins, or the carrot greens with liquorice. If I can't drink it, I can always smoke it,' said St-Cyr.

A wise one reeking of Sûreté and Paris and pissed off at having to wait his turn! The forlornly clutched pipe was empty, the tobacco pouch also, as further evidence. 'A moment, m'sieur. I will see if there is anything beyond ashes. Sometimes the urn contains a few leaves.'

Verdammt, Louis, how many times have you told me never to try to joke with a waiter? Hermann would have gone on and on about the 'lessons' in French etiquette he constantly received from his partner, but Hermann wasn't here as anticipated and perversity had won out!

Vichy's railway station stank of cold, damp soot, unwashed bodies, disinfectant and urine. Dirt was everywhere: in the saucer that was used for powdered saccharin, on the floor that hadn't been swept in months, in the shabbiness of the crowd that mingled or came and went but that held few happy faces. Papers being checked – plain-clothed Gestapo on the hunt; GFPs too, the Wehrmacht's secret police, looking for deserters; its uni-formed military police also, the *Kettenhunde*, the 'chained dogs' who wore their badge of office on a chain around their necks. Tough, brutal, no-nonsense men to whom even the Vichy goons and *flics* gave a wide berth.

The sculptress had taken the same train as Hermann and himself, but try as he now did, St-Cyr could find no memory of her having been in any of the waiting queues, either at the Gare de Lyon in Paris on Wednesday, the day after Céline Dupuis's murder, or at the Demarcation Line.

'Inès Charpentier,' he said. Oh for sure, her name had been in the register. She'd taken a sleeper – normally one would think nothing of it except that, as an artist and poor, how could she have afforded such a luxury when even detectives didn't dare to do such a thing?

Then, too, since the Defeat, the trains had been policed, not by the Sûreté, but by the German railway police. And everyone, including most especially the Résistance, was well aware of the respect and admiration given to wealth and position by the common and ordinary of the Occupier.

Even at the Demarcation Line they seldom bothered to disturb those in the *wagons-lits*, the *Schlafwagens*.

'A man and a woman, but one of the latter,' he said, 'who knows well how to come and go and now has a reason for staying here.' Had someone paid her fare, someone in the Résistance?

It was an uncomfortable thought and, as always these days, things could be so complicated. Many of the railway workers, especially in Lyons, had been communists until the party had been banned, and when the Germans invaded Russia in June 1941, the *cheminots* formed what was to become, in 1942, the FTP, the Francs-Tireurs et Partisans, but by then the assassinations they had initiated were being carried out in earnest. Prominent collaborators, Wehrmacht corporals and higher-ups. In December 1941, General Keitel signed the *Nacht und Nebel Erlass*, the Night and Fog decree. In retaliation for the killings, all those arrested whose innocence could not be quickly determined were to be deported to the Reich under cover of darkness.

Families could not even find out where their sons or daughters had been taken or if they had even been arrested. Brothers lost brothers; sisters the same. One simply vanished without a trace.

Hostages were also taken and shot. At first only a few, then ten for each German killed, then more, people being rounded up and held as *Sühnepersone* – as expiators – for those who'd been killed.

And yes, a civil war between Vichy's newest police force, the Milice, and the Résistance was definitely possible. And yes, Hermann and he himself would be caught up in it, his Giselle and Oona too; Gabrielle also.

But these killings, he reminded himself, these failed assassination attempts, if indeed that is what they'd been, might not have been the work of the Résistance at all.

First there was the extreme right of Paris who hated Vichy and wanted power. The Intervention-Referat, at 48 rue de Villejust, recruited and trained teams of assassins from among members of the Parti Populaire Français of Jacques Doriot whose newspaper, *Le Cri du Peuple*, didn't just shrill collaboration beyond that of Vichy, but total union with the Reich. True, these killers did the work of the Gestapo when they wished to appear dissociated from it and, true, they did the PPF's work as well, even when it didn't necessarily agree with the Gestapo's position.

Then, too, there was the Bickler Unit of the Alsatian, Karl (Hermann) Bickler, who trained infiltrators and agents for the Gestapo – assassinations, kidnapping and extortion also – but primarily directed against the Résistance.

'And otherwise?' he asked himself, for there were still possibilities of a political nature. 'A jealous wife or lover, but surely not with all three of the victims.'

There was still no sign of Hermann, nor the tisane he had ordered. When looking out of the restaurant at the crowd, he couldn't help but notice their footwear. Shoes indicated the health of the nation: carpet slippers in winter, but stuffed with bits of newspaper or twists of straw and worn sometimes even in mismatched pairs; open-toed high heels with thin straps, but with woollen socks instead of the silk stockings for which they'd been fashioned, hence the tightness, the rubbing, the painful chilblains one often noticed on the female corpses one had to examine. Wooden-soled shoes with their cleverly articulated hinges and cloth or ersatz leather uppers were everywhere, sabots also, and then, too, shabby leather or rubber boots that were far too big for the wives of those who were locked up in POW camps in the Reich.

'We've become a nation that will wear anything and that no longer cares about appearances,' he said and then, getting back to the matter at hand, 'Camille Lefèbvre's father will have to be interviewed. There is also Céline Dupuis's love of birds and her use of their quills that will have to be looked into. *Merde*, where is that partner of mine?'

Hermann functioned best with a set of wheels under him. In September 1940, when they'd first met, he'd seen that big, black, beautiful Citroën *traction avant*, that front-wheel drive, and had said blithely, 'You'd better give me the keys.'

'My car! The years of diligent service, the rise to Chief Inspector, and then ... then to have it all taken away!'

Hermann was a terrible driver. Heavy on the foot, careless on the straight and narrow, insane on the blind curves. 'It's a wonder I haven't been killed or forgotten how to drive.' But Hermann, for all his faults, was desperately needed.

'Bousquet has not come completely clean,' St-Cyr grumbled when, grinning and loudly exclaiming, 'I knew I'd find you here!' the Bavarian at last appeared in a rush. 'He's still trying to hide something, Hermann.'

'Cheer up and shut your eyes – come on, do it – and hold out your hand.'

Louis sucked in a breath as he felt for the thumbnail groove and carefully opened the blade to cradle the pocket knife in his hand. 'A Laguiole, Hermann. A woman's knife – there is no awl or corkscrew as with those of the men. It's an unwritten rule of etiquette that women flash only open blades. The bee under my thumb at the head of the haft supposedly symbolizes Napoléon's warrant but I doubt it. The village is well to the south of Clermont-Ferrand and a good distance from here. Still, the knives travel, and in the Auvergne it is preferred over the simple Opinel most of our peasants favour. Beautifully made, not cheap now, but razor-sharp because the steel is similar to that of surgical instruments – one per cent carbon, seventeen per cent chrome and point eight per cent molybdenum – but always the love of one's craft goes into them.'

Opening his eyes, Louis laid the knife on the table, the cinematographer within him taking in each detail: the length, in total, some twenty centimetres, the blade being a little less than half of that: silver-coloured, then brass and rosewood with brass rivets, then brass again in the softly curved end to fit the hand perfectly – any hand.

'She knew her weapons, Hermann, if she killed them all.'

'But had she the Maréchal in mind?'

'Or Bousquet, or Alain André Richard, Minister of Supplies and Rationing?'

There was a pattern in the steel along the back of the haft and this extended from the bee to the very end. One of art deco hills – volcanoes, perhaps, and each of a wide, low triangle with incised, deeper and much smaller triangular cuts both above and below to give the impression of the forested hills and valleys of the Auvergne.

'It's light,' said Kohler. 'It can't weigh any more than two hundred grams.'

'One hundred. A marvellous weapon and so easily carried in a handbag or pocket. The style is Spanish, though that of the blade goes much farther back in time and is Turkish, I believe. In the twenties and thirties the knives became increasingly popular outside of the Auvergne as tourists visited the village, and many were made to individual specifications, each client stating their needs and even the design on the haft and the choice of wood or horn. In short, the Laguiole became a cult item and expensive, a mark of distinction that others who also owned one would recognize and appreciate.'

'Let's hope we do.'

The tisane finally arrived in a dirty mug but was brusquely shoved aside. 'Bring the Chief Inspector St-Cyr a pastis. He's going to need it. I'll have a beer and *not* one of those near-beers, eh? Gestapo, *mon fin*. Gestapo, and don't you forget it or spit in our drinks either.' The Walther P38 was taken out and laid on the table. 'That's so as to have it ready,' he said to the waiter.

The knife and the pistol were stark against the worn glass of the table top beneath which a faded menu listed the brioches and croissants of long-lost days. 'It shall be as you wish, m'sieur. Who am I to object to your breaking a law that was made only for us?'

'Piss off!'

'Certainly.'

'Now he'll cough into our drinks, idiot! How many times must I tell you that a little patience is always necessary?'

'We haven't time. The Bank of France has been humping stuff from Paris for friend Ferbrave.'

'Pardon?'

'*Gut.* I've finally got your attention.'

As was their custom when on short rations and at other times, they shared a cigarette, Hermann managing to find one in a pocket. Damaged, of course, and dribbling stale tobacco, but still ... '*Merci.*'

'Take two good drags and take your time, eh?'

'Three murders, three supposed assassination attempts that failed to find their respective targets but chose another.'

'A lover, a mistress.'

'The first of whom was known to flaunt her liaisons and no doubt to laugh in the face of Madame Richard.'

'Did her husband know the vans were being used to haul rationed goods that had been purloined?'

'We'll have to ask him.'

'A shorthand typist with the Bank of France, Mademoiselle Lucie Trudel, asked Albert to let her into the Hall des Sources, Louis. A bottle of the Chomel for a sick father, at just after 5 a.m. last Saturday.'

'And not seen since?' blurted St-Cyr, alarmed, no doubt, by the prospect of a killing as yet undiscovered.

'Away on compassionate leave. I ... I forgot to ask where. Sorry.'

'We'll deal with it.'

'She lives in the Hôtel d'Allier.'

'And is not away at all, but staying in her room and able to enter Céline Dupuis's at will to leave these?'

Louis set the love letters on the table and then the *carte d'identité* with its head-and-shoulders profile. The knife was still there ...

'Someone who can come and go at will,' said Kohler, 'and must have damned well known the Garde Mobile and lift operator would be absent.'

'Ménétrel gave them the night off.'

The cigar band was added to the collection, the earrings also and the sapphires, lastly the cufflink's stud.

'And a dress, plus a pair of high heels,' muttered Kohler.

'Why leave the ID like that for Bousquet, *mon vieux*? In neither of the other killings was such a thing done. Though the reports are thin and add little, both of those victims had their handbags with them – Camille Lefèbvre's was found untouched with her clothes in the cabin; Marie-Jacqueline Mailloux's was in the lock-up at the *Grand établissement thermal*, also untouched and with her clothing.'

'They'll have sold Céline Dupuis's other papers. You know as well as I do there's one hell of a racket in stolen bread cards, to say nothing of the other ration tickets.'

Before the Defeat, the French had become accustomed to eating – and tasting – their food only if it was accompanied by bread. From around a kilo per day, the adult consumption had dropped to about 200 grams if one could get it, and then it usually came in the form of 25-gram slices of the grey National, or in its thumping-hard and very questionable loaves.

'If they were that desperate, Hermann, then our two assailants are not entirely the professionals we've come to believe and could well be *résistants*.'

'The one was sick, Louis. She threw up in the portable toilet when she dropped the knife. No sign of the cigar, though, or of its ashes. I checked just to make sure.'

'A killer with a queasy stomach!' Louis dragged out two *mégot* tins, one of which had once held mints; the other, dressmaker's pins. 'Camille Lefèbvre's,' he said of the former. 'Bousquet let it slip that she greedily smoked cigarettes whenever she could get them and that her father had accused her of selling herself for them. That's what made me take this from her bag, and then, that of Marie-Jacqueline.'

The wealthy, the middle class and the poor, it didn't matter, thought Kohler. Priest, cardinal and gangster, pimp, prostitute and disgruntled housewife, schoolboy, urchin and banker, these days all of them had become butt collectors. If one didn't smoke, one sold or traded the tobacco for something else. Seldom was anything but life wasted.

'Lucky Strikes from downed American aircrew,' he said, fishing about in Camille Lefèbvre's tin. 'Baltos and Russians.' He savoured several, crumbling one after another, was good at this, thought St-Cyr. A connoisseur. 'Gauloises bleues, with dried herbs, straw and other *Quatsch* added as usual, the bastards. Cigars . . . Three of them. No bands, but good. A cigarillo also. A wayside inn, I wonder. A place where both Occupier and Occupied can meet over drinks to discuss things.'

'Like songs, sex and using vans that belong to the Bank of France?'

'Chez Crusoe, and if you ask me, *mein Kammerad der Kriminalpolizei*, I think our groundskeeper's son must have watched a good deal more than those vans.'

They'd have to talk to Albert, have to get him alone and go to work on him, but gently. '*Merde*, we're going to be run off our feet, Hermann. Is that what Bousquet wants? To keep us so busy we can't possibly uncover the truth? And Ménétrel . . . What of the doctor? What, please, was his part in all of this?'

'That driver of Bousquet's refused to cough up, Louis. I tried. I used every threat in the book, but our Georges's mouth has been zipped so tightly, you could put a bullet in his brain and get more.'

'A cabin,' muttered St-Cyr. 'A small hotel downriver of it, to which Bousquet's driver conveniently goes to stay the night.'

'And a local inn to which some of the girls go after work.'

'And where one of them meets that same secrétaire général to bum a lift home in the small hours – is that how it really was?'

Kohler opened the other tin only to find an almost identical selection, but here there were also two carefully flattened cigar bands: another Choix Supreme perhaps, and a Romeo y Julieta, both bright red and with gold coins on either side of the brand name.

'Our nurse must have known Albert, Louis.'

'She had a private practice. Was he one of her patients?'

'Was she accustomed to caring for the girls at Camille Lefèbvre's school?'

'Where Céline Dupuis may have taught ballet part-time?'

'A bird lover, Louis. One who wore diamonds she tried her damnedest to hide.'

'But hadn't worn the dress, the shoes or this because she couldn't have had them.'

The beads of a very wealthy flapper.

'Which, by rights, should have been stolen from her room,' breathed Kohler. 'The Hôtel d'Allier, *mon vieux.* I think we'd better hear what our shorthand typist has to say if alive and still at home.'

The Hôtel d'Allier rose up from behind its iron fence, grey and slate-roofed against an even greyer sky. Shutters open, others closed.

In the foyer, a simple bell and desk stood before dark, wooden pigeon-holes with their infrequent messages. Keys absent or left on the run, others long forgotten. Maybe sixty or seventy rooms . . .

The head-and-shoulders portrait of Pétain in uniform, looking sternly down from the papered wall, was crooked.

'St-Cyr, Sûreté. Mademoiselle Lucie Trudel, and hurry.'

'Hurry?' yelped the ancient concierge, having ducked behind the desk. 'The police are always in a hurry, no more now than before. Nor have they changed their coats or their politics, only the weight of their truncheons.' Cloves of garlic spilled from his left hand. 'My lunch,' he hissed. 'There's no bread.'

'Kohler, *mon fin.* Gestapo, Paris-Central.'

'Concierge Rigaud, it's a matter of some importance,' tried Louis.

'My soup, is that not important? This place. The constant

comings and goings and no one signing in or out, eh? What's it this time? Drugs? Syphilis? Or did she have something worse? Is that why she had to go home? Well, is it?' he shrilled.

Sacré nom de nom, a tough one! 'Did she really go home?' bleated St-Cyr.

'Three messages now and not collected. Aren't they evidence enough?'

Rigaud, for all his years and apparent frailty, was fiercely protective of his territory but the snap of Hermann's fingers broke the air. Swiftly handed over, the slender slips of paper were quickly scanned and pocketed.

'She was rounded up, wasn't she?' rasped the concierge, biting back on his gums, then clucking his tongue for good measure. 'Grabbed off the street and hustled to the *commissariat*. Forced to strip for the doctor to have a look and a swab, eh? They're disgusting, the girls these days. Dropping their underwear whenever they get itchy. No morals. No sense of decency. These old ears of mine *don't* want to listen but cry when they hear the goings on!'

Venereal diseases had become so rampant in Paris that the Occupier had insisted the *flics* routinely round up for medical checks whatever females were available, not just the *filles de joie*.

'Yes, yes,' sighed Louis. 'The key, monsieur. Room 4-17.' He pointed to the empty pigeon-hole.

'She left very early on Saturday and has not returned,' said Rigaud spitefully.

'Stay here. If we need you, we'll get you. Louis, it's this way. I'm not taking that lift or any other.'

Caught once by the hanging thread of a broken cable, Hermann had a thing about lifts. Old or from the late thirties, repaired and constantly serviced or otherwise, it simply didn't matter.

'The exercise will do you good,' he said, only to gasp in pain on the stairs and grab his left knee. '*Ach!*' he shrieked. '*Scheisse!*'

He sat down hard. Pain blurred his eyes and twisted the whip scar on his cheek. 'Go ahead,' he managed. 'I'll join you in a minute. It's nothing.'

'*Nothing?* Remind me to fix that poultice for you tonight.'

'Who sleeps? Not us. Now beat it. Fourth floor at the back, since Céline's room in the attic was number 3 and at the front. Oh, here. You'd better take these.'

The messages.

Friday, 29 January

Chérie, je t'aime, toujours je t'aime. You know I want only what is best for you. Paris, *chérie.* Paris tomorrow. Though we won't be able to travel together, I promise I'll be with you when we get there.

It was signed: *Ton petit grigou.* Your little penny-pincher.

Saturday, 30 January

Lucie, please come back soon. We have to talk. It's urgent.

   Céline

Tuesday, 2 February

Chérie, I needed you. Every day without your warm embrace was a day of constant despair. Paris no longer held its magic and now I find that you went home in spite of our having discussed things and agreed.

This final note was unsigned but was obviously from her penny-pincher. *Merde,* were they to have yet another killing, wondered St-Cyr, or had it already happened?

As before, the stairs and corridors were narrow and poorly lit. Noises carried. Though most of the rooms would be unoccupied at this time of day, cooking was in progress somewhere, a gramophone was playing – Lucienne Boyer singing 'Sans Toi', Without You ...

The room was not at the back of the hotel as Hermann had thought, but at the front, though here the blackout curtains were still drawn, the bed mounded with covers. Slacks, a woollen pullover, a blouse, brassiere and underpants lay in a heap beside it. One sock, her shoes, her overcoat, ah *Jésus* . . . *Jésus* . . . The pale blue glass bottle of water was on the bedside table. Woven wicker where the hands would hold it. The Buvette de Chomel . . . the Chomel . . .

Switching on the overhead light, he hesitated, asked silently, Was she smothered – is that how it was done?

The smell . . . always there was that clinging, throat-clawing sweetness Hermann now found so terrifying.

Flinging back the covers, St-Cyr sucked in a ragged breath and held it, forced himself to look closely as, grey and bloated, cut open, festering and crawling with maggots, five dead rats lay belly up, their entrails trailing.

'Trapped . . . They were first trapped,' he heard himself muttering and wondered where her corpse must be. Her corpse . . .

'On Saturday,' he said, his voice stiff with control, '30 January. Almost six days now, but was Bousquet supposed to find these?' he asked when Hermann hobbled into the room to swear under his breath.

'Where's the girl, Louis?'

'Don't open that armoire. Let me.'

Dresses had been flung aside, others had fallen from their hangers. A brown velvet hacking jacket, a paisley silk cravat and brown whipcord riding breeches covered her. A slip, a half-slip, then a pair of lace-trimmed underpants, silk and expensive, were hooked over the end of the riding crop in her hand.

The cheeks were ashen to a contused greyish purple; her eyes were closed, sprays of petechiae dusting the lids, the bridge of her nose and forehead. Effluent and bloodstained oedematous fluid and froth had erupted and then oozed from her nostrils and mouth. There were blotches. The stench was terrible.

'Smothered,' he said softly. 'Held down under a pillow on the bed, Hermann, then carried here while unconscious to be crammed into a corner and finished off, the other sock no doubt jammed into her mouth. She's lost the child. About three months, I think. Laloux will be more precise. Aborted foetuses are a speciality with him, among other things.'

She had also voided herself.

'These rats are all males,' managed Kohler. 'Why only those, unless they're the next to get it?'

'De Fleury, Bousquet, Richard, this one's "lover", and Pétain, eh?' snapped St-Cyr.

'Mademoiselle Trudel was to have left for Clermont-Ferrand, Louis. There's a third-class ticket on the floor with her clothes.'

'Yet she changed her mind.'

'Was agitated. Didn't pick up Friday's message. Went out very early Saturday morning to meet Albert and get that bottle. Forgot her hat and mittens. Must have been freezing, yet walked all the way there and back in the dark.'

'Then took off her clothes and climbed into bed.'

'To freeze and wait for her lover?' hazarded Kohler.

'Who was to have checked in with her before the couple made their separate ways to catch the train to Paris, or to give her a lift to it, eh?'

'She's scribbled two items on a bedside note. A seven with a plus and minus sign and then a half-hour for the train to Clermont Ferrand, and an eight with the same for the early train to Paris, kidding herself that they still run so closely on time.'

'A *grigou*.'

'One of *les gars, mon enfant*.' One of the boys.

4

The room was quiet, the hotel also. Alone with the corpse, St-Cyr tried to get a sense of what had really happened.

Lucie Trudel, the common, the ordinary working girl – certainly it was unfair to use such terms, but best to get things in perspective – had had every intention of going home to see her father but had suddenly changed her mind.

On her return, she had hurriedly unpacked a rather shabby cardboard suitcase – one of thousands these days – and had placed inside it, at a tight fit, an all but new one from Goyard Aîné, at 233 rue du Faubourg St-Honoré in Paris, founded in 1792.

This second suitcase had been packed well beforehand and with loving care. The scarlet silk Charmeuse evening dress and velvet shawl were from Pinnel, at 18 ave. de l'Opéra – not designer originals but, especially with the shortages, exceedingly expensive. 'Eighty-five thousand francs,' he said flatly. The grey worsted suit that accompanied it was of an exquisite cut and worth probably fifty thousand.

There were slips and brassieres – two changes of everything – garter belts, silk stockings that most women *and* men could only dream about, silk underpants and nightgowns, all from J. Roussel, at 166 boul. Haussmann. Again, not quite designer originals but sufficient for all but the most discerning taste.

Two rough flannel nightgowns, some small, plain white towels and a bundle of sanitary napkins gave pause. The brown leather handbag was from Raphael, at 99 rue de Lafayette, the red leather high heels, with their thin and elegant ankle straps, were from

Bonnard, at 53 Faubourg St-Honoré, as were the brown Oxfords, except that no one used such terms in France any more. 'Pumps,' he grunted, 'but with laces.'

She'd have put the cardboard suitcase in the left-luggage at the Gare de Lyon, would have taken off the one overcoat and ... What? he demanded and, opening the Paris handbag, found a ticket for Chapitel, at 4 boul. Malesherbes. Dry cleaning was prohibitively expensive and all but impossible to organize, yet ... yet she'd been able to arrange it. 'A beige, cashmere overcoat, a small stain on the right sleeve. A smudge. Coffee,' she had thought. Real coffee.

Sure enough, the Paris suitcase contained brown leather gloves, a soft yellow cashmere scarf and cloche, the handbag enough jewellery to satisfy a banker.

'A *grigou*,' he said tartly and, taking out the notes, read them again.

'You would have seen that there was a message for you, yet you didn't collect it on Friday,' he mused, the doors to the armoire still open. 'Your penny-pincher had insisted you have an abortion – that was the reason for this particular trip to Paris. You'd spend a few days together beforehand but not afterwards. You understood clearly that you couldn't travel together. First and third class, the cardboard hiding the leather but no fear of its being searched at the Demarcation Line because ...'

Dumping the everyday handbag out on her dressing table, he picked up the necessary *laissez-passer* and *sauf-conduit*, the letter also that, especially since it was in *deutsch*, would have stopped any such intrusion.

It was signed 'Monsieur Gaëtan-Baptiste Deschambeault, Sous-directeur of the Bank of France'. 'You reached high, Mademoiselle Trudel, but then, so did he.'

Photographs in a bedside album revealed the girl she'd been: swimming this past summer at the tennis club's pool, on the far side of the Allier. Sunbathing in the buff on one of the little islands that were just downstream of the Boutiron Bridge and were used for just such purposes; riding near the racecourse, which was also on that same side of the river; even a snapshot taken on the leafy, shade-drenched terrace of Chez Crusoe, with Céline Dupuis, Camille Lefèbvre and Marie-Jacqueline Mailloux.

They had all known each other. All were smiling and dressed for an evening out, the dresses either off the rack or sewn by themselves. Delightful summery frocks that complemented the wide-brimmed, flowered *chapeaux* that had been all the rage in Paris last summer, here too, apparently. Marie-Jacqueline's hat even had small oranges tucked among the blossoms.

There were several other photos of the riding stables, one of a dappled grey grazing in a paddock, another with its saddle empty. Hugs and kisses, Lucie's cheek pressed close, the girl fondly stroking the mare's muzzle. Another with the riding crop hesitantly clutched, her expression one of . . . Ah *nom de Jésus-Christ!* Sex?

A girl of twenty-three, he reminded himself. A girl with chestnut curls and eyes, the face a pleasant oval, the lips slightly parted as if in expectation of some carnal excitement, the chin not defiant or proud but determined enough and greedy for it, yes.

'Born 28 August 1919, at 133 *bis* 12c, avenue Charras,' he said – the tone of voice, he knew, was businesslike. 'That's near the railway station in Clermont-Ferrand, mademoiselle. Nose: aquiline; mouth: average – my partner would have vehemently disagreed. "Lovely kissing lips," he'd have said. "A nice derrière."'

Again he looked at the photo of her with the riding crop. Hermann would have had much to say about it!

'Height: one fifty-seven centimetres; weight: fifty kilos; distinguishing marks: none.

'Why did this pregnancy have to happen, eh? No *capote anglaise*, no little English riding hood and cape because he didn't want to spoil things for himself? Was that it, eh, and you at your prayers and taking the chance? It's typical of such men, so please forgive my impatience but I've seen it too often. Deschambeault couldn't have married you even if he'd been single or a widower.

Not a graduate of the *grandes écoles*, not one of the *haute bourgeoisie* and product of the *système*. Certainly discretion was always necessary in such a little place as Vichy – there are no photos of him or any of the others' lovers, are there? But in Paris he could show you off and did to his friends and business associates to engender envy and gain admiration, hence the clothes and the jewellery, though he couldn't tolerate your keeping his child, could he, not even with abortion outlawed and its rare practitioners living in absolute terror of the breadbasket.'

Crammed into her corner, naked, stiff and soiled, she couldn't respond, yet he felt she wanted to. 'Why did he leave that note for you on Friday and then think it necessary to leave another on Tuesday? Come, come, Mademoiselle Trudel, you had refused him. That's what he must have thought, and a man like that doesn't take kindly to rejection. He should by rights have left you to suffer alone, yet he came here to the front desk also on Tuesday. A puzzle.

'But what I can't understand is why, if you were expecting him to give you a lift to the train on Saturday – and you were, I think – he left a note on Friday that implies he would meet you in Paris and not here first.

'Two visits, then, to this hotel, mademoiselle, the first not on Friday as the note claims but on Saturday. He knew you were worried about the abortion, knew you might not join him, so he told his driver to wait and came up here to this room, but what did he find?'

He would let her consider this, thought St-Cyr. He would pocket the snapshot of the four victims on the terrace of that inn and the one of her with the riding crop. 'Did he find you, not in bed as you'd hoped, but crammed into that armoire? Is that not why he wrote Friday's note and then ... yes, then returned on Tuesday to leave the other as proof positive that he hadn't been here on Saturday. Old Rigaud, the concierge, could well not have noticed that Friday's note had been hurriedly left on Saturday.

'The train took him to Paris, mademoiselle, but had he discovered why you couldn't join him?'

114

I was cold, she seemed to say. So cold in bed, but I wanted Gaëtan to make love to me. I needed that reassurance, Inspector.

'You had left the door unlocked. He was early – too early for the Paris train, but you said "*Entrez*" anyway when he knocked, only it wasn't him,' said St-Cyr, his voice gentle as he crouched to look closely at her. 'Did you know your killer or killers, Mademoiselle Trudel? There is no sign of a struggle – of course things could have been tidied, but I doubt this. You didn't scramble out of bed to try to escape, didn't scream – although others would have been awakened and would have rushed to your assistance. Had you drifted off? Had someone intercepted you as you carried that bottle of Chomel from the Hall des Sources? Did they demand you tell them where the key to the Hall was kept? Had they known then that Céline Dupuis, your friend, would pay the Maréchal a visit?

'Did they know your lover would pick you up on his way to the train and was their intervention the reason you decided not to go home?'

As the sous-directeur's shorthand typist, it would have been reasonable for her to accompany Deschambeault to Paris to cover whatever meeting he had to attend. 'But he was worried you would bolt for home. He had to be certain you would take that train, mademoiselle, and so had told you he would be giving you a lift to the station.'

Again the killer or killers hadn't chosen the logical target, but had left, in the rats, every indication that he, she or they would now do so.

There were 25,000 francs in the Paris handbag – more than a year's wages for a girl like this – all in brand-new notes with Vichy's *Labourage et pâturage sont les deux namelles de la France* on the reverse. Ploughing and grazing are the two udders of France. '*Merde alors*, some ploughing, some grazing, eh?' And no thought of theft on the part of her killer or killers, just as with their next victim.

An embossed, gold-lettered card allowed entrance to the Cercle

Européen, that supper club of the elite on the Champs-Élysées, which was owned and operated by Édouard Chaux of Lido fame.

Anyone who was anyone sought membership to the Cercle but only a select few gained it.

'And vans from the Bank of France were hauling things other than banknotes. Gaëtan Deschambeault's vans.'

A gold cigarette case from Cartier, at 23 place Vendôme, held only Chesterfields, the case filled in preparation for the trip. No *mégot* tin accompanied it – either she would have had no reason to scrounge while in Paris, or hadn't wanted others to see her doing so.

The tin was in her day-to-day hangbag and had once contained small, pearl-shaped bonbons, Anis de l'Abbaye de Flavigny; the illustration on its lid was of a shepherd and his girl at a well.

'Dijon,' he said, and taking out his own tin, which was far more worn than hers and one of several he used, confided, 'We share this love, mademoiselle. A tin that harkens back to a quieter, gentler time.'

Humbled by the coincidence, he prised off the lid of her tin to reveal six half-smoked cigarettes. 'A Balto, two Gauloises bleues, and three Wills Gold Flake – British,' he muttered. 'But why, please, did the girl you were talking to smoke only half of each of the last three cigarettes? Nervous ... was she nervous? Was it yourself and Friday night here in your room and alone? Alone, I think, with your thoughts.'

The lipstick on the cigarette butts had been thickly applied. When touched, a little of it remained on his fingertip, a sure indication of how cheap and ersatz things were these days. 'But you wear none, mademoiselle, and would not have applied it so heavily, not if about to kiss a lover who demanded discretion.'

Turning from her, he began again to look about the room, saw the records she had brought from Paris on previous trips. One sleeve was empty. No portable gramophone was in evidence, but a cleared space, square and empty, had remained.

' "Sans Toi",' he muttered as he read the sleeve's label and, looking uncertainly at the door, said, 'Ah *mon Dieu*, Hermann, be careful. I heard that song being played as I came up here.'

There were sixty-seven rooms in the bloody hotel, five of them kept as spares in case needed by visiting secretaries, accountants, pimps, card-sharks, assorted bagmen and hangers-on. Of the sixty-two registered residents, fully half had been here since the Defeat.

It would be a detective's nightmare to sort it all out, but as if this was not enough, the conservatory had been and still was used as a general overflow and dosshouse. Beds everywhere under the blue-washed, sticking-papered glass, clothing here and there, scant food on makeshift shelves, in trunks, on suitcases and in boxes. Hotplates warm, thin soup in a pot. A crust of the grey National, a half-eaten clove of garlic.

'And not one of these unregistered visitors,' breathed Kohler. 'Have they all vanished?'

The 'room' smelled of sweat, no wash-water and mould.

'Three males, two females,' he said, 'and the hotel, having learned by its bush telegraph of the murder and the presence of two decidedly interested detectives, has emptied itself.'

Ach! what was he to do? Go back up to Louis who would still be 'talking' to that poor thing, or try to find someone?

Rigaud was reading Proust! Closeted in his *loge*, the concierge was taking time out in a tattered club chair.

'Run the lift up and down for me,' said Kohler. 'Create a diversion. Do it twice.'

'The electricity ... The shortages, monsieur.'

'Fuck the shortages. Just do it or I'll have Herr Gessler and his boys turn the hotel upside down and tumble everyone out in the cold.'

'It's freezing in here anyways. Besides, most are away at work. Only the entertainers, the hat-check girls, night waiters, croupiers, telephone and telegraph operators and the sick are in their rooms, or were. After all, isn't the flu season upon us?'

A wise one to whom the offer of a cigarette, had he any to give, would only have been accepted but 'for later'.

The Gestapo is harried, thought Rigaud, but heard the voice of his mother saying, Daniel, have courage. This one and his kind are living like God in France, therefore you must show the muscle! Only then will he and his little Sûreté collabo gumshoe realize that the hotel is indeed empty except for the corpse they have found.

Maman had always had something to say about everything. 'Corpses should be removed immediately, Inspector,' he said testily. 'It's unsanitary to leave them for so long. The room is needed also.'

'*Nom de Dieu*, don't you listen? Stop at each floor. Open and close the cage door and don't bother to tell me you haven't an operator's licence or that you're not paid to run that thing!'

This Boche, like the others, just had to have the last word, snorted Rigaud silently. Well, he'd see about that!

When the lift started, it went down into the cellars and there it stayed. '*Salaud!*' muttered Kohler as he went up the back stairs. He'd find Lucie Trudel's floor and start there. He'd wait, he'd listen. Some may not have made it out yet, he told himself. And trying door after door, silently went along the narrow halls.

Even Louis was listening to the hotel. Caught like a thief with an empty record sleeve in hand, he was startled when the door opened without a sound.

Then he brought a finger to his lips and pointed to the room above.

Hermann indicated he would go left. A nod would suffice.

Louis softly closed the girl's door and eased its key around in the lock before pocketing it.

Guns drawn, they started out.

The staircase was old, the carpet thin and faded. Wincing, cursing the pain in his left knee, Kohler took the steps two at a time. There wasn't a sound but then, distant and deep below him, came the metallic clunk of a spanner, the noise rocketing up the lift-well from the cellars.

BANG! BANG! came the voice of a bloody great hammer hitting the spanner to jar the bolt and make it come loose.

'You'll bugger your tools, idiot,' he breathed and, going up the last of the stairs, saw Louis at the far end of the dimly lit corridor. He was pointing to the floor above. Ah *merde*, this was serious.

Again the hammering came, again it sent its shock waves through the hotel. Old Rigaud began to curse the *imbéciles* in Paris to whom instructions for repairs should have been sent had the ancestors of the members of the Ministry of Housing not been *sired* by incestuous Royalists and priests in the pay of the Sun King himself!

The gears to the lift had jammed, as Rigaud had known they would!

There was no sign of Louis in the sixth-floor corridor. Had he gone up to the attic, to Céline Dupuis's room? Had he met the assassin or assassins on the stairs between the fifth and sixth floors?

They're here, he said to himself. They're waiting. *Ach*, it wasn't good. No matter what the outcome, the Résistance would only think Louis was trying to protect the boys. A collabo.

Going up to the attic, he found all the doors were closed. Crossing the hotel, he started down, listened, heard nothing even from the cellars, but now the lift began its painful ascent. Straining, he waited for it to reach the ground floor which it did, the thing not stopping afterwards until the fourth floor and the end of its ride.

Still the cage doors didn't open. Still there was no further sound.

'Louis?' he asked under his breath. Had they come for Louis? Early last December he'd been put on some of their hit lists. They'd even sent him one of the little black coffins they reserved for those they felt were due special attention.

A patriot. And sure, Gabrielle had tried to intervene and tell her contacts in the Résistance that Louis was innocent and at one with them, but such communications were difficult at best.

Silently he descended the stairs only to find Louis sitting on the top step to the sixth floor. A copy of *L'Humanité*, the clandestine newspaper of the communists and Francs-Tireurs et Partisans, was in his hands.

Liste Noire Numéro 10, he indicated. The Black List. It began with a blocked-out Definition of a Savage, implying brutality, cruelty, child butchering and all else, and then in heavy type that sickened: ST-CYR, JEAN-LOUIS, CHIEF INSPECTOR OF THE SÛRETÉ, DOMICILED AT 3 RUE LAURENCE-SAVART, BELLE-VILLE, PARIS, AGENT OF THE GESTAPO CURRENTLY OPERAT-ING IN VICHY AND ITS ENVIRONS.

There were a good fifteen other names but Louis's was right at the top of the list. 'Almost fresh ink,' mused Kohler softly. 'It's dated Tuesday, 2 February 1943. Boemelburg hadn't even sent us on our way.'

Were there ears everywhere? Were the walls also watching? 'But it was left for me to find, Hermann, not you. Did our assailant or assailants know the very staircase I'd use?'

It was a good question, but something had best be said. '*Dummkopf*, it's simply coincidence. It can't have been anything else. Come on, we'd better see about the lift.'

'Monsieur Rigaud was certainly pissed off by your ordering him around. You did, didn't you? How many times must I tell you there's a way to ask and a way not to?'

'But has he paid for it? Have we another body on our hands?'

Again, as before, the hotel seemed to sense there was trouble and, keeping itself utterly still, waited for them to make their way down to the fourth floor. When they got there, Louis plucked at his sleeve and silently mouthed the words, 'Let me take care of it.'

Tucking the newspaper into a pocket and securely out of sight, he went on ahead, shabby in that battered brown fedora and threadbare overcoat, unassuming, broad-shouldered and tough, *mein Gott*, tough. The Lebel *Modèle d'ordonnance* 1873 six-shooter, with its 11mm black-powder cartridges that had been left over from just after the Franco-Prussian War, was in his right hand. Double action and weighing nearly a kilo, the revolver also served as a club. Though Louis could hit a sou at thirty paces with the thing, it wasn't even the 1892, 8mm smokeless, 'modern' version that had been lost in Lyons on another case!

The older Lebel was all that Gestapo Paris-Central would allow him and even then the gun was not to be handed over by his partner until after the shooting had started!

But rules were to be broken, especially at times like this.

Louis slid the gun away and, facing the brass and diamond-patterned mesh of the cage, stood waiting.

There'd been whispers – there must have been – but these had stopped. Unsmiling, Bousquet stood beside a tall, grim-faced, black-overcoated, broad-shouldered, white-shirt-and-tie man whose black homburg was loosely held in the left hand. Wedding ring and all, thought Kohler. Married and no doubt with a grown or nearly grown family. Wealth and power, the face broad and determined, the hair jet black but unfortunately thinning where vanity would be sure to notice, the nose wide and fierce.

'The lower lip is thicker than the upper,' confided Louis quietly, not turning to face his partner. 'The cheeks and chin are freshly shaven, Hermann, and still tingle from the lotion his *coiffeur* had just applied as the chair had suddenly to be vacated due to an important and unpleasant summons. He's missed his luncheon engagement and looks at us as if at a plate of soup in which a fly has had the audacity to make a crash-landing. Be careful. Let me do the talking.'

'Jean-Louis, I came as soon as word reached me,' began Bousquet, forcing a grin as he opened the cage.

'And Rigaud, Secrétaire?'

'Is at his desk. We just saw him.'

'Ah *bon*, then come with me. Hermann, please check the fifth- and sixth-floor rooms that are directly above that of the victim and her child. I heard something up there. Fire twice if needed and the three of us will join you.

'It's police work, Secrétaire,' he continued. 'I'm sure you know all about it. *Mes amis*, this way, please.'

*

121

Threads and patches of dark blood were interwoven with the waste she had evacuated. The umbilical cord was a deep bluish purple to flaccid grey and netted with dark veins, the child, the foetus, tiny and curled up in the puddle.

Eyes stinging as the stench rushed in at him, Deschambeault jerked his head back and clapped a handkerchief over his nose and mouth. Rage, fear, doubt . . . ah, so many things were in the look he gave. Bousquet, to his credit, exhibited only concern and worry, a touch of sickness also.

'*Enough, damn you!*' choked Deschambeault. 'How dare you force me to look at her squatting in her filth? She's gone. *Finie*, eh? Isn't that enough for you?'

'Jean-Louis . . .'

'Secrétaire, a moment . . .'

'A Sûreté? A Chief Inspector? René, is this *imbécile* the one that Laval insisted Paris send us? Well, is he?'

One should never back away from an insult, especially not from a *haut bourgeois* and a political! 'Monsieur, you will excuse the first-hand experience, but it's necessary. You see, she was rendered unconscious by smothering and then placed here. Look closely . . . Come, come, both of you. Another simple introduction to police work, eh? You see there are fibres in the frothy, bloodstained, oedematous fluid that has erupted from her mouth. Some cotton wool, perhaps, or ersatz cloth you ask? Her killer found that the pillow he had used was insufficient, *n'est-ce pas*? A sock was jammed into her mouth while she was unconscious, then the nostrils were tightly pinched until the body's convulsions had ceased and the child had been aborted. That sock, in so far as I can presently ascertain, is missing but I may, perhaps, have found its mate. Now talk. Give me everything. Avoid arrest for the moment, Monsieur Gaëtan-Baptiste Deschambeault, Sous-directeur of the Bank of France, since there are more pressing matters.'

'Arrest? What is this he's saying, René?'

'Jean-Louis . . .'

The room was close, the door closed, the hotel silently listening no doubt, but it was now or never and they had to be made to cooperate. 'Secrétaire, all four of the victims knew each other, yet you failed to tell us this. I need not remind you that such a lapse of memory could well bring arrest, dismissal, disgrace and a penalty of no less than five years.'

'You wouldn't,' breathed Bousquet, the life draining from him.

'Don't try me, Secrétaire. Please don't. This one went to Paris knowing of the murder yet failed to inform you of it even when he returned.'

'Gaëtan, is this true?' blurted Bousquet, sickened by the thought of such a betrayal.

'Two notes, monsieur. One written, I believe, not on Friday, but on Saturday morning early. Argue if you wish, but failing to report a murder can only add weight to the charges of counselling and arranging an abortion. That girl was expecting you, in any case!'

'*Salaud*, you're a cold one, aren't you?' retorted Deschambeault acidly. 'You don't like us much, do you?'

'Liking or not liking you has nothing to do with it. You came here on Saturday not only because you were afraid Mademoiselle Trudel would decide to go home but because you'd arranged to give her a lift to the train.'

'She . . . she was where you found her, yes.'

'And the rats?'

'Rats?' blurted Bousquet.

'Were in her bed.'

'Did you know she would go to the Hall des Sources for that bottle of the Chomel? That one. That one right there,' demanded St-Cyr.

'I did not. I arrived well before seven when I knew the hotel would be asleep, and I quickly left.'

'Pausing only long enough to write Friday's note?'

'Inspector, I . . .'

'Please just answer.'

'Then, yes. No one saw me enter or leave the note or building

– at least, I don't think anyone did. She hadn't been dead long, was still warm when I felt her neck for her pulse.'

'And you saw no one?'

'I'd been very lucky. After all, Marie-Jacqueline and Camille had been done in by this ... this assassin. I had to leave. The fewer who knew of my being here, the better.'

The urge to say, It sounds familiar, doesn't it, Secrétaire? was there but it was unnecessary. Bousquet was clearly unsettled and now extremely worried.

'Then it's true, Jean-Louis,' he muttered. 'The bastards intend to kill us one by one, having paved the ground with corpses.'

It would do no good to show them *L'Humanité*'s list. For now it would be best to let them think they alone were the targets. 'Who knew you would go to Paris last weekend, Sous-directeur?'

The abrupt softening of tone and absence of aggression were noted, Deschambeault taking out his cigar case and offering one. 'It will help, I think,' he said as only he indulged. 'My director knew of it, Inspector. My two most senior assistants, the wife and family of course, and those I was to meet in Paris.'

The cigar was lit, the fool even savouring it, thought Bousquet, silently cursing such stupidity. If St-Cyr thought anything of it – and he did, most certainly – he didn't let on. 'The ambassador also, Gaëtan.'

'Another telephone call, yes. To Paris.'

'Even members of the Government, myself included,' inter-jected Bousquet, 'must apply for and often wait days or weeks for a permit to cross the Demarcation Line.'

'Fernand is occasionally difficult, as René suggests, but usually such things are easily arranged,' said Deschambeault with a magnanimous wave of his cigar.

'Fernand?'

Jean-Louis must surely know who was meant! 'De Brinon,' said Bousquet gruffly. 'Delegate General of the French Govern-ment to the Occupied Territories.'

The former *zone occupée*. 'Our *laissez-passers* came through quickly, of course,' said St-Cyr, 'but only because Gestapo

Boemelburg requested them from the Kommandantur, as he does each time he sends my partner and me south of the line.' A glance of warning passed between the two but had best be ignored for the moment. 'How often did you see Mademoiselle Trudel socially, Sous-directeur?'

Socially . . . *En garde*, eh? Was that it? 'Twice, occasionally three times a week.'

'Alone, or in the company of others?'

'Both. It depended entirely on circumstance and who was in town. Sometimes we'd meet up with others for a few drinks or a bit of a meal, sometimes not.'

'Since when, please?'

St-Cyr had now taken to looking about the room. Being careful to touch nothing, he used the blunt end of a pencil when needed. He was still hunting for that other sock, thought Deschambeault, and answered, when asked again, 'Two years.'

'And how many weekends in Paris?'

'*Merde alors*, is this an inquisition, am I a suspect, René?'

'Please just answer him, Gaëtan,' said Bousquet. 'It's necessary.'

'Once a month. Perhaps less, perhaps more. My presence is often required at the bank in Paris, so it is only natural.'

There was the inconsequential wave of the pencil-hand. 'Of course. But each time Mademoiselle Trudel accompanied you, *laissez-passers* were required?'

'For both travelling to and from, yes. It's a fact of life, isn't that so? One does not argue. One compromises.'

The aroma of cigar smoke didn't mingle well with the stench of the body and the rats. 'And your wife, monsieur? Please, I must ask again, was she aware of the affair?'

'I hadn't realized you'd already asked.'

'I hadn't.'

'*Bâtard*, my Julienne isn't well and spends much of her time at a private clinic! Migraines, that sort of thing.'

'Dr Raoul Normand?'

Marie-Jacqueline had worked part-time at the clinic but did

St-Cyr know of this yet? 'A crisis of the nerves. Several of them. Somehow the good doctor manages to calm her, particularly after she's stayed in that hospital of his for a few days or a week or two.'

'And your children, were any or all of them aware of this infatuation of yours?'

'Jean-Guy? Martine? Thérèse? Why do you ask?'

'Monsieur Jean-Guy manages the racecourse and its stables, Jean-Louis. The Jockey Club and riding stables as well.'

Lucie Trudel would have known the son ... 'And the other two, the sisters?' asked St-Cyr.

'Thérèse teaches ballet; Martine, having taken her degree in horticulture, tries to brighten the Government's solitude with her flowers. We've a labrador retriever, also a cook, housekeeper, chauffeur, groundskeeper and two, or is it three, maids of all work. My wife keeps firing and then rehiring them.'

'But were your son and daughters or any of the staff aware of your running around?'

'My fucking Lucie? Why should they have cared, especially as it kept me happy and content?'

'It must have cost you plenty.'

'I've private money. I've always had it.'

'And the riding crop, monsieur? Why did her killer or killers place it in her hand?'

Ah damn this infernal Sûreté! 'I've no idea. How could I have?'

'It's curious, that's all.'

'Then if you're through with me, I'm already late for a meeting with Dr Carl Schaefer, the coordinator of the Bank of France and director of the Office for the Surveillance of French Banks.'

'*Das Bankenaufsichtsamt*,' said St-Cyr in *Deutsch* just to increase their uneasiness if possible.

'The reparations,' countered Deschambeault in French without a whisper of disquietude. 'Try as we consistently have, our friends refuse to reduce them.'

Five hundred million francs, nearly seventy per cent of the value of the whole economy, went to the Reich every day of every year. Two and a half million pounds sterling at the official rate, or eleven and half a million US dollars.

'Secrétaire, transport was promised and is urgently needed.'

'A Peugeot two-door sedan has been left for you and Kohler outside the Hôtel du Parc. The keys, together with petrol and food tickets, are with the concierge. It's the best I could do under ... under the circumstances.'

'Merci. Then please notify the sous-préfet that we again require the services of his iron man. Félix Laloux is to do the autopsy on this one also, and I'm grateful you arranged his release from prison. There were only four of you in your little group? If there are others, now is the time to say so.'

'Four only,' said Bousquet guardedly.

'An bon. Then for now that is all, but please remind the others to take precautions. No one leaves town. Not today, tomorrow or any other day until this matter is settled.'

'And the killer or killers?' demanded Deschambeault.

'Have ears that have been wrapped around each and every one of you. Let us hope my partner can pin things down a little more firmly.'

Already St-Cyr had gone back to his probing, easing a drawer open, leafing through a novel with the blunt end of that pencil. Totally absorbed as if he'd forgotten them.

'He won't,' swore Bousquet as they left the building and headed for the car where Georges sat behind the wheel. He had kept the engine running in spite of the ordinance to do no such thing. 'He'll remember every word you said, Gaëtan, every nuance. The cigar, the riding crop, the laissez-passers Fernand so generously parts with from that allocation of his when you grease his palm, as do I and others. How could you have gone to Paris without telling me she'd been murdered?'

'You worry too much, René. He's only a cop.'

'His partner's a Gestapo.'

'Who has yet to visit Herr Gessler to pay his respects.'

'Then let us hope he doesn't.'

'Gessler says Herr Kohler's loyalties are being constantly

questioned and that Gestapo Paris-Central would just as soon be rid of him and St-Cyr.'

'Idiot, both are considered far too honest and seek only the truth. But it's you I'm also worried about, Gaëtan. You *would* take Lucie to Paris. You know how I've warned you about Doriot and Déat and the others of the far right. Any excuse to let us have it is excuse enough for them.'

'The Intervention-Referat, the Bickler Unit?'

'Hired assassins who know how to hide behind the Résistance and have or have not the sanction of their Gestapo friends. Georges, drop the sous-directeur off at La maison des saumons plus beaux for a taste of that fish he and Lucie used to love, and where I know he's to meet with Schaefer, then run me round to the *commissariat*. We've found another one.'

As the car drove off, Kohler let the blackout curtains at the end of the sixth-floor corridor fall back into place. No sound came up from the lift, or from anywhere else. It was eerie how quiet the hotel could be; it simply wasn't good.

Room 6-11 was as close as peas in a pod to being above that of Lucie Trudel and below that of Céline Dupuis. And why the hell did the Résistance have to put Louis's name in print and do so in advance of their visit?

That, too, was eerie and not good.

Kneeling – ignoring the sore-tooth pain in his knee – he tried to peer through the keyhole only to find the key had been inserted into the other side of the lock. 'Okay, *mein Liebling*,' he muttered under his breath, 'two can play this game.'

Using a half-round feeler from the ring of lock-picking tools in his jacket pocket, he silently gave the key a gentle push and felt it move, hoped there'd be a carpet and heard the bloody thing crash on the parquet floor. Through the keyhole he saw a plump white rabbit suddenly lift its head and prick up its ears, then return greedily to its feeding.

Slices of dried apple had been tossed on to the worn Aubusson carpet to keep the creature quiet. Beyond it, there was a plain wooden coffee table, a carpenter's bench in years gone by perhaps, with books, ashtrays, a japanned chest, a bronze model of the place Vendôme's column, an Empire-style desk lamp with jade-green shade and, at either end of the table, two china mugs: blue as well, to match that of the carpet.

Steam issued from the mugs but there were no knees or hands in sight.

Beyond the table, beyond a narrow space with piled tin trunks, cluttered shelves with square openings rose all but to the ceiling. More books, some porcelain – Chinese perhaps – a few figurines, a soft purple tulip-glass with white silk narcissi and, at the very top, four experiments in beginner's taxidermy: a dove, a rook, a starling and a seagull.

'*Un moment*,' confessed a faint but carefully modulated female voice, the accent perfect. Not a trace of the rolling, singsong accent of an Auvergnate, more of Paris and the Sorbonne. Of wealth and place and the long, long tumble from it. Of hesitation too, and fear? he wondered.

Fabric moved to block his view as the key was collected. She didn't tremble when fitting it back into the lock, was outwardly calm. 'Monsieur?' she said, the look in her dark blue eyes empty.

'Kohler, Kripo, Paris-Central.'

Her throat was lovely and slender, what he could see of it, the collar of the black and crimson brocade dress all but touching the delicately smooth fantastic line of her lower jaw and chin. About thirty, he told himself, the hair a dark, rich auburn and long but pinned up and worn in the style of the *fin de siècle*, her brow partly hidden by it, the face thin and sharply featured, aristocratic, yes, the whole of her being from that other time and nervous. Yes, nervous.

'Well, Herr Kohler, to what do we owe this pleasure?' she asked.

It would sound foolish, but he'd have to say it. 'A moment of your time, Madame . . .'

'Mademoiselle Blanche. Everyone calls me that, but I suppose you will need another label. Varollier. Grand-papa was an architect. The *mairie*, the *hôtel de ville* – how do you say it in *Deutsch*, Inspector?'

The town hall. '*Das Rathaus*, but my French is good enough. Please continue using it and don't worry.'

'Forgive me. It's just that ... that so few of our visitors speak our language. Japanese, of course, at their embassy, Spanish, too, at theirs, and Italian at theirs, but seldom what is so often required, which makes me of some small service when needed. The *mairie* of the eighteenth *arrondissement* has magnificent stained-glass windows which cover its courtyards. The Église de Notre-Dame-de-Clignancourt, opposite it, was finished at about the same time, in 1896 and four years later, I think.'

She was almost as tall as he was, and the dress went right to her ankles, belted by linked art nouveau silver plaques with intriguing patterns in dark green, red, blue and white enamel.

'My brother, Inspector. Paul ... Paul, darling, this is Herr Kohler.'

Open book in hand, back to the door and facing one end of the shelving, the brother continued to read.

'Paul ... Paul, you heard me. Please don't be difficult.'

'We've done nothing. Why, then, does he have to bother us?'

Whereas she tried desperately to be calm, the brother was highly strung and wary and didn't seem to give a damn if it showed.

'Well, come in if you must,' he said. Her twin, he had the same height and build, the same blue eyes but much lighter, more reddish-brown hair, a hank of which had flopped down over the left side of his brow, the expression intense. 'Blanche, please ask the Inspector to be seated. Offer him some coffee, otherwise ours will just get cold.'

'It's made from wild-rose petals Paul and I collected and roasted, Inspector. It's sweetened with a purée of chestnuts we also gathered.'

The water was hot, the stove warm. Trays of the papier-mâché balls most people used these days as fuel were in various stages of drying. A few twigs were on the verd antique sideboard whose style Kohler couldn't determine. Floor-to-ceiling curtains – Russian Imperial, he thought – were parted and of a steel-grey blue. Lace hung behind them, and through it he could see a grimy window, no balcony and, probably from there, the river and Boutiron Bridge.

Paul Varollier seemed all bones and knuckles as he sat awkwardly in a brass-studded armchair with brocade cushions jammed in on either side and behind him, one mug now cradled for warmth in thin, long-fingered hands.

Kohler took the proffered mug from the sister. 'Our "coffee",' she said, managing to smile faintly.

'A tis sane. My partner loves them.'

'Was Céline really killed by this assassin everyone whispers of?' she asked, still standing before him. 'You see, we were good friends, Inspector. I often looked after Michel for her and now must salve his loneliness. He misses her terribly, poor thing. Rabbits have feelings, don't they, Paul? They're not just God's dumb creatures as Père Paquette preaches. They're almost like us.'

Knowing she had said too much, she found her mug and gracefully composed herself in one of three dining-room chairs. The rest of the set and its table and sideboard had either not been available at the sale or had been sold when the family's estate had been settled and the bailiff had taken damned near everything. Louis XVI, he thought. *Directoire* period anyway.

He'll flip open his little black notebook now and balance it on his knee, thought Blanche. He'll be very proper, isn't really like a Gestapo. Usually it isn't hard to tell with those, but this one *is* different and therefore far more dangerous. But such a terrible scar on his face. How had he got it? Duelling? she wondered and told herself, He's not of that class. Barbed wire from that other war, then? It's far too fresh. The slash of broken sugar, she said firmly. A pimp or . . .

'Céline Dupuis left early on Tuesday morning,' Kohler heard himself interrupting her thoughts. The hotel was still all but as silent as a tomb.

'The older students,' said Blanche. 'She was always so conscientious. This job, that job. She lived entirely for the day when she could return to Paris to be with her daughter. Will we soon be allowed to send letters to the former *zone occupée*, Inspector? Céline wanted so to write them to Annette. Every day if she could have. Now I'll have to do it when possible. Paul, I must send the child a postcard. How will I tell her what's happened? She'll be devastated.'

'She's not our responsibility. How many times must I tell you stray cats and rabbits are definitely not our concern unless we are to eat them?'

'Annette is not a stray,' she said petulantly, the Inspector noting the exchange and writing a terse comment. *Brother heartless: sister deeply caring,* or something like that. Impolitely, Paul started to read again. Not aloud as often, thank God. Balzac, a banquet scene probably. Oysters, chicken and fish, or is it cakes and ale and naked whores, my darling?

'We're not being of much help, are we?' she hazarded before taking a sip and, finding the coffee to her brother's liking, gave a curt nod his way.

The rabbit was looking for more to eat.

'I often cared for it. Céline was away so much, she gave me a spare key to her flat. Paul and I would gather grasses and other things for it. Sometimes a carrot or a few leaves of lettuce.'

Has key to Céline's room – was that what the Inspector scribbled? she wondered, wishing he'd leave. Just leave!

'Where is it?' he asked, and for the first time since their meeting, a lifelessness filled his pale blue eyes – eyes that until this moment she had felt certain would keep a woman happy, or several.

The key was found in the top drawer of the sideboard. Briefly their fingers touched and just as briefly warmth came back into the detective's gaze. '*Merci*,' he said.

'Your French is good,' she countered only to hear him reply, 'I learned it as a guest of your country in 1916. I was one of the lucky ones and have always been grateful for the holiday. Now the French is useful.'

I'm sure it is, she wanted so much to add in High German because his would definitely be Low, but didn't.

'Did you see or hear anyone go into or out of Céline's room on Tuesday?' he asked.

'Only myself. To . . . to feed and water Michel and give him a bit of daylight and company.'

'And on Wednesday?'

How sharp his voice was. 'Wednesday . . . ? Paul . . . Paul, didn't you say you'd heard someone up there?'

'The Secrétaire Général de Police and Dr Ménétrel, idiot. Why ask when you know?'

'He reads every day at this hour, Inspector. It's his only form of relaxation. Please forgive his appalling lack of manners.'

'*Blanche, just tell him!*'

'Twice we heard someone on the stairs, Inspector. At first I thought it was Céline and that she must have stayed overnight at a friend's to avoid being out during the curfew, but those steps faded away. Later the secrétaire did come, as Paul has said, and with the doctor.'

First visit: the identity card. Had Herr Kohler scribbled this? wondered Blanche, or had he written: Killer ducked into room before Camille's lover and Pétain's *éminence grise*?

'And today?' he asked sharply.

'Once. Before . . . before you and . . . the other one came here.'

Before our first visit to the hotel – did he write that? wondered Blanche.

'How long have the two of you lived here in the hotel?'

'Since the beginning'

'Jobs?'

How brutal of him! 'Translator, and croupier, though the casino is open only on weekends, with a consequent loss of promised wages which has, I am afraid, made my brother somewhat bitter.'

'Blanche!'

133

'Paul, we should be thankful for what is ours. Others have it far worse!'

Nom de Dieu, they were a pair. 'Do you know Albert Grenier, the groundskeeper?'

'Everyone knows Albert, Inspector,' said Paul spitefully. 'The fool makes a point of saying hello even when not wanted.'

'To those who like him, and to those who don't,' confessed the sister. 'Paul, you mustn't think Albert stupid. He's really very intelligent, just a little awkward perhaps, but in his own way he's himself. That is more than one can say for a lot of the others in this town, Inspector.'

Again the sister realized she had said too much. 'Who did the birds?' Kohler asked, indicating the stuffed one.

'I did,' she quickly admitted. 'I had such plans when a child, didn't I, Paul? But as you can see, my talent was sadly lacking. Céline loved birds – live ones. They were free to fly, she used to say when thinking of Annette and building dreams for when the two of them would be together again. She wanted me to give her one of the tail feathers from each of those. Paul wanted her to take the birds and be done with my memory of them, but she wouldn't do that and . . . and never brought the matter up again.'

'A quail,' muttered Herr Kohler, flipping back through his notebook. 'A male hen harrier . . .'

'A merlin, a peacock . . . Céline was going to try to write to her daughter using a tail feather from each. That way her words would appear as though they'd flown to Annette and every time the girl visited the zoo at the Jardin des Plantes, she'd think of her mother. Your coffee is getting cold, Inspector. Don't you like it?'

'Can't you see you've prattled on so hard he's been too busy?'

'Paul, please. I want to help.'

'Then why not tell him where Céline would have got the tail feathers! Go on, idiot. Can't you see that's what he's fishing for and he'll soon find out anyway?'

Ach! had the sister been trying to avoid doing so?

'Herr Abetz, your ambassador in Paris, keeps a château nearby,

Inspector,' said Blanche. 'Its . . . its custodian and former owner tends the birds he once collected.'

There, she said sadly to herself, now he's writing that down too. *A château*, his expression grim at the thought of Herr Abetz being even remotely connected to the killings. In a way she felt sorry for Herr Kohler, sorry for herself and Paul too, of course.

A mist of fear and anxiety was in the detective's eyes when he looked up at her to ask, 'Just how the hell did Madame Dupuis get to visit our Otto's birds?'

Paul should have kept quiet. 'The parties,' she said not daring to look at Herr Kohler. 'The dances and nights of games and . . . and other things.'

'And your brother and you, Mademoiselle Varollier? Did the two of you also attend these evenings out?'

These orgies, was this what Herr Kohler thought? To deny it would be foolish; to admit it, suicidal. Why did Paul have to force the issue? To get everything out in the open and over with in spite of what might happen to them? To get back at her, his sister, his twin?

'Occasionally, Inspector, but . . . but not in some time. Wasn't it well before Christmas when we were last there, Paul?' she asked acidly. 'My brother to deal the cards or tend the roulette wheel, myself to translate when necessary.'

Speaks *Deutsch* fluently – was this what Herr Kohler now scribbled? wondered Blanche, but when he looked across the table at her, it was to ask, 'Who else was there?'

Had Paul wanted this to come out too? 'Céline and . . . and others.'

'Lucie Trudel? That is her portable gramophone on the bureau next to your brother's chair, isn't it? When was the last time you saw her? You first, Monsieur Varollier, then you, Mademoiselle Blanche.'

Ah *Sainte Mère*! Herr Kohler had led them into believing he hadn't noticed the record on its turntable, hadn't thought it important. He had laid a little *souricière* for them.

A mousetrap.

*

135

The blood- and vomit-stained sock that had been crammed into Lucie Trudel's mouth and then taken from it had been thrown behind her killer or killers and had landed under her bed.

Lying flat on the floor, St-Cyr reached for it with the tweezers. He'd have to bag it but bags were in too short a supply even for murder investigations and Stores were obstinate. 'A leaflet, then,' he grunted. 'Two perhaps, and tightly folded over. Idiot, the ink will run. Everything these days is made not to last!'

The sock had been hand-knitted in four-ply white wool with a cable pattern above the ankle. He was certain it matched the other one he'd found. It, and this other one, had been mended not once but twice by the look of them. Both were definitely from the thirties, from when she'd have been eighteen or nineteen. Treasured because Maman or Grand-mère had knitted them. Used and mended until they unravelled during the Occupation to be used elsewhere.

'You came from a good home, didn't you,' he said, looking across the room at her. 'But they wouldn't have thought well of your returning with child and unmarried. Was that why the indecision, or did someone really interrupt your early-morning walk from the Hall des Sources and demand the location of that key?'

She couldn't answer, couldn't speak, yet he felt she would have liked to have said, Papa was very ill. They had trouble enough at home.

'Was he dying?' he asked gently. The leaflets in the inner pocket of his overcoat had been dropped by the RAF on a night-bombing raid over the U-boat pens at Lorient on the Breton coast. 'Target missed and town hit,' he said by way of explanation. 'My partner and I were lucky not to have left the living. I seldom empty these pockets,' he apologized. 'We were there at the beginning of January. A dollmaker, a U-boat captain who wanted to revive his grandfather's business of making beautiful dolls, the Royal Kaestners. Another difficult murder investigation. We always seem to get them. Well?' he asked suddenly.

Dying, she seemed to say of her father. I was torn between murdering my unborn child and returning home for a last visit perhaps, and ... and the funeral.

'And the interruption?'

The location of the key to the Hall, but why, she seemed to insist, would he, she or they have needed to ask me when so many others knew Albert?

'A warning then. Was that it, eh, or did your killer simply follow you back to this hotel?'

Two black leather thongs, each about a half-metre in length, were neatly coiled among the things in her Paris suitcase, and he had to ask himself, Had the riding crop also been packed? Had that been why her killer or killers had fitted it into her hand after they'd killed her?

Deschambeault had shed no tears, had expressed anger, yes, but not really remorse and regret at her killing. More a concern for himself, a curiosity and a thinly disguised sense of relief.

'Did you beat him during sex? Was he of that nature or did he beat you? Please forgive me for asking, mademoiselle, but it's necessary. Pain does, with some, increase pleasure; with others it's essential.'

She wouldn't have answered, would have ducked her eyes in shame, or would she? Accustomed to coming across all manner of perversions, he filed the thought away and again took to examining the contents of her bed.

The rats had all been caught in traps but not the usual, he felt. There were, in so far as he could see, no broken backs or broken necks and legs, nor was there any sign of the froth that poison often brought. Instead of this last, or a spring-loaded trap whose bar would snap down when the bait was taken, a wire snare had been used.

'Coroner Laloux will confirm this,' he said. 'Rats are very intelligent and not easily tricked. Each family quickly becomes aware of the consequences of poisoned bait and avoids it like the plague. Those spring-loaded traps are often of no use either. Bacon, cheese, bread soaked in wine or soup – whatever I used, even securely tying the bait to its little pan with thread, they would leave the trap set *sans* its little reward and the thread still perfectly in place. Wire cage traps, though expensive, are better. Of course I shot some, but with this bunch I think snares were used. The bait put in a difficult and out of the way place, the rat curious, then growing a little bolder until jerking frantically.

'But our killer or killers have been careless, mademoiselle. If not the trapper, then he, she or they both know someone who is good at his business, even to determining the sex of those he has caught. The livers are also missing. Tasty, no doubt, though I haven't yet had to dine on them, nor has my partner. At least, not knowingly.'

Still the hotel was silent. It was uncanny how news of their continued presence must constantly be telegraphed from room to room and past those that were unoccupied.

Deschambeault had left his cigar band on her bedside table next to the bottle of the Chomel. 'An El Rey del Mundo, mademoiselle,' he said, carefully flattening it. 'A Choix Supreme perhaps? Taste is everything to those who can afford to cultivate it. Taste in cigars and in mistresses. *Salut.* The band is glued to the cigar. Once plain, and used to prevent the fingertips from becoming strained with nicotine, the bands soon acquired great diversity of design. Gold coins to wrap themselves around Albert Grenier's finger. Does Albert know you were stopped on your way here? If so, then he's in even more danger than I had first thought.'

But had the cigar band from the Hall des Sources been left for them to find, or simply removed as this one had been by an automatic response of long custom and only when heat from the lighted cigar had softened the adhesive?

The *laissez-passer* she had been given by the sous-directeur had indeed been countersigned by Fernand de Brinon whose signature appeared beneath that of the Kommandant von Gross-Paris and its stamp. 'Deschambeault's wife is a neurotic, is she?' he asked, desperately wanting answers. 'Marie-Jacqueline Mailloux must have known her from the clinic of . . .' He flipped through his little black book. 'Dr Raoul Normand. Céline Dupuis left a message for you: "Lucie, please come back soon. We have to talk. It's urgent."'

'Talk about what, mademoiselle? About jealous wives wanting revenge or about vans from the Bank of France being used to haul cigars and other luxuries from Paris so that your lover and those of the others could enjoy the high life while the rest of us knuckle under? Or was it this?' He indicated the *laissez-passer*. 'They're so very hard to come by unless you know the right people. You see, it's rumoured Monsieur de Brinon, our delegate in Paris, sells them. Secrétaire-Général Bousquet is patently aware of this and afraid I am too. A little under-the-table business that's probably not so little. Certainly such things,' he said and shrugged, 'are never recorded and thus the income is never taxed.

'You ran with the pack. You all did, for various reasons no doubt. And now . . . now have paid for it while we must find your killer or killers but protect those we would most like to see taught a damned good lesson!

'*L'Humanité*,' he went on. 'It's only natural that I should dread what could well happen to me. Questioned first, and not kindly! Then up against the post, Mademoiselle Trudel, or with the necktie.

'Hermann . . . Hermann, why the hell are you being so quiet?' he asked.

Sans toi, she seemed to say. *Sans toi*. And when the voice of Lucienne Boyer filtered down the corridors and stairs, a wild moment of panic rushed through him and he heard himself blurting, 'Hermann . . . Hermann, are you all right?' Had they killed him? Were the Francs-Tireurs et Partisans really behind this thing, this so-called plot to *bousiller les gars*? The FTP had formed a secret murder squad in the winter of 1941–42 and it was still very active, still *selecting* its targets and not at random!

Softly closing and locking the door to her room, he started out, knowing only as that sincere and lovely voice permeated every part of his being that others also listened and waited. Bousquet, on making his deal with Oberg and Gestapo Boemelburg in Paris, had said the French had better become accustomed to 'a police force that intervenes ruthlessly'. Parisians and all others would be in for 'a shock at the sight of it'.

Of an all-too-willing collaboration, of often violent arrest for little or no reason, of brutality, cruelty and theft being carried out by ordinary *gendarmes, les flics* of cities like Paris and Lyons, but even in some little villages by their trusted *gardes champêtres.* The French Gestapo also, and now, too, the Milice who were to enforce the Service de Travail Obligatoire, the compulsory labour service that would send thousands to the Reich. And yes, too, the Bickler Unit, and the Intervention-Referat.

People had good reason to be very angry. A lot of people.

Putting the Lebel on full cock, he started up the stairs, listening always to that voice, thinking of it, of dancing cheek to cheek with his first wife. They'd been so in love, but the long absences, she never knowing if and when he'd return, had intruded just as they had with the second wife, with Marianne. And now there was Gabrielle who would sing that song as well or even better, but to 800 of the Wehrmacht's servicemen on leave at the Club Mirage on the rue Delambre, and to those in the front lines and barracks, for her voice was carried by German wireless to men on both sides of this lousy war.

Gabrielle Arcuri who was of the Résistance, her group so tiny she, too, could well be in danger from the mistakes and reprisals of other *résistants.*

'It's the shits, isn't it?' he said softly, as if to Hermann. 'While you want the quiet life with Giselle tending a bar in that little place you're always saying you'll buy on the Costa del Sol, and Oona keeping house for you and looking after Giselle's and your babies – you know I've warned you it will never work – I want to go fishing with Gabi and her son on the Loire in summer. Yet here we are and no one except Premier Laval – I repeat no one but him, *mon vieux* – wants us to be anywhere near here.'

The song came to its end. A big man, a giant with strong, capable hands and thick fingers whose nails were closely trimmed, Herr

Kohler used great sensitivity to lift the armature with its needle from the recording. Does he defuse bombs? wondered Blanche. Bombs that are meant to kill the unsuspecting?

Paul was suffering under the detective's gaze and nervously waited, but Herr Kohler deliberately didn't switch off the gramophone. He would let it unwind itself.

'All right,' he said. 'You say that the last time you saw Lucie Trudel you met her quite by accident Friday evening at just after seven, the new time. You were on your way to the casino, she was returning here to the hotel. You asked if you could borrow the record and the machine.'

'That is correct,' said Paul, the turntable going round and round. *Chéri*, be careful, begged Blanche silently, only to hear him saying, 'Look, Inspector, I was a little early for work and knew how much my sister loved that recording, so thought to surprise her and walked back here with Lucie.'

'The sleeve ... There's no sleeve,' said Herr Kohler.

'Of course there isn't!'

Paul *would* use sarcasm!

'The record was on the turntable. *That* is why we don't have its sleeve!'

Idiot ... Did Paul want to say, Idiot?

'Where had she been?' asked Herr Kohler.

'At work, where else?' Paul *would* snap back answers and think he was in control. You're not, my darling. Not with this one. The machine was still winding down, still making its little grinding sounds that went on and on and seemed to fill the room. The room ...

'What street were you on?'

'Street?' yelped Paul. 'Why, in the Park.'

'Near the Hall des Sources?'

'Yes. She ... she had just come out of the Hôtel du Parc.'

'From work?'

'Isn't that what I said?'

'The offices of the Bank of France aren't there, *mon fin*. Try the Carlton.'

'She had delivered some papers,' said Paul calmly, now very much the dealer of *vingt-et-un* who knows the deck in his hand is thin of fives and tens and therefore vastly in his favour.

'Your shoes. Let me see them.'

Paul was wearing carpet slippers. 'My shoes . . . ?' he managed. 'They're . . .'

'They're under his side of the bed, Inspector. I'll get them for you if you wish.'

'I don't.'

The headboard was against the corridor wall, the sister having that side closest to the door and window, the brother the one next to the far wall; the things one had to do these days to make do.

'One pair of boots without hobnails or cleats, one pair of leather shoes with soles of the same, pre-war and needing attention, and a pair with wooden soles,' said Herr Kohler.

Running those fingers of his over the wooden soles, he looked at Paul and then at her, didn't say a thing about their having to share a bed but . . . but for just a moment his fingers hesitated on the right sole and then . . . then began to trace something out. A gouge, a deep scratch? wondered Blanche, sickened by the thought. 'Inspector . . .' She heard her voice. It was too sharp. 'Inspector, you've not told us why you want to know when we last saw Lucie, or what has happened to her to make you ask. She met us on the avenue Thermal, if you must know.'

The main thoroughfare.

'She had just come from the Église Sainte-Jeanne-d'Arc on place Chanoine Gouttet, had been praying to the Virgin for help and guidance, and had gone to confession. I . . . I knew she was pregnant. Paul hadn't been told but . . but must have sensed the reason for her distress of late and . . . and has now tried to protect her reputation. She was a good friend, and she readily said we could borrow her gramophone and the record while she was away at home to see her father. She . . .' *Merde,* it was going to sound badly but Paul had to be rescued. 'She gave me her key and said to leave it in her box at the front desk, that she'd collect it later that evening.'

'Then she wasn't on her way here?'

'She . . . she said she had to meet someone.'

'Who?'

'Céline, I think, but . . . but she must have known Céline had already gone to work at the Théâtre de Casino.'

The girl was desperate. 'As one of its dancers?' he asked. Had the sister read the note Céline had left for Lucie on Saturday and said this simply to protect her brother? he wondered.

'The piano also,' she said. 'An . . . an operetta. *La Bayadère.* All I know about it is that it's the one that Dr Ménétrel thought would most please the Maréchal. It was only to run for a few nights, a week at most, and is still on, I think, or . . . or has it finished its run, Paul?'

The brother didn't answer. Ignoring her, he tried to find a cigarette but finally gave it up. 'You're not going to take those, are you?' he demanded spitefully.

'These?' Herr Kohler indicated the shoes. 'No. They're all yours for now.' And coming round to her side of the bed, took to examining the wooden soles of her shoes, then those of the others and of her boots. In summer it would be so hot in that bed, so cold in winter – was this what he was thinking, that they must hold each other, comfort each other, see and touch each other when naked? Satisfy each other?

'I think you both know that early on Saturday morning she was murdered in that room of hers,' he said. 'I think the whole damned hotel knows by now, but what I want are answers.'

'Murdered?' bleated Paul, throwing her a glance of alarm, not being able to stop himself, poor darling.

'Here,' said the Detektiv, and then . . . then, on noticing above the baseboard the hole in the plaster that she had plugged, 'You don't have a problem with rats in this hotel, do you? You ought to, from what I've seen of it.'

'*Rats?*' said Blanche. 'Why . . . why, yes, we do, but . . . but Albert comes and . . . and takes care of them.'

'Albert.'

'That is so,' she heard herself saying. 'He's very good at it and studies each problem thoroughly before setting his snares . . .'

In a rush, Kohler left them. Louis wasn't in any of the corridors or on any of the staircases, nor was he still in Lucie Trudel's room, which was locked.

He was with the concierge deep in the cellars, was jammed head and shoulders between two ceiling joists and the floor above, and bent double over the top of a stone wall, his feet no longer touching the backless chair he had used to get up there.

'I heard you talking in that room, Hermann,' he managed. 'I knew then that you were all right. Earth,' he grunted, his voice still muffled. 'Very fine earth has been mixed with the powdered white sugar that's been dusted over the tripwire and noose. I'm certain it's sugar and not potassium cyanide.'

'Rats,' confided Rigaud, cradling the Sûreté's overcoat and fedora, the Lebel also and suit jacket. 'He's curious about how ours are caught.'

'And butchered,' came the tunneller's voice. 'Butchered and sorted as to their sex, then saved.'

The metal doors to the service lift from the furnace room opened on to the pavement outside the Hôtel du Parc. Still smoking, the ashes and clinkers overflowed their metal drums, carrying the acrid stench of sulphur. A waiting *gazogène* lorry intermittently banged and roared as its engine fought to suck into its cylinders enough of the wood-gas to keep itself running. The tank and gas-producer's tubing were up there on the roof of the cab, the firebox in front, and God help anyone if the lorry should happen to run into them, thought Kohler.

'Inspectors,' said the elder Grenier cautiously, 'my son always sorts them. So many males, so many females. It does no harm, and helps him to keep track of how much he should charge each client.'

Louis crowded him, putting his back to one of the assistant groundsmen. 'And the livers?' he asked, hands jammed deeply into those overcoat pockets of his, collar up, breath billowing and fedora yanked down. Frost on the thick and bushy brown moustache too. 'They were, I believe, absent from the little corpses we found.'

'The livers,' murmured Grenier, only to hear the Sûreté breathe, 'Mystery meat?'

'Albert sells them, yes, to . . . to others.'

'Restaurants?'

'Sometimes. The meat is . . . is as good as chicken, Inspector. When boiled for ten minutes and marinated in a little wine with herbs and a little salt, one can't tell . . .'

'Yes, yes. These days especially. The British have even issued such instructions to their aircrews in case of their being shot down. The cellars, I think. You and I. Hermann, please ask the concierge for the keys to our vehicle.'

Following the elder Grenier, Louis stepped off the pavement to take the service lift slowly down into the cellar. As it descended, those same hands were still crammed deeply into the pockets of that shabby overcoat, the shoulders still squared. 'He may look grim but he's happy,' confided Kohler to an assistant groundsman. 'We're making progress. Where are the rats kept after they're taken?'

'In the shed behind the Grenier house. Now that it's winter, Albert can dress them when he has the time, though he usually sees to this right away.'

'Ten francs apiece – that's what they're asking for crows in Paris.'

'The rats are evidently much tastier. Albert does quite well with them but only charges five for those he traps; ten if the client wishes to keep them, as some do. The rest he sells for twenty. There are always buyers.'

Down in the furnace room, the elder Grenier pulled off his asbestos gauntlet gloves and said, 'Some coffee, Chief Inspector? A little something to warm us up?'

'A cognac? Ah, *merci*, that would be perfect, as would the coffee, but alas we haven't time. Your son, monsieur?'

'Is out on a job. The racing stables again. Monsieur Deschambeault, Sous-directeur of the Bank of France, came to tell us. His son ...'

'Runs the stables, yes. And your Albert?'

'Went with the sous-directeur and the Mademoiselle Charpentier, she to see the horses, my Albert to set more snares.'

'And the sculptress? How did she ...?'

'Albert was showing Mademoiselle Charpentier his books, Inspector,' said Grenier, indicating them.

Both were open, the fairy tale to the illustrations of Pétain sitting under that giant oak with the little children dutifully attentive to his *all the rats, the wasps and worms that had done so much damage ... the termites, too, and spiders ...*

'My son believes he's helping the Maréchal, Inspector. That not quite all of the rats disappeared as our Head of State says, but that a few of the really bad ones managed to stay behind.'

In Vichy.

Among the scattered newspapers that had been perused over lunch were copies of *L'Humanité* destined for the furnace, but Grenier was far too polite to let him know he'd read the Black List.

'The sculptress has left her valise,' said St-Cyr. Opening it revealed what he'd seen before, except for the absence of the perfume. Lifting out the tray, he found a clutch of white table napkins, cushioned by still others, and inside this, the face of Pétain in wax. Flesh-toned, the grey hair and moustache carefully woven strand by strand into the wax, the eyes of that same china blue.

'She showed it to my Albert, Inspector. It's really very good and only needs a little touching up.'

'Brought like this from Paris?'

'*Oui.* There is a bust in clay that she's been working on at the Musée Grévin. First they do that, then they make a plaster cast of the bust, the cast in pieces so that it can be easily removed when the plaster has set. This then becomes their mould, and into it they pour beeswax, making a layer a centimetre or two in thickness. Then carefully – very carefully, she said – they take the plaster mould apart and *voilà*, they have a bust in wax of the Maréchal. Surgical glass eyes are used, their shape and size exactly matching those of the subject. Albert ... my Albert was speechless, Inspector.'

'And the sculptress?'

'Apparently the École de Dressage in Paris is at the end of the street on which she rents a small studio. Like my Albert, she's fascinated by horses and often likes to help groom them, so was looking forward to seeing those at our racing stables. Dr Ménétrel had told her it would be impossible for her to see the Maréchal today.'

Merde, what the hell was she up to?

It was only as they were on the stairs to the lobby that Grenier stopped him to say, 'Inspector, that knife my son found. Will it really be possible for your partner to replace it? You see, he's ... Well, Albert's counting on Herr Kohler's finding another. If he's to be disappointed, could I ask that you inform me first? The tears, the anger, the frustration ... All such things are much easier to cope with if my wife and I know ahead of time. He's a good boy, and we want only what's best for him.'

'The knife ...'

Grenier nodded.

Taking it out of his overcoat pocket, the inspector looked at it, felt it, thought about it and ran a forefinger slowly over the design on its spine. 'Would Albert know whose this was?' he asked. 'You see, if he does, my concern is that the assassin or assassins may be all too aware of it.'

He opened the knife. There was a sharp click, a snap as the blade fixed itself in place.

It would have to be said. 'Albert may know, Inspector. He's very alert to such things and has quite a remarkable memory which he often keeps hidden in fear that people will only ridicule him if he says anything.'

'There was white sugar in that van he got the coffee from, wasn't there?'

'And cognac. A Rémy-Martin VSOP. Louis XIII, the 1925. There were, apparently, cases of it. Champagne also from that same year, the Bollinger Cuvée Spéciale, the Clicquot.'

'And when did your son find them?'

'Well back in December, I believe, but Albert, feeling he had been bad, didn't say a thing about it for weeks, and only at the end of that month produced them. A bottle of the champagne for his dear *maman* and one of the cognac for his *papa*. Both were magnificent and allowed us to ring in the New Year as never before, the coffee and sugar also.'

'And the chocolates?'

'And those as well as the scented handsoap, the candles, the flour and the ginger.'

'Now tell me about the wire he uses for his snares.'

'The wire . . . ? It's just some he found at the château where his grand-uncle is now the custodian. Ordinary wire, but fine and pliable so that it's very easy to work with. Why do you ask?'

'Simply routine. One always asks. It's in the nature of detectives to do so.'

5

Snow filtered down, and as the light over the Allier River and the hills beyond it became a deeper grey in the gathering dusk, the line of waiting traffic moved ahead a few metres. Homeward-bound farm wagons and *gazogène* lorries that had obviously hauled firewood and other produce into Vichy were ahead of them and, at the very end, this lonely Peugeot.

'*Merde*,' swore Louis bitterly. 'The nation that expects the Blitzkrieg from us at all times provides delays that can only impede progress! Deschambeault cuts short an important meeting to visit a racing stable but makes certain he takes along the resident rat catcher? Inès Charpentier insists on joining them and wears Shalimar when first encountered but no longer does so, and no longer carries the *flacon* in her valise because I was foolish enough to have mentioned it? The 1925, Hermann, and, as you well know, the same as Céline Dupuis was wearing when killed! That dress, the necklace and earrings could all be from the same year!'

And Marie-Jacqueline had had three-fifths of a bottle of the Bollinger Cuvée Spéciale in her, the 1925.

'Our sculptress worries me, Hermann. She's like a leech that has to draw blood, only with her it's a fascination with what we are about that is so troubling. Did she once possess a knife like this?'

Louis dragged the thing out. 'Does she know Paul Varollier and his sister, Blanche?' asked Kohler. 'The soles of Monsieur Paul's shoes matched those the *flics* circled in the snow.'

'And you let me wait in this line-up? You don't tell me things like that right away? *Sacré nom de nom,* how could you not have done so?'

'I just did. Blanche had keys to both Céline's and Lucie's rooms but says she returned the latter.'

'And was able to come and go at will, leaving love letters presumably to taunt Ménétrel; the identity card to warn Bousquet that *les gars* are indeed being watched?'

'Those letters are to Céline, aren't they?' asked Kohler.

'Of course they are! Ah *mon Dieu,* you doubt my word? Look, then!'

Madame Dupuis, Hôtel d'Allier was written on the top envelope, the hand firm enough, the cancellation stamp dated Monday, 1 February 1943.

'Read it,' said Kohler. 'Go on, don't be shy. Since when did you owe the Maréchal any privacy?'

'Must I?'

'And spoken like a loyal *poilu!* I might have known!'

They were both exhausted and bitchy. Kohler yanked the packet from him and tore it open, freeing the envelope to let him have it verbatim. '*Ma chère Ange,*' – my dear angel – '*your eyes are like the blue of the finest sapphires, your breath the soft, sweet nectar to whose scent the bee finds he must come.*'

'Foragers are females!' snorted St-Cyr. 'Doesn't the old drone know anything about bees?'

They'd just come off the case of a Parisian beekeeper ...

'*When I see you dancing, I want to make you my Goddess of the Water Sprites.* More bullshit, and even more of it,' said Kohler, flipping impatiently through the thing until ... '*There are places we can meet where no one else will know. Please say the word and still the quivering of a heart that longs to kiss its little flower and caress its soft and exquisite petals.* Oh-oh, the horny old goat, eh, Louis?'

The line of traffic moved ahead one space, the car jerked as Hermann let out the clutch, then slammed on the brakes.

'*I must embrace you. Bernard can arrange everything. Bernard, my sweet. Look upon him as a friend in need and his loyalty and absolute discretion will be yours, as they are my own.* No wonder Ménétrel wants the letters, Louis. They as much as say he arranged the liaison that led to her death, but why the hell would anyone, even Blanche Varollier or that brother of hers, remove and then return them?'

'To be found not by Bousquet or the doctor, Hermann, but by ourselves.'

'But ... but surely our killer or killers couldn't have known we'd go there soon? Surely Blanche and her brother couldn't have?'

'But someone did. Someone who knows us well. The very staircase I would take in that hotel, my name on that list before we even knew we'd have to leave Paris.'

'Someone so close to things here, he, she or they are not only aware of what's going on moment by moment, but can come and go at will.'

'And aren't even noticed, Hermann, because, like others in the Government and the town, they are a part of the woodwork. They must be, and they know this and are confident of it. Supremely so.'

Lost to the thought – feeling exceedingly uncomfortable because of it – Louis took back the letter and began to retie the ribbon. 'A good ten letters ... no, fifteen,' he said, 'but not all of the envelopes, though of the same colour, use identical statio-nery.'

'Pardon?'

'These ...' He quickly sorted through them. 'Are to a Madame Noëlle Olivier.'

'And the dates?' muttered Kohler, knowing now that they *had* been left for them on purpose!

'June, July, September, October and November 1925, Her-mann, and all from the Maréchal.'

'To another married woman? Another of his conquests? Was the bugger so arrogant as to have sent them to her home? Well, was he?'

'To 133 boulevard des Célestins, Vichy.'

'*Jésus, merde alors,* take the topmost one and read it, then. Let whoever's trying to tell us something, tell it!'

Paris, 15 November 1925

My dear Madame Olivier,

You will excuse me if it appears harsh when I tell you enough is enough. Should you wish to pursue your intentions, please do so through my solicitors. Remember, though, that such a scandal as you envision is always a two-edged sword. Your good name and those of your husband and children are at present free from all such concerns. To wound them so grievously is to wound yourself and gain nothing. Love is always a battleground. Some you win, and from some you must inevitably retreat.

Adieu.

Pétain

'A glacier, Louis.'

'*Oui.* But what did she do? This letter has been stained by a flood of tears and then tightly crumpled into a ball, only to be later flattened out.'

'Did she use the rope, take poison, drown herself, find a gun, or simply go on living?' asked Kohler.

'Only to keep the memory of him close and bide her time?'

'Or are we looking for the husband and is he the one who ducks into and out of rooms to leave things for us to find?'

There were always questions, seldom easy answers. Because of a bend in the road and its rise and narrowness, they hadn't been able to see the entrance to the bridge but now could. Instead of two men on the Boutiron Control, there were four. Instead of acne-faced teenagers in oversized greatcoats with Mauser rifles, this detail wore winter whites with hoods up and cradled Schmeissers in white-mittened hands to keep the grease on their weapons from congealing.

'A *Sonderkommando*?' asked Louis, sickened by the sight and quickly stuffing away the letters and the knife.

A special command. 'Waffen-SS,' breathed Kohler softly.

'Straight in from Russia via the glorious army of the South that's now based in Lyons. An airdrop likely. Unless I'm mistaken, *mon vieux*, Bousquet, thinking the worst and that *les gars* really were the targets, must have run to Herr Gessler and the nameless one, and they called in the fist.'

There would be motorcycle patrols and arrests – all manner of such things. 'And if we so much as question someone or take too great an interest in them,' said St-Cyr sadly, 'so will they.'

Unsettled by the thought, they waited, and when the car was finally noticed in the line-up, a mittened fist soon pounded on the side window.

Hermann rolled it down. 'Trouble, Sergeant?' he asked pleasantly enough in *Deutsch*.

Shrapnel had once torn the right side of the Scharführer's face from well above the half-closed, lead-grey eye to the raw-boned chin. The last three fingers of the right hand were missing, the left shoulder permanently hunched forward.

'*Papiere, mein Herr.*'

'Kohler, Kripo, Paris-Central. We're in a bit of a rush, Scharführer.'

'That does not matter.'

'Don't you need the password?'

'If you wish.'

Herr Kohler gave out with the *Quatsch*. Harvests ripe and all, the song perfect, thought Gerd Schepp. But this Kripo was known to point the finger of truth at his own kind and wore the scars of it. Disloyal, not a true believer, and one to be treated as if *Scheisse* were on the boots.

That thumb and forefinger were impatiently snapped. Finding the papers wasn't easy. 'Your right coat pocket, Herr Detektiv Inspektor,' offered Louis submissively.

'Ah! *Danke.*'

A packet of long-forgotten cigarettes – emergency rations – was now more than slightly crushed, Louis having tucked it in there and four left, only four.

Offered up, straightened and lit – one each and the French half of the partnership totally left out – the papers were found and handed over to be closely scrutinized.

'You're a long way from home,' tried Hermann. 'Ferleiten ... the Hohe Tauern, near the Italian border?'

He'd deliberately got the location wrong so as to encourage conversation, thought St-Cyr, only to hear the Scharführer grunt, 'Mathausen. I used to work in the granite quarry but now they have plenty of cheap labour though they could, perhaps, still use someone with a knowledge of explosives if you're interested.'

A concentration camp!

'The north bank of the Danube near Enns? *Mein Gott*, Louis, how could I have missed it? One tries so hard but I've been away too long, I guess. Here, sorry I forgot to light a cigarette for you. Have mine.'

'Destination?' demanded Schepp.

'A cabin downriver. A crime scene,' said Kohler blandly and never mind about their heading for the racetrack!

'Recent?'

'Not so recent.'

'Then there's no rush, is there?'

'Not really.'

'Length of stay?'

Verdammt, were they going to be watched that closely? 'An hour or two, Scharführer. More if we find something we need to follow up.'

'Curfew has been rolled back to twenty-one hundred hours. Make sure you're tucked in by then.'

The buzzing drone of a low-flying Storch interrupted them. Camouflaged, sand-coloured from the desert war in North Africa and looking like a skinny dragonfly with stiff legs, the plane roared overheard at 200 metres, then quickly throttled back to drop to river level.

'The tiny aerodrome below the village of Charmeil,' explained St-Cyr humbly. 'It's only five kilometres from here, Inspektor. The Maréchal Pétain has a large farmhouse in the village; Herr Abetz a château, I believe.'

Hermann paid no apparent attention, would continue to try to break through that armour.

'Were you at Stalingrad with von Paulus and the 6th, Scharführer? I ask only because my boys were there and still are.'

'And not on the long march into Siberia? They're among the lucky then, aren't they, Herr Hauptmann der Geheime Stattspolizist?'

Fish only when there are fish to be caught and then you won't be humiliated, thought St-Cyr ruefully. The whole of the 6th Army, what had been left of it, had been taken. Over 90,000 men were on that march, but the Scharführer was letting Hermann know his sons were heroes, their father something far less. Paris had informed Herr Gessler of who Hermann was, and Gessler had spread the word.

'Lucky, yes,' muttered Hermann tightly. 'What's going on here?'

'The same war.'

'*Banditen* in the hills? That was a spotter plane, wasn't it?'

'*Terroristen, ja.* Communists. FTPs. We'll soon clean them out. Who's he?'

'Him? The Frenchman they gave me to run errands. St-Cyr, Sûreté.'

'The Oberdetektiv Jean-Louis St-Cyr of 3 Laurence-Savart in Belleville, Paris? The one who gets his name splashed all over the papers?'

'Yes. Yes, that's him.'

'Then just remember the two of you are on your own. We have enough to do as it is and won't be lifting a finger to help should you get into difficulties. Oh, I've forgotten my hand. This finger.' The roof was banged. 'Pass. Erich, let this one pass,' called out the Scharführer. 'They have to pee.'

'Sorry, Louis,' muttered Kohler. 'You know I didn't mean that bit about running errands.'

The *Sonderkommando* would net the innocent, the terrified who would bolt simply because they wouldn't know what the hell was going on, and perhaps even a few *maquisards* would be

155

caught. But was the threat really from the Résistance as Bousquet and the others thought? And had the Führer not also used the opportunity to make absolutely certain Pétain didn't go over to the Allies?

The aerodrome would still have French aircraft sufficient for a night flight to Morocco or Algiers, and Hermann ... Hermann had been told by the nameless one that the Reich didn't want anything happening to the Maréchal or else.

They had reached the stables.

'Hermann, will you be okay in there?'

Louis was remembering the SS and the scar of a rawhide whip that his partner had earned in the stables of a château on the Loire near Vouvray early last December, the château of Gabrielle Arcuri's mother-in-law. 'Me? Fine. No problem.'

Perhaps. 'There are two cars parked outside, and one engine is colder than the other.'

'Ferbrave's come running, I think.'

'And Albert?'

'Has found more rats than he bargained for.'

Built at the turn of the century, their heavily timbered cupolas rising above the loft, the stables' stalls were arranged off an aisle that was more than 300 metres in length and held the accumulated tack of all those years. There were thoroughbreds, quarter horses, trotters, hunters and those for just plain pleasure. Lucie Trudel's dappled grey was a splendid gelding; the stall was immaculate, even with a snapshot of her pinned up for the horse to look at if lonely.

Stablehands, and the usual hangers-on every track seemed to have, were about, riders still coming in. Two of the *Blitzmädchen*, the grey mice who had come from the Reich to work as telegraphers and typists, et cetera, were rubbing down a bay mare and whispering sweet nothings to it. A Wehrmacht general and his orderly were dismounting to hand over the reins. Everything seemed quite normal. A busy place. Bicycles had been parked outside and at least two staff cars were at the far end.

'No trouble, then,' breathed Kohler.

'But trouble all the same,' sighed Louis.

To the north-east, there was the racetrack and, just to the west of this and in line with the stables, the grandstand with the Jockey Club's reception rooms, restaurant and bar on the ground floor and first storey.

The showjumping course and paddocks were closer to the stables. The whole area must be lovely even in winter, thought Kohler. Fantastic if one had the money and time. And good to see that the Wehrmacht felt at least some horses should remain in France. A necessity.

'Please don't forget the sports club and golf course that are behind us, Inspector,' said Louis tritely. 'The tennis club and its swimming pool also.'

'And the clay-pigeon shoot which is a little to the west so that the noise won't disturb things here, eh? *Merde*, where the hell are Deschambeault and Ferbrave and our two innocents?'

If one of them was indeed innocent!

Not here, one of the hangers-on seemed to say, nodding curtly towards the way they'd come.

Blue-blinkered lanterns were being lit, but above them were strings of paper ones, from the Mikado perhaps, which once would have illuminated the dances that the owners must have held at the Jockey Club after successful races. Champagne and *les élégantes de tout Paris* wandering up into the loft to soft lights and beds of hay. Cigars, too!

'A bloody firetrap, Louis!' snorted Kohler, the pungency of manure, hay, horse piss and oats mingling with that of occasional and not-so-occasional tobacco. 'Stay down here. I'll take a look above.'

Again St-Cyr asked if his partner was all right; again Kohler had to reassure him.

Torch in hand, Hermann began to climb one of the ladders. In many ways it was similar to the stable at Vouvray. He hesitated – that bad knee of his, cursed St-Cyr silently. He went on, was soon out of sight. Perhaps they'd come a third of the way along the main aisle, perhaps a little more, but ... Ah *mon Dieu*, what was going on? Everything had suddenly stopped. Even the *Blitzmäd-chen* hesitated . . .

Shrill on the damp, cold air came a high-pitched, *'no, monsieur! please, no!'*

From the far end of the aisle a stallion neighed in fright and began to kick its stall. Inès Charpentier shrieked again and again, which only frightened the horse more. It kicked and kicked and neighed, the girl trying desperately to dodge its hooves. Others became restless. Others began to join in . . .

Hermann moved past him in a blur. He ran, he reached the stall ahead of the stablehands, snatched a prod from the wall, opened the door and vanished.

Sickened by what they must surely find, for the sculptress had given one last, piercing shriek that had been abruptly cut off, St-Cyr brushed past the others to enter the stall. Hermann had a firm grip on the halter and had tucked the prod under an arm, having used a shoulder to force the stallion against a wall and away from the girl.

'Easy . . . Easy,' he said, his voice soothing. 'Now calm yourself, my beauty. You pinch them on the neck or cheek, Louis. That distracts them, then offer the carrot if you have one. You're a handsome devil, aren't you?' he went on to the stallion, a magnificent three-year-old but still very high-strung. 'You're worth plenty and are certain to take the Prix de l'Arc de Triomphe at Longchamp this October, only it won't be held there due to possible acts of terrorism, they say, so it and the other races will be held at Le Tremblay to the north-east of Paris. Please don't worry.'

On and on he went, talking to the horse. He asked about the cinder track at Vincennes and how it was, said he was sorry that racing at Deauville had had to be cancelled in 1940. 'The RAF simply don't understand, do they? Louis,' he said in that same carefully modulated voice. 'Louis, the sculptress.'

Curled into a ball, trembling so hard she couldn't move, Inès Charpentier cowered in a far corner. No tears, nothing but shock.

'Take her out now,' said Hermann. 'Just do it gently.'

Her wrists were cold, her hands freezing, that lovely coat from the thirties, with its deer-horn buttons, in a mess that she didn't even notice.

Clinging to him, she quivered as they squeezed past Hermann; she was so thin, could be a killer, but couldn't, St-Cyr told himself, and finally said, 'Let the tears come, mademoiselle. Please don't be ashamed.'

'I can't,' she gasped. 'I haven't cried in years.'

'And you're terrified of horses, aren't you,' he said, 'yet chose to come here anyway?'

'I have to sculpt them, don't I?' she snapped, pulling away from him to place a steadying hand flat against the boards of the nearby wall.

'Argue if you wish, mademoiselle, but anyone who claims to be fascinated by horses, as you did to Monsieur Grenier, must have been around them enough to know they can and will sense fear and often react accordingly.'

'I hit the horse. I was flung right at it!'

'But didn't think to try to calm it.'

'Ferbrave . . . Henri-Claude Ferbrave of the Garde Mobile saw you coming and wanted to keep you from talking to Albert.'

Closed for the season, the Jockey Club's bar and restaurant would be pitch dark, Inès told herself. Still terrified by what had happened, still shaking, she knew the building must be huge, knew the beams from St-Cyr's and Kohler's distant torches must be flickering over empty tables with chairs leaning inwards. Sometimes she could hear the detectives, most often not, for in their haste to stop Henri-Claude, they'd left her far behind, hadn't realized, *grâce à Dieu*, that her eyes were giving her such trouble. They couldn't know that always now it was like this for her when going from a lighted room into darkness. Everything totally black. No use in blinking the eyelids to clear the eyes, though she often did this and must learn to stop. Always the panic, the terror, that cloying sickness of never knowing if and when someone might grab her or her handbag.

The detectives must be going up a staircase, for Herr Kohler's voice suddenly echoed. 'Louis, you leave that *salaud* to me!' To me . . .

'Never, and you know it!' shouted St-Cyr.

Their shoulders hit a door, Herr Kohler shouting at the occupants as it burst inwards, 'Ferbrave?' The answer, one she knew the detectives could only dread: 'Outside.'

And in the grandstand.

Feeling her hesitant way forwards – telling herself that she absolutely must somehow continue to keep from them her not being able to see – Inès stumbled blindly into a table, knocked over a chair, then . . . then started up the staircase. Henri-Claude had cared only to find out how much Albert really knew of the killings and the knife he'd found, and what the groundskeeper's son had told the detectives of the transport of illegal goods by vans of the Bank of France. There'd been no time to prise such answers from him in the stables. Ferbrave hadn't cared a damn about what might happen to her. She was expendable. She must hide the darkness from him, too, for he could just as easily have slit her throat and might still do so. He had run after Albert. Monsieur Gaëtan-Baptiste Deschambeault hadn't cared either and had run after them.

And now? she asked herself, pausing to listen closely and to still the panic the darkness always brought. Now the curved iron of what must be an art nouveau balustrade was cold beneath her hand. Now Ferbrave would either protect himself and the others, and what had been going on for far too long, or fail.

The others, she thought and wept inwardly. Bousquet, Richard – Minister of Supplies and Rationing – the banker also and, yes most certainly, Honoré de Fleury, Inspector of Finances, to say nothing of their friends and associates.

'Louis . . . Louis, where are they?' asked Kohler, dismayed by what lay before them.

Ice clung to the rows of seats, and in the beams from their torches, falling snow swept along. Away towards the far side of the grandstand, Kohler knew that neither he nor Louis could make out more than this; towards the lower railing and the racetrack, they could see little else.

There wasn't a sound but that of the wind and the incessant flapping of what were, most probably, swastikas on the flagstaffs that rose from the lower railing to stand well above the roof overhead. Having arrived on 11 November last, the Army of the South must have held a parade here, a show of force, and still the flags remained.

'I'll work my way among the boxes,' muttered St-Cyr. 'You take the lower rows of seats.'

'They're not here. They're above us,' sighed Kohler, the beam of his torch having found a flagstaff cleat whose rope now trailed in the wind.

'There has to be a better way.'

Albert had shinned up the flagstaff; Ferbrave had used the ladder that was at the back of the grandstand, behind the seats. The one had thought he could reach the trapdoor to hold it shut by lying on top of it; the other had beat him to it.

'It'll be a skating rink, Louis. That's why they're so silent. Give me a moment, will you?'

Lowering a flag, he cut off its rope and let the wind take the rest.

'Me first,' said St-Cyr. 'Tie it around one of my ankles and anchor me to something. You know that knee of yours will only cause trouble.'

Gun and torch were handed over, hat and overcoat too. Up on the roof the little ridges, glazed and with wide and shallow troughs, ran straight downslope, the wind making mischief as it whipped the snow along.

'Albert . . .' muttered St-Cyr to himself. 'Ah *merde*, Hermann,' he yelled. 'Keep your light on them!'

Spreadeagled next to the lower edge of the roof, the groundskeeper's son clung by one gloved hand to Henri-Claude who, in turn, clung bare-handed to one of the flagpoles.

'*I didn't tell them anything! what vans?*' shrieked Albert. '*I'm not hearing you!*'

'*You keep that mouth of yours shut or else!*' cried Ferbrave.

'*Can't shut what isn't open!*'

'*Who used that knife and then dropped it?*'

'*Vipère! serpent! I'm not listening!*'

'*Then fly, asshole. fly!*'

Ah no . . . No! The roof was slippery, the rope loose, but was it long enough or too long? wondered St-Cyr.

Careering down over the ridges and hollows, he tried to slow himself by turning sideways, wasn't going to reach them, was going to shoot right past . . .

Snatching at Albert's ankles, he grabbed one and hung on as the rope tightened. Ferbrave winced at the strain. A moment passed and then another. '*Hermann, take up the slack!*'

'Now pray, messieurs. You, Henri-Claude, that he doesn't fall to his death and walk you to the guillotine; and you, Albert, because we need you.'

'I don't know who dropped that knife in the shit. I don't know anything about the vans. I thought I did but can't remember.'

Inès blinked and blinked hard but still couldn't see a thing. The door St-Cyr and Kohler had broken in was almost closed, but a wedge of light flooded out from an office of some kind, precious light that lifted her spirits and made her feel whole again.

Deschambeault and his son were in there – she knew this for she'd heard them arguing, their voices always muffled. But now they, like her, had to listen as, with agonizing slowness, Herr Kohler pulled his partner and Albert back up the roof.

Ferbrave had been left for the moment – he must have been, but where, exactly, he was located she couldn't tell and that, she warned herself, was a worry.

Pressing a cheek against the wall, she strained to hear the sous-directeur and his son above the noises from the roof.

'Jean-Guy, it's got to stop. Things are getting far too close,' said the elder Deschambeault.

'Stop, *mon père?*'

'*Merde, imbécile*, must you taunt me at a time like this? One van and no one was the wiser, but then another and another and what am I to do now, eh? Go to the Maréchal and beg forgiveness when there are assassins about? *Assassins*, Jean-Guy!'

'*Résistants?*'

'It's possible. Those people from Paris also. Doriot or Déat may have sent in the Intervention-Referat or the Bickler Unit to teach us a little lesson.'

The son took a moment to consider this, felt Inès, then she heard him asking suspiciously, 'Did you inform Secrétaire Général Bousquet of your concern?'

'Pah! Don't be a fool. He's the one who suggested it and knows far more about them than I do!'

Again the son took his time to reply but now there was sarcasm. 'You worry too much, Papa.'

'Will you never learn?' demanded the sous-directeur. 'Lucie's dead. It's over. Will that not satisfy you and that ... that mother of yours?'

That bitch of a mother? she could hear the son thinking.

'Maman hasn't yet heard of your loss, and neither have Thérèse or Martine. Was it a boy or a girl that *putain* of yours dropped?'

Ah *merde*!

'*Bâtard*, how can you speak to me like that? I who brought you here from Paris and saw that you were given the position you have? You were always the *lanterne rouge* of the class, Jean-Guy.' The rear light. 'Failure at mathematics, at chemistry, at everything else. This job, that job. Gambling, losing, cheating, lying. *Mon Dieu*, the number of times I've had to cover for you, yet you treat me like this? Ah! I admit you're good at what you do here. One of the best. And perhaps in time, when this Occupation is over and things settle down, these stables will be yours.'

Sugar there. Some sugar, thought Inès.

'What is it, then, that you want, Papa, the olive branch?'

'You know very well. Quit visiting that brothel Ferbrave knows you visit because it's his also. Leave it and stop all use of the vans. Tell the drivers they'll continue to receive their extra wages for the long runs but are to keep silent or face immediate dismissal. Enough is enough, Jean-Guy. Good while it lasted. Oh *bien sûr*, but finished for now because it has to be.'

'And Lucie?'

'I didn't kill her, if that's what you're thinking.'

'Admit it, she was trouble.'

'Trouble? Tell your mother I'll visit her soon. All right, tell her I'll even sleep with her if that will satisfy her.'

Again the son took his time before saying, 'Broken fences are never easy to mend.'

'And that doctor of hers? That quack who claims to calm her at my expense?' hissed the father. 'What part has he had in breaking those same fences, eh?'

'Has he been fucking her – is that what you think?'

'You know it isn't, but why should I care, eh?'

'She's very ill,' said Jean-Guy. 'Why can't you realize she's psychotic? Torn by delusions, lives in hell because of you and your mistresses! Not just Lucie. The others before her!'

Still they hadn't raised their voices. 'How self-righteous you are,' said the elder Deschambeault. 'You who prefer the tenderest.'

Girls of fourteen and fifteen, said Inès to herself.

'Ménétrel knows that "quack" as you call him, father. Everything Maman has ever said to Dr Normand has been repeated to Ménétrel.'

The father must have been taken aback, for he hesitated and then asked suspiciously, 'Have you seen him there when you visited her?'

Perhaps the son smiled. 'Of course. Thérèse and Martine have also seen him at the clinic with Dr Normand, discussing Mother's progress.'

'And Lucie?'

'Most certainly.'

'At Chez Crusoe and the parties at the château?' asked the sous-directeur.

'Just as he makes a point of knowing everything else, Ménétrel knows, Papa.'

'Because you told him? Or was it Thérèse or Martine?' shot the elder Deschambeault.

'I didn't!' retorted the son. 'I can't, of course, vouch for my sisters whose eyebrows are always raised when they speak of their father having sex with his latest, but in any case, since none of us ever attended any of those "sessions" at the château, how could we possibly have known of what went on?'

'Sessions? Meetings of the board, idiot! *Nom de Dieu*, you must hate me.'

'Not at all. I simply know you.'

Again the father paused. 'Then tell Ferbrave he'd better find out everything he can from Albert before taking care of him. We can't have the rat-catcher coughing up our blood to those two from Paris.'

'And Henri-Claude?'

'Must be told that it has to end, Jean-Guy, that I won't submit to blackmail from him or anyone, and that if he doesn't stop, I will go straight to Herr Gessler with things our Garde Mobile would rather not have the Gestapo hear.'

Inès nudged the door open a little farther. Both were standing, the father and son facing each other across the latter's desk, but the sous-directeur's back was to her and this partly blocked Jean-Guy from catching sight of her.

Silver trophies and ribbons adorned the shelves beyond them. Paintings of famous racehorses hung on the walls, a map of the course and grounds, one of the town of Vichy too.

Jean-Guy Deschambeault wore the buttoned-up, burnt-umber, single-breasted jacket she'd been told he would. Beneath it there was the charcoal turtleneck pullover he often favoured and yes, the whipcord breeches were of a soft shade of olive, and yes, the tan riding boots were well greased and polished.

No spurs, not now. No sand-coloured, tweed golf cap either.

Thirty years old, he was unmarried because he chose to be, but never lacked girlfriends who were willing enough, though none had been able to give him what that *maison de tolérance* could and did. Blue-eyed and handsome, of more than medium height, he was well built, masculine, ah yes, a polo player too, with thick, wavy, curly dark chestnut hair and the bluish four-o'clock shadow of one who often shaves but can never quite dispel that mildly dissipated playboy image. Cold, too, Inès reminded herself, but utterly charming in his own right when he wanted to be.

The two had stopped talking. The noise from the roof had ceased. Now there was only that of the flags.

'Mademoiselle, what did you overhear?' came a whisper.

Someone had switched on the corridor lights. Ah *merde*, it was St-Cyr, standing so close to her she could feel the icy breath of him and see the suppurating, black-stitched, throbbing bulge above his half-closed left eye. Behind him at a distance was Albert Grenier, behind that one, Henri-Claude Ferbrave and lastly Herr Kohler. 'Nothing. I . . . I was looking for you. Albert,' she tried. 'Albert, are you all right?'

'Inside, I think. Take a seat while we warm ourselves at the stove. Compose yourself, Mademoiselle Charpentier. You've had a terrible fright and are perhaps still in shock, but please prepare your answers better.'

The nineteenth-century, cast-iron stove in the office was decorated with a pair of turtledoves that drank from a birdbath above its little door, and through the mica windows Inès could see the flames. Herr Kohler had sat right next to her on the leather sofa but Albert hadn't wanted to sit anywhere else and had tried to ask him to move over. He'd refused, of course, and had deliberately driven poor Albert to tears, causing him to abruptly turn his back to them and sit down anyway, squeezing himself between them and satisfying Herr Kohler as to exactly how close a relationship she had managed to establish with the groundskeeper's son.

These days such friendships were often automatic, the old and the young enjoying each other's company as if their differences in age were of no consequence. Sculptresses of twenty-eight and boys, young men of what? she asked herself. With Albert it was so hard to tell. Thirteen perhaps, or six or seven, but sometimes a young man. And yes, both Kohler and St-Cyr thought she'd deliberately formed the friendship. And yes, she had to remind herself, Albert can be difficult. I must be careful.

St-Cyr had remained standing halfway between the desk and stove. He had helped himself to the container of pipe tobacco, even filling both pouch and pipe, and had offered his partner a cigar from the humidor, a Choix Supreme no doubt, which had yet to be lit. Hadn't offered one to the father who now sat stonily in one of the club chairs, the son tense and watchful behind that desk of his.

A bottle of the local marc had been found but this had been rejected by St-Cyr. 'The Louis XIII,' he had insisted. 'The 1925.'

It hadn't been available.

'Inspector . . .' hazarded the elder Deschambeault.

St-Cyr turned on him.

'It's Chief Inspector, Sous-directeur. Let's observe the formalities since this is an official inquiry and you are now under suspicion also of trafficking.'

'*Jésus, merde alors*, what the hell is the matter with you? A few cigars, a couple of bottles of champagne – gifts I'd managed to find in Paris for an old and very dear friend?'

'The 1925 Bollinger Cuvée Spéciale? Need I remind you that Mademoiselle Marie-Jacqueline Mailloux had been drinking that when found in the bath she shared with your colleague, Alain André Richard, Minister of Supplies and Rationing?'

'Look, I . . . I know nothing of this. Bousquet would never have told me what was in her stomach. *Mon Dieu*, why would he?'

'Inspector Kohler, please record what has just been said and get him to sign and date it,' said St-Cyr.

167

'Now listen, you . . .'

'No, you listen, monsieur. Last year in the Department of the Seine alone there were over four hundred thousand arrests for violations of the food regulations – that is, for illegally buying and selling on the *marché noir*. The courts and jails are clogged with *lampistes*. Never the big fish, always the small fry, eh, Hermann, but now we've landed one of the biggest!'

In the silence that followed, St-Cyr yanked the cork from the bottle of marc and, finding four cut-glass tumblers, poured goodly measures into all but the last. 'Albert,' Inès heard him saying. 'Albert, *mon ami*, would you care to join us? It'll warm you up a little.'

And there's much that you can tell us, thought Inès.

The big, raw hands, with their thick and stumpy fingers, were suddenly stilled atop the coarse, dark grey woollen gloves in his lap. Dirt lay beneath the cracked nails.

'He's trying to bribe me,' whispered Albert into her right ear. 'I knew he would!' The breath of him was warm with the anise he must have been chewing. Anise and garlic.

'He'd like to join us,' Inès heard herself saying too loudly, too awkwardly, she felt.

Abruptly a glass was handed to her and another to Albert. 'This friend?' went on St-Cyr, sucking on that pipe of his and causing the elder Deschambeault to curse under his breath and look to his son for help that was not forthcoming.

'The custodian of Herr Abetz's château,' said the sous-directeur flatly.

'His name, please?'

'Inspector . . . Chief Inspector, is this really necessary? He can't have had anything to . . .'

Kohler knew Louis would tell him that everything was of interest, and smiled when he did.

'Charles-Frédéric Hébert,' muttered Deschambeault.

Herr Kohler wrote it down, then flipped back a page in his little black notebook. 'The parties, Louis,' he said, not looking up but leaning across Albert's lap to let her see the entry, the names of Paul and Blanche Varollier, and below the first of these: A deep gouge in the right, wooden sole.

'Parties? Informal meetings. A few nights of cards, an occasional game of backgammon or chess, Inspector,' objected the elder Deschambeault. 'Brief respites from the affairs of state. Chances to discuss matters in private and away from the office. Often it's best that way.'

'Was any help called in?' asked Herr Kohler. Deschambeault was sweating, the son's expression empty, thought Inès.

'Help?' said the father. 'I really wouldn't know. One is too busy talking shop. The economy has been a terrible strain, the demands for new policy papers ... Surely there's hardly time to notice the help at such functions?'

'A translator,' muttered Herr Kohler, his partner watching everyone's reactions and filing them away, Inès told herself.

'My *Deutsch* is more than sufficient,' said Deschambeault.

'Then some of my compatriots attended these little gatherings of yours?' asked Herr Kohler.

To say, They're not mine, would be unwise. 'A few.'

'Girls?' asked Kohler.

'Lucie sometimes accompanied me but found it rather boring.'

'Birds?' demanded Herr Kohler.

Salaud! the elder Deschambeault must be thinking, thought Inès, and heard him saying, 'The custodian keeps a few, but I've never seen them.'

A lie for sure, she told herself, chancing a glance at Henri-Claude Ferbrave, who must have torn the skin from the palm of his left hand – frost on bare metal would have done that. He had bandaged the hand with the white scarf he'd worn but now was realizing the silk would cling to the wound ...

'Lucie Trudel,' sighed St-Cyr, deliberately pausing to relight that pipe of his and to drop the match into the stove. 'Lucie, Albert. She wanted a bottle of the Chomel.'

'Her father was sick!' yelped Albert. 'She was co-old.'

'You took her down into the cellars, to your nest.'

'She was free-zing!'

Taking him by the hand, Inès gently squeezed his fingers and then knitted her own among them. 'You're so very kind, Albert,' she softly confided. 'One of the kindest men I've ever met. The inspectors mean no harm, so please don't be afraid. Just try to remember what Mademoiselle Trudel said to you. They'll want to know. It might be important.'

And why, please, are you taking such an active part in this investigation? wondered St-Cyr.

A little of the untouched marc spilled over the rim of Albert's glass. 'Don't know anything. Can't remember.'

Merde, one would have to go so carefully and be so very gentle with him, thought St-Cyr, but the presence of Henri-Claude and what had almost happened on the roof was still very much with the boy. 'You reached up to the board for the key to the Hall des Sources, Albert. Lucie would have seen you do this.'

'She was cry-ing. She was co-old. I hadn't put the coffee on. Always I gets to make the . . .' Oh-oh, I shouldn't have said that, said Albert to himself, using the secret voice in his head. Henri-Claude was staring at him and so were Monsieur Jean-Guy and his father. 'I . . . I found a clean rag for her and she wiped her eyes.'

Albert had gripped her fingers so tightly he was hurting her. Inès winced, but better to be hurt than to have him take his hand away.

'You went outside to the Hall,' continued St-Cyr. 'You removed the padlock and chain, and opened the door. Could you see her tears then, in the torchlight? You must have had a torch.'

'Tears?' yelped Albert. 'What tears? She had just dried her eyes. Do you think I don't remember what I said?'

'Albert, what the Chief Inspector wishes to know is did Lucie tell you anything that might be useful?'

'Can't say. Don't know.'

'You filled the bottle for her,' tried St-Cyr.

'She hugged it. She was free-zing. She said she'd love to have a bathe in it, but . . .'

'But was too afraid to go to the *établissement thermal*?' he asked.

'My nurse was drowned there. Now I don't have my nurse any more. It hurts.'

'What hurts?' asked Inès.

'My back, my shoulders, my *spi-ine*!'

'Albert, did Lucie speak to anyone else that morning?' asked the Chief Inspector, his voice too insistent, Inès felt.

'Don't know. Can't say.'

'Inspector . . .' began the elder Deschambeault, only to be silenced by, 'Must I remind you it's Chief Inspector and that you will speak only when spoken to?'

'Albert, you'd best tell him,' said Inès. 'If you don't, I'm afraid the Chief Inspector will think I spoke to Lucie. I couldn't have, of course, for I wasn't here, hadn't yet met you, but he's a detective, and they are always suspicious.'

'No one spoke to her.'

'And the rats, Albert?' asked Inès gently. 'He'll want to know who you think might have taken them.'

'The owner of the knife.'

'A woman?' asked Inès.

'What do you think?'

'I . . . I don't know,' she blurted. Albert had released her hand and had turned to stare at her as if she had owned that knife, as if she'd taken the rats from his shed without even having paid for them! 'I . . . I *didn't* kill her, Albert. I swear I didn't.'

'Your eyes are wet. You're afraid. I can tell.'

Ah *Sainte Mère, Sainte Mère!* 'I'm just worried about you.'

'No you aren't.'

'Albert, *please!*'

'Hermann, take these three into another room and grill them. Leave me to deal with these two! Mademoiselle, you arrive supposedly on the same train as my partner and me, but take a sleeper so as not to be disturbed at the Demarcation Line. You say you are bringing cigars for the Maréchal, a gift from your director. You wear Shalimar, the perfume of the most recent victim, when found hanging about the lobby of the Hôtel du Parc. You then wander into the Hall des Sources to view that victim and leave your fingerprints all over the place thus destroying others we desperately needed. In the Chante Clair restaurant I find you hanging about watching my partner while he's having a little meeting with Bousquet, Ménétrel and Premier Laval, and now ... now we find you in the stable here and then following us to take a decided interest in the proceedings.'

'I ... I can't explain coincidences. I had time on my hands and wished only to help.'

'And have just provided one explanation but is it the truth? Your papers, mademoiselle. Papers, please.'

'Of course. Albert, they are in my handbag. I'm sorry but you will have to move a little.'

Handed over, the papers were scrutinized. St-Cyr was obviously unhappy with himself for having demanded them as so many did these days. Her place of work and residence were there – he'd see those quickly enough. Her age, physical features, all such things, but would he ask what he would need?

'You had a good look at the corpse of Céline Dupuis, mademoiselle. Why such interest?'

'The artist in me. Death has always interested that part of me. Must I apologize for something I, myself, don't fully understand? The compulsion, the drive ... Yes, that curiosity!'

And no mention of the tears Hermann had noticed. Tears she had since said she hadn't been able to shed in years. 'You attended the Sorbonne?' he asked.

'The École des Beaux Arts. Painting, life-drawing and sculpture.'

'And the uncle and aunt who raised you didn't mind?'

'I've already stated they encouraged me. Why shouldn't they have?'

'The expense.'

'Papa had left everything to Maman, and through her, since there was no male heir, it passed to me, as did the small estate my uncle and aunt left.'

'Your father was killed at Verdun?'

'Buried near there, yes. I've already told you this earlier.'

'Killed when, mademoiselle?'

'In May 1917. The ... the exact date I ... I was never told.'

'But tried to find out?'

'I was a child! I needed to know.'

'Was it during the mutinies, mademoiselle?'

'The shelling. You and Herr Kohler must surely have experienced this in that war? Men dying like flies. He ... he was ordered over the top as were the 137,000 others of his *compagnons d'armes* who manned the trenches along the Chemin des Dames and would die in that battle. He *obeyed*, Inspector. He did not run.'

'Forgive me. One always hates to force those under questioning, mademoiselle. Even a Chief Inspector of the Sûreté – this one at least – is not without compassion. Albert, would you get her another marc, please? A cigarette, mademoiselle?'

'I don't smoke.'

Damn you, was implied. And yes, said St-Cyr sadly to himself, as the horror of that ten-day battle swept back in on him, one could never forget the screams of the dying. But the battle had begun at dawn on 16 April and had lasted for ten days. In May the *médecin de l'Armée*, as the *poilus* had started calling Pétain, had been sent in to deal with the mutineers. Men who, for good reason, and with no shame attached to their terror, had thrown down their arms and refused to take the madness any more.

'Let me just see if my partner needs anything,' he said. With a sinking feeling in the pit of her stomach, Inès told herself he had realized Pétain had given the order to the firing squad's captain and that Papa had been buried in an unmarked grave with the other fifty-six the army had admitted to having executed. He couldn't know the love Papa had had for Maman, that at the last he would have cried out her name, that all he had wanted was to see her and hold them both.

The Jockey Club's boardroom was not nearly so wide as it was long. Always mystified by these ritual dens of the corporate elite, Kohler took a quick look around. Magnificent horseflesh here, there, and wouldn't Cro-Magnon man have been thunderstruck? Another Lascaux, as in the Dordogne on that stonekiller investigation Louis and he had had to settle, but a modern one.

Ferbrave sat midway to the side of the Luan mahogany landing field. The father was at its head, the son begrudgingly at his right; wasn't it marvellous how readily such rooms sorted people out, and didn't these three need sorting? There was even a portrait of Marcel Boussac, the textile manufacturer and racehorse owner who, after the Defeat, had got racing started again by hiring a Prussian baron to manage his stables.

Good thinking that. No better horsemen than those boys, but to be fair, had Boussac not done this he'd have lost his stables and France its leading bloodlines.

'Invincible,' he said, not turning to look at them.

'Gladiateur's line, Inspector,' offered the son, and by way of further explanation: 'The Avenger of Waterloo was winner of the Derby, the Grand Prix de Paris and the St Leger in 1865. Proof undeniable that France could at last not only produce champions but would take the lead.'

He'd mutter, 'History,' and still not turn from the photos and paintings. 'Normandy Dancer ... I gather Hyperion, 1933's fabulous British stallion, was felt necessary as that one's sire?'

'Inspector ...'

'*Oui?*' He would let the Chairman of the Board stew a little more.

'Inspector, shouldn't you clear things first with Herr Gessler?'

It was time to face them. 'Our Ernst? An unemployed shoemaker from Schrobenhausen?'

'I was merely suggesting ...'

'One of the beefsteak boys of the Sturmabteilung, the Assault Section of 1933?'

'Inspector, please ...'

'Red meat inside those brown shirts, eh? Must have kept a low profile or been whispering into Herr Goering's ear about his pals

174

in the SA before and during the purge of 30 June to 2 July 1934 – the Night of the Long Knives, that – because, *voilà*, he surfaces in the Berlin Kripo as a detective no less, and not a bruise on him. Even when I was assigned to the Lichtenberg district in '37 and then the Prenzlauerberg in '38, the boys in the cop shop used to whisper about him. I never met him, so can't really say, but it's a big city, or was.'

Merde, what were they to do? wondered Gaëtan-Baptiste. Gessler had warned that Kohler would be trouble but had also hinted he would let the two from Paris sort things out and trust the French would then take care of their own problems! 'He's a most proficient policeman, Inspector, and already has a firm grasp of things.'

'Poland in 1939, of course, and that ghetto in Warsaw in late '40 when almost a half-million of what Herr Himmler and others call the racially undesirable were bottled up until October '42, when they'd finally got the numbers down to a manageable seventy thousand and could spare him. Good at sniffing out trouble and valuables, the weak and deceitful. Came to the attention of several higher-ups. Sent to Rotterdam to deal with Dutch terrorists, then to Antwerp where he excelled in ferreting out housewives who were illegally hiding the enemy and still others of those R-people, the *Rasenverfolgte*, their children especially. And now . . .'

'Inspector . . .'

'No, you let me finish so that we all understand exactly who it is you want me to clear things with. Now considered so reliable that Klaus Barbie, over at the Hôtel Terminus in Lyons – yes, that's the SS-Obersturmführer himself – recommended his transfer to Vichy. Barbie's an old acquaintance, by the way. A case of arson in Lyons, a salamander. Now give. Cut the horseshit and don't ever try to threaten me.'

Just like the corporate elite, they would pull together, thought Kohler, but he'd had to tell them and somehow would now have to break them.

'I was merely suggesting that Herr Gessler could well offer

175

much-needed assistance, Inspector. After all, should anything happen to the Maréchal, the Führer would be most displeased.'

'And Louis and I'd be held responsible? Good *Gott im Himmel,* you don't listen, do you? Monsieur Jean-Guy Deschambeault, please stand up!'

'Up?'

'*Verdammt,* you heard what I said!'

Blanching, the son looked to Ferbrave for support but that one was busy gently teasing the bloodied scarf from his hand and sucking on a dead fag end.

'*Gut,*' snapped Kohler in *Deutsch,* just to remind them that he was Gestapo, before switching back to the lingua franca. 'That wireless set in your office had its dial glued to the forty-metre band. *"Ici Londres,"* eh, mon fin? *"Des Français parlent aux Français."* You've been listening to General de Gaulle.'

'I . . .'

'Jean-Guy, why must you be such a fool?' swore the father sadly. 'Inspector, I'm sure we can come to an understanding.'

Best to glance at the open door and the corridor beyond it, thought Kohler. Best to hesitantly wet the upper lip and softly say, 'I'm listening.' Inès Charpentier had also noted the position of that dial but had lowered her eyes when she'd realized that this Kripo had been looking at her.

'Three years' forced labour in the Reich,' he went on, letting them have it. 'Gessler will, of course, have to respond in the appropriate manner since I'll have to put it into my report to Gestapo Boemelburg and never mind what you've been told about how well we're regarded by the rue des Saussaies in Paris. My partner and I produce, and that's all Boemelburg really wants because, by doing so, we give some semblance of law and order to a nation that's sadly lacking in it.'

Gessler, if he wanted, could then easily take the heat off himself by claiming Jean-Guy was a suspected *résistant,* thought Ferbrave, impressed with what Kohler had just implied. Old money – and there was plenty of it with what had been added – would vanish into Gessler's pockets and the son would be shot, the father, mother and sisters deported to camps. 'You said you were listening, Inspector?'

This little *dur* obviously fancied himself as a 'number' – damned dangerous in the lexicon of such – and maybe he even had dreams of becoming an 'individual', but one must play it out. 'I am. Cut me in and I'll turn a blind eye to what's been going on.'

'And if your partner should notice those same things?' asked Ferbrave. A cigarette and a light were offered by the Kripo. The other two were seemingly forgotten for the moment, Jean-Guy still stupidly standing.

'Louis? He does what he's told. Don't get the wrong idea. He may be a chief inspector but I still pull the strings.'

The rope! snorted Ferbrave silently. 'What is it you'd like to know?'

'First, how many trips a month to and from Paris with the vans?'

'One a week.'

He would have to kill Kohler. St-Cyr's name was already on the FTP's latest list. No one, not even Gestapo Boemelburg, would question the loss. Ménétrel would be convinced the Garde Mobile was more necessary than ever and there would be no more threats of dismissal, no more shrieking about assassins lying in wait or about finding who had betrayed the Government, his precious Government!

'Four a month, then – I'd better jot that down,' said Kohler.

'Perhaps fewer, Inspector. Once or twice a month,' acknowledged Ferbrave.

'*Bon*. And for how long has it been going on?'

'Inspector, we've a crisis on our hands,' interjected the elder Deschambeault.

'And had best get this out of the way so that we can deal with it. How long?'

Kohler was just ragging them. 'A few months,' said Ferbrave cautiously.

'Sometimes a month would go by and there'd be no requests on the list, Inspector, no deliveries,' offered Jean-Guy.

'List? What list?' demanded Kohler.

'There was no list!' swore the father.

'*Requests?*' snapped the Kripo, not turning to look at him and still sitting across the table from Henri-Claude.

'Inspector, my son was merely trying to say that the whole matter didn't amount to anything. Enough flour for a child's birthday cake, a little powdered sugar for the icing. Alain André would . . .'

'Marie-Jacqueline's lover? Richard, the Minister of Supplies and Rationing?'

'Would kindly offer to assist and the child would have its cake.'

'And get to eat it from Government warehouses that are under lock and key?'

To smile ingratiatingly would be wrong. 'Look, I know such luxuries are forbidden,' acknowledge Gaëtan-Baptiste, 'but everyone bends the rules a little. *Mon Dieu*, these days one has to do many things one never would have done in the past. It was nothing.'

And like ripe fish, nauseating. 'When, exactly, did it all begin?'

'A year ago. One van. Only one. Two drivers and the security guard who always rides in the back,' said the sous-directeur.

'Armed?'

'Of course. Even with the policing our German friends provide and the tightening up of our own police, there are still those who will try their luck.'

Didn't he know detectives were only too aware of this! 'Began two years ago,' muttered Kohler, scribbling down the truth. 'The late autumn of 1940, Sous-directeur, when things came into such short supply it looked to you and the others as though what little remained would be hard to obtain through the regular channels. Who buys it – what you don't consume or give to those you need to pay off ?'

Jean-Guy was still standing. Shattered, broken – terrified and now utterly useless. 'Everyone who is anyone.'

'But you're so distant from it that you and Richard and the other lovers of those four girls are in the clear?'

'I was and, yes, I still am, as are they.'

Was that a hint, eh? wondered Kohler. Ferbrave and a little *accident*, the FTP getting the blame and everyone lamenting the loss of two detectives from Paris who were only doing their duty but couldn't have understood the difficulties of the terrain and the urgency of their being ever-vigilant? 'This Flykiller or killers of Monsieur Laval's, Sous-directeur. Who could have such an inside track?'

'I only wish I knew, but it can't have anything to do with the vans. *Merde alors*, why should it?'

'The perfume, the cognac and champagne from 1925. Who requested those?'

'I really wouldn't know, nor would my son or that one.'

Ferbrave.

'Inspector, you are only too aware of the scandal that will erupt if word of this gets out,' said the sous-directeur. 'Surely you must realize we could soon be on the verge of a civil war and that the Reich, for obvious reasons, doesn't want this to happen and wishes the Maréchal to remain in office and in Vichy. Ambassador Abetz is a personal friend and part-owner of the stables my son manages. If you were to speak to him, the Ambassador would satisfy you that what was done with the vans was necessary. *Pour l'amour de Dieu*, we had to keep up appearances. Thirty-two embassies, the papal nuncio among them. Constant delegations from the Reich, visiting dignitaries from all over the new Europe, submissions from our citizenry in the *zone libre* and even from the *zone occupée*. One couldn't have undertaken such receptions in an aura of defeat, could one? The nation had to maintain an image, and in a small and humble way what I and my associates did, helped.'

A saint. 'And the rats in that girl's bed, the knife that was recovered?'

'Albert Grenier may well know who took them and killed her but he's a difficult boy. I would not have harmed him in the slightest. Henri-Claude arrived unexpectedly and . . . Well, you know the rest, and fortunately no one was seriously hurt.'

'That hand,' said Kohler of Ferbrave. '*Merde,* it doesn't look good. I'd best get our sculptress to have a look at it. Hang on a minute.'

Ferbrave hadn't screamed when she'd done as Herr Kohler had asked and had poured the iodine on to that torn strip of flesh. He had simply looked at and through her, thought Inès, and she had realized he had been convinced she knew more than she was letting on. *Bien sûr,* Herr Kohler had warned him that if anything further should happen to her or to Albert he would be held responsible, but Henri-Claude would find a way. Albert hadn't revealed a thing. Adamantly he had refused to tell the detectives who he'd seen dropping that knife into the outhouse. And now? she asked herself, hunching her shoulders under her overcoat for warmth and cramming her hands deeply into its pockets. Now my ten minutes of utter darkness have again passed undiscovered by the detectives and moonlight bathes the snow-covered garden that runs behind the Grenier house on the boulevard de l'Hôpital. Moonlight that is so beautiful as it glistens off the rows of cloches beneath which vegetables will soon be started, the garden extending straight out to the railway embankment above the marshalling yards and the station beyond. And at its very back, next to the family's outdoor toilet, is the shed Albert uses.

Herr Kohler had gone to look at the railway lines and the ease of access. He would conclude there was no problem at all in getting to and from that shed unseen so long as one could avoid the patrols with their dogs. St-Cyr was inside it with the father; Albert indoors, in tears, his mother beside herself with trying to calm him.

While I . . . I stand out here where I've been told to wait by St-Cyr until he returns, she said, and the moon, so pure and silent, sails high above me, the innocent perhaps, or the condemned. And should I move from my little root, he will see my tracks in the snow.

But had the rats that had been found really come from here? Did Albert really know who had taken them?

She wished she could listen to what was being said but knew she daren't move . . .

'Inspector,' said the elder Grenier, 'my Albert was very upset when he returned from the Hôtel d'Allier last Friday evening. He said he had done well, and that with what he'd trapped in the cellars of the Hôtel du Parc, he'd managed six males and four females – he was positive of this – but that someone had stolen five of the males.'

'Stolen while he was still at the Hôtel d'Allier?'

'One of the tenants lets him play with her rabbit. Always when he's on a job there, he takes time out for this. She . . . she'd been to confession and was still very distressed.'

'That was Lucie Trudel. Céline Dupuis owned the rabbit.'

'Yes, but one of the others . . . a Mademoiselle Blanche – I'm sorry I don't know her last name – had returned to console Mademoiselle Trudel when Albert knocked on her door. Blanche had a key to the other one's flat.'

'And the sack Albert kept his rats in?'

'Was left in the cellars, as always. Dead of course. Albert finishes them off with a chair leg he keeps for just such a purpose. Even if they've hanged themselves in his snares, he gives them a good rap just to be certain.'

A rough-hewn bench served as butcher's block, its wooden-handled butcher's knife thin and old, but razor-sharp, the blade a good fifteen centimetres long but worn down at the haft to a width of about a centimetre and a half.

A tin pail caught the skins, the heads and entrails.

One mustn't alarm the elder Grenier too much. 'Monsieur, it would be best if you, or one of the others on your staff, could accompany him on his early-morning rounds and at other times. Do so as unobtrusively as possible. Make up some excuse that's logical, a little schedule with the others perhaps. Just for a few days, until this thing is settled.'

But would it be settled? Would Albert tell them what they

needed to know? 'Four murders, four lovely girls, Inspector. They were each very kind to him. Never a cross word or the disdain and impatience he gets from so many. Though very shy, he'd come to greet them whenever they passed through the park or he'd see them elsewhere in town. If they could, each would always pause to exchange a few words. If he could, Albert would have a little something saved up for at least one of them, a few flowers, an apple . . . We can't spare much, but always let him do this.'

'And Mademoiselle Charpentier?'

'Has taken their place, I think, until just recently.'

The furnace at the Hôtel du Parc had been banked for the night. At a word from St-Cyr, the firebox door was slammed, the lone man on duty begrudgingly excusing himself to leave the 'nest' to the three of them.

Herr Kohler set her valise on the workbench, then stood aside to let her open it. St-Cyr was to her left, the other one reaching up to hold the ceiling light a little closer.

Inès undid the catches. She would hesitate now, she told herself. The inquisition in the car on the return from the Grenier house had been hard: Mademoiselle, remind me of what street in Paris you and your uncle and aunt lived on while you were growing up? The rue Tournefort, *numéro* 47, she'd said and thought, It's not far from place Lucien-Herr and the house of Céline's parents, is it? Neither of them had made mention of this last, nor had they asked if she'd had one childhood friend, one very special person to whom she could confide everything. Well, nearly everything, and receive the same in trust.

The perfume . . . the Shalimar. Why had she chosen such a scent? It must have cost a fortune. It was my aunt's, she had said and they had left it at that, causing her to wonder if they'd believed her.

And where is the *flacon* now? St-Cyr had demanded. In my bag, she had answered, having fortunately resisted the gut-wrenching panic to throw the bottle away.

Boyfriends in Paris? Herr Kohler had asked, as if it was anyone's business other than her own. Boyfriends? she had asked in return. Haven't you heard where all the young men have gone?

Into the *maquis* to avoid the Service de Travail Obligatoire, or in one of the POW camps, or into the ground.

Every compartment of the tray she now removed was cluttered: her tools, her first-aid kit. Certainly the valise had been left here in the care of Albert's father, but would they wonder if this had been deliberate? Suspicious ... they were so suspicious of her, especially St-Cyr.

'Hermann, there's the smell of bitter almonds,' he said, having leaned over, his shoulder rubbing against her as he brought his nose closer to the case. 'Beeswax and that, *mon vieux*. This clear glass tube among your first-aid supplies, mademoiselle? What is the oil, please?'

She would have to give him a foolish smile and weakly say, 'A mistake. I was tricked. For toothache, the oil of cloves, only a switch was made at the last and what I was given was this.'

A little of the oil accidentally trickled down the side of the phial when, with difficulty, she had prised the cork out.

'Ersatz, Louis.'

'Strong, too strong,' grunted St-Cyr. He made no mention of her obviously having purchased the oil on the *marché noir*, his big brown eyes simply sweeping coldly over her.

'Ah *bon*, mademoiselle. For now the portrait, I think.'

Carefully she set the tray aside. She would pause again, though, and take a deep breath, Inès told herself. She would fight hard for control.

Uncovered and incredibly lifelike even though similar to a death mask, the Maréchal stared up at them.

It was St-Cyr who said, 'When we first met, mademoiselle, you stated that the Musée Grévin was always late in granting its commissions and that an update was felt necessary. You did not say it had all but been done. You gave us to understand that your work would take some time. Your room and board, I believe, was a bargain.'

'*Oui*. But is there anything wrong with a person wanting a little break from Paris? From hunger, from the endless queues for a cabbage, a few beets or the tops, a scrap of gristle and mostly disappointment? For six months now I've worked on this subject – first the bust in clay, the mould in plaster, then the portrait face.'

'And now must only check those little details.'

St-Cyr was the constant questioner; Kohler the watcher, content to let him. They would discuss her later, would question possible motives, her wearing the very perfume Céline had worn, the place even where she and Céline had grown up. Had the two girls seen their first film together, met their first fleeting loves, vowed to remain friends for ever? St-Cyr would ask, or would he want still more? Of course he would.

'Inspectors, must I also remove the portrait?' she heard herself asking. Not a quaver now.

St-Cyr nodded. Gingerly she lifted Pétain out, cradling him in his swadding clothes and finally uncovering the rest. 'Six four-hundred-gram blocks of beeswax, Inspectors. You may cut into each of them if you wish.'

It wouldn't be necessary, felt Kohler. The slight nod St-Cyr gave was curt. He was still not satisfied.

Lifting out one of the blocks, she held it up to him. 'Soft amber in colour and with the scent of buckwheat, isn't that so?' she said. 'It came from Normandy, from well before the war. Monsieur le Directeur, feeling things might become difficult, wisely laid in a substantial supply that the authorities have fortunately let us keep but only for our work.'

This one was almost too clever, thought St-Cyr sadly. They couldn't cable Paris to check her story. Gessler would hear of it; they couldn't even ask Ménétrel for the dossier he must have been sent.

'Hermann, take her to the Gare de Vichy to pick up her suitcase, then drop her off at her boarding house. I'll catch a *vélo-taxi* and we can meet up a little later.'

These two, they spoke in silent words, each holding a hidden dialogue with the other. Purposely St-Cyr hadn't said where they would meet, had left her to wonder. But she wouldn't ask, Are you satisfied now? She would repack her case and when it was done, softly say, '*Merci.* It's late and I've not eaten since breakfast.'

Kohler, she knew, wanted to feed her; St-Cyr was the one with the heart of stone.

6

Red, yellow, white and gold, with soft green-and-white seals that looked like the backs of exotic American dollar bills, the cedar boxes were neatly stacked behind art nouveau glass and mahogany doors in a walk-in humidor. Hundreds and hundreds of the finest Havanas – thousands of them, and still others from elsewhere. Bolivar, El Rey del Mundo, Hoyo de Monterrey and Upmann.

Punch, Montecristos, Ramon Allones and Romeo y Julietas.

Astounded by what the Marquis de Bon Goût held, St-Cyr went deeper into the humidor, to a room within a room. Deep red, morocco-covered *fauteuils* from the turn of the century sat round an inlaid table on which were cognac and glasses, and a superb collection among opened humidors. Macanundo Portifinos from Jamaica, the Duke of Windsors, Baron de Rothschilds and Crystals; Nat Shermans, too, as if straight in by transatlantic liner from New York's renowned Fifth Avenue shop: Morgans, Carnegies and Astors, the Metropolitan and City Desk selections, and the Gothams in their dark green boxes with gold lettering and clock emblem.*

The son had said the elder Paquet would be here. And there he was, fussing with a little galvanized pail of water and a tightly squeezed sponge. Eighty years of age at least and up on a roll-away ladder whose graceful lines melded so delicately with the decor that it would hardly be noticed. A small, slightly stooped

---

* Both older and more recent brand names are used, especially those of Nat Sherman, which so aptly suit the late 1930s, though the cigars themselves are not from Cuba.

man. Thin, with fine and carefully groomed iron-grey hair, gold-rimmed spectacles and faded, watery blue eyes that took him in, the closely shaven jowls stiffening momentarily, the blue smock coat, white shirt, tie and freshly pressed dark blue serge trousers immaculate, as were the polished black patent leather shoes.

'Monsieur . . .' hazarded St-Cyr softly. Ah! one was afraid he might tumble from his perch.

'A moment, please,' came the politest of answers, the voice no broken reed, but invested with utter calm, even though he must have realized the visitor was not only from the police but had been hit hard too. 'The humidity must always be as close to seventy per cent as possible,' he said, ignoring the half-closed left eye. 'Each day I watch it morning, noon and evening, then at day's end help to ensure it by wiping down the cabinets with a damp sponge that leaves no dust. The temperature must be between eighteen and twenty-one degrees, and always when one is in here, one experiences a little of the jungles, isn't that so? The perfume of cedars that must have reached to the clouds, their beads of rainwater constantly dripping as strange birds haunt-ingly call and monkeys chatter. Ah! forgive me, Inspector. I do go on, but you see, I've been doing this little task since well before you were born. Father founded the shop and when, in 1873, I was twelve years old, he took me in. What can I do for you that my son can't?'

'A few questions. Nothing difficult, I assure you.'

'But why should anything you would wish to ask me be difficult? Much of what you see here was acquired before the war and certainly well before this total occupation of ours.'

One would not argue the point nor mention the vans and a minister of supplies and rationing, or a *marché noir* that could gather up such things if the price was right. 'Four murders, monsieur. Four young women in the prime of their lives. Monsieur le Premier suggested you would know Vichy society like no other and might be able to help.'

'That one seldom comes here, since we have never sold

cigarettes or loose tobacco. For those one must patronize a *tabac*, I think.'

Methodically descending from his perch, Honoré Paquet told himself that one should always be polite even when speaking of men such as Laval.

'Please have a seat, Inspector. A little of the Rémy-Martin Louis XIII? It's superb and has such a bouquet. I find it whets the appetite but one can't, I'm sorry to say, enjoy one of our cigars here or that pipe of yours. Should you wish to smoke, why, we can go into the shop. Pierre-David will, of course, have pulled and locked the shutters by now.'

The Louis XIII . . . The 1925, and on a *pas d'alcools* day.

The hand that poured was steady. The elder Paquet sat only after he had finished, the son coming into the room to quietly say, 'Papa, shall I wait for you?'

The head was briefly shaken. 'Have the *vélo-taxi* pick me up on your way home. Don't worry so much, Pierre-David. *Mon Dieu*, if my last breath is to be drawn, let me take it here.'

'There's an early curfew, papa. You need to rest and then to eat something. The soup and bread, a little of the poached salmon and then the *pot-au-feu* or the chicken.'

'Inspector, you see what I'm blessed with? A miracle. How long do you think we will be?'

'A half-hour. Perhaps a little more. My partner is to meet me here but one never quite knows with him.'

'One of *les Allemands*?'

'They are our constant companions. Monsieur Pierre-David, please keep an eye on the time, allowing sufficient for you and your father not to miss dinner. And a black-market one at that! Could you bring us the register, though?'

The father gave the son the slightest of nods. Holding his glass in both hands to warm it and catch the light, the elder Paquet grew serious. 'Four *jeunes filles*, Inspector. *Très adorables, très intelligentes*, yet each murdered in a different way. It's curious, is it not? The knife for all, one would have thought. Guns are far too noisy, wires too brutal, too savage.'

'Did any of them come into the shop?'

'Each of them, and from time to time. A little present for the men in their lives, the theatre props also.'

'Pardon?'

'The cabaret, but only with Madame Dupuis or others of that group. She always chose the less expensive, machine-made cigars when she could, though we seldom carry them. The cost was not one for which she received any compensation, so we reached a little agreement. Piano lessons for my great-grandson in exchange. Surely that's no crime. If it is, I freely admit it.'

Barter most definitely was, but to prosecute him or anyone else for such a thing would only be to align oneself with an authority whose smallness one increasingly despised, as did Hermann. Women, though not allowed a tobacco ration, could have been 'given' the tickets to buy supplies for a friend or relative.

'From time to time such as these would come into our possession. A moment, please. Excuse me,' said Paquet only too aware of what must be running through this Sûreté's mind.

Pushing the ladder, he vanished round a corner and went right to the back of the humidor, returning a patient few minutes later with a pocket case.

The label was in English.

THIS AIRTIGHT TIN CONTAINS FIVE CIGARS, SELECTED AND PACKED FOR CAMPAIGNING.

' "Alfred Dunhill",' read St-Cyr with a sadness he couldn't help. ' "Thirty Duke Street, St James's, London, SW." Property of a "Thomas Almond, Esquire".'

'Inspector, I have no knowledge of where this flying officer, navigator or gunner was shot down, nor do I know if he even survived. The cigars are no doubt the best Dunhill's could provide at cost, given that the German naval blockade must surely have cut off virtually all such supplies, but I content myself with their having at least attempted to fit out their servicemen in such a proper fashion.'

One of the old school most definitely, since similar tins

including the use of the word 'campaigning' had been used in the Great War.

The son produced the register and retreated, the hush of the humidor closing in on them. And how many secrets are there here? wondered St-Cyr, for the register began on 14 June 1862 and contained the signatures, dates and purchases or special orders of every client since then. A truly remarkable historical record – tsars and tsarinas, kings and queens, et cetera, et cetera, but Laval hadn't wanted them to dwell on this aspect.

Running a finger down through the recent months, he found the signatures of several women, including those of Céline Dupuis and ... ah *merde*, Blanche Varollier. A Choix Supreme, purchased for 500 francs and part of a ration ticket, the balance to be held on account, on Saturday, 30 January 1943 at 4.45 p.m., the same day that Lucie Trudel had been murdered.

'The other cabaret dancers and singers, monsieur?' he asked harshly. 'Did they also choose only the cheapest for each performance?'

'Madame Carole Navaud prefers the Hoyo de Monterrey double corona, the favourite of many who know and appreciate a truly fine cigar. Madame Aurélienne Tavernier will smoke anything and always asks what I advise, and Madame Nathalie Bénoist purchases only the El Rey del Mundo Demi-Tasse, a small cigar, quite slender, smooth and mild, the aroma always delicate.'

This was all written down in the detective's notebook. 'And Henri-Claude Ferbrave?' he asked

'Is not a client.'

'A supplier?'

'Sometimes.'

'That's not good enough, monsieur.'

'Then often. Inspector, were we not to purchase what he brings us, others would sell it. These days one does what one can and hopes that one's stock won't be requisitioned.'

Otto Abetz was a frequent client, Charles-Frédéric Hébert, the custodian of his château, also Herr Gessler and, just recently, an

Arnolt Jännicke – the nameless one? wondered St-Cyr. A Major Remer was the district Kommandant.

As with the list of occupants of the Hôtel d'Allier, to go through even this small portion of the register would require far too much time.

Taking out Camille Lefèbvre's *mégot* tin, he opened it. 'Surely she wouldn't have mixed tobacco from the cigar butts with that from the cigarettes?'

Paquet lifted his gaze from the tin. 'To inhale such smoke would only make one sick, I should think. Far too harsh. The curing is quite different, *n'est-ce pas*?'

'Ah, *oui*, but are they . . .' The detective hurriedly flipped open his little notebook to the note he had just made. 'The Demi-Tasses of the cabaret dancer, Madame Nathalie Bénoist?'

'They are. At least, they could quite possibly be hers.'

'And these cigar bands?' he asked, opening another tin that had once held dressmaker's pins.

'An El Rey del Mundo Choix Supreme and a Romeo y Julieta double corona maduro. The latter's dark brown leaf is the result of extra maturing which produces a richly flavoured cigar with a mild aroma. The British Prime Minister was very fond of them.'

Pacquet turned the heavy register towards himself and, finding a page several years back, quickly located the name. 'A brief visit in the summer of 1913. Mademoiselle Mailloux was very much interested in seeing his signature. Winston Leonard Spencer Churchill, First Lord of the Admiralty then. A very determined gentleman with decided views as to his choice of cigar, the *français* atrocious, but I did manage to understand him. Two dozen of the maduras at twenty francs each. *Mon Dieu*, how prices have risen. Mademoiselle Mailloux laughed a little when I gave her that band but she didn't enlighten me as to what she saw as being so funny. Albert Grenier wearing it, I suppose. She was a bit of an imp and loved putting one over on the pompous stuffed shirts, as she'd have called them. Madame Dupuis was most upset to learn of her death, as were others, myself included, and especially Madame Lefèbvre and Mademoiselle Trudel. Four doves, I used to call them. Birds, wanting only to fly in these harsh times of ours, and now they've all been murdered. A tragedy.'

Céline's note to Lucie had stated they needed to talk. 'It's urgent,' she had said.

'Monsieur, when found, Madame Dupuis was wearing one of these. The stones are *blancs exceptionnels*, the earrings perhaps from the *fin de siècle*, or from the twenties.'

Paquet didn't need to touch them. 'Was there an exquisite strand of sapphires?'

It would be best to lay the necklace on the table and tell him of the dress.

'And why wasn't she wearing both earrings?'

'That is one of the questions we are trying to settle.'

'Then please don't avoid the obvious.'

'She tried to remove and hide them from her killers, succeeding only with one.'

'Was she also wearing the silver dress and the sapphires?'

'Ah no. No, she wasn't.'

'A white silk *chemise de nuit* and black-meshed underthings, the cabaret costume?'

Word must be flying. A nod would suffice, Paquet raising a forefinger to indicate he would need a moment.

When he returned much saddened, it was with a box of Choix Supremes, quite obviously a part of a client's private store but long forgotten. 'The Maréchal was not the only one to favour these, Inspector. Auguste-Alphonse Olivier and his wife would often come into the shop on their way to the theatre or casino, or to some function or other. There was also a tiara, a thin headband that had been purchased for Madame Noëlle Olivier in Paris, from Cartier's on place Vendôme by Monsieur Olivier, as had the necklace. The earrings had been his mother's, I believe. But . . . but why should Madame Dupuis have had them? Surely that one was no thief? She had a daughter she missed terribly. Always a postcard or two from the child, or the latest she was sending her. She was fiercely determined to return to Paris, felt she had saved up enough. "It's all been arranged," she said. "The *laissez-passer* and *sauf-conduit* will soon be here, the residence permit also." '

'Did she say who had arranged them for her?'

'Ah no, but ... but I felt it had to have been Dr Ménétrel, the Maréchal's personal physician. Inspector, why would such as these not have been in Monsieur Olivier's safe-deposit box? Oh certainly, there are now the lists everyone has to fill out just as they did in the north, in the *zone occupée* in 1940. All items above a value of a hundred thousand francs, the louis d'or one has kept against the devaluations and the inflation. Has anything happened to him?'

To admit that they didn't know would sound foolish but had best be done.

'He's never been the same, not since she took her life on 18 November 1925. Thirty cubic centimetres of laudanum and into the river with her. *Toute nue*, which only made the heads here buzz all the more, I'm afraid. She was only thirty-four years old. Lovely, so lovely. It broke his heart. A cuckold.'

'And now?'

'A bitter man who keeps much to himself and is seldom seen except in the late evening when strolling through our English Garden along the river. Solitary, the hat pulled down, the scarf tight, the walking stick and stride no longer purposeful.'

Olivier had withdrawn his last cigar from the box at noon on that fateful day.

'Monsieur Auguste-Alphonse used to love his after-dinner cigar, Inspector. It was then that he would contemplate the day behind him and plan for the one ahead. Madame Noëlle ... She was his life away from the world of finance, his constant ray of sunshine in a world that was too often clouded with difficulties. Not only had he been our mayor for several years, he was our foremost banker.'

Laval had said to take Paquet into their confidence but would it be wise to reveal more?

The inspector laid a number of *billets doux* on the table; the powder-blue envelopes and handwriting of the address were enough. 'God seldom makes us perfect,' said Paquet. 'Even a most esteemed and austere Head of State has weaknesses. The Maréchal set his cap for her and won, only to then leave her in despair. She and Monsieur Olivier had two children, a boy and girl. In spite of this, there were frequent trips to Paris by Madame Noëlle – too many, some said; others that she was young and beautiful and that to live in Vichy must be stifling for her after being raised among *les hauts* of Paris. The grandmother had left her a mansion in Neuilly, not far from the Bois de Boulogne.'

'But when the Maréchal wrote this, she killed herself?' asked the Inspector, tapping the missive.

'*Oui.* Auguste-Alphonse went in search of her, the letter in his hand, but found only her clothes and the empty dark blue bottle that had held the laudanum her grandmother must once have been in the habit of taking. There is a weir and a footbridge that crosses our river, the Pont Barrage. It leads to the sports club and golf course. Her clothes were found on it, the body downstream on one of the islands where, in summer, it is said couples sunbathe in secret.'

'The two children, monsieur, where are they now?'

This one would leave no stone unturned. 'In the north, in Paris. He sent them away to avoid the scandal that had erupted and ruined him. They were raised by his wife's family, and he has had, I believe, no further contact with them.'

'Their ages now?'

'They were twelve at the time.'

'Thirty, then, and a set of twins.'

'Inspector, there was one other item Madame Noëlle left with her clothing. A knife. A Laguiole. It was felt she had thought of killing herself with it but had, at the last, taken what she felt was a better way. The slumber. The water, though cold, would soon have overcome her.'

The inspector opened its blade, and, laying the Laguiole on top of the *billets doux*, tossed off his cognac, needing no further answer.

'You're sworn to secrecy, monsieur. What you now know could well be dangerous for you and your son. Just let it rest in peace among your cigars and leave my partner and me to deal with it.'

The gate to 133 boulevard des Célestins was rusty, the gilding of its heraldic fleur-de-lis gone. Above twin neoclassical pillars of black Auvergne basalt, single Grecian urns of the same would once have held spills of ivy and fuchsias in season but were now broken and devoid of all but the last of their earth.

His breath billowing impatiently, Hermann lowered the beam of his torch to the rusty bell pull. Seizing its loop, he gave it a yank and then another. Like death, the dull, flat sound of a cracked bell thudded in the near-distance.

No lights would come on. It was now almost nine, the blackout complete, the boulevard unlit except for the soft diffusion of clouded moonlight on snow.

Across from them in the Parc d'Allier, where Napoléon III had had the river dyked, its marshes filled in and acacias, sycamores and cedars planted, there wasn't a sign of life. But then, these days, when automobiles of any kind pulled in alongside a house and two men in fedoras and overcoats with raised collars piled out, people tended to wait and watch from a distance or vanish.

Hermann shook the gate but the lock was fast. 'And freshly oiled,' he swore, having dropped the beam of his torch to it. 'So why the uncaring disrepair of the recluse yet the oiling, in a nation that has so little of that commodity nearly everything squeaks, even its *filles de joie*?'

He was in rare form. Again he yanked on the bell and again! 'Patience, *mon vieux*. Patience. This is not one of Napoléon III's villas – those are downstream a little and nearer to the Parc des Sources and the Hôtel du Parc. This is simply a private residence, an *hôtel particulier*, a mansion but . . .'

'But another of your travelogues? Piss off. It's cold, I'm hungry and we still have to register at our hotel before curfew or those bastards will lock us up! They will, Louis. That Scharführer wasn't kidding. Those boys would like nothing better than to get their hands on two *Schweinebullen*. We should call back here tomorrow morning. Don't *you* be so impatient!'

Hermann had had difficulty in locating Inès Charpentier's boarding house, across the river on the outskirts of the suburb of Bellerive-sur-Allier. He had had to cross and then recross one of the bridges and had been hassled twice more!

'Messieurs . . . What is it you wish?'

Ah *merde*, a woman, a dark silhouette, stood just behind the bars of the gate, shrouded in the cloud-shadow of one of the pillars.

'Auguste-Alphonse Olivier. Sûreté and Kripo.'

'Detectives . . . Whatever for? He can't know anything of use to you. He never goes out during the day, never walks up into town. You'll only upset him. His supper . . .'

'*Ach!* Open up, Fräulein. *Sich beeilen! Dépêchez-vous!*' shrieked the Kripo.

Hermann would use *Deutsch* and then French! '*Verfluchte Franzosen*,' he went on. Cursed French. 'Always causing trouble.'

One shouldn't let that pass! 'I thought it was *les Allemands* who caused the trouble,' snapped St-Cyr.

'*Calme-toi*, Louis. *Calme-toi*.'

The key, though probably fashioned in the late 1860s, had difficulty finding the lock after that little exchange but once there, it turned smoothly and, surprise of surprises, the gate swung open without a sound.

'I can answer whatever you wish to ask,' she said determinedly. 'There is absolutely no reason for you to question him. Is it the house that you think to requisition? Well, is it?'

The path to the street had been cleared and freshly swept. Only her footprints dented the snow ahead. In the foyer, and once beyond the blackout curtain that shrouded all such doors these days, the light from a single sconce of mid-nineteenth-century brass and frosted glass was grey and dim. A plain walking stick leaned forlornly against a small, bare table. Another of those urns was to Hermann's left, on a short pillar of grey marble, the *fer forgé* balustrade and stone staircase rising majestically to a landing beneath a magnificent Beauvais tapestry before turning to lead to room upon cold room.

'All right, messieurs,' she said tartly, 'you will now answer me.'

Arms tightly folded across her chest, she blocked further progress. Severe was the word one would most use to describe her, felt St-Cyr. Dark and very widely set eyes lay under fiercely plucked brows. The long straight black hair was tied behind but pulled down in front to hide the left side of her forehead, making her look like what? One of Man Ray's photos, the stern *maîtresse* of a girls' boarding school?

The nose was prominent, the lips thin, the face with its slanting knife-edged creases on either side of that nose, sharply angular. The ears were pierced and held wedding-ring loops of gold; the neck was no longer youthful, the head perched as if that of a tortoise protruding from the loose and cable-knitted cowling of a grey-blue, woollen, long-sleeved dress.

'Well?' she asked harshly. 'If not the house, then what?'

'Your name, mademoiselle?' asked Louis, having raised a cautionary hand to silence his partner who was still taking her in, still trying to get a feel for this place. Ah yes!

'Pascal, Edith, secretary and, since some time now, cook, housekeeper and maid of all work.'

She was in her early fifties. The cheeks were indented, the complexion sallow, or was it the lack of lighting? wondered Kohler. Black eye shadow had been used only at the extreme far corners of her eyes to emphasize their shade and severity. The eyebrows were much, much thicker nearest the bridge of the nose so that their arch tapered swiftly to pencil thinness and the gap between them was reinforced by their blackness.

In 1918 there had been so few eligible men left in France, Germany and Britain after the Great War that spinsters like this had been minted in their hundreds of thousands.

'Employed here since November 1925?' asked Louis pleasantly enough.

197

'If you must know, yes,' she said, having read his partner's mind and not liked what she'd read.

'A few pieces of jewellery,' he continued, unruffled as usual.

'There is no jewellery here. Why should there be?'

'Perhaps if you would simply take us to your employer, he might allow you to stay while we question him?'

'Stay? of course I'll stay! Haven't I been at his side all these years since she ...'

'Drowned herself?' asked Louis, keeping up the heat.

'How dare you say that in this house?'

'Edith ... Edith, who is it?' called out a distant voice.

'Detectives, Auguste.'

'Then have them come into the kitchen. Could we offer them a little of our soup and some of the National?'

'No soup and no bread, Auguste. There's barely enough as it is.'

'A little of the wine?'

'It's a *pas d'alcools* day and the wine has been watered twice in any case.'

'Then at least some of the tisane, Edith. It's very cold out there. *Mon Dieu*, two pullovers on under my coat and still I froze! Inspectors, what brings you to us?'

He had finished his soup and bread. Though his cheeks were still coloured by the frost and he'd doubtless been outside recently, newspapers were spread before him. *L'Humanité, Paris-Soir, Je Suis Partout*, the *Völkischer Beobachter, Das Reich* also, and still others ... How had they come by them?

The couple had been arguing – that was abundantly clear, thought Kohler. Reclusive Olivier might be but those walks of his had served him well. The ex-banker's grip was strong, the hand roughly calloused. Once sure of himself no doubt, this *haut bourgeois* – never one of the *nouveaux riches*, for the house was of old money – had been reduced to avoiding the gaze of others but that's where it all stopped. On his lapel lay not only the red ribbon of the Légion d'honneur but that of the Croix de guerre and the yellow and green of the Médaille militaire. Though sixty-eight or seventy years of age, he was still quite handsome, if now rough and ready. The blue suit jacket had obviously been something he might have once worn to that bank of his, but now it had frayed cuffs and mismatched buttons. The pullover beneath it was one he must favour, the plaid workshirt beneath that, frayed right round at a collar that had already been turned.

There were bags and dark circles under the deep brown eyes and these made the still-averted gaze even more sorrowful. There was also the perpetual evening shadow of Paul Varollier, though stronger and definitely not sickly.

'Inspectors, we tend to live in the kitchen,' he acknowledged with a gesture. 'As a boy I spent much time here, so that is all to the good. Sit, please. Smoke if you wish. We've a fire as you can see, but the wood is from one of my own trees. A windstorm took it.'

Was the emphasized singsong accent of the Auvergnat deliberate? wondered St-Cyr.

Olivier slid a saucer their way, refusing Hermann's offer of the last of his partner's cigarettes.

'I gave it up,' he said. 'One has to. The tobacco ration alone can put more on the table than the francs that china vase* of ours issues. Butter at three twenty to the kilo on the *marché noir*, sugar at two thousand, coffee the same. Even the potatoes here have risen to over two hundred the five kilos. A new suit of haircloth is six thousand or half a year's hard-earned for many of our men. We refuse to deal on it, don't we, Edith? What others, including our bishop, will sanctify, we prefer not to.'

A louis d'or was spun on to the table, the eyes of the banker flicking swiftly over them to come to rest on it. 'In 1857 that was worth twenty francs and the same in 1869 when Napoléon III minted the second of them. I can trace back my family in Vichy to well before that.'

'Auguste, please . . .' attempted Mademoiselle Pascal, nervously fidgeting.

---

* A nickname Pétain earned, the country having been flooded with images of him. Vases, mugs, et cetera.

'No, Edith, let them hear it. What can that all but *lanterne rouge* of his class at the military academy trace himself to, eh? The farm of the peasant heritage he's so proud of that he never worked a day in the fields? The Victor of Verdun, the *médecin de l'Armée*? Oh *bien sûr*, I was there and worshipped him like so many others. That,' he indicated the coin, 'was worth one thousand francs in 1940 after the Defeat and now . . . why now it's close to eight thousand and the price of a new bicycle if one can find one. In Lyons the St Paul prison, and even the St Joseph's for women, are packed to overflowing. The Fortress of Montluc has been requisitioned by Obersturmführer Barbie, and it, too, is jammed. Five and six to a cell with only two bunks so they sleep in shifts but that's not allowed by the warders, is it?

'You're police officers. You should know all this. The Santé in Paris was built to hold a thousand and now houses between five and six thousand. One in every five men has been deprived of his liberty and all contact with his loved ones, and Secrétaire Général Bousquet and the others wonder why their lives are being threatened? *Sacré nom de nom*, do they need Laval's clairvoyant to show them the truth?'

'Auguste . . . Auguste, you're shouting. The . . . the inspectors, they want to ask you about Noëlle's . . . Messieurs, my employer apologizes. Isolation has made him incautious.'

And yet . . . and yet he knows we'll not arrest him for it, said St-Cyr to himself. Has he still contacts in Paris who can tell him how it is there for us?

'*Travail, Famille, et Patrie*, Inspectors. While one-third of our farmers languish in POW camps in the Reich, our remaining peasants sell nearly half of their butter, eggs and pork to the BOFs, the butter, eggs and cheese racketeers. One-quarter of all potatoes not sent to the Reich also go to them, and one-half of all chicken. And yet . . . and yet, our Head of State and the Government he has created wish us to *venerate* the noble peasant while making those same peasants far richer and more arrogant than they've ever been?'

He waved a dismissive hand. 'Seventy-five per cent of all oats grown in the country go to the Reich, eighty per cent of all pressed oils and now ... now they're no longer counting the cattle that arrive in Paris for transhipment to the Reich, only the rail trucks when full. I shouldn't be surprised if Parisians aren't wondering, as they did in the Franco-Prussian War, if they will not soon be reduced to eating rats!'

'Auguste, I'm going to my room.'

'Go if you wish, Edith. These two will listen. That one, though he's no collabo, has his name on *L'Humanité*'s list, and that one ... Well, if you'll forgive me, Inspector Kohler, I have to ask, did your rebelliousness not once consign you to a *Himmelfahrtskommando*?'

To being one of the trip-to-heaven boys, one of a bomb-disposal unit!

'Though I can no longer stop averting my gaze, still I've seen it in your eyes, Herr Kohler. Not just fear of what's going on here in France but of what's to come for those you love. Now toss out the jewellery and I will tell you what I can.

'Edith,' he said. 'Edith, the bilberry tisane for our guests. They say it's good for the sight, Inspectors. One has to try everything these days, so one steps carefully at night when one leaves a lighted room or else one falls on one's ass. Ten minutes it takes me now just to adjust the eyes. Ten minutes!'

Night blindness was a terrible problem, especially in the bigger cities. During the day vision would be normal, but at dusk it would become hard to gauge distances and define objects. One would step outside into the blackout as if totally blind, and would have to wait patiently for the eyes to adjust. A lack of vitamin A and fats in the diet, the doctors said; others, the blackout itself.

Bilberries *did* contain vitamin A.

'But there is only this *Quatsch* to sweeten them, eh, Herr Kohler, this crap?'

A bowl of saccharin was thrust their way.

'I'm a recluse, a stroller, and yes, I'm as well informed as I possibly can be, nor do I attempt to hide this or anything else from you. Small towns, and this is still very much one, are especially hard on those of their own, Inspectors. Between 1929 and '37 over seven hundred of our banks failed, mine too in '33, but even though I could not in any way have been responsible, since I was no longer there, still I'm castigated for its failure. The anonymous letters dribble in and occasionally in the dark of night a stone is thrown through a window. Of course, the pane is impossible to replace and the hole must be boarded up. I knew you'd have to come to see me. I've had time to think about things. Four murdered women, the most recent of whom was wearing some of my dead wife's jewellery. Since I've always been a target, I can only surmise that Premier Laval's Flykiller wishes you to arrest me. Please don't forget it was Laval who coined the name, just as it was Pétain who willingly coined the word collaboration and fed it to the Nation.'

But how had Olivier known of Laval's use of that name, wondered Kohler, and why was he being so incautious?

Louis seldom removed his overcoat or fedora during such interviews, preferring always to leave doubt in the mind as to when he'd depart, but this time he set the hat on the table with a finality that brooked no interference, and pulled off his overcoat.

As the jewellery was laid on the table, moisture quickly collected in Olivier's eyes. A quiver passed through him as he reached out to touch the trinkets.

'Edith, please take Herr Kohler to her room. Show him where these were always kept. Not in my safe-deposit box, Inspectors. Not registered or listed – I've yet to be forced into that humiliation, so you'll just have to believe me when I tell you they must have been stolen.'

'By whom?' asked Louis.

'Outside of the killer or killers, I've no idea. No one visits except for the postman. There are only the two of us, and when I'm out, Edith is invariably in.'

And suspect? wondered St-Cyr. *Mon Dieu*, this one was clever. Having decided the best course of action, and weighed up the risks, which were considerable, Olivier hadn't wavered from that course.

Hermann departed with the housekeeper, leaving the two of them to themselves.

'You were at Verdun, Chief Inspector. You were wounded twice. Like yourself I, too, saw the Maréchal in action. Instead of deciding to attack in an all-out suicidal charge, he practised two defensive lines, the second to still the panic of the first, and, in defiance of Foch and the other generals, he alone had the courage to say *matériel* kills men. The noria he introduced to quickly relieve men at the front was a godsend I greatly admired. He *was* my hero. That's how he met my Noëlle when he came here in 1924 to stay as a guest in this very house. I, who thought I knew men, had my life taken from me. So, yes, I have good reason to want him dead.'

Olivier had led him to this point, even to having Hermann removed from the room. In one hand he held the earrings, in the other, the sapphires.

'You know what it's like to be made a cuckold, Inspector, but Paris is not Vichy. In a big city one can easily hide. Here things are so close the walls come tumbling down and you stand naked before the very people you once served and who once respected you. Your second wife and little son were killed on their way home to you, I gather, and for that I am deeply sorry, but it was, in so far as I can determine, a tragic mistake.'

Improbable as it seemed, knowing the attitudes of *les hauts* as he did, St-Cyr had to wonder if Olivier was of the Francs-Tireurs et Partisans. 'A Résistance bomb that Gestapo Paris-Central's Watchers left in place for me took them instead.'

'War is never easy, is it? Dr Ménétrel knows all about that little affair of hers and the films the Watchers made of the couple and enjoyed. Naked and fornicating, that wife of yours crying out in ecstasy to another while you ... you have had to bear the shame of it and the laughter.'

Olivier had even tried to provoke him but a calm front would be best. 'Hermann had the films destroyed. The Hauptmann Steiner was sent by his uncle, the Kommandant von Gross-Paris, to Russia where he was killed in action.'

'And the chanteuse Gabrielle Arcuri, whose superb voice is regularly broadcast to the Boche and avidly listened to also by the Allies, came to know you.'

Then it was true. He was of the FTP. 'Hermann is aware she's involved with the Résistance.'

A cold, flat answer. So, good. Yes, that was good! 'I just had to hear it from you yourself.'

This upstairs corridor to the bedrooms had always seemed so long, thought Edith. A journey and a half that never ended because Auguste would never let it end. Herr Kohler was right behind her and she knew he had realized love had yet to be consummated but that she would wait for ever if necessary.

'They always had separate rooms,' she heard herself saying tartly. Would caution not stop her tongue? she wondered. 'Auguste rose early, his wife often late. In those days he had the duties of mayor as well as chairman of the bank. Madame Olivier should have understood he had only so much time to spare. Like so many, he went away to war in 1914 and we seldom saw him for four years but still, a wife waits, does she not?'

'Some do, some don't,' she heard Herr Kohler saying. 'Did she fool around?'

And before the Maréchal?' 'She had two little children. Perhaps they occupied her totally, perhaps not.'

'But she liked older men?'

'Her father felt she needed one and Auguste fitted that mould perfectly. He was thirty-six years of age and very successful, she not quite twenty. Guidance, *n'est-ce pas*, as if one could ever have guided that filly. Is not the key to a girl's heart that to the strongbox? I'm sure that father of hers thought this.'

Many are the ways to a girl's happiness, Hermann, Louis would have said, but the surest is the foresight of the father. *Les hauts* had a host of such expressions. 'But Olivier loved her.'

'Passionately. It's what every woman prays for but it wasn't sufficient. Married 13 June 1911, miscarried 27 October of that year when she fell off her horse, gave birth to twins 5 March 1913, and then lost Auguste to the war as so many did. I don't excuse her; I excuse his not realizing that in his absence she had not had the benefit of that precious guidance and was no longer the young girl he had married.'

'And her maiden name? It's just routine.'

Did he know the twins were in Vichy? *Did he?* wondered Edith. 'Varollier. An old family in Paris, once very wealthy and with connections to several banks including ours, but all of that was lost in the Depression. Oh for sure one could say, as many later did, that in marrying her Auguste was merely completing a business transaction and that she felt this terribly but it wasn't so. She was beautiful, was everything a man like him could desire, was tender when needed, vivacious, shapely, *voluptueuse*, and yet ... and yet ...'

Ah *merde*, had Herr Kohler somehow provoked her into speaking her mind or were things so close now she'd had to?

'The children, mademoiselle,' he said, having stopped her in the corridor, having taken hold of her by the shoulder and turned her towards him.

What should she say – what *could* she say? 'After what happened, he wasn't even sure they were his. Indeed, he had every reason to think not.'

'Then Pétain wasn't the first?'

Abruptly her thin shoulders lifted in a questioning shrug but she didn't turn from him. Wouldn't!

'There were others during the war. I'm certain of it.'

Jésus, merde alors, with what were they dealing? 'And you let him know this when he came back? It couldn't have been too difficult, could it, since you worked at that bank of his?'

'He wouldn't listen! Even when so many later called him a cuckold and laughed at him, he wouldn't! "Pétain and only Pétain," he'd always say and still does.'

'And the Maréchal, does he ever come here?'

'You can't know of our Head of State, can you? That one has probably forgotten all about her.'

'And the house in Paris, in Neuilly? The one her grandmother left her?'

Had the twins told him of it? 'Auguste sold it and gave the money to Les Soeurs de l'Immaculée Conception. Inspector, the room is just down these few steps. I'm not sure the electric light will work. Auguste ... Auguste ... hasn't been in there since she took her life.'

Herr Kohler must be thinking, A hard man to have sold the house on the children, hard to have sent them away like that, but he did not say so. Instead he said, 'The children's bedrooms?'

'Are just across the corridor. The nursery first and then ... then the girl's room and then that of her brother. Always she was close to them, always their very special friend, but even that was not enough to stop her. She was pregnant. Did they tell you that?'

'They?'

'Whoever told you of her suicide. Pregnant with Pétain's child!'

'And your room?'

'Is next to his on the other side of the staircase. One of the former guest rooms.'

A cold, bitter answer if ever there was one. The overhead light didn't work. Crowding her, Kohler flicked the switch on and off again. 'You knew this, didn't you, because you had removed the bulb from its socket?'

They faced each other in darkness, she standing just inside the room, he still in the corridor. 'We ran out. We had to have light. These days if you can find them in a shop, and have the necessary tickets, two used light bulbs are demanded as well for each new one, but there aren't any to be had. They've requisitioned them all for the Government. Pétain has light; the rest of us have to make do as best we can.'

The Nation's matches were brittle and often broke and threw flames or sparks or failed to work at all, but in the light of the two he held, Herr Kohler looked not into the room but at her. A giant with a cruel and recent scar down his left cheek from eye to chin, and others from the Great War, the graze of a recent bullet, too, across the brow. 'The newspapers in the kitchen,' he said. 'How did he come by them?'

He'd seen the dates, had seen that they'd not been less than a week old, except for *L'Humanité*, and had first been read by others. 'A friend saves them and I ... why I try to have a little something for him in exchange.'

Herr Kohler didn't ask the name of this friend, which could only mean that he sensed it must be Albert Grenier and that he wanted her to know he knew. 'Let me find you a candle, Inspector.'

'All the light bulbs are gone, aren't they?'

'All, I'm afraid.'

Olivier let the silence grow between them until the hiss of green wood in the kitchen stove was heard. Abruptly he lifted his gaze from the jewellery, passed it quickly over this Sûreté from Paris, then returned it to the diamonds.

He fingered their hardness, feeling how cold they still were, for diamonds always felt cold. He said, 'Two patriots have just exchanged those few words that would condemn them to death, Inspector, should either of them fall into the hands of Herr Gessler or Herr Jännicke.'

To say nothing of Gabrielle and Hermann, or of his Giselle and Oona! 'Why *did* you feel I needed to know you were of the Francs-Tireurs et Partisans?'

St-Cyr hadn't liked it one bit. Too dangerous, too cavalier, but sometimes one had to take such risks. 'As its regional leader I must ensure that nothing is done to harm our position. We want you to stop this assassin before he or she or they cause irreparable harm. As it is now, our sources have word well in advance and we can take steps to protect ourselves, but should Pétain and Laval be assassinated, should even Bousquet or one of his confrères be killed, the Boche will unleash a savagery that can only lead to their taking over here completely. Make no mistake, what we have worked so hard to build will be shattered. Herr Jännicke is here because he's the cure Berlin believes may be necessary. He's a *spécialiste* in interrogation and has been sent on orders from Himmler and Gestapo Müller.'

To know such things could only mean an inside source but could Olivier be goaded into revealing it? 'They're already raking the countryside for *maquisards*.'

'We have to let them. To attempt to intervene would be both foolish and futile. We had six hours' advance warning of the *Sonderkommando* and took what steps were necessary to save our own.'

'But not those of other Résistance groups? Not the innocent who had to shelter them, sometimes even at gunpoint?'

Was St-Cyr really so weak? 'We couldn't interfere. In war there are always casualties. You of all people should know this.' He tossed a hand.

'And putting my name on *L'Humanité*'s list?'

'Surely you must realize that was to convince the Boche of your loyalties? Though Gestapo Boemelburg in Paris doubts them, Monsieur Laval still wanted you and Kohler to deal with the matter; Bousquet and Herr Gessler didn't. In the end, Herr Kohler's boss won out perhaps simply because he's also that of Gessler.'

'*Merde alors*, you heard of our being sent here even before we did!'

'We have our ways.'

'*Radio-trottoir* or *Radio-concierge*?' St-Cyr all but shouted.

Pavement or concierge gossip. 'I can't tell you. The risk is too great.'

'Yet we're expected to deal with a killer or killers who have also an equal ear to the ground? Forget it, monsieur. Me, I'm taking my partner and myself out of this and back to Paris!'

'Calm down. Why else do you think I decided to be frank with you? Céline Dupuis wears jewellery my wife did? Who gave it to her? Who stole it from here and then asked her to wear it and for what reason except to remind that ancient roué of my wife? And why, please, did Madame Dupuis try to hide it, if not to protect the very person who had given it to her?'

Olivier spread the strand of sapphires on the table and, placing an earring on either side of it, said, 'Oh for sure, our little tragedy is well known here in Vichy, Inspector, but to think to use it against me only compounds it and raises questions about my leadership. Constantly I must preach caution to my fellow *résistants* and, like the Maréchal at Verdun, say, *"Courage, on les aura."*'

Take heart, we'll get them, but it was best to belittle the reference. 'Jeanne d'Arc said almost the same thing at Orléans and was later condemned as a heretic and burned at the stake.'

'Pétain simply stole the words, but women aren't supposed to lead armies, are they? In ours they could well do so again!'

Had he meant to say this last? Had he? The furrows across the brow had deepened. That shock of greying brown hair was irritably brushed to the left. The lips were grim-set, the strong oval of the face, with its full Roman nose, emphasizing his displeasure at inadvertently having yielded such a *confidence*.

There was a vertical, two-centimetre-long scar directly above the bridge of Olivier's nose.

'Shrapnel,' he grumbled, ducking his eyes away from such a close scrutiny. 'A centimetre to the left or right and we wouldn't be talking. Even so, I was out for hours and had blood all over my face, and when I came to, it was to discover that the Boche had overrun our position. Like yourself, Inspector, I managed to crawl away and use my *Deutsch* to good advantage, reporting back their positions and strengths when I was finally able to cross their lines and return to my own.'

So we're blood brothers now, was that it? 'Who told you the jewellery had been found?'

'Bousquet. I knew beforehand, of course, and had prepared myself. Edith took him up to the room this afternoon.'

And made no mention of the dress, the shoes and missing love letters? 'Your former secretary's loyalty is admirable.'

Did St-Cyr suspect Edith? 'With some women, as with some men, Inspector, life must always be on the horizon. Her father was a *cheminot*, her brothers still work on the railways, and yes, you're wondering how I, a former businessman and owner, could no longer say as most still do, Better Hitler than Stalin. After all, this Occupation has been good for many businessmen, and for the upper crust also. For them and the professionals and other *hauts* to support the Résistance would be to deny their most cherished beliefs. But after eighteen years of Edith's *socialisme*, even I, who in 1936 feared another October when one and a half million voted for the communists, now pray it will happen. The communists are the only ones with guts, and guts are what is going to be needed in the struggle to come.'

Ah *oui*, but had Olivier deliberately used their Résistance connection to throttle further suspicion and ensure that Hermann was told as little as possible?

'Inspector, even though Ménétrel presumably now knows where this jewellery came from, he won't go to the Germans with the news since he has no love of them. He'll play it safe by alerting his Garde Mobile and waiting for you or Bousquet to tell him of it. And since our Secrétaire Général won't do this because Laval has ordered him not to, it will be left to you and Kohler. You see, for all his sources and intrigues, the doctor has blind spots, and without the Maréchal, he knows absolutely that he is nothing. With Pétain, there is still hope for him, even if it is to go over to the Allies, for our Head of State won't travel without his precious doctor.'

'And Laval?'

'Dismisses Pétain by asking who needs a flag except to stand in its shade in summer. Of course he's the true authority. He has always been very anti-British and still tries constantly to form an accord with Hitler so that France can be restored to her rightful place in the new European Order.'

'Does he really consult a clairvoyant?'

'If he does, he believes only the half of what he hears, but believes that half all the same.'

'And her name?'

'Madame Ribot, Hôtel Ruhl, 15 boulevard de l'Hôtel de Ville.*
Don't talk to her. Leave her out of things.'

'That may not be possible.'

'*Sacré nom de nom,* is your head so thick you can't take a hint,
eh? *L'Humanité*'s list, remember? Don't tread where you've been
told not to.'

'Or you will arrange a little Résistance accident for Hermann
and me?'

'Anything is possible. Anything. Edith . . . Well, Edith, what is
it? Where is Kohler?'

Rooted in the doorway, her expression one of shock at what
had so obviously been revealed, she seemed unable to react.

Outraged, she finally spat, 'You fool, Auguste!' and, finding a
candle, departed.

The flame from the matches had gone out almost as soon as
Edith Pascal had left him. She hadn't wanted to go, Kohler told
himself, but had needed to get away from him, to check on her
boss and Louis, to be alone, if only momentarily to settle herself
and gather her thoughts. A very troubled woman. A heart that
had yearned for far too long.

The smoked-glass, trifold mirror of the dressing table was off
to his left through the darkness. Beautiful cut-glass bottles, too,
some a soft blue, others clear or citrine and all with silver caps or
glass stoppers. A comb and brush set – Russian that had been, in
blue enamelwork and silver. Jars of face cream, rouge and
powder, lipstick too . . .

A small, cut-glass ashtray served as a lamp, perfume as the fuel.
Within a minute or two of her leaving him, he had what was
needed, a beautiful blue flame just like that from burning cognac,
but *Jésus, merde alors,* there were no dustsheets in the room. The
soft grey satin-and-lace spread on the gilded Louis XVI cane bed
was rumpled; the generous, white silk-and-lace-covered pillows

* Now the boulevard de Russie.

were propped against the headboard as if the bed had only just been slept in.

The armoire, of perfectly matched walnut, glowed richly in the softly flickering light, and was still crammed with Noëlle Olivier's dresses and suits. A hacking jacket, waistcoat and whipcord riding breeches, silks and soft woollens, satins too. Cotton summer frocks, crêpes de Chine, grey flannel slacks, blouses, shirt-blouses, some sheer, some with ruffles, some with lace, a ball gown, another and another. And yes, that silvery silk halter-necked dress and the shoes must have come from here.

A Boulle *commode* held lingerie one couldn't buy now except at a fortune: chemises and half-slips, several brassieres, a black lace teddy, black mesh stockings, a black garter belt and frilly pink peekaboo undies *à l'Ange bleu*, but that film had first come out in Berlin in *Deutsch* in 1930 and who could ever forget Marlene Dietrich singing 'They Call Me Naughty Lulu' and 'Falling in Love Again'?

Peacock lariats hung from one of the footboard's posts, their black-centred eyes greeny-blue to a deep coppery-orange ringed with white. Why, really, do some birds dress up?

The thongs were black, not more than a metre in length and tightly bound by spirals of silver wire at both eye and loop, but had she liked to be tied up with them?

On a bedside table there was a Sèvres gold-and-enamelled cup and saucer. Empty, of course, but the tisane's leaves were still damp, not frozen, and the ashes in the fireplace still warm.

A photo of her standing, leaning against the edge of a half-opened door, was behind the bedside lamp. Only the fingers of the left hand could be seen gripping the edge just above her head. The right hand, with its cigarette, was pressed against that forward thigh, the diamond ring catching the light, the sequined dress with black halter-neck and deeply plunging neckline, the laughing smile coy and alluring and full of fun, the hair jet black and bobbed.

Another framed photo found Noëlle Olivier wearing a black bowler hat, cabaret costume and smoking a cigar.

'Louis has to see the room,' he muttered. 'Louis is always better at this.'

Books – novels – a photo album were also on the table. Laying the latter on the bed, Kohler quickly flipped through it, could hear Edith Pascal saying something downstairs, had little time now, must hurry . . . Hurry.

There were snapshots of men on leave behind the lines of that other war, none of the boys actually in the trenches, of course. No, wait, there was one, and to send such things home, if one could get them past the censors, had been definitely against the rules, yet here it was. Two men in uniform, wearing open trench coats and officers' caps, were sitting face to face with a board between them on their knees. Mud and pools of water around their boots, ammo boxes strewn about and barbed wire – skeins and skeins of that fucking stuff – up above them, the timbers shattered and not, tin mugs of coffee and cognac to hand, the one man not much older than the other, if at all.

Rain, too, and the ruined remains of a canvas fly strung above them to sag and piddle its constant stream. *15 April 1917. Chemin des Dames.*

'Ah Christ,' he said as he read the rest of the pencilled note on the back. *Playing chess in the warmth and comfort of the Hôtel des belles tranchées, our Lieutenant Charpentier and Captain Olivier await the game of war.*

Charpentier.

'Louis . . . Louis . . . ,' he croaked and, feeling moisture welling up in his eyes, cursed himself, for detectives should never get sentimental. *Never!*

Blurred, the light from the little lamp that was cupped in his hand was reflected in the mirrors of her dressing table and he saw himself first in one, then another and another, old now and beaten. 'I was there, too,' he said of that other war, 'and so was Louis, but he took part in that battle, I didn't.'

Dreading what he'd found, for that lieutenant had to have been Inès Charpentier's father, he pocketed the snapshot, closed the album, then reopened it to the back, to more recent snapshots of Noëlle Olivier on horseback, a goddamned grey gelding, a stable ... 'And as a cabaret dancer. A château, a party...'

These last two photos joined the first but Edith Pascal would be certain to realize he'd taken them. The pungently sweet and heady smell of burning perfume was now everywhere.

Quickly crossing to the dressing table, Kohler wet a tissue with the perfume, tucked it away for Louis and replaced the stopper. Quipped guiltily when the woman sucked in a breath, 'Oh, sorry. I had to have light and had run out of matches.'

Louis was right behind her. 'Hermann, please have Mademoiselle Pascal show us where the jewellery was kept. Check the window catches for signs of forcible entry. The usual, *mon vieux.* Spare nothing, even if it takes us all night.'

These two were hateful, Edith told herself. They pried into everything, but unlike the one called Kohler, St-Cyr had infinite patience. For hours it had seemed, while she'd shown the other one the drawer in which the jewellery had been kept, St-Cyr had stood in front of the dressing table, unable to take his gaze from it.

'I remember this,' he had said, marvelling at it and the thought. 'It was in one of the room exhibits at the Exposition Internationale des Arts Décoratifs et Industriels Modernes, Hermann. Paris, summer, 1925.'

Had he now memorized the position, style and use of everything on that table? He hadn't touched the clear, fluted crystal *flacon à parfum* his partner had half emptied, hadn't even said anything about its distinctive fan-shaped sapphire-blue stopper, but must have known it was Shalimar.

For some moments Herr Kohler had deliberately distracted her. St-Cyr, she was positive, had opened the top drawer of the table – he'd have seen the *billets doux,* would have noted the soft blue envelopes, the handwriting, would have surmised that not all of them were there.

Perhaps he'd asked himself why Auguste had not burned the

Maréchal's love letters to Madame Noëlle; perhaps he understood that Auguste had locked the room after her death and hadn't since set foot in it.

But had St-Cyr noticed what had been lying among the garters and pins in her little porcelain box? Had he taken that cork that once came from a bottle of Bollinger Cuvée Spéciale, the 1925 Madame Noëlle and the Maréchal had drunk?

He had, she thought when next she was able to glance his way, not touched a thing, or so it seemed. His hand still cupped that cold and empty pipe of his . . .

'Her hair,' he said.

'Jet black and bobbed, Louis,' Herr Kohler muttered, still engrossed in searching through jewellery that hadn't been taken but should have been if robbery had been the motive.

The Sûreté spread a printed leaflet of some kind on the only free space and pulled hairs from the brush, didn't ask, Are you in the habit of using this, mademoiselle? Just did it, and made sure he had what he wanted.

'A *téléphone*?' he asked. 'Is there one in the house?'

'No,' she heard herself yelp. 'Not since he . . . the monsieur was forced to leave the bank. So many made such cruel calls, he . . . he had to have the instrument disconnected. He who had invested so much of his own money and had worked so hard to bring a modern exchange to Vichy, had to sever all links with it.'

An old exchange, and then a new one – would St-Cyr think to remember this?

He gave no indication, said only, 'Hermann, Madame Olivier's clothes,' and pointed to the chair on which Auguste had set them eighteen years ago on his return from the Pont Barrage. The laudanum bottle was still there on top of her things. St-Cyr took out her knife and laid it there, too . . .

His voice broke over her and she knew he was watching her closely. 'Mademoiselle Pascal, is this how you remember its being there?'

That dark blue bottle on its side without its stopper, the Laguiole next to it, Madame Noëlle's crumpled French silk

215

pongee step-ins so soft and cold. 'Yes ... Yes, that is approximately as I first found them but that was nearly two months after she had killed herself. Auguste had locked the room and had tried to shut it all out of his mind. I . . .'

'You were to have packed away her things, weren't you?'

'He wouldn't have given them away. "The town's too small" – too spiteful is what he really meant. "Burn them," he said but later I knew he had realized I hadn't, though we never spoke of it.'

'How often do you come here?'

To lie in Madame Noëlle's bed, to touch her things and smell them, to care for them and wonder why Auguste had loved her so much that he had been blind to her affairs, blind until that moment she had drunk the contents of that bottle and had thrown herself into the river?

'I came. At first it was not often, and only when he was away on one of his walks, but then, as the years progressed, I needed to discover things and came more often.'

'Waited?' asked the Sûreté softly.

'Waited, yes, for him to come to me, to me!'

'*Toute nue?*' he demanded.

'Sometimes,' she answered.

'Louis ... Louis, don't be so hard on her. It's life, *n'est-ce pas*? Mademoiselle, come and sit down. Rest a little. We'll soon be done here.'

Done, having stripped her feelings naked!

'The château in this photograph?' Herr Kohler asked.

'Aux Oiseaux Splendides!' she blurted tearfully, couldn't help herself. 'Monsieur Charles-Frédéric Hébert made certain she and the Maréchal were alone together in the late summer of 1924. He had always envied Auguste and saw a chance to destroy him.'

'And recently? Have this Monsieur Hébert and your employer spoken?'

'Never.'

'Ah *bon*,' said Louis sadly. 'And now, mademoiselle, please tell us if you've recently seen your employer's children.'

'I *what?*' she shrilled from where she was now sitting on the edge of the bed. 'Surely they're not in Vichy? Well, are they?' she demanded fiercely.

Anger tightened the lines in her face, making it appear even more sharply angular in the candlelight. 'Hermann, remind her of to whom she's speaking.'

'Louis . . .'

She would clench her fists, thought Edith, but keep them in her lap, would let her voice erupt in a torrent of derision. 'Inspector, *quelle folie*! I could not possibly have seen them. *Mon Dieu*, they were children when they left. I . . . Why, how could we have met? They wouldn't have remembered me. A secretary at a bank they seldom went to with their mother? Believe me, Inspector, to keep such news from Auguste would have been for me to have denied everything I've felt for him.'

'Then you saw no signs of forcible entry?'

She must not yield! 'None. Had there been any, I would have told Secrétaire Général Bousquet of them when he came here this afternoon to tell us of the theft.'

He'd shrug nonchalantly. That would be best. 'Hermann, the housebreaker must have entered unobserved and vanished just as easily.'

'Auguste . . . Auguste often leaves the gate unlocked.'

'Especially if he's out for a stroll after curfew?' asked St-Cyr. Ah *Saint Mère!* 'I . . . Why, yes. Yes, then, too.'

'Louis, go easy, eh?'

'The truth is often so hard to reach, *mon vieux*. Blanche Varollier, her hair, please?'

'Auburn, Chief. Long, dark and fine,' replied Hermann perfectly and on cue, even throwing Mademoiselle Pascal a questioning glance and a shrug as if he, too, didn't know what the hell was up.

'The brush, mademoiselle, suggests other than what you've told us. Someone with just such lovely hair has recently thought to use it frequently.'

Ah no. 'They . . . they forced me to let them in.'

Tears streaked her mascara. Agitated fingers tried to stop this as she bowed her head in defeat.

'They ... they said that if I did not let them in they would go to *les Allemands* and cause trouble for Auguste. Much trouble. Don't you see that I had to?'

'When first?' asked Louis. There had been a German Embassy in Vichy, and still was for that matter.

'A year ago, then again in midsummer and last autumn. In October, and ... and since then two more times. Never long, I swear it. An hour, perhaps a little more. They would speak quietly to one another, rediscovering their childhood haunts. The attic, the cellars, their father's study, the kitchen. I ... I could not stop them and was always so afraid Auguste would suddenly turn up.'

'But were they left alone in here?' asked the Sûreté.

Bâtard! she wanted so much to shriek at him. 'They ... they insisted, went everywhere they wished, even into their father's bedroom and mine. Mine!'

'And the most recent visit?' asked Louis. Her head was now bowed again, fingers agitatedly twisting and untwisting tightly.

'Last Monday afternoon.'

With Lucie Trudel already dead. 'And you didn't realize anything had been taken?'

The knife, the dress and shoes, the earrings, sapphires and a sample of Noëlle Olivier's perfume, also some of the *billets doux* Pétain had written to her. 'They'd never taken things before. Why should they have done so then? I was only too glad to see them gone from the house!'

'And when Secrétaire Général Bousquet came here did you inform him of what Paul and Blanche Varollier must have done?'

'I ... I couldn't. Auguste ... Auguste would never have forgiven me if he'd found out I'd let them into his house and not told him they had returned. Each visit had to be arranged so carefully, the moment seized only when he was certain to be absent for more than an hour.'

You're the fool, not the monsieur, one wanted so much to say,

St-Cyr told himself sadly, for those same times could so easily have been used to pin down Olivier's meetings with others of the FTP.

Repocketing the knife and taking the laudanum bottle – feeling like examining magistrate, judge, jury and hooded executioner, and not liking himself one bit – he said as gently as he could, 'For now we've seen enough, Hermann. Mademoiselle, please don't think of leaving Vichy. You will only be hounded down.'

'And Auguste?'

'Will, I believe, have gone for one of his strolls.'

A Peugeot two-door sedan can't outrun a Wehrmacht motorcycle patrol in the dark of night, in a strange town where armed controls are on every bridge. It can try, of course, but when it finds itself wedged into the narrowness of a medieval street in the heart of the old town, with all exits blocked, it has to give up.

Unblinkered headlamps – an emergency – blinded them. Steel helmets hid riders' heads, goggles their eyes, black leather their massive shoulders and bulging arms.

Gauntlets their hands.

VAROOM ... VAROOM!

BANG! BANG! farted a wounded muffler. The shortages these days ...

'Talk to them, Hermann.'

'Louis, you let Olivier go!'

'I had to! I had no other choice.'

'And Giselle and Oona and Gabrielle, eh? Did they have a choice? Gessler won't stop if he lays his hands on him. It won't just be you and me!'

'I'm sorry, but ...'

'Admit it, that son of a bitch is Vichy's section head of the FTP and your patriotism got to you. *Jésus, merde alors*, don't I know all about it!'

Hermann got out from behind the steering wheel, leaving his door open so that the thirty degrees of frost and its softly falling snow would find his little Sûreté Frog, his constant passenger.

Strolling into the light, he gave the boys a nonchalant wave, a rush of banter, which was cut off by an Unterfeldwebel shouting, 'Arrest? *Ach! mein lieber* Hauptmann Detektiv Inspektor, we aren't to arrest you. *Mein Gott*, what gave you such a crazy notion? We're to escort you to a meeting with the Chief of Police.'

He didn't say anything. For once Hermann was at an absolute loss for words, didn't even lift a tired hand to indicate they would obediently follow.

Tears frozen to his cheeks, he got back into the car to grip the steering wheel with bare hands.

'You left your gloves on the bonnet, *mon vieux.*'

'Fuck my fucking gloves! *Think*, Louis! Gestapo Gessler! We've got to have answers for him we can readily give.'

'Like, you examined Madame Olivier's bedroom and the scene of the theft, while I interviewed the recluse who was just that, lonely, bitter, very difficult and of little use to us.'

'*Bonne chance.* It isn't going to work.'

'All right. Four murders that could just as easily have been eight and should have been if the boys were the targets, forgetting of course, for the moment, Pétain, Laval and Ménétrel!'

'Gessler will like it if we say it must be a sadist who's sexually incapable of rape. I'll tell him the girls were killed because the assassins had a thing about marital infidelity and wanted to put the fear of God into their lovers.'

'Who were obviously up to mischief, not just with them, and who needed to be taught a damned good lesson before the scandal of their using vans from the Bank of France erupted in the Government's face.'

'Give me that again, will you? Christ, I need a fag!'

The car started off with a jerk – water in the petrol, always water these days. Following the eight bikes, they watched as the headlamp beams fled up and over the walls, revealing stonework and doorways from the days of the Célestins perhaps, when in 1410 a monastery had been established at one of the sources, not far from Olivier's house.

Louis repeated the thought, adding, 'Is that not why Céline Dupuis's note stated, "Lucie, we have to talk. It's urgent"?'

A scandal of massive proportions in an already shaky Government, not just one of an unfaithful wife and Pétain to titillate the local ears. 'Madame Dupuis was afraid they, too, would be killed – is that what you're saying?'

'Marie-Jacqueline Mailloux and Camille Lefèbvre already had been. All were friends – fast friends, I'm certain.'

'Four girls, then, the first of whom constantly flaunted her affair with the Minister of Supplies and Rationing whom we've yet to meet.'

'We've simply been far too busy for such social calls, but yes, our thirty-seven-year-old nurse must have made a nuisance of herself.'

And Bousquet hadn't exactly been telling them the truth.

'Lucie was pregnant, Hermann, and had had a *crise de conscience* over the abortion Deschambeault had arranged. I think she may have been threatened early last Saturday morning on her way home from the Hall des Sources and that this is why she changed her mind and got into bed to await Deschambeault's comforting embrace. She could well have become a considerable problem both to him and that family of his, judging by what little we've seen of it so far. Old money never appreciates a mistress who imperils the family fortune and drives an unhappy wife and mother to seek costly help in a private clinic.'

'But Camille couldn't have become a nuisance to Bousquet, could she?'

'A Secrétaire Général de Police whose wife and children reside in Paris and who must have come to know the others here only last summer and not two years ago after the Defeat? He'd have had to take his rightful share of the rewards of their little scheme wouldn't he? One of *les gars*?'

'Laval trusts him, Louis.'

'Laval told him to work closely with us and to keep him advised of our progress. An embarrassment, then, at the highest level, Hermann. Let us not forget this.'

'They didn't kill them, did they?' It was a plea.

'And try to pin it on Olivier?'

'Who, in the first place, suggested that they had, right? Or at least that the killer or killers had.'

They were now heading north along the river beside its park, the billowing snow from the motorcycles sometimes hiding the road ahead. The villa the Turkish Embassy used came into sight. Herr Gessler's was next. Was God not watching? wondered Kohler. Did He really have to allow things like this to happen to honest, hard-working detectives?

'An assassin or assassins, Hermann. One or two who move about this town so unobtrusively as to be seen but not seen, accepted but ignored, passed over and forgotten only until that final moment when truth arrives.'

'One or two who have his or her ear – or both – to the ground at all times, eh?'

'And who know well beforehand when things are about to happen and must have impeccable sources.'

'Olivier, *mon enfant*. Olivier and his Edith, and you damned well let him go!'

7

Chez Crusoe was Hermann's kind of place: loud, brassy and crowded, the tobacco smoke pungent, the girls half naked, their legs wrapped in black-mesh stockings and garters, their songs lewd, ribald, saucy or coy and sweetly virginal, with black bowler hats, stick canes and lighted cigars under spotlights, the keys of twin pianos furiously rippling to a thunderous drumbeat . . .

'*Gott im Himmel*, Louis. Paradise instead of prison and the firing squad!'

'Don't count on it.'

'No sign of Gessler.'

Fin-de-siècle decor was everywhere if a trifle moth-eaten, the main dance floor huge, its timbered ceiling smoke-stained from the turn of the century and before. Probably 1890, or 1880.

'I'll get us a couple of drinks and see if there's any food left.'

'You won't get through the crush.'

'Pastis, right? Beer for me. It's straight in from home.'

Hermann was like a small boy greedily eating stolen chocolates at his first film. Mesmerized by it all, rejoicing and automatically joining in because that's the way he was. Giselle and Oona would certainly have their hands full if he ever *did* get that 'little place' on the Costa del Sol.

'Your hat, monsieur, and coat?'

She wasn't any more than fifteen, reeked of cheap perfume and underarm talcum powder. 'I'll keep them. These days that is often best.'

'Suit yourself. Monsieur le Secrétaire Général Bousquet makes the telephone call while that one, he . . .' Her bare arm pointed

223

to a distant corner table all but hidden by the dim lighting and the smoke. 'He awaits your pleasure. Personally . . . and I'm just saying this for myself, you understand,' her childlike eyes widened mischievously only to duck away at the fierceness of a Sûreté frown, 'he can have you.'

Alone, Alain André Richard, Ministre des Vivres et du Rationnement – Supplies and Rationing – seemed impervious to the grey-green uniforms of the Occupier intermingling with the Occupied, the constant commotion, the comings and goings of cigarette girls selling everything including tobacco, and waitresses who should have known better than to wear such draughty costumes among soldiers and Government employees who only wanted to forget the war and their humdrum lives.

An intense little man in his mid-fifties, the face was pinched, the black hair thinning and carefully groomed, its dye-job perfect just like the rest of him. Even the blue serge suit had a gold *Francisque* pinned to its lapel.

'Ah *merde*,' muttered St-Cyr under his breath as he all but reached the table. 'Must our top civil servants always be so difficult?' The glass before Richard had remained untouched, perhaps because it was dirty or because he simply didn't think a gin and *gazeuse* would help the stomach that had been giving him trouble of late. The cigarette that wasted its little life in the chipped ashtray had company of the same, but what, really, had Marie-Jacqueline Mailloux seen in this one besides money?

'Monsieur . . .'

'You're late! Why is this, please?'

Even the voice was tight. 'A small matter, Monsieur le Ministre. Unfortunately detectives can't always determine before-hand if their time will be used unnecessarily. Please pardon the delay.' And never mind that we weren't even aware we were to meet you!

'St-Cyr, Sûreté. I know all about you.' Richard sniffed in as if wishing a pomander were to hand.

'Good. That's as it should be.'

The despicable fedora was summarily dropped on the table,

the dishevelled overcoat removed to be perfunctorily dumped over the back of a cane chair.

'It's hot in here,' said St-Cyr. 'Now perhaps, monsieur, while we have a moment to ourselves you would be good enough to provide me with a clear statement of your illegal activities?'

'*Cochon! Imbécile! Bâtard!* Do you think you can mess with me?'

Pig, and the rest of it, and not bad for a start. 'Ah *bon*. Let's see now. How can I put this down?'

A little black notebook was opened to a half-scribbled page, the Sûreté, with that black-stitched bulge above his left eye, wetting the end of his pencil, to write and say: 'Opportunity given.'

That bushy moustache was touched with a knuckle, the fist clenched.

'A few cigars, Inspector. A little flour and sug—'

'Ministre, we've heard it all before. One blows the dust away, *n'est-ce pas*, only to find that the floor needs to be washed, only to then find that the varnish is cracked and the boards are in need of replacement, the joists also.'

'I came here to discuss the murders, damn you, and whether they're the work of one or more assassins!'

Spittle, too, had erupted. 'Then please proceed.'

'And we'll get to the other later, is that it, eh?'

'Begin, monsieur, by telling me about Marie-Jacqueline Mailloux.'

A hand was irritably tossed, a shrug given.

'The silly bitch made a mockery of me. Always flaunting her ass when at the office on one of her impromptu visits. Always cheeky. Did she think others would not notice?'

'Your wife and children perhaps?'

'Are among those who noticed, yes. Scene after scene. I had constantly to warn her that she was going too far. She shouldn't have ridiculed my wife in front of others. *That* was unforgivable but Sandrine should also have understood Marie-Jacqueline meant nothing to me. Nothing, absolutely!'

'Elaborate, please.'

Again a hand was waved. 'It's not important.'

Patience, *mon vieux*, patience, St-Cyr counselled himself. 'Everything is important.'

'A party. A small gathering. A little fun – what could have been more innocent? *Nom de Jésus-Christ*, the stress has to be relieved now and then, does it not?'

Mon Dieu, the arrogance! 'Where?'

'Le Château aux Oiseaux Splendides.'

'And your wife turned up. A little surprise?'

'*Oui*. It . . . Ah . . .' He threw out both hands, gesturing with them and raised a cautionary finger. 'It was nothing. Marie-Jacqueline and I on a . . .'

'A staircase?' It was just a shot in the dark.

'To the small tower that was off the bedroom we were using. The beam of Sandrine's torch found us. Instead of trying to cover her *parties sexuelles*, Marie-Jacqueline leaned back on the stairs, laughed at my wife and . . . and spread her legs. We'd . . . we'd just had sex.'

'Unprotected?'

'Inspector . . .'

'It's Chief Inspector, Monsieur le Ministre, and unless I'm mistaken, which I'm not, you are already guilty of misuse of your office and misappropriation of goods you yourself are in charge of rationing, so let us have the truth.'

'Not protected.'

One could imagine the rest, the wife with her gaze riveted on the offending female, jealousy, hatred and unbridled rage in her eyes and acid on her tongue. But it would be best to sigh and say, 'Let's have the date and time.'

'The Saturday six weeks before she drowned. As to the time . . . perhaps my wife found us at midnight, perhaps a little after that.'

'And she had clearance to be out after curfew?'

Ah damn this one! 'I have a pass, the car its *Service Public* sticker.'

And signed by the Commissaire de Police, a petrol allocation also. *Party, château, 24 October 1942*, was jotted down. 'These parties, Monsieur le Ministre, who else was there and how often were they held?'

Maudit salaud! 'One never really knows at such gatherings.'

'Just tell me.'

'René and the others, as well as still others. Maybe forty, maybe a few more. It depended on...'

'On what?'

'The success of...'

'Your little enterprise?'

'*Oui.*'

'So, a party every fortnight?'

'Perhaps.'

'Netting how much a month, please, this enterprise?'

Was St-Cyr a saint? 'Four or five hundred thousand francs, seldom more.'

'A *week*?' asked Hermann, setting a double pastis without water on the table before his partner and chum, and two of Paulaner's Münchner Hells for himself.

'A week,' sighed Richard, realizing only too clearly that Bousquet had buggered off and had left him to face the music on his own.

'One and a half to two million a month, Louis. Between eighteen and twenty-four million a year. Among how many shareholders, monsieur?'

These two... René had been *warned* not to let Boemelburg assign them to the investigation. Laval *would* intercede on the detectives' behalf by personally telephoning the Gestapo Chief! 'Fifteen. No more. It's always best to minimize such things.'

'All well-placed in the Government ministries or doing business with it? Good business?' asked Kohler.

'All.'

'That four or five hundred thousand a week is too little, Louis. Think of the expenses, the buying on the *marché noir*, then selling on it. Two breaches of the law, of course, but the commissions also, the pay-offs. Travel to and from Paris and other cities and

227

towns. The price of flour alone tells us it has to be more. What's Henri-Claude Ferbrave's cut?'

Ah *merde*! 'Ten per cent.'

'And Jean-Guy Deschambeault's?' demanded Hermann.

'Another ten.'

'And the guards and drivers of those armoured vans of his father's? Their hush-money?'

Must Kohler threateningly lean over the table and not sit down? 'Ten again.'

'Five million a week, Louis. At least five and probably fifteen.'

'Look, I . . . I don't know the details. How could I? Ask Honoré de Fleury. He . . . he oversees the accounts.'

'Our Inspector of Finances, Hermann. Supplies and rationing, the police, the Bank of France, and finance.'

'And no income tax because none of it's reported, since de Fleury makes certain of that, and Bousquet lets him.'

'Four murders, Hermann.'

'The threat of further and more important assassinations, Louis.'

Hermann would now leave the rest of the interview to his partner and enjoy his beer and the scenery. 'Monsieur le Ministre, unless you fully cooperate you will accompany me to the morgue where we will continue our little discussion over the corpse of your former mistress.'

Must the fun, the laughter, the sound of the pianos, the singing and dancing swirl around the island of their little table? wondered Richard acidly. 'Marie-Jacqueline told my wife that Sandrine couldn't possibly be any good at making love since I had not only sought her company but had done so repeatedly and for almost two years. They fought. They screamed at each other and tumbled down the stairs and out on to the carpet next to the fireplace and the fire. Sandrine's coat was torn open, her hair pulled, the dress and blouse ripped and a breast repeatedly grabbed and squeezed; Marie-Jacqueline's skin was deeply scratched and bled in several places. Threats were shrieked. Fists pummelled one another. Sandrine did cry out several times that she would kill Marie-Jacqueline but it meant nothing, I'm certain.'

'And that one's response?'

How cautious of the Sûreté. 'She laughed at Sandrine and then cheered the crowd who'd gathered to watch, and turning back to my wife, shrilled, "Why not strip and we'll see which one of us causes his cock to lift?"'

Ah *merde*! 'Had you told the nurse you'd get a divorce and marry her?'

'Inspector, surely you are aware that family is everything to a man in my position and that what I say to such women is of little consequence? She knew it was impossible but couldn't resist making the taunt.'

'And your wife?'

'Spat in her face, slapped her hard, and left.'

'Then I'm going to have to interview her.'

'That's impossible. I can't allow it.'

'You will whether you like it or not, and that is final.'

Six of those little grey pills of Benzedrine the Luftwaffe's night-fighter pilots took to stay awake were shaken from Hermann's inexhaustible supply, to lie like gravel on the linoleum-topped table.

'Down those, Louis. You're going to need them.'

'Six! We've been up for nearly forty-eight hours! You know those won't sit well on a stomach that has had only beer or pastis to wet it!'

Unsteadily Herr Kohler got up and, a head and shoulders above nearly everyone else, picked up his two empties and began to make his way back to the bar.

'He'll be awake all night now and asleep tomorrow when I need him,' grumbled St-Cyr.

'Don't you two ever stop?' demanded Richard caustically.

'Never. Now where were we? Oh yes, the older scratches and bruises the coroner noted on Marie-Jacqueline Mailloux and this supposed threat to assassinate *les gars*.'

*

Caught unexpectedly, their voices low and urgent only to be suddenly silenced, the cabaret troupe remained motionless in their dressing room. 'Oh, sorry,' quipped Kohler. 'I was looking for the toilets.'

Still the three of them didn't move, nor did they grin or laugh at such an obvious lie. They'd left the stage, he the bar and right after them. Now they knew he'd deliberately invaded their privacy and they didn't like it one bit.

Their gazes taking him in, their black velvet chokers setting off the kind of women men imagined them to be, their expressions were, as one, cold, and silently demanded, why is it that you want us to be the way you do? But then ... each, in her own way, realized why he must have come.

'Kohler,' he heard himself saying, his throat still dry at the accusation but also at having interrupted something he should have quietly listened to from the corridor. 'Kripo, Paris-Central.' The dressing room was crowded. Underthings, skirts, blouses and winter coats hung on wooden pegs even around the much-stained mirror. Stage make-up, grey rolls of unbleached toilet paper, lipsticks, et cetera, cluttered the shared dressing table. In a far corner, a rusty iron hole in the floor with stirrups, a pull-chain and one hell of a rush of icy water – a Turkish – was not only wet and slimy but reeked.

'A detective,' croaked the one with the clarinet, moisture rapidly filling wounded dark brown eyes that only moments ago had wantonly gazed down the length of that instrument she had blown into and fingered on stage. Her thick chestnut hair was long and still shaken out but now it fell forward, for she was lying, tummy down, on a lumpy, moth-eaten day bed and had had to turn her head his way. Ass up a little, legs slightly parted, knees dug in and waist bare, the off-white satin bra no doubt binding her so tightly it pinched and chafed her nipples.

Unbidden, Herr Kohler's faded blue eyes fled emptily over her body, Aurélienne told herself – Madame Tavernier to you, Inspector. He didn't pause at her frill-clad bottom and black-meshed legs, but noted the holes in her stockings and, realizing that they couldn't be mended because they helped to create that seedy, sluttish, twenties look of Berlin that was so in demand, especially now, paused only at her black high-heels and cleats. Was he thinking of footprints in the snow? *Was he?* she wondered desperately.

He blinked as if a little drunk and tore his gaze from her to look suddenly at Carole – that's Madame Navaud to you, Inspector – who stood with lighted cigarette poised. The flowered grey silk kimono was thrown well off that bare left shoulder, that hand placed firmly above a provocative hip, while the barbed tattoo of a wild rose climbed from her belly button and the equator of pink peekaboos to just below her satin bra. Black garters and black net stockings too, and her long, light brown hair all over the place and all but hiding the hard hazel eyes that looked sideways at him.

'Kohler,' Carole said in that way she always did when forced to caress some bastard's quiverins cheek. 'Here to find a killer or killers.'

'Not us,' whispered Nathalie, her expression unchanged, and still sitting facing the back of that Thonet chair of hers. Its bentwood waist was slender and curved beautifully upwards just like her own, her thighs tightly gripping it, her chin on the hand that was folded delicately over the top rail as if she was caressing the back of a lover's neck. A chair that she often used as a stage prop and had insisted she must have when she'd arrived in Vichy in the late autumn of 1940. Madame Nathalie Bénoist, Inspector. Nathalie who holds us all together and writes our songs and routines and makes us work. She has such lovely shoulders hasn't she? And yet ... and yet her expression can be so hard and uncompromising.

Nathalie's black teddy gave Herr Kohler's swift scrutiny a glimpse of lace, flesh and garters, of smooth white thighs and black lisle stockings that had no holes above the tops of her jackboots.

'What's to happen to us?' she asked at last, but with that same

231

penetratingly cold voice she used on insufferable men. 'Are we to be next?'

'Just who the hell is doing this?' demanded Carole, abruptly taking a quick drag, then curling back her upper lip to spit, 'Detectives! *Merde*, haven't you *salauds* from Paris thought it could well be the wives?'

'A knife?' Nathalie said softly from her chair. 'Noëlle Olivier's, is that so, Inspector? Well? Damn it, tell us.'

'*Yes!* Louis ... Look, my partner has it.'

Had Herr Kohler been startled by Nathalie's vehemence? wondered Carole. Did he, too, think there could well be a connection to that little legend? Edith Pascal, eh, Inspector? *La Mégère* as we call her – the shrew – when she hounds Albert for newspapers and about other things.

'And is it true that Albert Grenier found it?' bleated Aurélienne from where she lay, her back still to him.

'Yes, again.'

'Ah *Sainte Mère!*' she cried, and, shutting her eyes, bowed her head to press it against her own stage prop which Albert had seen her lewdly sucking and fondling often enough. Albert ...

'*Chérie*, it can't have been him!' insisted Nathalie.

'*Ma foi, quelle stupidité, idiote!*' scathed Carole. 'Albert loves us all. You know he'd never touch a hair on your head. He'd die for us just as he would for the Maréchal. He couldn't hurt a fly.'

'Just the rats, eh?' blurted Aurélienne, defiantly swinging her legs off the bed to sit on its edge. 'He presses a thumb under the chins of those that haven't quite been done in and watches as they struggle for breath or all but cuts off their heads by tightening that wire of his!'

'Or uses the chair leg, so why make such a thing of it?' shot back Carole.

'Because I've seen him watching me! Oh *bien sûr* we used to say he should at least have a little fun in his life and why not let him watch us, but now I'm afraid of him. I am, Nathalie. *I am!*'

Hurriedly Herr Kohler pushed things aside on the dressing table to set his drinks down but knocked over the bottle of cologne that was always left open as an air-sweetener. Futilely he made a grab for it only to realize he was too late as it shattered on the concrete floor. *'Verdammt!'* he swore and desperately searched his pockets for a cigarette until Carole gave him hers.

'Merci,' he said. 'Christ, I needed this! Four girls and Albert knew them all. Did he watch them too?'

'Getting undressed?' asked Nathalie.

'Fucking their lovers?' went on Carole. 'Céline was one of us, Inspector. The others were friends.'

'And she was killed with that knife!' wept Aurélienne. 'I knew she was going to be next. I begged her not to go to the Hôtel du Parc when Honoré de Fleury came in here to give her that nightgown and told her to put it on. Albert knew what she was up to with Pétain. I'm certain of it. Certain, do you understand?'

Svelte and looking taller than she was, the one called Nathalie lifted herself from that chair of hers, its back slipping between and behind her legs in one gracefully fluid motion. Putting a bare arm about the clarinet player's shoulders, she kissed that tear-streaked cheek and, pressing her forehead against it, rocked her head from side to side, saying soothingly, *'Petite,* don't worry so. Albert couldn't possibly have killed Céline or any of the others. *Mon Dieu,* didn't he leave flowers for you in your room last summer, in mine also, and now sometimes a gingerbread his mother has baked especially for him?'

And gazing up with superb china-blue eyes under bobbed and parted jet-black hair *à la* Madame Noëlle Olivier – yes, damn it! thought Kohler – said, 'It was nothing, Inspector. Albert overheard Lucie telling Aurélienne and Céline that she was going to have to go to Paris. Gaëtan-Baptiste, her banker, was insisting on it and had . . .'

'Had what?'

Ah *merde!* 'Arranged everything.'

'An abortion?'

'She wasn't going to refuse, Inspector,' said Nathalie. 'She couldn't, she said. But for me, I think she wanted very much to keep the child.'

'And Albert? How did he react?'

She shrugged. 'He got angry. He thinks girls lead men astray – at least that's what his mother has told him often enough. She's very religious and had wanted a child so badly but had had to wait nearly for ever, so Albert, he doesn't feel abortion is right either.'

And neither does the Maréchal he worships, thought Kohler. 'Where is this peephole of his?'

'Actually there are two of them,' said Carole. Picking her way round the day bed and past the doorless armoire, she found the crack high up in the wall and ran a finger along and right into it. 'He stands on the wooden crate he uses as a footstool when reaching difficult places to set his snares.'

'The other one is in the ceiling above Aurélienne, Inspector,' said Nathalie dryly. 'There's a storeroom in which Albert must also set snares. Chez Crusoe would rather their kitchens and our dressing room were inundated every spring during the annual floods, than have all that stuff up there get wet.'

'Cigarettes and pipe tobacco?'

'Sugar, flour, chocolate, wine and champagne,' said Carole, giving him the blankest of looks.

'Orders are placed here, then, and the vans come and go?' he asked, not missing a trick.

'Yes,' she said, 'but please don't tell anyone we let you in on it.'

'And you all have rooms at the Hôtel d'Allier?'

'Yes,' said Nathalie. 'Inspector, forget about Albert. Think about the wives, as Carole has said. You see, they came here to Chez Crusoe. Not Bousquet's – she's in Paris – but Richard's, de Fleury's and Deschambeault's. What they saw they did not like and were only too vocal about it. Everyone in the audience laughed, of course, ourselves especially. *Mon Dieu*, to be presented with such an opportunity for humour was too much to resist, but . . . but their husbands had left the club by then.'

'Marie-Jacqueline, Camille, Lucie and Céline had gone with them to the Château aux Oiseaux Splendides,' said Carole, lighting a cigarette for herself. 'We joined the party later.'

Louis had shown him his notebook: ' "Party, 24 October",' he muttered, 'and just before the Allied landings in North Africa and total Occupation . . .'

'But there have been other parties since,' confessed Aurélienne, taking Nathalie's hand in hers to kiss and grip it tightly. 'Like Camille, Inspector, each of us has a husband who is a prisoner of war in your country, but unlike Céline's, ours are still alive. *Alive!*'

'Those bitches had the nerve to accuse us in public of being unfaithful,' snorted Carole. 'Oh for sure, they despise us for letting a little fun come into our lives now and then, but to threaten to tell our husbands we've been unfaithful? To write letters to the Maréchal demanding that he get *les Allemands* to send us to the Reich and into forced labour in a munitions factory? *Merde*, how could anyone *think* of doing such a thing to another?'

'We're not saints, but we didn't deserve what they said of us,' said Nathalie. 'I've two sons I board at a farm on the other side of Charmeil where I know they will get enough to eat. Carole has a daughter she left with her husband's parents.'

'I couldn't stand to live with them any more. It drove me crazy, their constant carping. Now I work and save and hope we'll have a future when my husband is released.'

'Aurélienne comes with me, Inspector,' said Nathalie. 'Every second Sunday we visit the farm and take the boys to Mass at the same little church Pétain sometimes attends. They call her auntie, and as for me, I know she loves them as much as I do, if not more.'

'I haven't had any of my own yet,' confessed Aurélienne, shyly blinking away her tears. 'There . . . there wasn't time. One day we were married and the next my Yvon was sent to the front. Now a heavily censored letter still comes every once in a while but what's a girl to do, eh? Pine away the whole of her life?'

'Starve?' said Carole.

'Wear black?' said Nathalie.

'Wait when one never knows if her husband will ever come home and if he does, will he still feel the same way about her; will she still love him? Me, I can't even remember his face!' swore Carole.

'We're not here to judge.'

'Don't men always judge?' she snapped. 'And their wives too? Especially those who have everything and consequently think they're better than those of us who have nothing?'

'And at this château party, did any of the other wives join in the fight between Marie-Jacqueline and Sandrine Richard?'

'Madame de Fleury found Honoré with Céline and wept but couldn't seem to move or say a thing. She just stood in the centre of that room with her head bowed and fists clenched,' said Nathalie. 'Never have I seen a woman more devastated.'

'And Madame Deschambeault?' he asked.

'Her?' snorted Carole. 'For that one, Inspector, you have to understand that her mind isn't at all well. She remained in the car with Madame Pétain.'

'Ah Christ!'

They were subdued, these men of influence, said St-Cyr to himself and, for just this once in their corrupted lives, reduced to silently watching two overworked detectives enjoy a much-needed meal. Bousquet, again absenting himself had gathered the unfaithful around their table at Chez Crusoe, but Laval had made certain of the meal. From one of the restaurants he frequented along the Allier, the Premier had sent a splendid sampling of the rustic fare for which the Auvergne was justly famous.

Pounti could be no more than a hash of bacon with onions, Swiss chard and eggs, but here it was golden brown, piping hot, cut into wedges, containing chopped ham, pork, raisins, cream and herbs – tarragon and chervil especially – and was accompanied by the dark green lentils that were grown only in the Puy de Dôme and had such a remarkably distinctive flavour.

Two bottles of the Chanturgue red – ah, not a Beaujolais of course – were totally acceptable. *Truffades* were waiting. A kind of potato cake, but shredded coarsely, fried in lard with Cantal

236

cheese cut in strips over them and left until melted only to be then turned over, the fire now low, the aroma *superbe.*

A *salade de lentilles aux saucisses* also waited – dried country sausage cut in rounds, the lentils, which had been soaked overnight with onions and carrots, simmered and drained, the carrots, et cetera, saved for the never-ending pots of *soupe aux choux,* the lentils cooled, mashed with a fork and given a drizzle of whisked egg yolks, vinegar, olive oil and Dijon mustard.

The bread? he asked himself, refilling Hermann's glass and then tearing off a fistful from the round and golden cross-hatched loaf, was a meal in itself.

But, to business, he said, looking silently round the table and asking himself, Marie-Jacqueline Mailloux and this acid little Minister of Supplies and Rationing, this Alain André Richard? A patently indiscreet nurse with a private practice who was on call at the girls' school where Camille Lefèbvre was a teacher, and who had also worked part-time at the clinic of Dr Raoul Normand where Julienne Deschambeault sought constant help? Marie-Jacqueline, monsieur, age thirty-seven, not thirty-two or -three, and born in Tours. A divorcee at the age of nineteen who had just given birth to twin girls she had given· up to the Carmelites. A woman with jet-black hair, dark blue eyes, an angular face, sharp nose and chin and dimpled apple cheeks. What, please, had Julienne's reaction been when attended to by such a creature? Intense hatred, a traumatic fit perhaps, or did Madame Deschambeault simply swear to drown her?

Gaëtan-Baptiste Deschambeault, the husband and Sous-direc-teur of the Bank of France, was tall and not unhandsome, broad-shouldered under an open black overcoat, the black hair thinning, the aristocratic blue eyes swift to every nuance. Was he thinking of his little Lucie who'd been smothered at the age of twenty-three? His very personal shorthand typist, the one he'd got pregnant? Was he remembering the foetus between her blotched and putrid thighs, the effluent and bloodstained oedematous fluid that had still oozed from her, or was he thinking instead of her chestnut curls and dark brown, mischievous eyes, the riding crop clutched licentiously – was that not so, monsieur? – and leather thongs waiting, but to tie up which of you?

And Honoré de Fleury? he asked. For the first time we get a good look at you and I have to say you're quite ordinary, even for an inspector of finances, all of whom look ordinary. Nervous still, and not liking being forced to sit here – Bousquet must have told them all they had no other choice. And Laval would have made certain his secrétaire général did just that!

De Fleury's faded green eyes were closely set in a finely boned and freckled face. Age fifty-six and greying, the reddish hair rapidly receding, the hands small and light. A man of numbers, an accountant and yet . . . and yet he'd had a mistress who'd been knifed. Age twenty-eight, a dancer, a piano player, teacher, singer . . . blonde, blue-eyed, a widow with a little daughter Annette to whom she had written postcards using the quills from increasingly exotic birds. Céline Dupuis, formerly of 60 rue Lhomond. Taught ballet part-time to the girls at Camille Lefèbvre's school, as well as at the ballet school of Thérèse Deschambeault. Ah yes!

Céline, who had worn two costumes and a black velvet choker, and whose hair, of below shoulder length, had been all over the place due to someone's desperate search for something they'd left behind.

As always, one had to wonder what such a gorgeous and hard-working woman could possibly have seen in such a moth-eaten older man. Position, money, the good times, the 'fun', but really oughtn't there to have been something else? Unattached in a place like this, a girl would always be badgered. Attached, she would have got a good meal every now and then, and others would have left her alone. And she hadn't believed de Fleury could possibly divorce that wife of his, that Élisabeth. A little game they had played, he had said to Hermann. A game! But had Élisabeth de Fleury wanted Céline Dupuis murdered? Had she hired a professional?

All three victims had been friends of Camille's, the teacher with thick auburn hair and brown eyes, her *carte d'identité* had stated. Chestnut hair and deeply warm brown eyes with flecks of green and gold, Bousquet had said. Her husband a POW, a captain; her father one of the disbanded Army of the Armistice who hadn't liked his daughter playing around and had always bitched about what a coward his son-in-law was. Garrotted savagely by another professional, or the same one. Born in Lyons – had she, too, been caught in flagrante delicto but with Bousquet at that infamous château party?

Real coffee, black and strong and made over a wood fire in an iron pot, nothing fancy, awaited, as did *fouaces*, pancakes made with fine, unleavened flour, cooked *sous la cendre*, under the ashes, with butter, egg yolks, saffron, cinnamon and nutmeg and filled with that marvel of marvels of the Auvergne, its crystallized fruit, with even a few glazed walnuts being added for good measure.

Wedges of Cantal and Saint-Nectaire also waited, bringing moisture to this poor detective's eyes. It had been years since he'd seen such simple, wholesome fare but, alas, he'd best continue to deal with the matters at hand.

'Messieurs,' he said, as the racket of the club constantly swirled around the table, 'we are presented with a plot to kill you. *Résistants* perhaps. A Flykiller, in any case, or two of them, and the ominous threat of an imminent civil war and yet . . . and yet.' He stabbed the air with his fork. 'We find the mistresses are the victims and that in each case, not only is the intended target passed over and no attempt made on his life, but that he, to save his reputation, keeps silent and buggers off, leaving the corpse for others to find and tidy up.'

'Now listen, you . . .' began Deschambeault, still not even having bothered to remove his coat and scarf.

'No, you listen, Sous-directeur. If what my partner has just learned is true, your wife was not alone in that car on her little visit to the château you boys use, but was sitting beside Madame Pétain.'

'That woman interferes, Inspector,' swore Richard acidly.

'Why not tell him she wields enormous power?' shot Honoré de Fleury.

'Which is always veiled,' sighed Deschambeault. '*Merde*, I've no idea why she was there. My Julienne was to have been at Dr Normand's clinic. Total rest and further treatments. The *hydrothérapie sauvage* and *électrothérapie*. Thirty cubic centimetres of the Chomel six times a day . . .'

'And your wife, Monsieur de Fleury?' asked Louis.

'Knew only that I would be late and not home for dinner.'

Louis wouldn't let him get away with that! thought Kohler.

'And where, please, is home?'

'The Hôtel Majestic. We've three rooms just along the hall from Dr Ménétrel and his family, and . . '

'Near Madame Pétain's suite?'

'Near enough. All right, they know each other. They talk. Élisabeth and Madame Pétain use the same *coiffeur* and . . . and visit the *Grand établissement thermal* every Thursday, as does Madame Richard.'

This was getting better and better! 'And do they share a bath?' asked Kohler. 'The steam room perhaps?'

'I've no idea.'

'Tea once or twice a week, or coffee and cakes in the Chante Clair?' he asked, ripping off more bread and still eating like a soldier in the trenches of that other war, as if it was his last meal.

'Often enough, yes,' flustered de Fleury. '*Mon Dieu*, you're not suggesting my Élisabeth entered into some pact to kill them? She's not like that. She's meek and mild, the perfect stay-at-home mother and wife. Certainly she's upset about how crowded things are, living as we have to, but . . . but I've made a full confession that she has accepted. Never again will I . . . Well, you know.' Agitatedly he passed worried fingers over that brow of his.

'Stray from the fold?' quipped Hermann, helping himself to more of the *truffades*.

'Sandrine has been appeased, Inspectors,' said Richard dryly. 'Revenge, yes, but as to her drowning Marie-Jacqueline . . . ? It's impossible. Nothing could have been further from her mind.'

'And yet . . . and yet,' motioned Louis with his fork. 'You and your lover shared a bath at the *établissement thermal* and your wife, since she also visits the baths, must have known the two of you were accustomed to doing this, as did Madame Pétain. It wasn't the first time, was it?'

'Inspectors ... Inspectors,' chided Bousquet, grinning affably as he rejoined them, 'in the heat of a jealous rage a woman will say anything!'

'And Madame Pétain?' asked Hermann, wolfing most of a *truffade*. 'Just what the hell *was* she doing there last 24 October?'

'In the middle of the night, messieurs?' demanded Louis. 'Was it raining? And which of you escorted Mesdames Sandrine Richard and Élisabeth de Fleury to the car, only to find the Maréchal's wife staring out through her side window at him?'

'I did,' said Bousquet, that lambskin-collared overcoat of his falling open to reveal the very finest of suits – did he change his shirts several times a day? wondered St-Cyr. Image was so often everything to the Occupier. Wealth and power went hand in hand with that.

'I told her the matter had been taken care of,' said Bousquet stonily, 'and that there was no cause for further alarm.'

'When, really, it hadn't been taken care of at all,' sighed Louis, helping himself to the salad. 'Further parties at that same château led to further flagrant infidelities; here, too, I should think, and at the Jockey Club, wouldn't you say, Hermann?'

'I'd give him a month's wages, Louis, just to hear what Madame Pétain had to say!'

'*Mon Dieu*, how were we to know then that all four would be killed?' demanded Bousquet.

The dishes were, of course, covered, the porcelain not Sèvres or Limoges but eminently serviceable. Renowned for his love of the table, Laval had stood them proud, but why?

'Messieurs,' said St-Cyr, 'let us admit that you were up to mischief and that it had to stop if for no other reason than that of the scandal and embarrassment to the very Government you serve. Marie-Jacqueline was killed but the rest of you carried on as if nothing had happened, and certainly for you, Ministre Richard, this first killing was a blessing in disguise. She was trouble – you, yourself, have stated this. She was drunk – she must have been, a little at least – and had slipped below the water in that bath. The electricity had gone off – another power failure you went to investigate – and when you returned, you stated to the investigating officer later that you thought she was still alive, wanting only to caress you with her foot.'

'That was 9 December, Louis, at about 6.50 p.m. Then all but a month later, Monsieur le Secrétaire Général meets Camille Lefèbvre at a cabin he rents out for just such a purpose, and let's not kid ourselves about that.'

'And at 2.45 a.m. finds her garrotted, fires two or three shots into the wilderness but can't remember how many and buggers off to Paris to an important meeting.'

'Inspectors . . .' attempted Bousquet.

'No, please,' cautioned Louis, taking more bread with his salad. 'Lucie Trudel then dies and she, too, could have been a substantial embarrassment to you, Sous-directeur Deschambeault, so much so that you even failed to inform your friend and business partner, our Secrétaire Général de Police, of the murder.'

'Then Céline is persuaded to agree to do something she didn't want to do, and is taken to the Hall des Sources at 10 p.m. on Tuesday, 2 February,' said Hermann. 'Trouble is, *mon vieux*, if this one had owned up as he should have, Céline might still be alive.'

'Two of those murders rest on your shoulders, Sous-directeur. I'm even certain you read her note: "Lucie, we have to talk. It's urgent".'

'What was?' asked Hermann. 'The abortion? The murders of Marie-Jacqueline and Camille and were they to be next, eh? Or had Céline discovered who the killer or killers were?'

'Jean-Louis . . . Herr Kohler . . . listen to me, please,' urged Bousquet, no longer dashing, just damned worried. 'It can't have been the wives. *Merde alors*, it's crazy to even think such a thing.'

'It's the terrorists,' said Deschambeault vehemently. 'Why else would your name be at the top of *L'Humanité*'s list? Those bastards are out to get us!'

'The Résistance,' said Hermann. 'There's only one problem. Since when did they start killing the innocent only to forget entirely about their intended targets?'

'They want to make us afraid of them!' seethed Richard.

'To prolong our agony!' hissed de Fleury.

'Or is it, messieurs, that the killer or killers wish you to blame the Résistance, as you have?'

'Herr Gessler and Herr Jännicke will sort it out, Jean-Louis,' said Bousquet gruffly. 'I had no choice but to ask them to bring in a little help.'

'To snatch people from their farms and streets?'

'By questioning anyone they think necessary,' he countered.

'Then let us hope we're allowed to continue unhindered, or is it, Secrétaire, that you still want roadblocks thrown up in front of us?'

'Not at all. We're here to cooperate.'

'Then do so. Begin by realizing that we're dealing with one or perhaps two persons who not only know Vichy extremely well, but are also in on everything you do.'

'They know beforehand when things will happen,' said Kohler.

'Yet so far we really know very little about our victims,' lamented Louis.

At a curt nod from Bousquet, Deschambeault said, 'Inspectors, Lucie carried letters to Paris for Céline. Who they were to, I've no idea, but I warned her to be careful. Innocent . . . I'm certain the matter was perfectly innocent.'

But against the law.

'She simply posted them for her in Paris,' said Bousquet.

'One or two or more per trip?' asked Louis, draining the last of the bottles.

'One, always, and to the same person,' replied Deschambeault uncomfortably. 'I know this because she told me not to worry so much, that they . . . they were simply to an old friend of Céline's.'

'And not to Madame Dupuis's daughter?' asked Louis, who

was always such a stickler for detail, especially when someone had tried not to give him the whole truth.

The head was shaken.

'Secrétaire,' said Louis, 'I found no such letter among the things Mademoiselle Trudel had packed for her Paris trip. Not in her day-to-day handbag, not in the one she would have used in the city, nor in her suitcase.'

'Maybe there wasn't one,' said Bousquet. 'Maybe Céline, thinking that Lucie was going home to see her father, hadn't given her one.'

'Maybe, maybe,' sighed Kohler. Louis hadn't liked Bousquet's response either. Had the letter been taken by her killer, or by Deschambeault? Was it all a cover-up?

Bousquet gave another curt nod, this time to Honoré de Fleury, who said, 'Inspectors, after Camille's death, Céline felt certain Marie-Jacqueline hadn't just drowned accidentally and that she would be next. She had always wanted to leave Vichy and return to her daughter, but she ... she then became desperate.'

'Thus agreeing to the little proposition Ménétrel had put to you,' said Louis sadly. 'Monsieur, exactly what reward did the doctor promise?'

The others must know, thought Kohler, but even so it would hurt to have to say it.

'He said that if I could convince Céline to answer the Maréchal's love letters with a little visit, he, the Maréchal's personal physician and confidant, would see that I became Directeur de Finance, but that if I didn't, I could kiss my crummy job goodbye.'

'And Céline ... what was she offered?'

'Two hundred thousand francs as well as the *laissez-passer*, *sauf-conduit* and necessary residence papers.'

'Fernand de Brinon, our Government's representative in Paris, is a shareholder of our little enterprise,' confessed Deschambeault, not looking at any of them.

'Everything had been taken care of,' offered de Fleury. 'Céline was happier than I'd seen her in weeks but was still very worried about Lucie having an abortion. That, I think, is why she wanted to talk to her.'

'And the earrings, monsieur?' asked Louis.

'Believe me, I knew nothing of them, nor do I know why she would have tried to hide them from her killer.'

'Jean-Louis, you spoke to Auguste-Alphonse Olivier. How did you find him?' asked Bousquet.

'Withdrawn and very reticent to discuss the robbery. I did get him to admit that the jewellery hadn't been in his safe-deposit box but had been left where his wife had always kept it. When Hermann and I came downstairs from examining the room, he had gone out for another of his walks. A defeated man, Secrétaire.'

That was good of Louis, thought Kohler, but God help them if Gessler found out the truth!

'And the robbery?' asked Bousquet.

'The housekeeper confided that he often forgets his key and that she has then to leave the door unlocked.'

Good again.

'Ah *bon*,' nodded Bousquet. 'A veteran, a war hero. It's sad what life can do to a man.'

'Pétain made a cuckold of him,' snorted Richard, 'but fortunately Olivier poses no threat.'

'Sadly none whatsoever,' said Louis. 'A recluse no one pays the slightest attention to. And now, Monsieur de Fleury, since you keep the accounts, would you tell us, please, who the other shareholders are?'

'Charles-Frédéric Hébert at the château – it was only proper of us to include him.'

'Ménétrel?' asked Hermann, only to see de Fleury shake his head.

'The doctor has always the well-being of the Maréchal in mind,' said Bousquet gruffly.

'And the others?' asked Louis blandly.

'Inspector, is this necessary?' asked Deschambeault.

It was. 'Jean Bichelonne, Minister of Production and Communications,' said de Fleury. 'Philippe Henriot, Minister of Propaganda and Information.'

Radio-Paris's Number One Boy.

'Herr Otto Abetz, the German Ambassador.'

And owner of the château.

'Édouard Guillaumet, Sous-directeur of the Tabac National at Vanves.'

And necessary.

'Gérard Ouellette, Inspecteur des caves de la Halle aux vins.'

The huge Paris wine store: champagne and cognac too, of course – perfect.

'Jean-Louis, the rest are prominent men of industry and commerce and members of the Cercle Européen,' said Bousquet, as if this ought to put them beyond reproach. 'Aeronautics, automobiles and lorries, locomotives and railway trucks, coal, iron, steel, aluminium, beet sugar, cement and textiles, chemicals also. All keep horses at the racing stables.'

'And occasionally enjoy a party or two?' asked Hermann, having momentarily lost his appetite.

'Of course.'

'Then the vans aren't the only vehicles that are used to transport goods, are they?' he said.

'That is correct.'

'And anything you need you can get at a price?'

'That, too, within reason, is correct.'

'So last December who ordered in the 1925 Bollinger Cuvée Spéciale that Marie-Jacqueline downed, and the Shalimar that Céline Dupuis was wearing when killed?'

'Charles-Frédéric Hébert,' said Bousquet. 'He's very fond of the Maréchal, though he no longer sees him and hasn't since the tragedy. The Bollinger and the Rémy-Martin Louis XIII were, I believe, Christmas gifts, but extra arrived with the consignment. As to the perfume, I don't think any was ordered.'

'What tragedy?' asked Hermann innocently.

'Why the suicide of Noëlle Olivier. It was Charles who brought

246

the couple together and he still blames himself for what subsequently happened. He was a major shareholder in Olivier's bank and lost a fortune when it failed in 1933. Oh, by the way, Jean-Louis, I'll take those *billets doux*, if you don't mind.'

'Later, Secrétaire. Later. For now they must be considered as evidence.'

At 10 a.m. Berlin Time, Friday 5 February, the sun was ringed with frost. The wind, gusting like a bastard, swept snow from every ridge and hill, and in the valley of the Allier below, the river was gripped in iron, the gunmetal light enough to make the bones ache.

'*Mon Dieu*, Hermann,' said Louis, reverently ignoring the weather, his breath fogging an already iced-up windscreen, 'it's *exactement* as Caesar would have seen it in 52 BC. He'd been defeated by Vercingetorix and his Arverni at Gergovia, their hill fort, and had had to cross the ford down there to lick his wounds in the hot springs.'

Christ, were they to have another tiresome lecture at a time like this? They'd just driven through the little village of Charmeil, some seven kilometres north-west of Vichy, had first crossed the Boutiron Bridge without a murmur from the boys on the control, a bad sign. 'That little aerodrome with the swastika wasn't there, *mon enfant*, nor were the two Storchs or that Dornier that are warming up!'

Grumpy still and no imagination! 'Nor was the railway spur that's at the foot of this hill from which Herr Abetz's château commands such an imposing view.'

After leaving Chez Crusoe, they'd spent the rest of the night in yet another of the lousy flea-bitten hotels honest detectives had had to become accustomed to. Searing pain in that left knee and no time to boil chestnuts and mash a poultice as promised. 'Caesar wouldn't have campaigned in the dead of winter!'

A sigh had best be given. Hermann had tossed and turned all night. Sleep had been impossible! 'You're missing the point. Every schoolchild in this country your Führer thinks is his has to

247

memorize the heroics of that twenty-year-old warrior, less now, of course, due to the Maréchal's policy of collaboration. But still, when he or she hears that Vercingetorix was defeated later that same year at Alesia, they learn that, like all noble Celts, he praised his vanquisher and led the Arverni in the victory parade, only to be courted by the Romans and then put to death. I tell you this simply to emphasize first that treachery is common to the Auvergne, though not limited to its natives.'

'And the château?'

Hermann found a cigarette and, breaking it in half, lit both halves to pass one over.

'*Merci*. Is like Vipiacus, the former estate of the Roman, Vipius, now corrupted into Vichy and owned by one of your countrymen.'

'When in Rome, do as the Romans, eh; when in Occupied France, as the Occupier?'

'Buy up everything you can.'

'Then let those who once owned it, look after it.'

'You're learning. I'm certain of it.'

'And second?'

Ah *bon*, Hermann had risen to the bait. 'That those same natives, having kept their beloved Auvergne independent of Paris for over a thousand years until Louis XIV made the mistake of finally taking it, are still tough but toughest on themselves. Just look at this château of your ambassador. Its towers and square keep, which have been often repaired, are all that remain of the lava-stone feudal fortress. The villagers have repeatedly raided its ruins for building materials, not only out of necessity but because of a deep-seated hatred of its owners and former owners, all of whom had not only robbed but brutalized them. Of course the Revolution also took its toll, although even then it was the peasants who suffered. But then . . . then along came new money and a gentler time to give us the gracefully sloping roofs that are covered with *lauzes*, the walled gardens, fishponds and statuary of a *maison de maître*, the baronial mansion of a *grand seigneur*.'

'Who, like as not, is still from outside and still keeping the peasants in thrall. *Mein Gott*, haven't you heard that "effort brings its own reward"?' snorted Hermann, quoting the Maré-chal.

' "Salvation is above all in our hands," *mon vieux*. "The first duty of all Frenchmen," and I count you one of us, "is to have confidence".'

'You sort out the former owner and bird lover. Leave the staff to me.'

'*Les bonnes à tout faire?*'

The maids of all work. 'Only those who have eyes and ears and are pretty enough to have been chased at parties! Coffee and cakes in the kitchen when you're ready, Chief?'

Hermann had been lifted out of his slump and was now looking forward to opening this little can of worms, so it would be best to let him have the last word since he always liked to have it, except . . . except that, having now passed through the last set of gates, they had a visitor.

A black, four-door Citroën *traction avant*, just like their own in Paris, was drawn up in front of the main entrance, empty.

'The bonnet is still warm,' said Louis, noting its melting snow.

'Hot, if you ask me. There are even skid marks.'

Sandrine Richard was waiting for them. Not in the *grand salon* with its *Régence* furniture and floor-to-ceiling murals of the hunt. Eighteenth-century, those, thought Kohler. Flemish by the look. Gorgeous paintings of long-necked swans and geese hanging upside down to mature, pheasants too. Stags, boars and lunging hounds, the wounded at bay under crystal chandeliers whose light would be reflected from the gilded frames and bevelled mirrors.

Even the parquet underfoot would gleam, their quickening steps echoing as they passed a seventeenth-century harpsichord and followed the maid with the short blonde pigtails and blue, blue eyes. One of the *Blitzmädchen*. Eighteen, if that, and with an urgent, self-deprecating walk, her arms kept stiffly to the sides of the prim black uniform with its *dentelle* of white Auvergne lace.

Black lisle stockings, too, and glossy black leather shoes with low and slightly worn heels.

Madame Richard, wife of the Minister of Supplies and Rationing, wasn't in the billiards room either, its life-sized Hellenic nudes of Carrara marble gracing the decor of dripping, tassled green and maroon velvet, lozenges of crystal dangling from the low-slung lights above the table, the smell of cigars lingering in the musty air. Nor was she on the staircase that rose beneath baronial shields and crossed pikes to landing after landing, opening on to a long corridor that led to an even older part of the château.

She was in a high-ceilinged bedroom whose canopied bed was of dark rosewood and whose walls were covered with faded, patchy Renaissance frescoes but had the remarkable added touch of perched, exquisitely mounted birds. Hawks in full flight or having just come in to roost; eagles too, an owl . . . Another and another, one so small it was no bigger than a fist. All looking at the intruders, all caught as if alive. A snipe, a rail, a cock pheasant, a partridge. Eighty . . . a hundred . . . two hundred of these birds, the chicken-coop smell of their feathers mingling with that of cold wood-ashes.

'Messieurs . . .'

'Hermann, interview our guide and what staff remain. Leave this one and Monsieur Hébert to me!'

Turn-of-the-century, long-necked glass lamps with rose-coloured globes and wells of kerosene would shed the softest of lights on the assembled aviary, thought St-Cyr. An ormolu clock, its Olympian gracefully raising her garland from above the blackened fireplace, gave the exact time, even to its minute hand moving one step further into the current hour beneath a sumptuously reclining, all but life-sized nude whose back was slightly arched, throwing her pubes into full view.

Leaded windows let in the cold, grey light of day.

Madame Richard wore no hat or scarf – even the charcoal-grey woollen overcoat hadn't been buttoned, so eager had she been to jump into that Citroën of her husband's.

No gloves either, and watchfully tense, he noted. A woman in her late forties with straight jet-black hair that had been pulled to the right and back but had remained unpinned in haste, her eyes the hard and unyielding chestnut brown of the betrayed wife, socialite and mother, one of the Parisian *beau monde*, no doubt, with money, lots of money. Hers and his, ah yes. No wrinkles furrowed that most diligently tended of brows. Only at the base of the neck, above the everyday woollen dress, were there the cruel signs of ageing. A woman of more than medium height but not tall, the figure trim not because of the rationing, but because she ate only enough and never too much.

'Inspector,' she said, her voice tight. 'We have to talk.'

'A few small quest—'

'Don't you dare patronize me! That . . .' She pointed accusingly to an oaken door, centuries old, which had seen the hammering blows of countless invaders. 'Is where I found them and.'

She waited, still watching him as the hawks and eagles did.

'Is where I had them photographed not once but several times!'

A dark Renaissance table was swept bare of its lamp and sundry other items. 'Here, damn you!' she shrilled as the sound of the breakage died and, sucking in a breath, snapped down print after twenty-by-twenty-five-centimetre print. 'See for yourself what we were expected to put up with week after week, month after month. Élisabeth's Honoré de Fleury and that . . . that dancer of his; Madame Bousquet's husband, our Secrétaire Général and his school teacher; Julienne Deschambeault and her Gaëtan-Baptiste and his secretary. You should see what he's done to that wife of his. *Ruined* her life. Made a decent, healthy woman into a nervous wreck who is constantly ill!'

She stamped a foot. 'Of course I swore I'd kill Marie-Jacqueline Mailloux. That slut was always in heat.'

'And those photographs, madame?' asked St-Cyr, his voice somehow remaining calm while hers had climbed.

'Were taken by the photographer I hired to accompany us.'

Trust the husbands not to have mentioned it! 'And the negatives?' he asked.

How good of him to worry about Alain André being blackmailed by the photographer! 'For now I will keep them.'

'No, madame. For now you will allow me that privilege.'

'They're not with me.'

'Then when we leave here, you will take me to them.'

'They're at the clinic. I . . . I couldn't keep them at home. Alain André would . . . would only have found and destroyed them.'

Had she threatened to blackmail her husband into behaving? 'Did Monsieur le Ministre tell you to come here?'

His use of the word Ministre had been deliberate! 'What do you think? That to save his career and reputation he begged me not to and I compromised by saying I wouldn't give them to Herr Gessler who knows all about what went on here in any case?'

'Madame, please just answer.'

'Ménétrel, you *imbécile*! That bastard telephoned to say that it would be wisest of me to destroy them.'

Then she *had* threatened Richard and he had then asked Ménétrel to intervene.

'If I could have tarred and feathered that slut I would have, Inspector. Instead, when I realized fully what was happening to my marriage, I was fool enough to take my troubles to Ménétrel who suggested I masturbate to relieve the tension! *Mon Dieu* I hate it here. I always have and always will. The hypocrisy of the Maréchal's return to family values. All women are chaste, all girls virgins, is that it, eh? Pah, what idiocy! And what about the husbands? The *fornicateurs*? And Pétain himself? A dancer? Well, he got what he deserved and so did she!'

Ah *merde*, her voice was echoing and she shouldn't have said that. 'I . . . Forgive me. This room. The memory of it. You can see the state I'm in. Well, can't you?' she shrilled.

'Certainly.'

'Then *look* at the photos. See for yourself!'

'I will, but first, madame, who informed you of the party on 24 October last, and gave you not only the appropriate time to strike

252

but also the precise locations of the four pairs of lovers that you would confront and have your man photograph?'

'My husband was the last we surprised. As to who helped us, I can't say.'

'You'd best.'

'Or you will arrest me?'

'Just answer!' At last the inspector had been moved to raise his voice.

'Mademoiselle Blanche Varollier.'

'Hired to inform on her employers?'

'It was she who first came to me, but yes, I agreed to pay her ten thousand francs.'

'One hundred thousand?' It was a shot in the dark.

'Two hundred and fifty.'

'Then where were you, please, during the *cinq à sept* of Wednesday, 9 December last when Marie-Jacqueline Mailloux was drowned?'

The briefest smile of triumph was not reflected in the hardness of her eyes.

'A dance recital at Thérèse Deschambeault's ballet school. Élisabeth de Fleury's daughter is very good and presently needs all the support we can give her.'

Merde, this town, this investigation! 'And was Céline Dupuis there?'

No hint of triumph passed her lips.

'Monique de Fleury was her best student. A dance from the Ballet Russe. It was marvellous. Madame Dupuis played the piano.'

Sacré nom de nom, the acid of that put-down! But did everyone know everyone in this town? 'And were Madame de Fleury's daughter and Céline Dupuis close, as a teacher and her prized pupil would have to have been?'

'Very. So you see, Inspector, Céline did not just betray Élisabeth, but her daughter as well!'

The kid with the pigtails was uneasy and with good reason, felt

Kohler. In November, when the Wehrmacht had suddenly taken over the *zone libre*, her boss had been recalled to Berlin. Urgent consultations, questions about his loyalties and loving the French and all things French too much. Abetz's wife, Suzanne, came from France's de Bruyker family and was a sensation when the couple had taken up residence in Paris in July 1940, never here. *Mein Gott*, who'd want to live near Vichy in a draughty old château in a winter like this when the City of Light beckoned? France and Germany together in happy alliance and marital bliss in the showcase of showcases. Reception after reception, designer dresses, jewels, champagne and all the rest, the races too. Abetz and Fernand de Brinon, that pedlar of *laissez-passers* and Vichy's ambassador to the Occupied Territories, had been old friends from the mid-thirties when Abetz had got de Brinon and other like-minded collabos to join his Comité France-Allemagne. A hotbed of sympathizers, some of whom had willingly spied on their own country and helped to place Sicherheitsdienst agents in France.

But now, as could happen with the most loyal of former drawing instructors – and Abetz had been one of those – there were doubts.

And this little *Mädchen für alles*, this *bonne à tout faire*, had been up to more than mischief and had realized he knew it.

'Look, relax,' said Kohler and grinned. 'All I want is a little information.'

'*Sicherlich!*' – I'll bet! she swore and pulled away to stop in the corridor with her back to him. 'I only did what I was told.'

'*Befehl ist Befehl*, eh?' An order is an order.

'All of us used to report to Herr Schleier who came from Paris once every so often, but now . . . now we have yet to be informed of who our new contact will be.'

Schleier – who was Abetz's assistant and, at forty-one, the embassy's oldest member and most senior Nazi of the 568 Paris staff, of whom 367 were from home – was now temporarily in charge.

'*Ach!* don't worry so much,' he said, chucking her under a chin that could, no doubt, be soft and tender when necessary. '*Gemütlichkeit* prise useful information. Rudolph won't forget that such cosy friendship with the Occupied is useful and that your loyalty is beyond reproach. He's just busy. *Mein Gott*, doesn't he like uniforms, medals and official receptions even more than Herr Abetz? He'll delegate someone. Just give him a chance to put his glass down.'

'They'll close this place and send us home. I know they will!'

To live like God in France had been everyone's dream, except that this kid was Alsatian and her bilingualism had been deemed useful.

'Show me your room and tell me what went on.'

'My room ... ?'

'We've lots of time. That partner of mine's a bird-lover.'

As she stabbed at the photos, Sandrine Richard sucked in a breath and said, 'A *bordel*, Inspector? A *maison de tolérance*? Oh for sure in such places these things go on, but here? Here in an official residence of the German Ambassador?'

'Calm down, please.'

'Why should I? Look, damn you! See for yourself what those bitches were up to with our husbands. Feathers ... torn pillows? Does she have to pee? Is that why she holds a fistful of feathers against herself and also blows them from her lips?'

Jésus, merde alors, Bousquet and Camille Lefèbvre had been caught in a state of total undress and more than a little drunk, their laughter frozen by the camera's intrusion!

Deschambeault and Lucie Trudel were *tout nus* also, the shorthand typist stretched up on tiptoe, her wrists bound tightly together to an iron ring in the wall of a tower room or dungeon, the sous-directeur with the riding crop raised to fiercely strike her shapely but already welted buttocks. Fear, tension, excitement and apprehension – lust, that pent-up urgency for the *grand frisson*, the great shudder – were only too evident in her expression as, puzzled that her lover had paused, she had looked over a shoulder past him and into the camera.

Honoré de Fleury and Céline Dupuis had been caught on their hands and knees on a leopardskin throw before a roaring fire, the Inspector of Finance having taken the dancer and instructress from behind while tightly gripping her breasts, her hair in his teeth and her head thrown back as if in ecstasy.

'Can you imagine how Élisabeth must have felt?' shrilled Madame Richard.

Céline's eyes were closed and there were tears, but it would be best to say nothing of them.

'Monique de Fleury is fifteen years old, Inspector,' seethed Sandrine, 'but now no longer wants to dance or strive for excellence in anything, her schoolwork especially. Endless tears for the mother who was betrayed; floods of them for herself because, like girls of that age, she adored her father and idolized him. Must Vichy corrupt everything? That child worshipped Céline Dupuis only to discover her father was fucking the woman!'

'But surely she needn't have been told?'

'Then you don't know Vichy and how crowded are the rooms in which we live! Madame Pétain, who is *présidente* of the Committee on which Élisabeth and I serve, has tried repeatedly to get better housing for us, but all our complaints only fall on deaf ears. "It's the Occupation and we must set an example." Some example!'

Caught among the onlookers at the fight between this one and Marie-Jacqueline were several whom St-Cyr recognized from their photos in the Paris press and other sources. Léon Aubriet of Aluminium Français, the giant cartel that had been set up to guarantee the country's former position in producing the metal business and to supply the rapacious appetite of the German aircraft industry, was with the *Blitzmädel* who had guided Hermann and himself to this very room. That one had a pleasing figure and a lingering hand on Aubriet's bare shoulder. His arm was still around her naked waist. Antoine Chaudet, of La Samaritaine – the Paris department store which, with Le Printemps, Les Nouvelles Galeries and others, had entered into agreements with Karstadt, Erwege and Hertie, their German counterparts – was with a girl far less than half his age. Charles Lenoir of Matériel Électrique and Pierre-Denis Martin of the Compagnie Générale du Téléphone were there with older girls that had, no doubt, been brought in especially for them. So many prominent men were in states of undress and drunkenness, the girls with their garlands of ivy having slipped.

'There's more!' hissed Sandrine Richard, finding a stark photo of Abel Bonnard, Minister of Education and Member of the Academie Française, whose tear-streaked baby cheeks were stained with mascara. Bonnard had frantically thrown up a hand to shield himself from the camera's flash. This little man with downy, snow-white hair, this asthmatic, part-time poet and collector of porcelain whose blatant love of high living was legendary, was with two naked schoolboys both of whom had obviously been recently fondled.

'It's disgusting!' spat Madame Richard. 'He takes care of them and they take care of him, and we have that on photo too!'

'Ah *merde*, if I don't confiscate these and destroy the negatives, madame, all hell will break loose!'

Standing behind the crowd of onlookers, a head and shoulders taller than most and fully dressed, were Blanche and Paul Varollier. Both translator and croupier were withdrawn from the proceedings, their expressions passive and yet ... and yet so much a part of things.

'*Ich heisse* Ellinor Schlesinger, Herr Inspektor Kohler.'

The kid handed over her passport and ID as a good German maiden should. The room, in a newer part of the château and above the present kitchens, was plainly furnished but private, considering the crush in Vichy. The single, iron-framed bed, small desk, washbasin and jug, lamp and chair, armoire, *vase de nuit* and throw rug were neat as a pin.

Even the shrine could pass the stiffest of inspections. Crossed swastika flags flew over carefully laid-out knick-knacks. The stainless-steel Victory Rune of the SS; the Mann Rune, the sign of the German Women's Corps; the red lanyard, whistle and badge of an Untergauführerin, an under-leader of a group of BdMs, Bund Deutscher Mädel, the League of German Girls; sayings of the Führer on printed, unbleached cards in black Gothic script: Strength Through Joy; Blood and Honour; Learn to Sacrifice for your Fatherland; Who wants to Live has to Fight, and Whoever refuses to Fight in this World of Eternal Challenge has no right to Live.

'In your Race is your Strength,' he read aloud, picking up the card as if impressed.

There was the usual portrait photo of the Führer under the crossed swastikas and he knew that this carrier of National Socialist dogma, this little Nazi, would stand stiffly to attention on waking to the cold light of dawn or clanging bell from Herr Whatever, the major-domo, to proudly say, *'Morgens grüsse ich den Führer,'* et cetera, and before bed – this bed – *'Und abends danke ich dem Führer.'*

In the morning I salute my Führer. And in the evening I thank him.

'My boys grew up with this, too,' said Herr Kohler, having only glanced at her papers. He did not explain further, this giant with the cruel scar, but was, Ellinor said to herself, much saddened. Had he lost someone dear? she wondered.

He opened the little drawer of her bedside table but found no prayerbook or Bible, though the rest of her family were still staunchly Lutheran. He said, 'I remember Strasbourg as being a lovely city. Number 42 rue des Hallebardes ... the street of the pikes with the battleaxes at one end ... It's near the cathedral, your home?'

What did he want of her? she wondered. He had such a way with him. Easy-going and then suddenly he'd be after something, but would sometimes come at it obliquely. 'It's right in the cathedral's shadow, Herr Inspektor.'

'Born 7 September 1925. That was quite a year.'

He gave no further explanation of why the year of her birth had been so notable, but leafed through the thin pile of letters from home in that drawer, found her pessary and took it out, found the jar of petroleum jelly, too, and a clutch of *Kondoms* and, laying them with the other things, said, 'Four have been murdered, so you know why we're here and had best answer truthfully. Is that understood?'

There was nothing in his pale blue eyes but an unsettling emptiness. 'I know little, Herr Inspektor. The girls of whom you speak were informants, yes, but Herr Schleier was always wondering if they had given him everything they had overheard their lovers say when among themselves. Marie-Jacqueline seemed to treat it all as a joke – saying the pay was never enough for such a risk, and she constantly threatened to go on strike even though Herr Schleier could have had her taken away to one of the *Konzentrationslager*. Camille Lefèbvre was quite possibly the best, he thought. Everything of interest that Bousquet said in her company she would dutifully report in hopes that her husband would be freed and sent home, but that was not possible, though we were to continue to encourage her to think it was. Lucie Trudel had much to offer also and often brought papers and documents from the bank, but of late, she and the others had become "hesitant", he said, and needed to be reminded.'

Louis should have heard that. 'And Céline Dupuis?'

'Did not like reporting things at all and gave Herr Schleier much cause for concern. She was always asking when she would be permitted to leave Vichy and return to her daughter in Paris as promised.'

Then Céline, in addition to being very worried about being murdered, had realized the other just wasn't going to work and had agreed to give Pétain his little moment ... 'Were they recruited before or after they'd first taken up with their lovers?'

'After, of course. It's not hard, is it, to convince such girls to cooperate once they know what could happen not only to them but to their families? Temptation is also dangled but only as a sweetener.'

This kid was really something. 'And are the others who come here required to report what they overhear?'

Was he thinking of the rest of the cabaret singers and dancers, or of Blanche and Paul Varollier? 'The four who were killed were the most important and were recruited long before the Gestapo had an office here but, yes, the others also. Herr Schleier, you understand, does not report directly to Herr Gessler, but only to his superior officer, Herr Abetz.'

Whom the SS and SD seldom if ever listened to!

'You collect *goldene Zigarrenbände*,' he said, having opened her tin to fish about in it with a nicotine-stained forefinger.

'A few, for Albert Grenier when he comes. Blanche usually brings him when Monsieur Hébert or Frau Nietz, our German cook and housekeeper, feel it necessary. This old place . . .' She shrugged. 'We can't have vermin, can we? Albert should be sent away, I know, but . . . but he's very good at his job, so they must keep him, I think.'

'And on the night of 24 October last was Albert busy here?'

Had Albert watched – was this what the detective was wondering? Albert who had secretly been in love with each of those girls and had been so ashamed of them for their having had sex with men who were not their husbands. Sex like animals. 'He was asleep in the chapel. Monsieur Hébert has a straw mattress brought in for him and the bed made up. Albert always sleeps there when he visits. It's close to the kitchens and the main staircase to the cellars, and is "safe", he says, but he never looks at any of us. He's very shy, isn't he, as well as being . . . well, mentally retarded.'

'And Hébert and Albert, how do they get along?'

'Very well. Both of them are fond of the Maréchal. Monsieur Hébert is Albert's grand-uncle, so always Albert is asked for news. How is the Maréchal's health, does he still take his daily stroll in the Parc des Sources, or have the affairs of state so saddened him he no longer listens to his operetta recordings? And of course, now that he is having a wax sculpture made, is the sculptress doing a good job?'

'Wait a minute. How did you hear about that? Is Albert here now?'

'*Ach!* I thought you knew. He'll be in the stables or cellars, or out where the birds are kept.'

'And Blanche Varollier?'

'Is in the kitchens with the sculptress, I think. Both will be patiently waiting for him to finish so they can go back to town. Or maybe they're out with the birds? *Ja*, the sculptress did say she wanted to gather some feathers to take back to Paris for Madame Dupuis's little girl.'

8

Snail shells, along with oyster shells and fishbones, were being smashed to give the birds their necessary minerals. Dried apples, pears and apricots were being finely chopped with walnuts, chestnuts and acorns, carrots, beets, potatoes, brussels sprouts and the green tops of still-frozen leeks. Cheese was being crumbled, hard-boiled eggs, too. Dried redcurrants, seeds, buckwheat, barley and lentils by the handful were tossed in to be blended with the rest.

A truly domestic scene, given the shortages, thought St-Cyr wryly. Not a word was being spoken between Blanche Varollier, Inès Charpentier, Albert Grenier and the former owner of the château who'd put them to work and to silence, no doubt, at the present intrusion.

Alone on the squared lava-stone floor, the white rabbit named Michel stood on hind legs looking for more of the dried grapes it had found so sweet.

'I gave the rabbit to Céline, Inspector,' said Hébert, the loose, dark blue smock, the *biaude* they called it here in the Auvergne, the *sarrau* elsewhere, ending well below his knees to reveal the coarse black trousers and hobnailed boots of the peasant he'd never been. A man of sixty-five perhaps and of medium height and build, with rapidly thinning, greying dark brown hair that was worn straight back to expose an almost bald pate, the side whiskers iron-grey, the eyebrows bushy, the look in the faded blue eyes not straightforward but evasive. 'One breeds them for the table, of course,' he said, 'but I knew she could never have brought herself to kill it. Blanche felt it best to return it to me since her brother did not wish her to keep it in their flat.'

In Vichy one room becomes a 'flat'? snorted Kohler inwardly. Sandrine Richard, tense and silent, had remained behind them, in the arched doorway to a kitchen that couldn't have had much, if anything, done to it since the sixteenth century. There was a roaring fire in the blackened hearth beneath a mantelpiece that would have taken a small army to move. All along a side there were lava-brick stoves with black, sheet-iron tops above their fireboxes. No need for an overcoat in here, none either for a woollen pullover. Bunches of herbs hung from medieval spikes in the ceiling timbers. Rope after rope of garlic, onions, dried peppers, winter beans and dried mushrooms were there, too, with coils of sausage and hams that alone could bring a fortune in Paris and probably did, since why return empty vans?

Crocks of goose fat, lard and buttermilk stood alongside wicker-clad bottles of oil, wine and vinegar. Just who the hell was eating rats with all of this available?

The aromas of soup, spices, tobacco- and wood-smoke mingled with those of the cheese and other foods.

'Monsieur,' hazarded Louis in that deferential way of his that often hid so much, the rabbit hopping across the floor to examine detective shoes whose repeatedly broken and knotted laces caused it to gaze questioningly up at him, as if thawed soles needing better glue and nails had best be overlooked. 'Monsieur, the birds in that room . . .'

Hébert let his hands rest on the chopping block. 'One learns by experience, Inspector, but the taxidermy is not mine. What few attempts I made as a boy I gave to Blanche.'

Who had lied about them by saying they'd been attempts of her own, thought Kohler. A dove, a rook, a starling and a seagull! Blanche silently defied him to admonish her. Hands still gripping a pestle and mortar that were as old as the hills, she stood with shoulders squared, and only when he didn't say a thing, not even asking, Why did you want us not to know of this place? did that lovely slender throat of hers constrict.

Again, as before, her dark auburn hair was pinned up, but several wisps had come loose to spoil perfection and indicate nervousness.

The dark blue eyes were watchful. A breath was held.

Inès Charpentier, her mouth full of deftly palmed almonds but jaws stilled, had plunged her hands into one of the mixing bowls, not missing the exchange; Albert neither. Albert with a butcher's knife that bled beet juice on to the floor at the sculptress's feet.

'Though my grandfather shared his love of birds with me, Inspectors,' said Hébert, 'the taxidermy that so impresses was not his either, but that of the man to whom I owe all I know of the wild. Our head gamekeeper, long since deceased. Aurèle Mandrin.' Again his gaze was averted.

In 1754 Mandrin, since elevated to a folk hero, had been a smuggler from Dauphine, so the choice of name, beyond that of pure inspiration, was perhaps appropriate, thought St-Cyr.

'That room was always mine, Inspectors. I loved it as a boy and still do. The predatory instinct in their eyes is everywhere, especially when one looks out and up from that bed. One can't help but come to admire it, to want it too, and yet ... and yet, there is also that immense sense of freedom and joy that the power of flight must...'

'You let my husband use that room with that woman of his!' spat Sandrine.

Stung by this, Hébert tossed his head back but said nothing for a moment, then coldly, 'Madame, was he not the predator, she the quarry? In any case, I had no say whatsoever in the matter. As you well know, this château and its remaining sixty hectares, which had been in my family since before the Ducs de Bourbon were betrayed by their constable in 1527, were lost to others, due to bankruptcy. Your husband could well have chosen any room he wished, or was it that Mademoiselle Marie-Jacqueline Mailloux wanted to bring out the predator in him and loved to be hunted?'

Oh-oh, thought Kohler, only to hear the woman shriek, '*Maudit salaud,* how dare you?'

The custodian waved an indifferent hand. 'Ah, I dare because for me there is nothing left but that. Albert, are we ready?'

'Monsieur ...' interjected Louis.

'*Fornicateur, don't deny it!*' shouted Sandrine. '*we know everything that went on in this place!*'

'*Soixante-neuf,* madame?' taunted Hébert. '*Les grands specta-cles? La fellation, le sadomasochisme et le fétichisme?*'

'Orgies!' she shrilled, rocketing into the kitchen to take up one of the bowls and dash it on the floor. 'Rapist! We know you regularly kept a concubine in that room of yours, sometimes two and three of them to fly, eh? Fly while you and others took them, eh? In the ass, in the mouth, seldom where it's natural. *Salut, mon brave.*' She gave him the thumb. 'This one has a reputation, Inspectors, for both arranging the *liaisons sexuelles* of others and for often participating in them!'

'And your poor Madame Deschambeault, that sexually repressed neurotic, what of her son, madame?' shot back Hébert from behind his chopping block. 'A son whose taste runs to schoolgirls in uniform who must be held down? Has he got his eye on Monique de Fleury, eh, or need we ask?'

'Blanche ... Blanche has told us everything, monsieur.'

Oh-oh again, thought Kohler.

'*Vermine!*' hissed Hébert, turning on Blanche. 'Was it you who unlocked the doors and let those bitches in? An informer, is that it, eh? Well, is that how it was, Blanche? Did you think it would help your cause with that father of yours? Inspectors, this one and that brother of hers want what's rightfully theirs. To think that I offered them help, that I considered myself their friend and in no way asked anything for myself!'

He paused a moment, then said, 'Albert, *les oiseaux, mon vieux.* We can deal with this *lâcheuse* later.' This rat who has betrayed us.

'Monsieur, your birds can wait. While we have you gathered, we will settle a few things,' said Louis.

'Or call in Herr Gessler and his boys if needed,' said Hermann. 'Not that we want to, but if we have to, we will.'

265

'Then please don't forget that the château and grounds are an embassy, and that its employees, myself included, have diplomatic immunity.'

'But not from me, *mon fin*,' said Kohler. 'Not from me.'

The tension in the kitchen had become unbearable. Inès warned herself to be calm, to ignore the covert looks, the suspicion – even the outright hatred between Sandrine Richard and Charles-Frédéric Hébert – and to think clearly ... always clearly, but Albert was sitting so close to her, his right leg was deliberately pressed hard against her and he didn't move, wouldn't move, and was making her feel so uneasy. Did he sense she was an enemy? Did he somehow intuitively know she was a danger? What danger, please?

How could he? she asked. The butcher's knife lay on the table next to his thick, stubby fingers. Hébert had noticed this, too. Hébert who'd known Blanche and Paul's father ...

'Mademoiselle Charpentier,' said the Chief Inspector St-Cyr, 'I asked you a question.'

Madame Richard was watching her closely. Was the woman afraid the truth would come out, that she, the wife, had killed Marie-Jacqueline Mailloux in a fit of jealous rage as sworn?

Blanche Varollier was watching her, too, but Monsieur Hébert had now quickly averted his eyes. Again Inès heard St-Cyr ask his question – the letters that Lucie had carried to Paris for Céline, had they been posted to the studio on the rue du Douanier? To her studio.

One must either lie or confess, said Inès to herself, but to lie skilfully, one must impart elements of truth.

Mentally she crossed herself, kissed her fingertips as if the rosary was in her hands, and said silently, Bless me, Father, for I am afraid.

'Céline and I grew up together, Inspectors. She in that fine house of her parents on place Lucien-Herr and the rue Lhomond, myself with my uncle and aunt in a fourth-floor flat on the rue Tournefort. We met one day quite by ... Well, it wasn't by accident.' Could she manage a faint smile of memory? she asked herself and, more confidently when that was done, said, 'I'd planned to have my path cross hers, she mine, as it turned out, so when we bumped into each other, it was as if by accident, yet both of us knew we would.'

'You were lonely,' said Herr Kohler – was he always so sensitive? she wondered. 'You'd lost your father and then your mother. It was as if they'd abandoned you.'

'Yes . . . Yes, that's exactly how I felt as a child. Was it so wrong of me?'

'Mademoiselle,' said St-Cyr harshly, 'you are attempting to conceal things we need to know! Did you receive letters from Céline Dupuis that had been illegally carried across the Demarcation Line by Lucie Trudel?'

For which the penalty would be prison or transportation into forced labour. 'Yes. Yes, I did, Monsieur l'Inspecteur Principal. Céline was afraid.'

'Of what?' asked Herr Kohler, the sensitivity still there.

Blanche and Sandrine were again intently watching her, Hébert chancing a glance, Albert so still that she could feel the continued pressure and warmth of his leg. 'Of being killed – what else?' she heard herself hotly demand. 'I . . . I don't know what she and the other victims were involved in. Really, I don't. She . . . she did say she had to do things for *les Allemands* that she didn't want to, and that . . .' Now calm yourself, *ma chère*, she warned herself. Look at each of them as they sit around this lovely old table. 'That someone important had found out about what they'd had to do and, not liking it, had . . . had then had each of them killed – "removed" was the word she used. But I haven't got the letters, so can't prove this, since they made their little fires in my studio stove as soon as they'd been read.'

Herr Kohler scribbled something on a page of his notebook and thrust it across the table to that partner of his. Panic made the creamy skin of Blanche's cheeks become paler as the blood drained, but what had the Hauptmann Detektiv Inspektor Kohler just written to cause the girl such distress? wondered Inès. Was it:

They were all informants, Louis, but did Ménétrel order their removal? Ménétrel, Mademoiselle Blanche Olivier? An *éminence grise* and *confident* of the Maréchal's? A hater of *les Allemands* and lover of Vichy?

Blanche had gripped the edge of the table with both hands but, unlike Monsieur Hébert and Sandrine Richard or even Albert, hadn't noticed she'd done this.

St-Cyr *had* noticed, Inès told herself. He quickly wrote something in return and shoved it back across boards scratched and gouged through centuries – gouges, Mademoiselle Blanche, like the one in your brother Paul's wooden-soled shoe? she asked silently.

Blanche waited, knowing only too well the gouges in the table had been a reminder to the detectives, though none had been needed, but did she say, *Paul!* to herself, or, *Paul, my darling, beware?*

But what did St-Cyr write? wondered Inès. *Hermann, Blanche purchased a Choix Supreme on Saturday,* 30 *January at* 4.45 *p.m. the very day Lucie was killed and three days before Céline* – was that what he had jotted down? Or was it: *Paul Varollier must have taken Céline to his sister who waited in the Hall des Sources?*

The answer, if such it was, came with the Chief Inspector's next question. A shiver ran through her – Inès tried not to let Albert feel how nervous she was, but he couldn't have missed it.

'Mademoiselle, were those letters from anyone else?'

From Capitaine Auguste-Alphonse Olivier, Inspector? From the *compagnon d'armes* and dearest friend of my father, Lieutenant Pierre-Thomas Charpentier, who was put before the firing squad on orders from Général Pétain, orders that Auguste-Alphonse had then to carry out?

Blanche's cheeks had stiffened; the look in those dark blue eyes had hardened. Charles-Frédéric Hébert, the organizer of the little games of love, lust, rape and predator power, was watching her closely and no longer averting his gaze.

Albert's fingers touched the haft of that butcher's knife . . . Did St-Cyr ask himself of her, wondered Inès, Are you the threat

Albert Grenier thinks you are? Always sniffing around, drifting in and out of our company, turning up at the most opportune times – coming here early this morning even though you must have had to leave your boarding house just after curfew to walk – yes, walk – through the bitter cold to meet Albert, whom you knew would be in his 'little nest', putting the coffee on?

Your valise, mademoiselle. Did you leave it there again? You must have.

Father, help me, she said silently, and then ... then, 'The letters were from no one else, Inspector. Céline and I were like twins. Each of us shared equally the life of the other. Annette Dupuis is my goddaughter; I was bridesmaid at Céline's wedding, and it was I who found her when she had slashed her wrists.'

Mon Dieu, the control, Hermann, thought St-Cyr. Those sea-green eyes aren't full of tears as they should be, but reveal a coldness that brings back the very words she spoke when rescued at the stables and told to cry: 'I can't. I haven't cried in years.' But of course she had cried at the sight of her friend.

Some strands of the fine, reddish hair were hastily brushed from her brow; the freckled, turned-up nose was touched with a knuckle.

'I am what I say I am, Inspectors. When Céline convinced herself to take the job here in Vichy, we vowed we'd meet; either I would visit her, or she me. Monsieur Gilbert, my directeur at the Musée Grévin, was well aware of this and when the opportunity arose, he allowed me to come only for me to then find my dearest friend had indeed been murdered.'

'Hence her interest in the corpse, Louis,' said Herr Kohler gently.

'*Merde alors, idiot*, must you always go soft when the pretty ones put the squeeze on! Mademoiselle, that little dissertation in no way justifies the answer you gave my partner: that death has always been of interest to the artist in you.'

There are enemies and there are enemies, she warned herself, and was Herr Kohler not taking just that line of approach so that his partner and friend could then be hated, himself liked, so as to prise further answers? 'I couldn't tell you the truth, could I?' she heard herself ask. 'I didn't even know who either of you really were or what you were doing in Vichy.'

'You most certainly did!' said the Chief Inspector and, reaching for that cold and empty pipe of his, took it up, only to put it down as if furious with her! 'What brand, please, of cigars did that director of yours give you to bring to the Maréchal as a gift? Choix Supremes?'

'Yes. Yes, I believe that is what they were but I had to hand them over to Dr Ménétrel, so am not positive.'

'Albert . . . Albert, *mon vieux*,' interjected Hébert, 'please go to the storehouse in the big barn and get the Chief Inspector a tin of our Dutch pipe tobacco. The one that smells so good, *n'est-ce pas?*' A black iron key was taken from a ring and slid across the table to his grand-nephew. 'Bring the Inspector Kohler one of the tins of fifty Wills Gold Flake cigarettes. These last are courtesy of the RAF, Inspectors, and were included, I believe, in some of the *parachutages* they have now taken to illegally dropping to the terrorists.'

The Résistance, as if that battle, in itself, justified everything else, thought Inès, relieved that Albert hadn't said to his grand-uncle, I *can't* hear you!

Madame Richard, though wanting badly to leave the château and get free of the detectives and of Hébert, had listened avidly to everything, but had remained apart as much as possible. Forgotten, her cigarette, the third, Inès told herself, gave to the room its little pillar of smoke . . . Smoke that reminded one of the burning barns and farmhouses during the Blitzkrieg and the exodus from Paris when Annette and she had become separated from Céline and her parents. Their automobile was found in flames, as were countless others. The road had been a carnage of shattered prams, wagons and bodies . . . bodies everywhere, the wounded crying out for help, having been machine-gunned and bombed by Messerschmitts and Stukas bent on clearing the roads for advancing armour.

Albert had taken the butcher's knife – *why?* she asked. Had he been afraid she might have put it somewhere – on the floor under her feet, perhaps?

Or had he felt Herr Kohler or St-Cyr would remove it?

'Mademoiselle,' said Herr Kohler, having received the curtest of nods from his partner and friend – and how was it, please, that these two could be friends even if St-Cyr was, as Monsieur Olivier had confided, a patriot and Kohler the arch-doubter of Germanic invincibility and Nazi dogma? Like brothers? she had asked Olivier. Not quite, he'd replied, but be careful. The two are birds of a feather. A feather!

'Mademoiselle,' Herr Kohler continued, 'your father and this one's.' He indicated Blanche. 'Was Olivier forced to give the order after the Battle of Chemin des Dames and the mutinies of May–June 1917? Did Pétain order him to do it?'

She must give the faintest possible answer as if stricken, thought Inès, and then ... then must divert their attention to Blanche. 'I ... I can't believe it possible, Inspectors, but have no way of knowing. Mademoiselle Blanche, I ... I thought your name was Varollier?'

'*It is!*' came the harsh retort from one who knew only too well that she and her brother had been using Edith Pascal to get them repeatedly into that house of their father's when he was absent from it. Olivier had been adamant about this, though he hadn't yet confronted Mademoiselle Pascal. I'll wait, he had said, until I know more.

'Then perhaps you can enlighten the inspectors?' said Inès.

You bitch! – everything in Mademoiselle Varollier-Olivier's expression registered the thought.

'A knife,' said the Chief Inspector and, taking it out, laid Noëlle Olivier's little legacy open on the table as Albert returned.

The Laguiole was gone, Albert's shriek of anguish at the sight of it still reverberating. He had snatched it away as the tins and butcher's knife had fallen from his hands. No one had been prepared for his reaction, thought Inès, sickened by what had happened. No one. It's blade had gleamed, for it had been lying on the table pointing straight at her. At her!

'Inspectors,' cautioned Hébert grimly as he turned to pick up one of the tins. 'Let him be. I'll get the knife back.'

'My bag. My papers,' cried Inès. 'I wouldn't have killed Céline. How could I have done such a thing?'

'Louis, I'll go.'

'*Et moi?*' she shrilled, frantic now, for Albert had also taken her handbag and lost papers were all but impossible to replace and would cause extreme trouble, especially since she was not in her designated area of residence!

Though the reaction had been a shock, deliberately pointing the knife at the sculptress had done its work. 'Hermann, take her along. Mademoiselle Varollier, please show them the way.'

'Try the chapel first, and then the cellars, Herr Kohler,' shot Hébert and, when they'd left the kitchen, 'Let us hope Albert behaves himself. That boy can be a master of deceit and trickery. Certainly he worshipped each of those murdered girls but was also most distressed to find them participating – "doing filthy things", he called them – things that mother of his constantly condemns in the sight of God while the boy is on his knees with her.'

'And Blanche, monsieur. Did she "participate"?'

Sandrine Richard had paused while lighting herself another cigarette, noted Hébert. The slut was still listening intently, but had everything now suddenly gone her way? 'Blanche didn't join in, Inspector. She and her brother are very close – too close, perhaps. One never knows with twins, does one, especially when of the opposite sex and living alone? They remained indifferent – aloof perhaps – or so I had thought until she betrayed us so that this one could then drown Marie–Jacqueline and hide her guilt behind others.'

A sweet little smile would be best, thought Sandrine. 'And did Julienne Deschambeault smother Lucie Trudel? Did her madness allow for that, monsieur, and the hiding of the corpse in an armoire? Did Élisabeth de Fleury, that most gentle of women, drive that knife into Céline Dupuis after first smoking a cigar, something Élisabeth would never do since she can't stand the smell of them and vomits every time!'

Ah *nom de Dieu*, had it been said deliberately? wondered St-Cyr. And what of the armoire? Had Albert done it, madame?

'Madame de Fleury would have nothing if Honoré deserted her, Inspector,' said Hébert. 'A woman with two young boys and a teenaged daughter? The jealous wives hired an assassin. If enough is paid – and this one must have paid Blanche Olivier to inform on us; please let us not forget that last name – an assassin can be found even in Vichy with the Garde Mobile on the alert twenty-four hours a day!'

'But not, monsieur, when Céline was to offer herself to the Maréchal,' countered Sandrine swiftly.

Hébert tossed his head back as if struck and gestured with both hands. 'It was perfect, wasn't it, madame? Henri-Claude Ferbrave and his boys are given the night off – you would have known of this. Admit it!'

'And Ferbrave, monsieur?' she seethed. 'Did he do the job, eh? That one has got too big for his boots, Inspector. Why not take a look in the "warehouse" this one sent his psychotic nephew to? Ask, then, how big Henri-Claude has become?'

Psychotic . . . ? Did she feel she had to drive the nail in? wondered St-Cyr.

'All she wants is to protect her family's fortune, Inspector. Hers and that of her husband. Grasping . . . always grasping, eh, madame? Well, grasp this then. Albert saw you talking privately to Henri-Claude last Friday at noon. "Huddled," he said, and . . .'

Hébert ran a thumbnail through the paper seals of the tin of Wills cigarettes and, opening it, shook them out sufficiently for one to be easily removed.

'Huddled, Inspector, and money handed over. A "bundle", Albert said.'

'I . . .' Ah *sacré*! 'All right, I paid Henri-Claude twenty thousand.'

'Francs or Reichskassenscheine?' shot Hébert, his cigarette still unlit.

Flustered, she stubbed hers out. 'The Occupation marks. He . . . he wouldn't take francs. He said that . . . that in Paris some of the shopkeepers were afraid they'd soon be discontinued.'

'Four hundred thousand francs, madame?' hazarded the Chief Inspector, giving their value.

'I *didn't* pay to have him kill them! I . . . I paid for lingerie and perfume, a special order, and . . . and for a small collection of objects of virtu in tortoiseshell. A cigar case for the pocket, a cigarette case, comb-and-brush set and box for the cufflinks . . . Alain André has always been fascinated by the fact that, after heating and pressing, the shells of certain types of sea-turtle can be used for such things. He loves the look and feel of them. A gift, that's all it was. A set Henri-Claude had seen in an antique shop and on the rue du Faubourg St-Honoré. I paid in advance and for that purpose and no other.'

'Other than to convince her husband to return to the nest, Inspector, since the one he'd been so deliciously roosting on had become ice-cold!'

'*Bâtard*, why are you trying to pin her killing on me?'

'Yes, why are you?' asked St-Cyr.

'One only tries to help,' said Hébert.

A lighter was found, the cigarette lit, the custodian taking up the butcher's knife to start in on preparing more feed for his birds. Everything was finely and swiftly chopped, as he had done thousands of times before.

'Each of those girls massaged the neck of a collabo, Inspector,' he said gruffly, not looking up from the butcher's block. 'Find the leader of the FTPs and you have your man. Setting an example has always been foremost in the minds of the communists.'

'*À chacun son* Boche?' snorted Sandrine. To each his German, the communists were rumoured to urge one another. '*À chacun sa putain*, eh? Why not tell him whom you have steadfastly blamed and hated for your losing this château? Our resident recluse whose housekeeper's brothers are railway workers,

Inspector. Auguste-Alphonse Olivier, the father who disinherited Blanche and Paul Varollier and sent them away at the age of twelve when this one, having caused the suicide of their mother, forced Olivier to resign in shame and leave his bank so that others could take over. Others led by no other than Charles-Frédéric Hébert, who was the first and most vocal of those to call his former friend and business partner a cuckold!'

The slut, but how good of her to have inadvertently responded as wished when pricked! snorted Hébert inwardly. 'Alain André enjoyed Marie-Jacqueline, madame. He often said that fucking her just once made up for all the years of boredom. Now, please, Inspector, my birds. They get nervous if not fed on time.'

Through the iron-grilled stained-glass windows of the little chapel where Albert slept when at the château, light filtered, causing slashes of ruby red, emerald green, dark blue and amber to be cast upon the floor. The crucifix, to one side behind the stone slab of the altar with its antependium of gold brocade on white, was nailed to the wall with spikes as thick as her thumbs, thought Inès uncomfortably.

Black *torchères* with beeswax candles flanked the arched sanctuary. A banner hung above, and to her left. The lectern, to that side of the altar, though all but hidden in shadow, still held what must be its original vellum-bound, illuminated book of prayers for every Mass of the year.

The water in the stone font was frozen solid; the worn black prie-dieux exuded centuries of piety. These simple wooden stands had plain, forward-pointing boxes for the knees and three thin stilts that rose straight up to the briefest of forearm rests and, *Ave Maria grátia plena: Dóminus tecum. Benedicta tu in muliéribus: et benedictus fructus ventris tui...*

Without even thinking, she crossed herself and genuflected as she ducked her head and touched her brow and lips.

'Albert's not here,' said Blanche, a breath escaping softly.

The chapel would have held forty, if crowded, thought Kohler. Two iron rings and an inscription marked a tomb in the floor of the sanctuary. '*Honoré Hébert*', he read aloud. '*From 1480 to 1527, Chevalier de Charmeil et de Vichy, Compagnon d'Armes des Ducs de Bourbon. Sans peur et sans reproche.*' Without fear and without reproach.

'It's one of the coolest places in summer,' said Blanche, who had nervously stayed just inside the entrance.

Dear God, where was Albert? wondered Inès. She had the feeling that coming here wouldn't be good for her, that it was the beginning of the end.

'Did couples use this for their lovemaking?' she asked. Wrong of them if true, of course, but then so little was right about this place Céline had found herself in.

It was Blanche who said, 'Is that what she confided in those letters of hers?'

'We ... we didn't discuss things like that.'

'Ménétrel ... did she mention him?' demanded Blanche.

Inès told herself not to answer. Blanche would get angrier then – that had been anxiety in her voice, hadn't it?

'Céline told you Ménétrel would let her go home to Paris but only if she first went to Pétain. Ménétrel controls everything. Whether we like it or not, we're all in thrall to the doctor. Surely she confided that?'

'Did you take care of her for him? Did he order you to kill her?' asked Inès fiercely from behind the altar. 'She'd been an informant. She'd given away state secrets she'd overheard.'

'I ... I did no such thing,' retorted Blanche, flustered.

These two, thought Kohler. Had Céline told the one about the other?

'You bought a Choix Supreme the afternoon of Lucie's murder,' he interjected.

'For Nathalie Bénoist, one of the cabaret dancers!'

'But she prefers the El Rey del Mundo Demi-Tasse.'

'I ... I made a mistake, that's all.'

'A five-hundred-franc one?' he taunted.

'Not when Nathalie provided the cash.'

'A woman with two little boys she boards at a nearby farm?'

'She pays the price, but gets it back later.'

'In here?' asked Herr Kohler, still baiting her.

'Sometimes. In summer, of course.'

'*Nackttänze auch?*'

Nude dancing also. 'Sometimes,' countered Blanche hotly.

'And Albert?' asked Inès. 'Did he watch from ... from in there?' She indicated the sacristy whose stained-glass window let in a little light. One had to duck one's head to enter. 'There's a smell,' she said.

'Rancid oil,' said Herr Kohler, brushing past her to stand, stooped, in the enclosure, for people hadn't been nearly so tall when this place had been built.

Blanche did not enter.

A large, coloured poster of the Maréchal in uniform stared at them, the seven stars on his sleeve, with the phrase *Je fais à la France le don de ma personne pour atténuer son malheur*, under it. I make to France the gifts of my person to lessen her misfortune.

Upturned snail shells were on the table, the altar Albert had built. There was still oil in some of them, their wicks blackened, the shells placed in rows that pointed to the poster. Cigar bands had been pressed flat and these lay alongside the little lamps. There was a plaster bust of Pétain – one of the thousands and thousands that were still sold in shops or found in family shrines all over France. A mug bore his benevolent countenance; flags and coins, the image of the *Francisque*. A medallion of him hung on a tricolour ribbon. Printed cards gave quotes, pamphlets bits of his speeches. The Lord's Prayer had even been rewritten under Ménétrel's guidance, with Pétain as God on earth.

A wire – a length of the thin and flexible wire Albert used for his snares – was there as if in dedication.

A knife – a Laguiole, open so that its blade and softly curving haft lay between the rows of snail shells and cigar bands – was also there. 'But ... but it has a corkscrew,' Inès heard herself saying, aghast at what they'd found and at what Albert had done. 'He's kept Noëlle Olivier's knife and has left another.'

And now you're gut-sick, thought Kohler. 'It's a man's, and

nothing fancy. The usual for the Auvergnat shepherd or peasant. This one's seen a good fifty years of use but is still razor sharp.'

'But why did he leave it?' she bleated. Would Albert cut her throat? Would he knife her in the chest?

'Probably he thought you wouldn't even notice the substitution, Inspector,' snorted Blanche on joining them, her voice grating. 'Albert's often like that. If he can fool you, he will, but sometimes he doesn't quite think it through.'

Beneath the knife there was a card on which the motto of Les Jeunes de France had been printed: *Toujours Prêts*. Always Ready. Beneath that, and folded tightly, was the letter the Ministry of Education had sent Albert's parents, telling them the boy was unfit for the Chantiers de Jeunesse, the young men, the over-twenties of France, who had each to do their national service of five months of physical training, community service and rural tasks, in lieu of service in the Army which, of course, now no longer existed, even as the much-shrunken Army of the Armistice.

'Albert couldn't have read it, Inspector, and probably believes he really is one of les Jeunes,' said Blanche.

The date was 13 March 1941.

He'd been twenty-one then, thought Inès, was now nearly twenty-three. Turning swiftly aside, she threw up the grey National she had had with weak ersatz coffee at 5 a.m., and the nuts and dried fruit she'd palmed in the kitchen.

Just emptied herself, poor kid, thought Kohler. Couldn't have stopped, but sympathy ought not to be allowed to intrude.

'Come on. He must have gone into the cellars.'

Guinea fowl made their racket, quail too, and ducks. A peacock shrieked.

'Inspector,' spat Hébert, turning swiftly to block the way, the wind tugging at the blue smock, the open black cable-knit cardigan and black felt fedora. A large bowl of feed was in the crook of each arm, the cages just beyond him. 'That Richard woman and those other bitches have it in for me. Always

278

gossiping, always the little tête-à-têtes with Madame la Maréchale at their "committee meetings". Committee of what, I ask? Of dried-up housewives who are terrified of losing their meal tickets!'

Ring-necked pheasants croaked and beat their wings, a bantam rooster cocked its head. 'Monsieur . . .' began St-Cyr, only to hear Hébert retort as if stung, 'Please let me finish! Oh for sure, in 1924 and '25, when they were not together in Paris, I allowed my friend Henri Philippe Omer Pétain and Noëlle Olivier to meet in secret here to spend a few quiet hours in each other's arms. What else are friends for when the dice have already been cast? Auguste-Alphonse had been told many times by myself and others that the Maréchal was not the first of her lovers. *Mon Dieu*, he was too busy at that bank of ours, too concerned with squandering our money on bringing a modern telephone exchange to Vichy. Officers . . . for years we've had a military hospital. Not the badly wounded, you understand. Colonials mostly. Convalescents and men on special leave who came, and still do, for the cure. Noëlle would often help entertain the boys with games, walks, *thés dansants* and concerts, *bals masqués* and cabaret nights in which she loved to take part and was always the favourite. *Le cigare, la figure*, the black stockings, eh, and garters. The bawdy songs and gestures.'

He paused. He waited to see if his words had sunk in, so one had best let him talk it out!

'Please remember that Auguste-Alphonse was away for all but a few weeks during the '14–18 war, Inspector. Four years can be an eternity to a young woman who is *très sensuelle, très adorable et élégante* and outstanding even among the Parisian *hautes mondaines* who came to Vichy for *la saison des curistes* after that war. Men were always at her feet – Auguste was well aware of this and proud of what he'd married. Ah yes, he loved to show her off to friends and business associates! But is it any wonder then that she found what she wanted in the *buffet* he himself had provided?'

Cage after cage faced the sun, each with its shelter, the tiled roof of the barn extending well out for further protection.

'The bank, monsieur. You said, "Our bank".'

Hébert continued to the nearest of the enclosures, that of the guinea fowl, whose little tribe hurried relentlessly round and round it.

'*Oui*. It was his and mine and that of others,' he said, turning sideways to look, not directly at him, but slightly downwards.

'During the war I had to take over in his absence and things went well. It was only later, when he returned, that the problems started. A fortune I lost when that bank went bust in '33. A fortune!'

'And now?'

'Now I am little different than the cuckold himself!'

Fresh hay had been strewn about the enclosures, their shelters insulated with it.

'Ah *bon*,' he said. 'Albert never forgets – one doesn't need to remind him, Inspector. Once a task has been assigned, he does it. Look . . . the snow has even been swept from each of the cages!'

'The telephone exchange, monsieur?'

'The old one was perfectly suitable. Adjacent to the Hôtel Ruhl and only needing a small amount of upgrading. We should have left it at that. Instead, what did our chairman do but plunge the bank's resources into the most up-to-date exchange outside of Paris? A new PTT, new building, new everything, including far more employees than were ever needed. And where did he insist on putting it? In what had always been the Auvergne's loveliest of covered markets on the rue du Marché and avenue du Président Doumer. A meeting place, yes, yes, of course, for all our citizens but one we loved not for the chance to queue up and listen in to the telephone conversations of others, but for itself!'

'But . . . but in 1933 he had long since resigned from the bank.'

'Having sowed the seeds of its demise!'

The new Poste, Télégraphe et Téléphone hadn't been opened until 1928, or was it 1930? wondered St-Cyr, deciding on the latter. The old PTT had been left empty for a time, due to the Depression, but would surely have now been put to use.

Feed was scattered, Hébert going from cage to cage by interconnecting side doors. Ring-necked pheasants, partridges, even a covey of ruffed grouse from Canada and two pair of snow-white ptarmigan were all spoken to, the custodian frequently getting down on his knees to coax the birds to eat from his hand.

'They are God's creatures,' he said, looking sideways up through the wire. 'Céline and Albert often shared this little task. The girl loved to help him. Never the harsh word from her if he was clumsy or did something he then tried to hide. In turn, he adored her and had, I'm certain – yes, certain – all those confused feelings of guilt and apprehension a young man has for a girl he secretly wants. When she told him she was using quills to write postcards to her daughter, Albert plucked tail feathers for her until I had to tell him to stop!'

Rock doves were cradled; captured finches perched on the brim of his hat.

'Albert wouldn't have hurt any of those girls, Inspector. No matter what you hear from others, understand that my grand-nephew is incapable of such a thing. Certainly he has uncontrollable rages when things seem not to be going the way he believes they should be, and certainly he has sworn to protect and help the Maréchal in the best way he can, but a killer . . . ? Ah no, it's impossible.'

A master of deceit and trickery, a prude, and now the rages? 'Olivier, monsieur. Would he be aware his children are in Vichy?'

'Aware? Not likely. Edith wouldn't have told him, and neither would those two. That father of theirs does not forgive easily, Inspector. Disinheriting them? Blaming them as much as myself for the suicide of their mother? Claiming they wanted her to leave him for Pétain, for the father of her unborn child and that they, too, weren't even his own? His own! The man was insane and still is. A recluse who hides from his community and former associates? A man who hates!'

'A killer?'

One could not gesture with the hands full but could toss the head. 'It's possible. Weren't the victims marriage smashers? Hadn't one of them a husband who'd gone off to war only to discover from behind barbed wire that his wife had been playing around in his prolonged absence?'

'Camille Lefèbvre.' The birds, chickens of several varieties – white, russet, big, small – were making a hell of a racket!

'And what of the rest of the cabaret group Céline was a part of, Inspector? Aurélienne Tavernier also has a husband who is a prisoner of war, as do Carole Navaud and Nathalie Bénoist. Your killer uses Noëlle's knife on Céline who wears his dead wife's earrings to a *liaison* with the man who had made him a cuckold? Wears even the perfume that wife was so fond of because Henri Philippe had bought it for her? What more evidence do you need?'

'A dress was left in Céline's room . . .'

'Dress . . . ? What dress? Come, come, you must tell me.'

'A halter-neck . . .'

'Silvery, with see-through panels?'

'High heels to match.'

Flustered – sickened – his mind so obviously in a turmoil that he felt betrayed, Hébert turned swiftly away. 'Monsieur, that dress, do you know of it?' demanded St-Cyr.

'Know of it?' Hébert sucked in a breath, held one of the hens too tightly, then released it. 'Who wouldn't among those of us who'd seen her in it? Noëlle . . . Noëlle wore it to the party I threw here in the late summer of 1924 to celebrate the Victor of Verdun's return to Vichy.'

Then why can't you turn to face me? wondered St-Cyr. The chickens crowded round the custodian who, oblivious to their commotion, knelt among them, forgetting entirely that they were now greedily ravaging his bowls of feed.

Merde, who the hell had put that dress in Céline's room for St-Cyr and that partner of his to find? wondered Hébert. Had it been Auguste or . . . or Edith? Could it have been them? How could it? Had they learned of the earrings and the knife?

'Auguste-Alphonse felt particularly honoured to have Henri Philippe stay at his house, Inspector, before coming out here to spend a few days away from the crowd. A man of the soil. Noëlle visited frequently. Alone, of course, for Auguste was far too busy to take notice. There was, I believe, a strand of blue sapphires which Noëlle wore with that dress and the earrings. Like everyone else, Henri Philippe couldn't help but take notice of her at that party, even though married himself.'

Find the leader of the Francs-Tireurs et Partisans, Hébert had said in the kitchen, but did he suspect Olivier was that leader?

He'd have had him arrested! And what of the dress and the necklace – Hébert hadn't known of their having been left in that room, had been badly shaken by the news. 'Monsieur, the Bollinger Cuvée Spéciale, the 1925, and Rémy-Martin Louis III?'

Had the detectives told no one else of their having found the dress? wondered Hébert. He'd have to stand, would have to face this Sûreté. 'Ménétrel let it be known he was going to have de Fleury present a little gift to Henri Philippe. Naturally I searched my mind for something suitable, something which would also remind the Maréchal of a friendship gone cold since the loss of fortune. I'd had an equally fine Cuvée and cognac sent to the couple's room that first summer. What better way, then, for me to toast his latest conquest and remind him of our friendship? A man in his eighty-seventh year whose wife, I must tell you, when she discovered the affair with Noëlle, took his service revolver out of a drawer and told him in no uncertain terms to choose!'

Ah *bon*, the ultimate target, then, and either the betrayed wives as the killers or the cuckold. 'Yet it wasn't Céline who drank the Cuvée, monsieur. It was Marie-Jacqueline Mailloux.'

A last cage was ignored but for a few handfuls of hurriedly tossed feed, the hawks and eagles still to come.

'Didn't you find the bottles I sent for Céline to take with her? A picnic hamper? Saint-Louis crystal, caviar, a little pâté, a baguette and some of the Cantal and Saint-Nectaire? I packed these especially for the Maréchal and even included a corkscrew he would not fail to recall. My knife ... ah, not so handsome as

Noëlle's and much worn, but still ... I knew he'd recall it and remember the affair.'

'A Laguiole?' hazarded St-Cyr.

'Why, yes. It was one I'd had since a boy. Albert can confirm, since it was he I asked to deliver the hamper to Céline at Chez Crusoe early last Tuesday evening.'

Albert ...

'Inspector, the hamper ...'

'Has not been found.'

'Was it taken – intercepted?' demanded Hébert.

'Perhaps.'

The Laguiole, with its opened blade, was fixed in memory as Inès fought to see and again stumbled blindly. Cascades of what must be seepage clung to the passage walls of these cellars they were now in, cellars that had been built in the twelfth or thirteenth century. At each breath's escape she knew a little cloud of vapour would appear in the torchlight but still she couldn't see a thing. Blanche was ahead of her, blocking the light; Herr Kohler well out in front of her, and with the torch. Water trickled distantly, the taste of its sulphur in the air and on the tongue. And wasn't that what Vichy was all about? she demanded. A coldness that made one cringe, a warmth that was as if subterranean and filled with innuendo, its sound constantly hollow, the air acid?

Céline hadn't mentioned the château's spring in her letters, nor had Monsieur Olivier said anything about it. But, then, after his first letter, the rest, without names or addresses on their little envelopes of thin paper, had been concealed in those from Céline, and she had had to courier them to others to his contacts in Paris, had *wanted* to do this. Never the same café, never, even, the same contact. No names there either. Just greet as if old friends – the contact always recognizing her from a photo perhaps?

She didn't know, was not to know, and had accepted this. Simply telephoned a number from a café no one could trace her to when a letter arrived, the time and place of meeting then being assigned eight hours before that given and always two streets away to the south from the one given. Even the telephone number to call had changed with each letter.

Wear Shalimar, Céline had said in her last letter. *That way, if anything happens to me, M. Olivier will know it's really you.*

St-Cyr had been quick to notice the perfume but would he see that she'd worn it expressly for that purpose?

These days so much had to be hidden. And, yes, Céline had said she would be wearing it too.

'Stay here,' said Herr Kohler.

'*No!*' implored Blanche.

'Please don't leave us,' Inès whispered.

'I'll only be a minute. Either Albert took the left fork or the right.'

'Or went straight ahead,' she managed but, suddenly, Herr Kohler was gone from them and Blanche and she were left alone to listen in the dark. No images, no anything. Just a deep, dark, black emptiness before her eyes ... Her eyes.

He made no sound, gave no further indication of his whereabouts, must even have switched off the torch. Had he really done so? Had he?

Uncannily the water bubbled forth, its sound echoing in the distance.

'Albert's unpredictable,' swore Blanche, not liking their being left alone. 'Edith Pascal can get him to do anything simply by bullying and because he's terrified of being berated by her.'

Somehow Inès found her voice. 'Did he put the rats in Lucie's bed?'

'He'd have taken the livers if he had, but Edith could well have done it herself. Edith hates Pétain and all he stands for. She blames him not just for my father's rejection of her but for all the pain he's suffered.'

'So she killed the four of them, is this what you're saying?'

To not even ask about Edith first implied knowing her. 'Just what the hell are you really doing in Vichy?' grated Blanche.

285

'Albert's certain there's something wrong with your being here. He wouldn't have taken that knife otherwise.'

'And my bag? Why would he have taken that?'

'To find out everything he can about you.'

'But he can't read more than a few words. Even if he looks at my *carte d'identité* and travel permits, he won't be able to understand them.'

And you're still so very afraid of him, aren't you? silently demanded Blanche. 'He smells and gets the feel of them. He'll try to surprise us first and then ... then will hole up somewhere to examine every little thing you've got in that bag of yours. Be grateful you parked that valise of yours with his father or he'd have taken it too. Admit that you met with Lucie in Paris.'

'Céline's letters were simply posted to me!'

'You're lying! Lucie told me you'd met each time she went to Paris.'

'Now you're the one who's lying!' cried Inès as Blanche grabbed her by the arm only to suddenly release her hold.

'Look, let's stop this!' swore Blanche. 'Let's help each other. My father was the best friend of yours. Céline had him write to you about the firing squad.'

They'd been whispering urgently but had yet to realize this, thought Kohler, having moved back along the corridor to stand nearby.

'Céline did no such thing,' countered the sculptress. 'Oh for sure she knew Monsieur Olivier was my father's *compagnon d'armes*. Since the age of seven or eight she had to listen to the details of my searchings for what really happened to Papa. One evening she took it upon herself to speak to Monsieur Olivier in the English Garden by the river. Tears leaped into his eyes at her mention of my father and, asking her to follow in a few moments, he led the way to his house. They did not go inside because Edith Pascal was there. They simply sat and talked in the dark.'

And he told you a little about Edith, did he? 'Admit it, letters were exchanged. Not only did you write to Céline, but to my father!'

But why, please, does this upset you so? wondered Inès. And if a little is yielded, will not the same be done in return? 'All right, we exchanged letters. Lucie and I did meet. The Louvre, the Sorbonne, the Bibliothèque Nationale, the Musée Grévin . . . She first found me there, but after that would always telephone ahead or leave a message.'

'Didn't you think that dangerous?'

All calls were monitored, all such messages were read by others, but was Mademoiselle Blanche fishing for something else, a Résistance connection? wondered Inès. 'Of course I thought it dangerous – the penalty alone for carrying or receiving such letters is extremely harsh and totally unreasonable, but . . . but Lucie was my only link with Céline and it was the only way I'd know she was back in the city.'

'And your only link with my father!' spat Blanche. 'Did he tell you he knew Paul and I were in Vichy and had been in that house?'

Olivier hadn't even mentioned them in his one and only letter to her, but when they'd met yesterday he had revealed as a warning that he was certain they'd been in the house, certain that they had somehow forced Edith Pascal to let them in when he was absent. 'You took that knife and the earrings from your mother's room, didn't you? Your brother's footprints were found in the snow outside the Hall des Sources.'

There'd been both sadness and defeat in the sculptress's voice, thought Kohler.

'Those footprints were from earlier on Tuesday,' said Blanche tightly. 'Paul had to go to the Hôtel du Parc late that afternoon. Ménétrel had asked to see him again.'

Had she weighed up that answer before giving it? wondered Kohler.

'See him about what?' demanded Inès.

'The STO, what else?'

And wouldn't you know it, a little blackmail of the doctor's, thought Kohler. The Service de Travail Obligatoire, the forced-labour draft. All young men born between 1 January 1912 and 31 December 1921 had to register . . .

'Paul's not well,' offered Blanche, her voice conciliatory. 'If selected, he'd not come back. We both knew this.'

The sculptress's sigh was heavy. 'So you agreed to do what Ménétrel asked in exchange for a letter exempting your brother?'

'After the photos were taken at that party in October, Ménétrel demanded that we tell him what had been going on at the château – that Céline and the others had been Herr Abetz's key informants and that there'd been a huge breach of security. In a rage, he threatened not only Paul and me, but must have made certain that Honoré de Fleury knew exactly what had been going on and that Céline would go to Pétain's room or else!'

Then Bousquet, Deschambeault and Richard must also have been told by Ménétrel that their girlfriends were informants, thought Inès. Time had then been necessary in order to decide the most appropriate course of action to rid them of the problem.

'We had to take the earrings and a sample of her perfume from Mother's room on Monday and give them to Ménétrel. We had no other choice!' cried Blanche.

'But why the earrings and the Shalimar?' demanded Inès.

Why not the dress and the rest also? wondered Kohler, or did Blanche not know of them?

'To remind the Maréchal of Maman,' said Blanche.

'But she wore only the earrings and the perfume, didn't she?' said Kohler, causing them both to suck in a breath at the unexpected nearness of him and Blanche to blurt, 'Only . . . ? What is this, please? Was something else taken? The knife . . . who took the knife?'

He would not answer her, thought Kohler. Blinded by the torch beam, they blinked and tried to shield their eyes, the sculptress having gagged in panic and moved herself a good two metres from the translator.

The raptors, the birds of prey, were some distance from the others, separated by a screen of chestnut, oak and fir and long stacks of cordwood. Much larger enclosures allowed for exercise but not for soaring high on thermals or hunting over field and farm or marsh. Small openings, in the adjacent barn, allowed for shelter; each hawk or eagle kept itself to itself, with the owls more distant from them.

Still, in all, they were a sad, cold lot, thought St-Cyr, looking along the cages. Perches here and there – dead branches being used, their curled-up leaves caked with snow. Prisoners, even if royally fed on fresh guinea pig, mouse, rat or rabbit. Forbidden to migrate just as Pétain had been forbidden to travel south to his beloved Ermitage, his farm near Villeneuve-Loubet, for fear the view over the Bay of Angels would tempt him to join the Allies in North Africa. And just like him from his lofty perch, they sulked over lost freedom, even while watching their master closely for the prey, the little crumbs, he might or might not release.

Blood on the snow, torn flesh, sudden little shrieks and jerking, twitching legs, the corpses carried up to be pinned to each perch by razor-sharp talons. Kites, peregrines, kestrels, hen harriers, buzzards and Montagus ... A merlin.

A guinea pig was dangled by the tail and thrown – taken, killed, ripped to pieces and gulped down, each bloodied, furry lump still wet and warm. Intestines were pulled out until they snapped, the livers, heart and lungs devoured.

'Ménétrel, monsieur. I hate to interrupt your little hobby but time is of the essence. You stated earlier that the doctor had informed you he was going to have Céline Dupuis visit the Maréchal?'

Just who the hell had put that dress and those beads in her room? 'I learned of it from Honoré de Fleury,' spat Hébert, choosing a mouse from a little cage of several, his hand poised then pouncing to grasp the creature, take it out and fling it high. 'Honoré, Inspector,' he said, not lowering his gaze this time. 'Henri Philippe was much taken with the girl – everyone knew this. Did you find the love letters he must have written to her? Bernard was certain he had sent some.'

But you hadn't thought of them until now – was that it, eh? wondered St-Cyr. 'Bernard?' he asked pleasantly.

'Dr Ménétrel.'

'An old friend?'

'From before, yes.'

From 1925, when Ménétrel's father had been the Maréchal's personal physician, friend and confidant, and nearly always accompanied Pétain, the doctor's family often joining them.

'An acquaintance, Inspector, but, like Henri Philippe, the doctor keeps his distance.'

'You don't meet in Vichy when you go there as you must?' And often? 'We pass in streets that are crowded and nod deferentially to each other, that is all and as it should be.'

A wary answer. 'And yet . . . and yet the lives, not only of four high-ranking Government ministers and employees but of the Maréchal are threatened? Surely the doctor must have questioned you, at least about the party of 24 October last?'

'I told him what little I knew, if that is what you're after. Others were far better versed. Indeed, as I no longer live in the château but am housed in the former gamekeeper's lodge, I slept through it all and could offer only second-hand comments.'

'The organizer of these little escapades *sleeps* through them? Come, come, monsieur, we haven't time for this. You saw, you watched – you probably even participated or at least encouraged couples to have their little moments and were as caught by surprise as the others. If Céline Dupuis was the chosen one, and she *was* chosen for his patient, surely he'd have had a look at her?'

A rabbit was released, the poor creature zigzagging around the enclosure until its piercing shrieks signalled it had been taken.

'Your former bedroom, monsieur. My partner and I can, and will, rip that stuffed menagerie apart for its hidden eyes, its *chambre de divertissements détachés*!' Its hidden little room.

'Ménétrel secretly watched her, yes, but some weeks later and at another party. He said he had to see what Henri Philippe was getting. Later, in town, he even confronted her and . . . and insisted on giving her a thorough check-up. Honoré left him to it.'

'And wouldn't listen to her outrage?'

'That is correct.'

'Then you all weren't just pimping, were you, but had, in effect, made sex slaves of those girls.'

'She agreed to visit the Maréchal.'

'She was forced to agree. Let us not forget that!'

Trapped in the passage – pinned to the wall by the beam of Herr Kohler's torch and realizing he'd overheard everything they'd said – Mademoiselle Blanche's dark blue eyes were moist and filled with apprehension. 'Paul didn't take Céline to the Hall! I wasn't waiting there to kill her! Please, you must believe me! All we did was take Mother's earrings and a little of her perfume from her room for Ménétrel. *Ménétrel!*'

'Then why the Hall des Sources?' asked Kohler.

'Yes, why?' asked Inès.

'Pétain . . . The Maréchal met Maman in the Hall the day she took her life. He'd . . . he'd posted a last letter earlier from Paris but she had begged to see him again and he agreed. It . . . it was there that he told her in no uncertain terms to take whatever cure she wished but that, as far as he and his lawyers were concerned, their affair was over. *Tout fini. Absolument!*'

'Does Hébert know of this?' asked Herr Kohler.

'As he knows everything,' cried Blanche. 'He . . . he hates my father and still blames him for the loss of fortune and the loss of this place which, if you question him closely, I'm sure you will find he desperately wants returned. Why else the parties and the constant attempts to ingratiate himself with the doctor? Why else his involvement with the vans and the money it brings?'

'And Albert and that knife?' asked Kohler.

Blanche sucked in a breath. 'Albert listens to what his grand-uncle tells him and does exactly as he's told!'

'Albert knows who killed Céline, Inspector. I'm certain of it,' said Inès. 'You see, when we were at the Jockey Club, I overheard

Monsieur Deschambeault tell his son that Henri-Claude Ferbrave had better find out everything he could from Albert before taking care of him. "We *can't* have the rat-catcher coughing up our blood to those two from Paris." '

'Yet when stopped in that corridor after we'd pulled Albert and Henri-Claude from the roof, you told my partner you had overheard nothing.'

'Yes. Yes, I did, and for this I apologize. I . . . I wanted to think about it first.'

'And Henri-Claude?' asked Herr Kohler harshly. 'What else did those attentive ears of yours pick up?'

She must face him and not waver, thought Inès. She must try to recover lost ground. 'That the use of the bank's vans had to stop. That Monsieur Deschambeault would not submit to blackmail from Henri-Claude or anyone else and that if Henri-Claude didn't listen, he'd go straight to Herr Gessler to tell him things the Garde Mobile would rather not have the Gestapo hear!'

Like who really killed those four girls and had probably been paid to do so! 'What else?' demanded Kohler.

'That . . . that Ménétrel is on good terms with Dr Normand who treats Madame Deschambeault at his clinic, and that he is kept informed of everything she says.'

'You're a fund of information, aren't you?'

'I *want* to help. Is that not what you wish me to do?'

'Albert watches those portable toilets in the Parc, Inspector,' interjected Blanche to save herself perhaps, thought Inès. 'He'll have figured out who took that knife into one of them and then threw up and dropped it.'

'But didn't leave the cigar,' said Inès quickly, too quickly. 'A Choix Supreme, was it not? A brand the Maréchal favours.'

'As Pétain did in the Hall des Sources when he gave Maman the final brush-off!' spat Blanche, only to apparently regret having reacted so vehemently. 'That . . . that I really don't know,' she confessed. 'Edith Pascal told my brother and me this, of how the Maréchal had then left his cigar on one of the counters and how deserted the Hall had been at that time of year, the season all but ended. She . . . she was always telling us things about Maman when Paul and I went to the house. How the Maréchal and Charles-Frédéric were to blame for everything and had conspired to allow Pétain to seduce Maman. How they had joked about how easy it would be, that Mother . . . She had wanted to be set free and had had many lovers.'

'Edith would kill for Auguste-Alphonse, Inspector,' hazarded Hébert, as he warmed his hands at one of the kitchen stoves. 'That one has never looked at another man.'

They'd come in from the feeding to find Hermann and the others not back, and Sandrine Richard still sitting alone, nervously smoking the last of her cigarettes, the packet tightly crushed in a fist.

'Kill?' said St-Cyr. 'Isn't that a little harsh?' One had to keep the custodian talking now that he'd recovered a little from the news that the dress, the sapphires and the *billets doux* had been left in Céline Dupuis's room for Hermann and his partner to find.

'Not at all. Many times, when I was chairman and manager of the bank, I would see her at her desk secretly fingering a photograph of him in uniform. A cut-out from a larger photo of the directors. She knew all about Noëlle's infidelities and was incensed not just that a wife should betray a valiant husband but that she did so openly. Always the caution, though, when Noëlle visited the bank to make a withdrawal that I personally attended to. Always the little birthday gifts for Blanche and Paul who were in awe of her but laughed at her behind her back, a thing that, when she found out about it, enraged her. A woman, Inspector, who, if what Blanche has told me is correct, has kept the dead woman's bedroom as some sort of shrine and exactly as Noëlle left it. Why, please, would she do such a thing unless deranged?'

Hébert had to be grasping at straws to take the heat off himself! 'A motive, monsieur. Even if the assailant is mad, one is demanded.'

'Protection. Ah! I'm only suggesting this, but what if Edith felt those girls had discovered something Auguste-Alphonse couldn't have them repeating?'

'Such as?'

How swift the Inspector was to be cautious and suspicious. 'That those solitary walks of his are not so solitary as many have come to believe. That he has ways of finding things out and knows ahead of time what others are planning?'

L'Humanité and its list and a certain detective's name, was that it, eh? The leader of the FTP? Did Hébert really know of Olivier's position in it or did he simply suspect it?

In either case, things were not good – *bien sûr* this Sûreté was a supporter of the Résistance – but must one submit to such blackmail?

Sandrine Richard took a last drag at her cigarette and, with sharp jabs, stubbed it out in the overflowing saucer she'd used as an ashtray. 'Perhaps, Inspector, you should ask him how well he and Edith Pascal got on at that bank when Monsieur Olivier was defending his country at Verdun and other places. Edith noticed irregularities in the transfer of funds and took him to task.'

'Small transfers! It was nothing, I assure you, Inspector. That virginal puritan mistakenly thought she'd caught me out only to find everything had been returned with interest!'

'He's lying. Ask him what she did.'

'All right, all right, I'll tell him, shall I?' shouted Hébert. 'She notified Auguste-Alphonse – yes, yes, Madame Richard. That woman went right through the chain of command to Pétain himself! *Pétain*, madame!'

'Olivier returned, Inspector, ostensibly on leave, and for the last year of war, Edith, a mere secretary from the wrong side of the tracks, had the right to challenge every transfer this one made and to sanction it only if correct and honest.'

'*Jésus, merde alors*, you bitches certainly talk!' snorted Hébert, tossing his smock and fedora into a chair. 'Did that lantern-jawed witch, Madame la Maréchale, tell you all of this?'

'And more, monsieur. Much more. How you, yourself, during his absence had seduced Noëlle Olivier, your friend and business partner's wife. How you had wanted her to leave him for yourself. Many times you had had her out to this place, to parties just as wild and licentious as the ones you now hold for your friends and business partners. How, when she refused to leave her husband for you, you then continually introduced her to other men who made their attempts and sometimes succeeded!'

'*Trou de cul*, the dried-up wife has really been stung, hasn't she?'

'Asshole, am I? Then what about this, Inspector? His first wife left him in despair; the second . . . ah! should I tell you of her? All but a virgin and only twenty-one, she fell down the cellar stairs here and bled to death behind . . . yes, yes, Inspector, behind a door that should not have been found closed and locked after her fall but was, it is whispered, *slammed* on her!'

'*Imbécile*, she was drunk and had pulled the door closed behind her!'

'But she couldn't have locked it, could she?' shouted Sandrine, getting up from the table to face him with clenched fists. 'Not when naked, terrified and running away from two of your friends who'd been at her in that bird-room of yours because she'd sworn she was going to leave you! A girl whose wealth was more than your own and went straight into your pockets!'

'*Espèce de salope! Putain!*'

'Fucking bitch, am I? A whore, eh?'

'Talk is cheap, madame, and that is all you women ever do!'

'Ah *oui, mon fin*, but surely we do it not for entertainment? Surely it is to get at the truth of vermin like yourself!'

The warehouse, the barn, was chock-full of dehydrated food. 'Enough for an army,' breathed Kohler, in awe of what lay before them.

For as far as they could see, sealed crates were stacked to the roof timbers. Narrow aisles threaded their way through this maze. There was no sign of Albert beyond the last of his footprints in the snow and now . . . now, thought Inès, only the droplets of blood that, on either side of him, had shadowed those footprints.

'He'll have built himself a little nest in here,' said Blanche. 'He'll have gone to ground and will wait until you and the Chief Inspector leave.'

'Then he's got a long wait,' grunted Kohler.

'Must we find him?' bleated Inès, sickened by the thought. 'He ... he might do something.'

'Just why are you so afraid of him if you've nothing to hide?' he asked.

'Because these days even when one has done nothing, one can still be blamed.' And why, oh why did Albert suspect her? She'd given him no sign she'd cause trouble, had done nothing but try to befriend him. Had even shown him the wax portrait of Pétain in her valise and had watched as his eyes had searched it for each detail, in wonder, yes, but had that been when he'd first decided to take exception to her, or had it been later at the Jockey Club?

They came to cases and cases of pipe tobacco, then to those of cigarettes, one of which had been opened at a corner to reveal tins of Wills Gold Flake. 'Fifty to a tin,' quipped Kohler, 'and wouldn't you know it, these never saw the underside of a parachute.'

There was tea and there was coffee, cognac too – case after case of it and no concern about its freezing; the champagne and wine were kept in the cellars, no doubt. And cigars? wondered Inès.

'They'd have picked up the aromas of too many other things,' said Herr Kohler. Had he read her mind?

Blanche had said nothing further but had stayed close, too close. Sunlight, pouring through the cracks between the boards, filtered in. At a turning, the translator's hands touched her shoulders, lightly, so lightly ...

At another turning, the corridor ran straight to the very centre of the barn and to a ladder up into the loft.

There was blood on the first of the rungs, then only on every third and fourth one and its side rails. The rats ... had there been dead rats? wondered Inès. Had they banged against the ladder as Albert had climbed it?

He was right under the cupola, had made himself a little shelter and was sitting, legs sprawled on the floor, with the beige dust of dehydrated beef-and-noodle soup showered all over his tricolour scarf, knitted cap and *bleus de travail*, along with the diced, rock-hard carrots and peas, the tomato, too, of a minestrone and the pale white of a leek-and-potato. Several packets had been torn open, sampled, consumed or discarded. Two silver foils of Swiss, dehydrated bar chocolate were half gone. The soup and the chocolate were smeared all over his face, guilt in his eyes, and four dead rats hanging by their tails from wires that were hooked to his belt.

Slim and sleek, Noëlle Olivier's Laguiole lay open in his lap. The butcher's knife was on the floor next to his left hand. The contents of her bag were strewn about, having been well thumbed. Her *carte d'identité, sauf-conduit*, lipstick and compact, some photos of Céline and herself as teenagers, the phial of perfume ... Again Blanche touched her shoulders. Instinctively Inès ducked. Albert leapt! Herr Kohler hit him hard and he dropped like a stone.

'Get him some snow to eat. Not too much or he'll swell up like a balloon.'

'He was hungry. He wouldn't have hurt anyone,' swore Blanche, frantic but not, perhaps, at the sight of Albert or of what he'd almost done. 'Now he's bleeding. He's cut his head.'

'Mother him. Pet him like you let him pet that rabbit of Céline's.'

Kohler plucked the Laguiole from the floor where Albert had dropped it as he'd lunged at the sculptress. 'Look after it,' he said, pressing it into Inès's unwilling hands. 'I've got to find my partner.'

'The butcher's knife,' she managed, pale and badly shaken.

'Oh, sorry. Look after that one too.'

The noise was really something. It sounded like a cross between a

PzKw IV tank and a *leichter Schützenpanzerwagen*, a 'light' half-track, and when it appeared on the road from Vichy, cresting the final approach to the château, snow swirled around its dark, heavily plated body, sunlight glinting from the blue-tinted bulletproof windscreens.

On and on it came, rocking gently from side to side, lumbering yet travelling at a good fifty kilometres an hour and capable of much more.

'An armoured Renault . . .' began Kohler, having come from the barn to find Louis waiting in the yard.

'Built at great public expense for King George VI of England and Queen Elizabeth's visit in July 1938,' said St-Cyr drolly. 'Typical of such visits, it was used only once for a little side trip the consort made to Versailles. Boemelburg and I were in the lead car and defenceless from ambush. The tyres can't be punctured. That's why it sways. They're far too thick. It's Laval.'

'Louis, we have to talk.'

'Hermann, is there something going on that we've been missing? Those who knew that Madame Dupuis would wear the earrings and the perfume, didn't know that the dress, et cetera, would be taken from Noëlle Olivier's room and deliberately left for us to find. There was also, apparently, a hamper that was intercepted.'

'A hamper with a knife that has a corkscrew just like this one, eh?'

More couldn't be said.

The *durs* who got out of the front seat wore the grins of long, expenses-paid, pre-war holidays in the Santé, Fresnes and other such prisons. Tattoos were on the fingers that gripped the Schmeissers and barred polite progress. Three dots, two back and one forward, in the web of skin, the tobacco pouch between the thumb and forefinger. *Mort aux vaches*, death to cows – cops. The five dots too, for *All alone between four walls and solitary*.

'Ignore them,' said St-Cyr. 'It's always best.'

A rear door opened, a pinstriped trouser leg appeared, then another. Black kid boots negotiated a rut so as to avoid the deeper snow, their grey cloth uppers each closed with a neat little row of mother-of-pearl buttons from which the sunlight struck rainbow hues.

'Ah *Sainte Mère*, Hermann!' swore Louis, furiously fishing deeply into an overcoat pocket until, at last, he had what he wanted.

The plain, tin-plated stud, the post, the back of one of those goddamned buttons and memories of Céline Dupuis's corpse lying in the Hall des Sources behind the counter of the Buvette du Chomel!

9

The wind swept the granules of snow past those carefully planted boots, bringing with it, St-Cyr noted, the tired pungency of stale cigarette smoke. Long-moist, a stained fag end clung to the Premier's fleshy lower lip, the bushy black moustache half hiding it, the bull neck scarfless.

Dark eyes, swift to all meaning, detective or otherwise, took in Blanche Varollier and Inès Charpentier, for they'd come to watch from a distance, with Albert Grenier between them. Albert, who was terrified and in tears, of course, but for his own good necessarily out of commission, his wrists bound by the shame of Kripo bracelets he could not remove.

Sandrine Richard and Charles-Frédéric Hébert were also attentive, the two sworn enemies unaware they stood shoulder to shoulder in that side entrance to the kitchens. But one must say something.

'Premier ...' began St-Cyr, the gangsters moving discreetly away to allow privacy as commanded.

'Inspector, surely that ...' Laval indicated Albert. 'That *can't* be our killer?'

'He's a part of it,' grunted Hermann. 'He tried to kill the sculptress with this.'

'Pah!' snorted Laval, impatiently tossing his fedora-ed head in acknowledgement of the almost brand-new Laguiole of Noëlle Olivier. 'The doctor vets every visitor his God on earth receives and is most fastidious about it. Surely Mademoiselle Charpentier poses no threat to the great one, or are we to hire Albert to head up security?'

'Premier, the body of Céline Dupuis . . .' hazarded Louis.

'Inspectors, the boy loves the Maréchal as he would a grandfather who dotes on a little grandson. Certainly Pétain fails to acknowledge his existence, but Albert's loyalty never wavers, not even when the great one's autograph has to be purloined by other means, namely the Maréchal's batman!'

'Premier, you went to have a look at Madame Dupuis after the doctor had pronounced her dead.'

'My button . . . You found its backing! Certainly I have a stock of them, a few extras, but they're impossible to buy these days. I'm always misplacing them. *Merci.*'

Louis's fist was tightly closed and snatched away, the words spoken, though Kohler knew them by heart. 'That is evidence, Premier. Your unauthorized visit to the corpse?'

'And before the local gendarmes could even get a look at it? Ménétrel, *mon cher détective.* Ménétrel makes a great thing of his medical expertise. Electrical shock treatments for the Maréchal, daily massages, injections of ephedrine, it's rumoured, and it is not all beyond that charlatan, but even I, a simple peasant, have doubts. I had to decide for myself. Was it yet another killing – the third of those girls – or a planned campaign of terror?'

'But . . . but, Monsieur le Premier, by not informing us of your visit and by leaving this little memento, you have caused us to believe that a woman might have killed Céline Dupuis! Two assailants, not one, as has been indicated by the sketchy police reports of the other killings. *Merde alors*, how could you have done this to us?'

Hermann let him have it flatly. 'They were all informants.'

'For Herr Abetz and Company?' asked Laval swiftly, his dark eyes narrowing. 'Then let me tell you why I'm not surprised. Vichy's like a sieve, Inspectors, the Hôtel du Parc its main orifice and Ménétrel its incompetent dyke-plugger who runs from hole to hole with cork and hammer. But that's not why I came to find you both. Are the boys next, as they are given to believe?'

'And yourself and the Maréchal?' asked Louis.

The fag end was plucked from that lip and flung away. 'Pétain doesn't count. Only a fool would make a martyr of him. The terrorists, the *résistants*, if you wish, are too well versed in the national psyche for that. As a people, we love our martyrs, so we're stuck with that reedy skeleton, and until the coming of the Divine Reaper he has taken to praying to, he'll go on playing Gilbert and Sullivan and other operetta recordings in that "bedroom" of his, and if I have to hear the *HMS Pinafore* again while trying to write letters or decide something crucial, I swear to God I'll smash his machine! The boys?' he asked calmly. *Les gars.*

Richard, Bousquet, Deschambeault and de Fleury. Hermann indicated that for the moment he would leave that one to his partner and Chief. 'I don't think so, Premier,' said Louis guardedly. 'Though Herr Kohler and I are badly in need of a chance to compare notes, everything we've uncovered so far indicates exactly the opposite. Whoever killed them did so because of what they'd become.'

'Lovers and informants. The wives, then, or the doctor, who is not above murder, I must say, but ... but come. Before we decide, let me show you both why I've left a perfectly good lunch to find you. Réal,' he called out to one of the *durs*. 'Take Herr Kohler's vehicle and follow. Tell the others to pile into it. Albert in the back seat with Mademoiselle Varollier. The sculptress in front, but keep an eye on her and your weapons.'

'Monsieur le Premier,' called out Inès, 'would it be possible for me to go with Madame Richard?'

Laval looked to each of them, Hermann giving him a nod.

'Then it's settled. Madame Richard and Mademoiselle Charpentier to join us as we view the latest artwork.'

LAVAL AU POTEAU! 'Laval up against the post' had been plastered in huge, dripping, now-frozen black letters over the wall of Charmeil's eighteenth-century school. Above the Premier's name, and just beneath the tops of its letters, were two side by side and freshly mounted posters. *BEKANNTMACHUNG* – Official Notice – as if any of the kids or their parents could read *Deutsch*!

snorted Kohler to himself. *AVIS*. Notice *APPRÉHENDÉS*. Apprehended. *PEINE DE MORT*. Penalty of death. *FUSILLÉS*. Shot. Ah, Christ! Paul Panton, Edgar Guerledan, Francine Aubret and Marcel Boulanger. Kids, just kids.

'Herr Gessler's quick off the mark, isn't he? Ages eighteen to twenty. Fools!' swore Laval, indicating the names of the dead and angrily finding himself another cigarette to light hurriedly.

Everyone had got out of the cars, Mademoiselle Charpentier sickened by the notices, thought St-Cyr. Beyond them, and the letters, its whitewash faded by the years of the Occupation so that the wall became a mirror of the times, were the words that had been written in despair by retreating soldiers in early June 1940, not realizing then that the Government would soon be installed in Vichy. *QUI NOUS A TRAHIS*? Who has betrayed us?

No one had apparently thought to enquire about the bicycle that leaned against the wall. A sturdy, pre-war Majestic, its worn seat rested against the edge of the stripped-away stucco. Below it, the bare lava-stone blocks had been scratched by centuries of schoolboys and girls who had wished to leave their little mementos to posterity. A woman's bike, then, said St-Cyr to himself. Tallish, long-legged and long-armed.

The faded wicker carrier basket was frayed to twigs around its edges and held an all but empty, two-litre tin of coal-black paint and a ten-centimetre-wide brush that must date from 1930 and had been used many times to whitewash the inside of a cowshed. A good farm, then, and well above the usual, but perhaps this was the very brush the soldiers had found to use?

'There are also these, Inspectors,' said the Auvergnat, giving a quick wave of salutation to schoolchildren who had found the view from the classroom windows more interesting than their lessons.

Cartoons had been cut from a magazine and a newspaper.

'Both date from 30 October 1940,' said Laval. '*Punch Magazine* and the *Daily Mirror*. I had them checked.'

The first portrayed him as the Great Laval in white bow tie, black waistcoat and tails and juggling swastikas, holding a

Francisque rolling pin with rubber spikes like those guaranteed to remove excess fat, and bottles of his very own Vichy water, one of which had shattered at his feet.

The second clipping, that of the newspaper, depicted the Premier as a hideously grinning, squat and moustachioed bullfrog cradling a bouquet of chrysanthemums – the press's funereal choice had been perfect! – as he came courting to knock at a door whose emblem was a large black swastika.

'Vichy is Vichy, Inspectors. There is no other place like it in the world. There never will be nor can be, and I am at the centre of it. Inheritor of the decisions of others, cementer of bargains that are seldom adhered to. Reviled, hated, ridiculed by an ever-growing number, ah *oui*, but to be ill thought of and yet useful is better than to be ill thought of and useless. That bicycle must have been stolen; God knows where the artist found the paint. Footprints indicated the general direction of retreat but the children soon put paid to them, though they did establish the time of the atrocity, since the paint they touched on first inspection was then not frozen.'

'It doesn't belong to one of the teachers, does it?' asked Kohler of the bike.

'*Merde alors*, you sound like the great one! Is pedantic logic always foremost in the mind of detectives too? Come, there's more to see.'

'A moment,' cautioned Louis. 'The clippings, Premier?'

'Slid in an envelope under the door to my office at the Hôtel du Parc late last night or early this morning.'

'In spite of the Garde Mobile's redoubled presence?'

'Perhaps because of it. The doctor is, of course, in a rage and once more Henri-Claude Ferbrave has been threatened with immediate dismissal. Derelict. Spending too much time with the *horizontales* of that *maison de tolérance* he favours. Ménétrel, in spite of the coarseness of his tongue, is very much a prude and family man, and is offended by the unbridled appetite of his chief lieutenant. The Hôtel is, I'm afraid, abuzz.'

Workmen, among them the elder Grenier, were busily erasing the damage with scrapers, wire brushes and kerosene. Spectators stood about, lots of them. Passers-by paused. A Wehrmacht lorry dropped off a squad of burly Felgendarmen, the military police.

The Hôtel du Parc and Hall des Sources had also been decorated.

COURAGE ON LES AURA faced Pétain's office and balcony, from where the Maréchal could be seen sadly gazing down at words he'd spoken to the troops at Verdun in 1917: Take heart, we'll get them.

BOUSILLER LES GARS! Smash – bump off – the boys! had been splashed directly below him on the ground-floor wall of the hotel, between its sticking-papered and blue-washed windows. And then, as if to rub it in, the artist had used one of the Ministry of Agriculture's innocent campaign slogans for children. LUTTEZ CONTRE LES DORYPHORES! Fight against the potato beetle. Children all over rural France had been excused from classes, armed with bottles of water and, accompanied by their teachers, encouraged to swarm into the potato fields each summer to catch, drown and squash this pest. But now, of course, *Doryphores* also meant the Boche and everyone knew it!

'Premier, the Hall, I think,' said Louis determinedly.

'I can tell you little.'

'Sometimes even a little is enough.'

'Are the boys next, now that you've seen the slogans for yourselves?' Laval was clearly worried but calm.

'Let us reserve judgement, Premier. Let us adopt one of yours and the Maréchal's very first policies with the Occupier in 1940, that of *attentisme*.'

'Wait-and-see has never been my way, Inspector, but had you the opportunity then, what would you have done?'

'Exactly the same thing. You . . . we . . . had no other choice.'

'Then let us go in and settle this little matter before Herr Gessler and his gang of thugs trample everything.'

'And the thugs you, yourself, employ?'

'Are Ménétrel's men, the very ones who were among those who arrested me on 13 December 1940 after my first term here.

Ménétrel, of course, begged Pétain to have them assassinate me, but Herr Abetz intervened. Now I employ them. That, too, is of Vichy. I insisted they guard me. One has to do things like that when one is Premier. Every day that they are with me they must worry about being killed in an assassination attempt that has not been of their own making, but also ... Ah *oui, mes chers détectives*, they and that little doctor of ours are forced to realize not only the opportunity they missed but the mistake they would have made! Now, of course, if they were to kill me, they'd have no one.'

Merde alors, the wily peasant at heart! 'And Bousquet and the others?' asked St-Cyr – Hermann would leave him to deal with Laval.

'Are worth saving if for no other reason than to hold together what's left and prevent anarchy. No scandal is going to erupt out of what they've been up to. Shocking as it was, and a severe embarrassment to my Government, that little business venture of theirs has been stopped. You, in turn, will find the murderer or murderers of those girls and then quietly leave.'

'And if it's more than that?'

'The Résistance? We'll deal with it.'

'And if it's one or more of the boys?'

'Then he or they will be dealt with.'

'And if it's the wives?'

'Those too.'

'And if it's the doctor?'

Laval grinned.

'Personally I would like nothing better than to present to the Maréchal the *procès-verbal* his *éminence grise* had to sign under the stern gazes of a Sûreté and a Kripo that I, myself, had requested. What better an example of mutual cooperation between our two nations than for the Général, the *Vainqueur de Verdun*, to acknowledge that our two police forces, united in the battle against common crime, have found my Flykiller? Of course, the lance corporal with the Iron Cross Second and First Class would appreciate it too. Even Herr Hitler has, I'm sure if one searched desperately enough for it, a certain sense of humour.'

From inside the Hall des Sources, where she stood next to frozen Kentia palms and near-dead, pollarded lime trees, Inès could see the workmen quite clearly as they scraped away the COURAGE ON LES AURA. Like blue-clad flies in winter, they were pinned to the tall, arched windows from whose delicate friezes long icicles hung, and where sheets of discoloured ice had lain beneath the artist's brush, those segments of the letters rapidly vanished.

Beyond the workmen who faced her, others across the street at the Hôtel du Parc had their backs to her, and wasn't that also like Vichy? she asked herself. To confront, to shun, to erase the truth and turn the back on so many?

Laval, St-Cyr and Kohler had gone over to the Buvette du Chomel, to where Céline had been finally cornered and slain, but had she known her killer or killers? How had she got away from the one, only to then be trapped by the other? What words had been said? Last words . . .

Sandrine Richard stood near the entrance, perhaps not wishing to come closer for fear of betraying herself. And Blanche? asked Inès. Blanche was halfway between herself and the others but had found that she, too, could approach no closer.

Voices echoed. The detectives made no attempt to hide their questions or the answers given. Perhaps they did this to taunt her and the others, perhaps it was simply for expedience. Laval's description of the corpse fitted Ménétrel's – St-Cyr acknowledged this. The Premier had, on crouching to examine the body, lost a button from one of his shoes and, having heard it clatter away, had searched for and found it, only to then find that its backing had slipped out and been lost.

Her hair had been gone through. Had he opened her nightgown? St-Cyr had asked – one of its ties had been snapped. 'No had been the answer.'

'Yet you moved her legs and hips,' St-Cyr had challenged.

'I had to,' Monsieur le Premier had answered, lighting a fresh cigarette and erupting in a hacking cough.

'Why didn't you tell others of this?' Herr Kohler had demanded. 'Ménétrel, certainly the investigating police?'

'I didn't want the doctor knowing I was concerned enough to have come in here to see her for myself. Convinced that it could well be a threat to Richard and the others, I personally telexed Gestapo Boemelburg requesting assistance and then telephoned him. Boemelburg agreed to my request and I told Secrétaire Général Bousquet that even though he was opposed to my choice of you both, he was to work closely with you.'

'They've all tried to cover things up!' said St-Cyr.

'They had much to hide,' countered the Premier.

'Then what, please, other than another victim, another of your flies, convinced you of the threat?'

'Yes, what?' Inès heard Herr Kohler ask, and then . . .

Then from Laval, 'There was a burnt matchstick, broken and left in the sign of a V.'

'Ah *merde*, Hermann, now he tells us!'

'And I ask again, Inspectors,' replied Monsieur Laval calmly, 'is it a campaign of terror that now threatens us?'

And never mind the victims!

'Where is it, please, this matchstick?' demanded St-Cyr, clearly very upset with him.

'I removed it. I felt I had to. I didn't want to compound the matter until we had further information.'

'Did you tell anyone of it?' the Sûreté demanded archly.

'None.'

'And yet Ménétrel made no mention of it, Hermann. Why, please, did he not think that necessary?'

'Security,' snapped Laval. 'Ménétrel is terrified our friends will move in *en masse* and kick his precious Garde out!'

And that, too, was of Vichy, thought Inès, holding her breath and waiting for their answer.

'A Garde who are excused their duties . . .' muttered St-Cyr.

'Who miss an early-morning postman they should have

caught, Louis,' said Herr Kohler – referring to the press clippings Laval had shown them.

'A Flykiller or killers who can come and go at will, Hermann, and know beforehand exactly what the boys are planning.'

'Premier,' said Herr Kohler, obviously not liking this new piece of evidence one bit, 'how was it found?'

'Placed on the back of the right hand that clasped her breast. Here . . . here, I have it in my pocket. A sharp splinter underlines the burned half of the V when the match is opened.'

A pair of earrings, a knife from the past and a touch of perfume, a cigar band, the tin-plated post from a small, mother of pearl button, and a V for Victory, for that is what the match had meant: such little symbols, this one taken from the now-familiar gesture of the British Prime Minister, were increasingly to be found.

'The Résistance, Louis,' grated Herr Kohler. *Mon Dieu,* he could put such feeling into those few words! thought Inès.

'Or the killer or killers wish us to blame them, Hermann,' cautioned his partner and friend.

'So as to unleash a campaign of terror which has now already started?' scoffed Kohler, referring to the *ratissage* the *Sonderkommando* were conducting.

'Premier, the doctor pronounced her dead at 7.32 a.m. on Wednesday,' said St-Cyr. 'At what time did you step in here?'

'At just before eight. The police hadn't yet been notified. The door was open. Staff were hurrying past to their offices. I simply ducked in unnoticed.'

'Having learned of the killing how?' asked the Sûreté.

'One overhears everything in that Hôtel,' snorted Laval. 'Ménétrel was in a frightful turmoil, claiming he'd been betrayed and that there'd been a flagrant breach of security. Ferbrave was, of course, to blame and had been dismissed, but it wasn't the first time our ranting doctor had made that little threat, so I paid it no mind and simply went to see for myself.'

'Your footprints in the snow must have been noticed by the police,' said St-Cyr, 'yet none were mentioned in the report?'

'Clearly I had no reason to kill her and was above suspicion. I'd been at home, at my château in Châteldon, and could prove it. I simply pointed out my footprints to the sous-préfet when he and his men were deciding which prints might be useful.'

'Among those that hadn't been trampled?' asked St-Cyr as if stung by such incompetence on the part of the local police.

'We were, I'm afraid, all caught by surprise.'

'Yet all of you knew of the little visit she was to pay the Maréchal,' said Kohler.

'I didn't. I hadn't the slightest inkling of it.'

'Even though one can overhear everything in that hotel?' he demanded.

'Even then.'

'Nor did I,' said Sandrine Richard. 'How could I have?'

'But Mademoiselle Blanche and her brother knew of it, Louis.'

'Yes! Yes, a thousand times,' cried Blanche, 'but we *didn't* kill her, I swear it! We took the earrings and a little of mother's perfume in a phial I had brought along but only because Dr Ménétrel had demanded this.'

'And when did you leave them with him, mademoiselle?' asked Louis.

'On Monday afternoon, late.'

'And the knife?' asked Herr Kohler, quickly leaving the *buvette* to stand before her.

'Was lying on the chair in her room, with the laudanum bottle.'

'This one?' asked St-Cyr, showing the bottle as he joined his partner.

'Yes!' Blanche's voice quavered. 'My father had brought it home with the clothes Mother had left on the Pont Barrage the day she drowned herself. It was, I think, the last time he ever set eyes on that room of hers. A broken man.'

'And neither you nor your brother touched this knife?' asked St-Cyr, the bottle in one hand, the weapon in the other.

'Paul . . . Paul did open it on our first visit. Edith . . . Edith was so upset, he . . . my brother put it back.'

'With the blade open or closed?' he asked.

'Would it really matter?' she yelped. 'We *didn't* take it! We're not killers. At first we only wanted what was rightfully ours, and then ... then we agreed to do what was asked simply to protect Paul from the forced labour.'

Head bowed in despair, Blanche clenched her fists at her sides. 'Please, you must believe me. If Papa would have listened to us, Paul and I would have gone straight to him, but we knew he wouldn't. When we first went to her, Edith had told us it would be useless to try.'

It was Herr Kohler who gently asked, 'Could Mademoiselle Pascal have noticed you'd taken the earrings and come after them?'

'To the Hôtel d'Allier?' blurted Blanche. 'It's ... it's possible, yes.'

'And the love letters?' demanded St-Cyr.

'Were any of them taken?' she asked, caught suddenly by surprise.

'Please just answer.'

'Then no! Edith ... Edith would have noticed right away if we'd so much as touched them. She goes into that room every day to finger Mother's things as if in doubt, in hope. I know she's read those letters often, know she sleeps in Mother's bed. Why ... why does she do such things if not demented?'

'The dress, mademoiselle, and the strand of sapphires?' he asked.

'Dress? Which dress, please?'

'Left in Madame Dupuis's room after the killing,' said Louis gruffly, the sternness of his Sûreté gaze not leaving her. She tried hard to meet it and finally succeeded.

'One that we would find and not Bousquet,' said Kohler, watching her intently.

'Who had earlier been left Céline's identity card,' breathed St-Cyr.

'As a warning from the Résistance, Louis. A warning!'

'Premier, although you've already given us a reason, why,

please, did that telex you sent to Paris really use the name Flykiller?' asked St-Cyr.

'Those damned girlfriends were like flies,' spat Laval. 'Always buzzing about their men and threatening to spoil things for us. I was all but certain they were informants and have now been proven correct!'

They sat alone, those two detectives, in the Chante Clair Restaurant where the ladies, the *crème de la crème* of Vichy, wore fashion's latest whim, the colourful turban. The wives were at afternoon tea and gossip, the sound of their voices suddenly rising to a shrillness that frightened before dropping to a whisper that only served to increase anxiety.

Sandrine Richard had curtly been given permission to join Madame Pétain and Élisabeth de Fleury, their heads close in urgent conference. Blanche, alone and looking lost, sat at a table beneath the stained-glass lights of tall, streaked windows that overlooked the snow-dusted statuary of the inner courtyard. And I? mused Inès. I, instinctively not wishing to sit with Blanche, nor she with me, sit alone, having just learned that Albert has been released into his father's recognizance.

St-Cyr had agreed to do this, perhaps out of kindness, but had he also wanted to see what would happen? she wondered.

Kohler, in defiance of the hour, the head chef and the kitchen staff, had loudly ordered pea soup with ham, sausages and sauerkraut, and 'good German beer'; a pastis for his friend and partner. 'A double.'

Since he sat with his back to her, she could only clearly see St-Cyr who, from time to time, an unlit pipe clenched between his teeth or in a fist, would look across the crowded dining room to see her sitting primly beneath one of the wall mirrors, her back to that very wall, knowing she couldn't possibly overhear them now or see what lay before them. That tin-plated little post, Inspector? *Laval au poteau?* Had it been a coincidence, post and post? Would Monsieur le Premier wonder if it had meaning and make a hurried visit to his clairvoyant, Madame Ribot, of the Hôtel Ruhl, at 15 boulevard de l'Hôtel de Ville, to ask her advice?

Would he believe what the cards, the stars, the moon and conjunctions said?

'Hermann, our sculptress is still without her precious valise. Just what the hell is she really doing here?'

'Blanche asked the same thing.'

'Ah *oui*. She makes Albert edgy and now she's got me edgy too.'

The understatement of the year! 'Relax. Eat up.'

'And try to concentrate? *Merde*, I've no appetite. How can I when I know Herr Gessler must be watching the clock – our clock – and counting off the minutes? If he gets his hands on that one . . .' he indicated the sculptress, 'neither of us will be able to save her.'

Stripped naked, shrieked at constantly, her head shoved repeatedly under water in the bathtub those bastards were fond of using, she'd be strung up and further clubbed with rubber truncheons if she didn't tell them what they wanted, or thrown to the swill-soaked floor to be kicked by hobnailed boots until dead.

'Please don't let us forget that, Hermann.'

'You know I won't. How could I? It applies also to Blanche and that brother of hers as well as to Albert and others, especially Olivier and his Edith.'

'Olivier,' said Louis, opening Noëlle's knife. Quickly arranging the items and ignoring the food, he set the V for Victory beneath the knife; the earrings, laudanum bottle and *billets doux* to the left; the button-post to the right and isolated for the moment.

'One killing is a drowning, quick and easy, and no one sees it as murder, Hermann, until much later. The next is a garrotting, embellished only in that the wire, similar to that which Albert Grenier uses, is found embedded in the victim's throat. The third killing is further embellished by a riding crop, dead rats, a corpse that is hidden in an armoire, as if a child, a young man, a naughty boy, had done it.'

'Albert again.'

'Only with the fourth killing, as we now know, do we see further embellishment. A cigar band, cigar ashes, a knife with a past; earrings and perfume of the same; but since we may no longer be dealing with two assailants, a man and woman, we had best go carefully over things.'

Steam rose from the waiting soup. 'Blanche claims that Edith told her and her brother that Pétain met their mother in the Hall the day Noëlle took her life, Louis.'

'Then everything with this fourth killing is to point to Olivier as the killer.'

The soup would still be too hot in any case and Louis was trying hard to face up to the worst of this affair.

'A body is found by Albert just after curfew, and at 7.32 a.m. Ménétrel pronounces Madame Dupuis dead, Hermann.'

'Laval fails to mention the V for Victory, as does Ménétrel, but was it there at 7.32 or is it left afterwards, but before Laval's arrival?'

Sadly it was a good question, for if it was present overnight, the Résistance could well have killed Madame Dupuis; if not, then the matchstick could either have been left just before or after Ménétrel's viewing the corpse, either as a further warning to *les gars* or, if left by someone other than a *résistant*, to implicate them. 'Left there overnight, perhaps,' said St-Cyr, not liking it but motioning to Hermann to eat. 'Crush up some bread. Here, let me do it for you.'

'You know I can do that for myself!'

'Yes! but I want the sculptress to see that we look after each other.'

'A Résistance killing,' muttered Kohler. Louis had seen that their discussing it couldn't be avoided, but had the civil war begun? They did tend to leave other tokens of their presence, not just painted slogans. 'But why, then, did Ménétrel fail to mention it?'

That, too, was a good question. 'Fear perhaps. Also a need to first find answers for himself. Remember, please, with what we are dealing.'

'An *éminence grise* who's accustomed to holding things close and is fiercely competitive, Louis, but let's set that one aside for the moment, eh? It would still have been dark at 7.32 Berlin Time. The police hadn't yet been notified. Albert would have had to give the doctor his torch or lantern.'

The sun not up for an hour. 'Darkness, then, and yes, someone who could come and go at will and with no one the wiser, but with less than twenty minutes in which to complete the task, since Laval was there at near to eight.'

'Someone who has an ear glued so closely to the ground that he, she or they would know beforehand what's to happen,' said Kohler.

'They'd have had to know Laval would leave his office. It's too tight a timing, Hermann. The V for Victory was left when she was killed.'

'Or afterwards but before her body was first discovered.'

'The girl is killed, the knife removed and dropped into a portable toilet, one that Albert is sure to investigate. But why remove it in the first place if one wishes to focus attention on Olivier? Just what the hell is really going on, Hermann? Love letters are left for us to find? Sapphires that the Résistance should, by rights, have stolen? Press clippings for Laval?'

'An identity card.'

'Charles-Frédéric Hébert knew only of the earrings and the perfume, but was taken aback when he learned of the dress.'

'As was Blanche Varollier.'

'Light would have been needed if one was to duck into the Hall after the killing and Ménétrel's visit to the corpse. Light and then darkness, Hermann. Night blindness. Olivier told me he suffered from it. Ten minutes were required for his eyes to adjust. He knew Céline Dupuis. The girl had asked him to write to Mademoiselle Charpentier and send the letter with Lucie Trudel . . .'

Kohler set his soup spoon down and sighed. 'He'd have walked behind Céline along that corridor in the hotel, would have let her lead the way to freedom – was that what he told her, Louis? That the FTP had organized an escape for her? No struggle, the girl not trying to get away until in the Hall.'

'Only to then be killed.'

'Having tried her damnedest to remove and hide the earrings.'

Herr Kohler methodically added more bread to his soup and stirred it in. He was not happy, thought Inès, was disgruntled.

'Could Céline have been trying to protect Blanche and Paul, Louis? She must have known they'd taken the earrings for Ménétrel, would have known de Fleury had been given them and had been told to tell her to wear them.'

'Mademoiselle Charpentier was her friend and confidante, Hermann. She would have wanted to protect Olivier if only to protect the sculptress.'

'Then Olivier didn't walk her to her death – is that what you're saying?'

The Sûreté's plate of soup was offered and accepted, Herr Kohler's empty one set aside.

'Not at all. What I *am* saying is that, by openly confiding that he suffered from night blindness, was Monsieur Olivier attempting to convince us that he couldn't possibly have done it? Ten minutes, Hermann. They walk from light into darkness and Céline escapes when they reach the Hall. She goes to ground having realized it and he . . .'

'Holds the doors shut while the other one – Edith – hunts her down and kills her.'

'Why?'

'Because she knew too much, had become a danger to them.'

Their sausage and sauerkraut arrived. More beer, more pastis and bread were called for, noted Inès, the two of them digging in as if at a last meal. Some cheese and even a few of the petits fours the ladies were enjoying were also requested. The noise of the dining room was seemingly everywhere, yet they ignored it totally.

'Even if Olivier did send messages for Inès Charpentier to deliver to the FTP in Paris, Hermann – and I'm not suggesting he didn't, given the opportunity, or denying that the girl would probably have willingly agreed to carry them – Lucie Trudel would not have been aware of them. Olivier's no fool. After that first letter of his to Mademoiselle Charpentier, all others would have been enclosed in the envelopes from Madame Dupuis. He'd have insisted on it.'

Herr Kohler gestured with his fork, stabbing it towards his partner to emphasize the point, but what point? wondered Inès, still unable to take her eyes from their table.

'Lucie could have opened one and read it, Louis, and if so, and if he'd learned of it, as he surely would have, Olivier would have gladly smothered her.'

'I found no such letter in her room.'

'Precisely! It had been removed because it had to be!'

'And when she came downstairs to fetch a candle for that room of Noëlle Olivier's,' muttered St-Cyr, 'Edith Pascal realized Olivier had confided to me that he was the FTP's district leader, and had called him a fool. The night blindness would cover him for the death of Mademoiselle Marie-Jacqueline Mailloux, Hermann – an unlighted *Grande établissement thermal*, in a few minutes which were certainly not enough time for the blindness to clear. It would also suit with the death of Camille Lefèbvre since how could one so afflicted readily escape into darkness as our secrétaire général fired at him?'

'But Lucie would have gone from darkness outside into light,' said Hermann, cutting off another piece of sausage and then heaping his fork also with sauerkraut.

'But . . . but you're forgetting that her killer would have had to step into darkness to escape.'

Herr Kohler took a pull at his beer and then put two sausages on his partner's plate, some ham, too, thought Inès, and potatoes, gesturing that St-Cyr absolutely must eat.

'Now what about the husbands, Louis? Each of them had a great deal to lose and Ménétrel would certainly have put it to them in no uncertain terms that their girlfriends were informants.'

Good for Hermann.

'Create the myth of a Résistance threat, Louis, by leaving that little V for Victory. Get the Garde to paint a few slogans, et cetera, and use it all not only to get rid of the traitors, for that is what the doctor would have thought of those girls, but to emphasize the need for increased security before that responsibility is taken from him.'

'Find someone everyone knows about. A recluse,' muttered Louis. 'A cuckold, Hermann. One who must hate Pétain with a passion.'

'But do they suspect he's of the FTP? Could they? If he does suspect it, the doctor would damned well make certain Vichy took care of its own. He'd not want Gessler knowing that the resident recluse had had his ear so close to the ground that he'd found out everything ahead of time and had made a mockery of the Government.'

'But does Olivier have that ear, *mon vieux*? *Bien sûr*, he implied he was well informed and couldn't reveal his sources, but . . .'

'Ménétrel could damned well have left that little V for Victory, Louis, knowing Laval would be certain to have a look at the corpse and become convinced of the campaign of terror.'

The doctor would have too. Ah *merde*, it didn't bear thinking about, but had they stepped into a power struggle, each side now desperately making its countermoves – the rats, the corpse; the corpse, the knife and then the identity card, and then . . . then the dress and sapphire beads, the love letters, too, not only to complete the costume and the legend of the unfaithful wife but to emphasize the guilty husband?

Except that Hébert, and presumably Ménétrel, had not known the dress and necklace had been left in Céline Dupuis's room. The love letters too . . . Had they been left, then, by Olivier or Edith Pascal?

'Admit it, we need answers, Louis.'

A curt nod was given to indicate the occupants of a nearby table, Inès noted and again held her breath.

'From that one in particular, *mon vieux*. The one in the vermilion suit, the Indian brass and pearl necklace and the North

African turban. That thing on her head is from Morocco, isn't it? My eyes ... The lack of vitamin A ...'

And Auguste-Alphonse Olivier, the years 1924 and '25 when the Victor of Verdun had been married to that one for four and then five years. 'Wounded ... *Nom de Jésus Christ*, Louis, that hatchet wouldn't just have threatened Pétain with his service revolver for fooling around on her, she'd have shot his balls off!'

'Ah *oui, certainement*, but remember, please, that Ménétrel warned us to leave her out of things.'

'Then go and talk to her and let's hope he's not been scheming and dreaming behind our backs.'

They were still at their table, St-Cyr now standing and about to leave to talk to Madame Pétain. 'Inspectors, excuse me a moment, please. There ... there is something I must tell you,' said Inès. She would have to endure their suspicious gazes, she must! 'The vomit Albert found in that toilet. It ... it was mine, I think.'

'*Nom de Jésus Christ*, Hermann, what the hell is it with Vichy? Does it bring out the liar, the arch-schemer, the thief, corrupter, cheat and killer in everyone we meet? Mademoiselle.' Louis calmed himself. 'Please explain yourself.'

'Yesterday morning, after Dr Ménétrel had come to find you in the foyer of the Hôtel du Parc, but before I went to see Céline's body for myself and Herr Kohler was surprised to find me in the Hall, I was so upset I ... I had to throw up. Albert must have seen me dash into that outdoor toilet. The men were clearing the snow. Has he confused me with her killer and is this why he feels I'm such a threat? It must be. It must!'

'She did look like death warmed over, Louis. I thought ... Ah! that the iron man and his flash were what had made her so pale.'

'And sickly? Talk to her, then, Hermann. Try to force yourself to wring every last drop of juice out of this grape, but if she lies, give her a pair of bracelets to wear and throw the key away! You are not leaving us, mademoiselle. From now until the close of this investigation, you are staying with us!'

'That might not be possible, Louis.'

'Possible or not, she has just given us information we should have had long ago!'

'I didn't kill her. I can have had nothing to do with any of the killings.'

'But for some as yet unknown reason, mademoiselle, Albert Grenier has come to consider you a threat.'

'Yes, but he's confused. The knife dropped in there after her killing, the vomit only yesterday – you yourselves and your questions . . . questions are always very difficult for one such as he is. The portrait mask . . . Perhaps I shouldn't have shown it to him. Maybe he has confused it with death. I . . . I don't know. Really, I don't.'

The kid was desperate. 'Louis, for her to have come forward like this took courage. Go and talk to the ladies. Leave this one to me.'

'With pleasure!'

The tightly bound, Moorish turban, a lamé of irregular patches of ochreous silk on a crimson background with thin, interlaced black lines, had flashes of silver everywhere. Beneath it, the wrinkled, well-powdered brow was further creased by a ruthlessly plucked and defiantly raised eyebrow, the expression accusative, the nose prominent, the lips wide, grimly pursed and turned down in distaste, the wrinkled upper lip, jaw and jowls fierce, the broad shoulders squared.

Formidable, thought St-Cyr, as he introduced himself, but then . . . then one of Houbigant's scents delicately emanated from her. A woman of great taste . . .

'Well?' demanded Madame la Maréchale. 'Why have you released the one and not arrested the other?'

At sixty-six years of age, Eugénie Hardon-Pétain could still defy time, but this one, he felt, would fight it to the end. Large teardrops of pearl, ruby and brass, one on either side and curving inwardly, flanked the many strands as if the necklace was a breastplate of office and she the female counterpart of the Wehrmacht's *Kettenhunde.*

'Albert Grenier is constantly confused, madame, and for some reason feels the sculptress is a threat to your husband. But since she is to remain with my partner and me at all times, and his father is looking after him, the boy is no longer a threat.'

'And the other?' she demanded fiercely.

It would be best to appear simple-minded. 'Who?'

'*Nom de Dieu,* are we to expect this from a chief inspector with an enviable reputation? Enviable, I say, if one is not guilty! Hébert, of course. That *fornicateur* deliberately introduced those girls to Bousquet and the other. He made certain they were tempted!'

'The girls or the boys, madame?'

Ménétrel had been in a rage when he had learned of this one and his partner coming to Vichy; Bousquet hadn't liked it either, but the *Jamaick* had insisted on it. St-Cyr and Kohler and no others! 'You know very well whom I mean, and if you so much as breathe a word of what was to have gone on in that room of my husband's, I will personally see that you are not just stripped of your rank, but are court-martialled and shot. Do I make myself clear?'

'Abundantly, Madame la Maréchale. A few . . .'

'*Questions?* Inspector, for your information, neither of these two ladies were anywhere near those girls when each of them was killed. I should think you would have discovered this by now!'

'Then let me just jot that down. Ah yes, here it is. Friday 7 January at about 2.45 a.m.'

'Camille Lefèbvre . . .' hazarded Sandrine Richard, as the three of them swiftly exchanged glances. Bousquet's woman of course.

Visibly withdrawn and obviously finding it hard to come forward, Élisabeth de Fleury said quietly, 'One of my sons was ill, Inspector, and had a very high temperature. The flu – we all worry so much about it, for when it arrives it spreads like wildfire throughout the hotel and everyone can hear its first coughs and sneezes. I . . .' She looked to Madame Pétain for guidance.

The rock curtly nodded.

'I hurried along the hall to Dr Ménétrel's suite in my nightdress and awakened him. He gave me a few of the aspirins he keeps in a special store and advised the damp cloths and a cold sponging, but . . . but it wasn't until nearly noon the next day that . . . that my little Louis let the crisis pass and slept soundly. He's only ten years old and looks so like his *papa*, I . . . Naturally I had moved the other two children out of the room and had let them sleep in my bed, daughter and son together, you understand, but only during such an emergency.'

Merde alors, and not like Blanche and Paul Varollier, eh? 'And your husband, Madame de Fleury?'

Downcast, her sky-blue eyes rapidly moistened until two single tears were squeezed. 'Had not come home,' she whispered, her fists desperately clenching.

'Didn't he have to go into the office that morning? A Friday, madame? It wasn't a day off, was it?'

How harsh his voice was, but her look must be frank, Madame Pétain had warned. You must face the Chief Inspector and answer truthfully as if your life was nothing more than an open book, *ma chère*. A little book, of course, and one not read even by your husband! 'It would be best, Inspector, if you were to ask him where he was that night.'

'He was with that woman of his, Inspector,' charged Madame Pétain. 'Céline Dupuis, a widow, yes! First at Chez Crusoe and then . . . then, *mon pauvre détective*, in a hotel room those men had rented for just such a purpose.'

And damn Bousquet and the others for not having told them of it! 'The Hôtel d'Allier?' he bleated.

'Pah! And advertise their identities like that? Isn't an element of secrecy necessary with such as they? An overcrowded hotel like the Allier would not have been suitable. People coming and going at all times. Friends knocking at the door or, as is usual, I understand, in that place, simply barging in.'

And never mind Lucie Trudel lying naked in hopes Deschambeault would come to her the morning she was smothered!

'The Hôtel Ruhl, Inspector,' said Sandrine Richard. A fresh packet of cigarettes lay in front of her but none had been taken since Madame Pétain did not use tobacco. 'Room 3-17. An old bed with a sagging mattress that reeks of stale urine, a plain washbasin, second-hand water pitcher, mirror whose backing is clouded, thin towels . . . Always there are the hand towels and the notices, now in *Deutsch*, too, warning of unsafe sex!'

'Near the lift? Was the room near it?' he heard himself asking. They were all watching him closely. Élisabeth de Fleury moved her cup and saucer from in front of her, the teaspoon telegraphing a nervousness that alarmed the others.

'Next to the service staircase,' she said, not averting her gaze though she must have wanted to. A rather pleasant-looking, very pale and fair-haired woman in her early forties. 'Inspector, I . . . I know this only because I had to see where my husband and Madame Dupuis had been meeting.'

'And you're certain he spent the night of 6–7 January with the dancer?'

Ballet instructress, piano player, cabaret singer and whore. Honoré would have his alibi, and she herself? she asked, and answered, I will have mine. 'Yes. Yes, I'm absolutely certain.'

Ah damn the woman! 'Then please explain how you know this.' He held up a hand. 'Neither of you ladies are to answer for her.' Hermann . . . why the hell hadn't Hermann come to listen in and help? The sculptress, he reminded himself. Inès Charpentier is with him. The table was directly behind and he couldn't, daren't turn to throw a pleading glance that way. *Merde!*

'I . . .' began Madame de Fleury only to hesitate.

'Madame, one of your sons was gravely ill. You were at his bedside. You couldn't have left him until what? Well after noon that Friday? You were exhausted, hadn't slept, were sick with worry . . .'

'All right! All right! I asked my daughter, Monique, to stay home from school while I went to that hotel to . . . to touch the pillows!'

And smell their cases before throwing back the covers to examine the sheets of an unmade bed? 'You had a key, did you?'

'No! I . . .'

'She paid the concierge two hundred francs, Inspector,' said Sandrine Richard, taking out a cigarette only to remember suddenly, at a look from Madame Pétain, that she shouldn't have. 'We often did this, she and I, if you must know. Eugénie also, for proof. Solid proof!'

Fresh tears wet Élisabeth de Fleury's cheeks. Madame Richard reached across the table to take her by the hands, scattering shreds of tobacco, for she'd unconsciously crushed the cigarette.

'Can't you see how upset she is?' spat Madame Pétain, having seen that this Sûreté had taken note of the spilled tobacco. 'Aren't the photographs sufficient for you, Inspector? Must you have all the details, coarse as they are?'

'Everything,' he said.

'*Merde*, how can you be so insensitive? A man whose first wife left him with an empty house . . . the house of his mother, I understand, the second wife running off with the Hauptmann Steiner, only to be blown to pieces by a Résistance bomb on her reluctant return to that same house? Her child as well!'

Ah! what could one say? 'We police are seldom sensitive, Madame la Maréchale. It's part of the job. The victims, the blood, the oedematous fluid and aborted foetuses . . . Always a certain detachment is necessary, but they don't teach this at the Academy, of course, and wisely, I think, as it might dissuade some from taking up the profession.'

'Touché, eh? You didn't even know of that room, did you?'

'We're learning.'

'Then listen, Inspector. Though the doctor is certainly no friend of mine, he will tell you Élisabeth did awaken him that evening at about 2 a.m., and if you press him, I'm sure he will confess to having made a little joke of it. The first words uttered to her by that jackal were that if she desired extramarital sex, she must come to his office during the day, never to his home!'

One had best let that pass. 'And this room at the Hôtel Ruhl, madame. How long have you ladies known of it?'

'Since early last summer. Since Sandrine and then Élisabeth found the courage to admit their suspicions were more than justified. It was Sandrine who first saw her husband leaving that place just before that nurse of his, he going to the right, she to the left.'

Marie-Jacqueline Mailloux.

Would it hurt to volunteer a little without first consulting madame? wondered Élisabeth. 'It's an old place, Inspector, whose rooms are mostly taken by long-term residents who are not well off.'

'A few of the rooms are reserved for visiting civil servants whose positions demand little better,' said Madame Pétain tartly. 'Gaëtan-Baptiste Deschambeault found it for them.'

Julienne's husband, Lucie's lover . . .

'That *grigou* would have made certain the bank covered the cost, Inspector,' shot Sandrine Richard.

'*Grigou*, madame?'

Visibly flustered – realizing she had inadvertently said something she shouldn't have – she managed a brief and self-conscious grin. 'A nickname he uses with his wife and family when they demand too much.'

Had she read the notes Deschambeault and Céline had left for Lucie? he wondered. Had these three 'ladies' murdered that poor girl, the others also, or hired someone to do it? 'Is the hotel a *maison de passe*?' he asked.

'Haven't we just said it was used for that purpose?' spat Madame Pétain.

'Committee members know the hotel well,' he muttered, jotting it down in front of them. 'And at the *Grand établissement thermal*, Madame la Maréchale?'

This one was trouble. *Vipère* that he was, the little doctor had been correct about that! 'Mademoiselle Mailloux couldn't resist letting us know she and Alain André often shared a bath.'

The three exchanged glances, Sandrine Richard taking up the

thread of it. 'About three months before she was drowned, that woman entered our steam room as if by mistake, Inspector. No towel, *le costume d'Ève complet* and flaunting herself in front of me and my friends. I . . . I was so taken aback, I didn't know what to do. Eugénie calmly told her to leave.'

'Calmly?'

The Inspector had put his question to Élisabeth and was again holding up the hand of justice to prevent interference.

'She . . . she shrieked at her to leave,' confessed Madame de Fleury. 'Mademoiselle Mailloux blanched and muttered, "Sorry".'

'What, exactly, was shrieked?'

That we'd kill her if she didn't go? 'I . . . I can't recall the precise words. "Get out!" I think.'

'But she lost her smile, lost composure, was frightened and turned abruptly away? Apologized?'

'There was not time for that, but as to the rest, yes.'

'Three months . . .' he muttered.

'Prior to 9 December, Inspector. I didn't kill her. I swear it!' said Madame Richard.

Élisabeth de Fleury quickly took her by the hands to anxiously say, 'We're in the restaurant. Others will hear you!'

'The 9th of September,' he said. 'One always has to jot these little details down.'

'The 10th,' grated Madame Pétain. Others *were* trying hard to listen but not let on! 'Thursday afternoons are always our times at the thermal palace. First the steam and then the baths, the hot and then the cold, and then the douche to tighten up the pores. Mademoiselle Mailloux really did want to embarrass Sandrine in front of us, Inspector. That tart was shameful and totally without conscience.'

'And like Noëlle Olivier, Madame la Maréchale?'

To say, How dare you, would be of little use. 'Eventually you had to get at that, didn't you, Inspector? The knife, the earrings – even the perfume that bitch wore? Well, listen closely then, *mon pauvre* Sûreté. The Maréchal and I have always had two places of residence. His and mine. It's very discreet and convenient, and he has always made certain of this. In Paris, after our marriage in September of 1920, he rented and furnished two flats at 6 and 8 square de Latour-Maubourg – you know the Left Bank well, I'm sure – and then . . . then in the house at *numéro* 8 when a suitable one became available for me. Here, too, in the Hôtel du Parc, myself in the Majestic. *Bien sûr*, in our marriage we live apart and together, my being invited only to some of the many dinner parties and functions he attends; he and his current mistress, if he has one, to others. That's how it has always been with us.'

'Madame, I merely . . .'

'Did you think to insult me so as to let my anger give you an advantage? Did you think I wasn't aware of Madame Olivier's infatuation or that of the countless others Henri Philippe has had? In June 1920, not three months before our wedding – the banns had been announced well ahead of time, let me assure you! – he took up with Marie-Louise Regad, an old flame who had recently been made a widow. Then just a few months *after* our wedding, it was Madame Jacqueline de Castex, another widow and old flame whose daughter and her husband now live in the Hôtel du Parc to constantly remind me of that affair and to whom he regularly makes visits, not me. Never me! The Maréchal has a reputation for going after the married ones, hasn't he, even to chasing myself, and widows especially! But . . . but I must tell you.' She would pause now to catch a breath and hold it, Eugénie said to herself. 'No other woman in France can lick the back of her husband's head every time she mails a postcard to the north, or a letter in the south. *Moi-même, seulement*, Inspector.'

Only myself. 'Did all, or any of you, pay to have those girls killed?'

'And not kill them ourselves – is this the reason you sigh? Really, Inspector, that is so typically male-chauvinistic of you! Not capable of killing to save our marriages? Not able to vote, of course, nor to open a bank account without one's husband's or father's permission? That, too, is only understandable in such a male-dominated society, though one has to wonder about it when so many of our men are either dead or in prisoner-of-war camps. But women *are* allowed to go out to work and each day eight million of us do. More than in any other country in Europe, even now during this dreadful conflict. And of course, when they get home, there are always the meals, the washing, the cleaning, the children, the endless queues for food . . .'

'Madame, please just answer the question!'

'And not complain about the disgraceful conditions in this and the other hotels to which we have been assigned? Cooking on a single hotplate? Washing the clothes, the sheets and blankets in a hand sink if one is lucky? The tisane of linden blossom here, an occasional meal, but endless days of drudgery in overcrowded quarters, and on top of all of this, we are expected to ignore the philandering!'

'Madame, the question.'

'First, the *billets doux* that old fool wrote to Céline Dupuis.' Her fingers snapped!

'There were others he wrote to Noëlle Olivier,' cautioned St-Cyr.

Her eyebrows shot up. 'Is it that you wish to strike a bargain?'

'It could be arranged. A small fire.'

'Then listen closely once again. Ménétrel found out those girls were informants for *les Allemands*. Though he has swelled far beyond the mediocre capacity of his head, even I would never underestimate his loyalty to my husband. He'd have definitely had those girls singled out and killed, both to teach them a lesson and to set one for others, and to remove the breach of security they represented.'

'And even though you must hate him for what he did to you with Noëlle, Charles-Frédéric Hébert would have been the one to do it for him?'

'*Yes!*'

'The Hôtel Ruhl, then. Would the doctor have been aware of Room 3-17?'

No glances were exchanged. Madame Pétain noticed a pulled thread in the tablecloth and plucked fastidiously at it.

'Sandrine and Élisabeth haven't had to watch that place in

some time, Inspector. Even when they did, their surveillance was limited to those occasions when they felt certain something must be going on, often during the *cinq à sept*. Fortunately there is a café just across the boulevard de l'Hôtel de Ville, one not much frequented by those of the Government.'

'Seedy?'

'A little.'

'Madame, these two would have stood out like sore thumbs. Yourself also!'

'Certainly, but the *patron* is a very understanding man, a White Russian who is married to a Jewess. Ménétrel, to his shame I must say, is our most violent anti-Semite, so you see he could not possibly have been aware of our having used that café unless . . .'

Merde, what the hell were the three of them after now?

'Albert Grenier,' said Élisabeth de Fleury softly. 'On several occasions I saw Albert going into or coming from that hotel, and often just after Madame Dupuis had left it.'

The resident rat-catcher . . .

'And once, Élisabeth, someone else,' prompted Sandrine.

'Ah *oui*. His mother. At least, at first that is who I thought it was, but then Madame la Maréchale corrected me.'

'Edith Pascal,' sighed St-Cyr, for Edith obtained newspapers from Albert. *Sacré nom de nom*, must he feel so completely out of his depth with these three?

It was Madame Pétain who said, 'Albert would have told his grand-uncle of that room, Inspector.'

'And Charles-Frédéric Hébert would have told Dr Ménétrel,' said Sandrine Richard, 'but more recently, I think, and just before the killings started.'

This thing goes round and round, Hermann would have said.

'Inspector,' confided Madame Pétain, her forearms now resting on the table, 'Charles-Frédéric is indebted to the doctor for the position he holds at that château of Herr Abetz's and for the dreams he harbours of its return. Hébert must have known those girls were informants. Once the doctor had learned of their betraying the country, he would not have let that one forget it.'

'So Hébert and Albert killed them?'

'Perhaps.'

'And when, please, Madame de Fleury, did you first see Albert and Mademoiselle Pascal going into that hotel?'

'First?' she bleated.

'First,' he said.

'Last August. The 16th, a Sunday afternoon. Honoré and I were to have taken the children to the town's swimming pool in the Allier, but . . . but at the last moment, my husband said he had to go in to work and that I should take them myself. "The children mustn't be disappointed," he said. "Here, let me give you a little something for their ices."'

The bastard. Saccharin and ersatz flavours, and well before the raid when photos were taken at the château.

The sculptress had had some soup and a few of the egg-salad sandwiches from one of the trolleys and was now on her first cup of tea – 'Real tea,' she had exclaimed, 'and petits fours like Céline and I used to buy from Monsieur Bibeau's *pâtisserie* in the rue Mouffetard.'

Kohler knew he shouldn't have let her enjoy herself. He hadn't put the squeeze on her all the while Louis had been at that other table – still was, for that matter – though they desperately needed answers from her, if for no other reason than her own safety. Yet he couldn't ask if she'd delivered messages in Paris for Olivier – that would be far too risky for Louis and himself, should Gessler get his hands on her. Somehow he had to go around that one and yet prise what he could from her about it.

'You get sick a lot, don't you? First in that snow-bound toilet and then in the sacristy.'

Flustered – caught out as if having taken something she shouldn't have – Inès reluctantly set aside the half-eaten little wedge of Genoese sponge cake, with its filling of butter cream, glaze of apricot jam and coating of white icing. The meringues had looked so heavenly, the miniature éclairs also, but had Herr Kohler fed her simply to loosen her tongue?

'My stomach hasn't been right since the Defeat, Inspector. The constant diet of vegetables is impossible. Carrots always; rillettes and chops of rutabaga when I can't stand the taste and woody texture of swedes and know the hospitals are full of appendicitis cases and other bowel complaints. The "rabbit stew" in the little restaurant I sometimes go to only tells me Monsieur Lapin has leaped the casserole and made good his escape, leaving mystery meat behind. The grey National causes gas and diarrhoea, and I can understand fully the concern of the doctors. I once dissolved some of that bread in a bowl of water to see what rose to the top and sank to the bottom, and have ever since wished I hadn't. What one doesn't know is often better than what one does, *n'est-ce pas*? Sawdust, little bits of straw, the wings and carapaces of beetles or weevils perhaps, fibres of some kind – cotton, I think, but hemp also from the grain bags – and a slimy coagulation of grey-green to black particles that are greasy and not of pepper.'

Rat shit but *merde alors*, hadn't she unwound her tongue about it! 'And at the bottom?' he asked.

'Sand-sized grit and larger particles from the grinding stones. That is what gave me the toothache I complained of and still have. A hairline crack, I think, in an old filling.'

'And oil of bitter almonds instead of cloves . . .'

Had he not believed her? 'Yes. Cheated twice. First by the Government adding weight with sand, and then by the *salaud* I had to deal with on the *marché noir*. He swore it was oil of cloves and I . . . I was stupid enough to have trusted him.'

Dentists seldom could offer anaesthetic. These days everyone was avoiding the drill, even Louis. 'Albert didn't just reject you. At the Jockey Club he tried to stick as close to you as possible and then, at the château, tried to kill you. Any ideas?'

'None. I know it looks bad and, believe me, I'm trying hard to understand and forgive him.'

Her tea was getting cold. 'Then start by telling me why that one is also wary of you.'

'Blanche . . . ?' Did Herr Kohler suspect Monsieur Olivier had warned her about them, that Blanche and her brother had forced

Edith Pascal to let them into his house? 'Perhaps it is that she's afraid of what Céline might have told me in the letters Lucie brought.'

'That she and her brother live alone and share the same bed?'

Incest . . . was this what Herr Kohler wanted her to say? 'That Blanche and Paul, being all but identical twins, are very close and that she worries constantly about his health and looks after him as a mother would.'

'And doesn't wonder what Céline told you of Olivier, or that one of himself, or even whether the two of you have met since you arrived in Vichy?'

So there it was: Olivier. 'We haven't met. I want to but . . . but there hasn't been time yet.' A lie of course, but would Herr Kohler accept it?

'Too busy following us around, eh? What about Edith, then? Have you met her?'

She must force herself to gaze frankly at him. 'Neither one nor the other, Inspector, and as for my "following" you and the Chief Inspector around, it is, as I've said, only because I'm waiting to get on with the job the Musée sent me to do and because I want, also, to find out who killed my friend.'

'Lucie doesn't seem to matter much to you.'

'Yet we met in Paris and so I should be concerned? *Mon Dieu,* I am, but naturally more about Céline.'

Pas mal, pas mal. Not bad for an answer. 'That wax portrait in your case . . .'

'Needs only a touch-up, yes. If okayed by Monsieur le Maréchal and Dr Ménétrel, I may, I suppose, need do nothing further.'

Honesty at last, was that it? 'Then you're not here for as long as it takes.'

'Well, in a way I am. Of course, I should have told you it was all but complete. I . . . I had thought to but . . . but wanted to give myself time to find out what I could about Céline's murder.'

'And you're certain you've never met or spoken to Olivier? You wouldn't have used the telephone to contact him? Few do these days if they can avoid it and there isn't one in that house of his in any case, is there?'

'I ... I wouldn't know. He ... he did write to me once, as I've said, Inspector, and Céline did know he was my father's *compagnon d'armes.*'

'*Verdammt!* I knew I'd forgotten something.'

Taking three snapshots from a jacket pocket, he looked at her and then at each of them. 'This one, I think,' he said. 'But first, admit that you knew Olivier had been forced by Pétain into giving the firing squad its orders.'

After the Battle of Chemin des Dames ... after the mutiny that followed in May 1917. She mustn't let her eyes moisten, must gaze steadily at him and say clearly, 'That just can't be true, Inspector. Monsieur Olivier would have told me of it in his letter and begged my forgiveness. Instead, he wrote only of what a fine comrade Papa was, how brave and kind and honest, and how he had spoken constantly of me, the child he was never to see.'

The photo showed them playing chess in the trenches, and for a moment Inès couldn't stop her eyes from smarting, her fingers from trembling. 'Could you let me have this?' she asked, her voice unfortunately faint. 'I ... I haven't many, and none like it.'

Jésus, merde alors, just what the hell was she hiding? 'Later, when we've our killer or killers.' The photos of Noëlle Olivier as a cabaret dancer and with a grey gelding just like the one Lucie had kept were hardly noticed. 'Now let me have that handbag of yours Albert was so interested in.'

'You've already seen its contents. Would you scatter them in front of all these ladies and treat me as a common criminal, Inspector, when I'm most definitely not? Believe me, there's nothing but the usual. A lipstick I seldom use because of the ersatz things they put in it. The key to my studio. My papers, I assure you, are fully in order. There are some tissues, a pencil and paper to sketch with if I wish ...'

'The phial of perfume. Let's start with that.'

The Shalimar ... 'My aunt loved that scent.'

'And so did the Maréchal who gave it to Noëlle Olivier and insisted she wear it.'

'As did Céline and myself. A coincidence.'

'And nothing else, eh?' he snorted with disbelief.

Though he didn't dump her bag out on the table, Herr Kohler found the phial and, unscrewing its cap, brought it to his nose, holding it there until satisfied. 'Now tell me why the one with the almond oil isn't here?'

But is it with the portrait mask, the blocks of beeswax and sculpting tools? Sticking plasters, too, and iodine with which to patch up battered detectives . . . 'I simply tried the oil, Inspector, and finding it wasn't what it was supposed to have been, put it in my case with my other first-aid supplies.'

'Having spilled a touch of it?'

'Yes, unfortunately, since I could, quite possibly, have used it for baking if . . . if I could have somehow managed to find the flour.'

'Then tell me why that one has just brought your valise into the restaurant?'

Her back had been to them, but now the sculptress turned as she hesitantly got to her feet to look towards the entrance.

From her solitude next to the windows, Blanche Varollier had done the same thing.

Inès's hand was limp. The kid didn't even tremble. Too frightened and with good reason, thought Kohler, having stepped close to her.

Without a fedora, but with briefcase crammed under one arm and valise gripped in the other hand, Gessler stood with Herr Jännicke just inside the entrance, potted Kentia palms in dark blue jardinières to their left and right, the ex-shoemaker short, broad-shouldered and bull-necked, the top button of the lead-grey overcoat undone; the other one tall, and with his black overcoat all buttoned up, the scarf loose, the black homburg in hand, his thick black hair receding and combed straight back off the high, wide brow.

Gessler's expression was grim and sour, for he'd not liked the

334

sight of all these ladies indulging themselves so frivolously when there was a war on, and for him there had always been a class war, ever since the days of the Blood Purge.

The big ears stood out, the eyes squinted with distaste, slanting downward to the left and right of a nose that had, no doubt, been bloodied by barrel staves more than once for the sake of the Party.

His tie was crooked; Herr Jännicke's was perfect. Gessler's moustache was grey, not brown like the Führer's, so he hadn't dyed it like many did. The face was grey too, and wide, the close-cropped Fritz haircut all but reaching to Herr Jännicke's right shoulder.

'You let me handle this,' breathed Kohler. 'Don't you dare disgrace me.'

'My valise . . .' It was all the kid could manage, for the two had now set out to join them. Gessler knocked against anyone who happened to be in the way. The gossip died as arrest seemed imminent until silence swelled to fill the void and all other motion had ceased.

Louis hadn't got to his feet. Louis knew his revolver was in his overcoat pocket here at this table.

Heels didn't clash, salutes were not given. The valise was set on the table, smashing things and causing the sculptress's teacup to tip. Milk and cold tea flooded into the tablecloth.

They didn't shout, didn't shriek. They simply blocked any exit, Herr Gessler speaking rapidly in *Deutsch*, Inès trying desperately to fight down her sickness and pick out a word or two of meaning. Berlin . . . Kohler's reputation as a . . . Slacker? she wondered, watching each of them closely, trying hard not to bolt and run but to remain still so as to fathom what was happening to her . . . to her!

'*Dieser Fliegentöter*, Kohler. *Ich warte schon . . .*' I've been waiting . . . For your report? Four murders and you arrest an *Idiot* and then let him go? '*Was ist mit ihn los*, Herr Jännicke?' What is it with him?

'Herr Oberstleutnant, I can explain.'

335

'*Verfluchte Kripo, Verfluchte Franzosen ...*' Cursed Kripo, cursed French ... '*Vermehrende Idioten.*' Breeding idiots ... '*Alle Halbheit ist taub*, Kohler.' Half-measures are no measures. He can't be '*dieser Fliegentöter*'. The Flykiller. But better in '*den Zellen*', than free.

'*Jawohl*, Herr Oberst.'

'*Gut*,' but you'll ... not find him in the cellars of the Hôtel du Parc ... '*Dieser Handkoffer*, Kohler,' this case ... was open. That father of his can't ... can't find him either. Ah no!

'*Bitte*, Fräulein, go through your case. Damage, theft ... we must know of this.'

Her valise ... She must empty it for them ... '*Oui*, monsieur. I ... I had forgotten Albert's father was looking after it for me.'

Kohler translated what she'd said. Gessler lit a cigarette and offered one to Herr Jännicke. The kid lifted out the tray ... The phial of almond oil now held only dregs, just dregs. Had Albert sampled it? he wondered. Wet ... the tray was wet and reeked of bitter almond. The mask, swaddled in its white linen cloths, stared up at them.

She nodded. Faintly she said in French, 'Nothing has been taken or damaged. Albert must simply have wanted another look at the portrait and ... and accidentally emptied the phial when putting it back.'

Herr Kohler translated.

'Then please be more careful in future.'

'Bernard ... Bernard,' sang out Madame Pétain as Dr Ménétrel came into the restaurant on the run only to stop dead at the sight of Gessler and Jännicke. 'Bernard, the Chief Inspector St-Cyr was just telling us of Paris. Not a word about those dreadful murders or your part in them.'

Stung by her words, furious with her and with them, no doubt, the portly doctor turned on his heels, collared the maître d' and bent his ear before retreating to the lobby and the Hôtel du Parc.

It was the maître d' who, on coming to their table, quietly confided, 'Mademoiselle, the doctor wishes you to present your

portrait to the Maréchal for his appraisal tomorrow morning at
9.50.'

'Where?' she asked, her voice far from strong.

'Why here, of course. Behind that.'

The screen that kept the great one from prying eyes while he
ate.

'Right after his breakfast briefing. A few minutes can be spared,
mademoiselle. No more.'

A few minutes ... 'Yes. Why, yes, of course. I understand
perfectly. *Merci.*'

10

As the dining room was cleared, the detectives again sat alone at their table. Blanche had remained at hers, Sandrine at Madame Pétain's. And I? mused Inès silently. I sit to the far side looking beyond hurrying waiters and across vacated tables to Herr Kohler, and he at me. Kripo that he was, Kohler had realized exactly how terrified of arrest and torture she'd been. He had watched her closely as she'd taken the valise with her and had set it carefully on the floor at her feet. He'd known she'd been silently repeating Aves; had known she had all but run from Gessler and the other one.

Madame Pétain and Madame de Fleury had gone to dress for the trip the detectives had insisted on to the clinic of Dr Normand and his patient, Julienne Deschambeault. Sandrine Richard would drive the two ladies to the clinic. And I? Inès demanded and answered, I must go in either car. And Blanche? she wondered. Would Blanche come with them or . . .

Herr Kohler nodded at her. 'Gessler's just given us a reminder, Louis. Having sealed the town off and put the *Sonderkommando* to work scouring the countryside, he and Herr Jännicke will quietly let us do the job here. If we foul up, we'll get the blame; if we succeed, he'll take the credit.'

'*Merde*, this investigation, Hermann. Vichy is like a Pandora's box and Chinese puzzle all in one. Every time we lift a lid, there's another waiting!'

Tobacco was needed; crumbs from the meal were carelessly scattered on the tablecloth. Did they have the bits and pieces arranged before them again? wondered Inès. Would St-Cyr insist on the plodding, methodical approach in spite of the need for haste?

Would Herr Kohler's impatience get the better of them both?

When it was time to leave, they refused to let her travel with Madame Richard and the others. Though it couldn't be so very dark outside the Hôtel Majestic, due to the snow cover, everything was jet black to her. No details at all, no silhouettes. Just nothing but an empty, empty darkness, she wanting desperately to reach out and feel her way yet knowing she mustn't, that she must hide the blindness from them at all cost.

Suddenly she went down hard at an unseen step, Herr Kohler grabbing her. 'Easy,' he said. 'Don't worry so much. You're not under arrest.'

Arrest? Ah, Sainte Mère, why had he to say it? No lights were on that she could see but she knew there must be the blue-blinkered torches of pedestrians, those of the tail lights and headlamps of *vélos, vélo-taxis* and horse-drawn carriages. Wasn't that a cyclist she heard call out a warning?

They crossed some pavement, went out on to a road, reached a car, any car – their car – she clutching her valise and handbag tightly and telling herself it's a two-door Peugeot. The back seat . . . You'll have to squeeze into it . . .

'A moment, mademoiselle,' said St-Cyr, the door opening at last . . .

Now put the valise in carefully ahead of you, Inès told herself. That's it, *ma chère.* You're doing fine. Now follow it. Say something. *Anything* to hide your blindness. 'It must be late. People are hurrying home.'

Still there were none of the firefly lights as there were in Paris every time she'd had to go out at night and had had to wait, leaning against a wall or lamp-post, until her eyes had adjusted and her terror had abated with relief at the sight of them and their owners' silhouettes.

'You must drink bilberry tisanes,' Monsieur Olivier had said well before dawn yesterday when she had arrived in Vichy, he having come to meet her at a café near the railway station.

'Vitamin A, mademoiselle. Too many are suffering from its lack, not here, though. Here, in Vichy, the problem hasn't surfaced because we've only had a full blackout since 11 November. Before that, every second street-lamp was always lit.'

He'd been able to see perfectly when walking from a lighted room into darkness, she abysmally not at all.

When the car pulled over, Inès felt they must be near the main casino, which was at the far end of the Parc des Sources. St-Cyr got out; Kohler lit a cigarette, then offered her one, only to say, 'Oh, sorry, I forgot. You don't use them, do you?'

'Is there some trouble?' she asked, turning to look behind them but knowing she still couldn't see a thing.

'Trouble? Louis is just telling them we've had a change of plan.'

She blinked. She would concentrate hard on where she felt his cigarette must be, but each time she had experienced night blindness, it had taken a little longer for her eyes to adjust, each time it had become more terrifying. To not have one's sight, to be totally blind and a courier, a *résistante* ...

Quickly the kid crossed herself and kissed her fingertips, had forgotten to wear her gloves.

'They're not happy,' grunted St-Cyr on returning, abruptly yanking his side door closed. 'A visit to the morgue will do them good, Herman!'

The morgue ... Ah *Jésus, cher Jésus*, Céline, what have you got me into?

The lights were blinding. Always, too, it was like this when coming straight from darkness into strong light, the pain suddenly searing.

'*You should have told me of this!*' Olivier had said of her night blindness. He'd not been happy to have discovered it, had hauled her up sharply and had said harshly, '*You can't see, can you?*'

They'd been on the street, had just left the café and its crowd of railway workers ...

The morgue was cold and brightly lit, the stench of disinfectant, attendant cigarette smoke, blood and rotting corpses, formaldehyde and bad drains causing her stomach to tightly knot.

Madame Pétain took a firm grip on her. Blanche and Sandrine Richard were behind them.

'This way, ladies,' said St-Cyr, as if enjoying the discomfort he was causing. 'We will only be a moment but the visit is necessary. Either we have one killer or two, and Dr Laloux may, perhaps, now be able to enlighten us.'

'Laloux . . .' muttered Madame Pétain. 'Isn't he the socialist Henri Philippe put on trial at Riom in the spring of '41 with Daladier, Blum and the others of the Front Populaire? You'll get nothing useful from him, Inspector. No matter what the courts decided, people like that are parasites.'

'*Doryphores*, madame?'

'*Précisément!*'

'Then you'd best meet him.'

Élisabeth de Fleury had stayed in the outer office with Herr Kohler, Inès told herself. They went along a corridor, a steel door was opened, the sound of it echoing, the air now much, much colder, the stench sharper. Water . . . water was running. A tap? she wondered.

The sound of it was silenced at the sight of them. Hands were now be being dried – coroner's hands.

'Mademoiselle, you don't look well,' hazarded Madame Pétain. 'Inspector, surely it's not necessary for this one to join us? Here, let me take your case.'

Smile faintly, Inès told herself, say, '*Merci*, Madame la Maréchale, it's most kind of you.'

'Get her a chair, *imbécile!*' said the woman to the attendant. 'A chair! Surely you know what that is?'

'There are none,' the man replied. 'No one ever sits in here.'

'I'm all right really. I . . . I've already seen Céline.'

Her left hand was quickly guided to a railing of some sort, her fingers instinctively wrapping themselves around it.

'*Merci*, madame,' she heard herself say again as the sound of metal rollers grew louder and one drawer was opened, then another, another and another.

'Draw back the shrouds,' said St-Cyr.

'Fully?' yelped the attendant.

'*Merde alors*, had I not wanted this, I'd not have asked for it, monsieur, and if you smirk again at these ladies, you can kiss your job and pension goodbye!'

Although they were still clear enough, the images were blurred by her tears, Inès knew. Madame Pétain had left her at some distance, standing beside an empty pallet. The large hats she and Madame Richard wore were of felt and widely brimmed, Madame la Maréchale's with a silvery pin and of a striking blue to match the woollen overcoat, scarf and gloves, the back straight, the woman tall; Sandrine Richard's *chapeau* had a wide band and was charcoal grey, the overcoat the same.

Blanche stood alone, a little apart from them. Her back, too, was straight, her head held high but not proud, for apprehension was in her look, despair also.

'The rats, Jean-Louis,' said a scruffy-bearded, grey little man with wire-rimmed spectacles whose right lens was broken. A man who'd been in prison, Inès told herself. 'One can always tell with them,' Olivier had said.

Hurriedly the coroner threw Madame Pétain a glance but otherwise ignored her.

'The rats,' said St-Cyr, 'five of which were found in this one's bed.'

Their putrid little corpses lay belly up and split open, the mush of entrails puddled. Madame Pétain was curious, seeming to tower over St-Cyr and the coroner; Madame Richard stood back a little and tense, so very tense, not at the sight of those little corpses, ah no, Inès told herself, but in expectation of what the coroner might have to say about their butchering.

'Snared, Jean-Louis, by one who is very skilful at such things. Two of them finished off with a stick of some sort.'

'The leg of a kitchen chair,' acknowledged St-Cyr. 'And the

342

others?' he asked, raptly leaning over them himself in spite of the stench.

'Death by strangulation in their snares, the time at least a good twenty-four hours before that of the victim.'

'And then?'

'All of them more recently butchered with one of these, I think. The blade has a deep nick in it – one that hasn't yet been ground out and is burred. As it cut towards the scrotum, it caught on the penile bone and tissues and ripped the genitals out of three of them. A hasty butchering. One that took, I would estimate, no more than three or four minutes. The blade was then wiped on the sheets, tearing the cloth as well.'

Coroner Laloux took from his smock a worn, black-handled Opinel pocket-knife, its blade more robust than that of a Laguiole, somewhat shorter, too, and wider, not nearly so graceful or piercing a weapon, though a knife that sickened all the same, if not more . . .

'Albert Grenier uses a butcher's knife,' Inès heard herself blurt. 'Albert doesn't have a knife like that, but . . .' She caught herself and turned away, saying silently to herself, But I know who does. I do!

'As to whether a man or a woman, Jean-Louis, I can but say that whoever it was knew anatomy well enough.'

The sex and the livers . . . Sandrine Richard hadn't moved in all this time. Lips parted in apprehension, her gaze was fixed on the little gap between St-Cyr and Madame Pétain and her cheeks were drained of colour. She was swallowing hard, and one could imagine her thinking, Gaëtan-Baptiste killed his mistress, Honoré his, and Alain André his. Or did she simply think, St-Cyr knew who had done it?

But could he?

They moved to the victims, Blanche trailing them, herself staying put because Céline had been so beautiful, so full of hope and yet . . . and yet so worried.

Scared shitless – why can't you admit it? Inès asked herself harshly, only to hear St-Cyr saying to Madame Richard,

'Madame, please take a good look at this one and tell me if you killed her?'

Marie-Jacqueline Mailloux . . .

Revolting to look at, putrefaction's suppuratingly livid encrustations of bluish green to yellow and blue-black blotches were everywhere on her legs, mons and stomach, her breasts, shoulders, throat and face. A network of veins, dark plum-blue to black, ran beneath an opalescent to translucent skin. The brow was high and wide, the skin like wax where not yet discoloured, the chin narrow, the nose sharp, the stench terrible.

Discharge webbed an unplugged nostril, the cotton wool having fallen out.

'There are bruises, Jean-Louis, and scratches,' said Laloux. 'Though drunk on champagne, Mademoiselle Mailloux fought hard and her killer must surely have borne evidence of the struggle.'

'Scratches?' demanded Madame Pétain.

Dr Laloux did not look at her. 'Though mostly removed during the initial autopsy and not saved or detailed sufficiently, some scrapings of the assailant's skin were left.'

'How can you be sure it was a male?' Madame Pétain asked.

'I can't, nor can I say it was from a female, madame, but . . .'

'Hair . . . the colour of the killer's hair?' she demanded. Sandrine Richard winced, St-Cyr noticing the exchange as he noticed everything.

'Hairs would, I feel, have been present, madame. At least one or two, but whatever evidence was present has since been removed.'

And lost, but deliberately: was that what he implied? wondered Inès. It must be, for Laloux was not at all content.

Blanche couldn't take her gaze from the corpse. Revulsion, fear . . . ah, so many emotions were registered in her expression, thought Inès, having at last joined their little group.

The Sûreté's voice was harsh. 'Sandrine Richard, I ask you now in front of these witnesses, did your husband, Alain André

344

Richard, bear any such scratches on the evening of 9 December last or in the days following?'

They would have all but healed and vanished by now . . .

'Since we were no longer sleeping together, Inspector, I noticed none.'

A cold answer.

'And you yourself?' he asked.

Madame Pétain caught a breath and held it.

'Have a conscience that is clear.'

'The other victims, then,' he said, swiftly turning to the coroner and obviously furious with Madame Richard's response.

'With this one, the same wire, as you noted before,' said Laloux, 'the assailant at least of medium height and perhaps a little taller.'

'Then not Albert Grenier, Louis,' said Herr Kohler, having reluctantly joined them.

Laloux acknowledged the contribution. 'With this next one, perhaps the assailant who drowned the first victim, smothered the third. There is that same sense of downward force, that same weight, that same ruthless determination.'

'A professional?' asked St-Cyr.

'Why then the necessity of finishing her off in an armoire? Surely if that were so, the killer would have completed his task in the bed.'

Not a professional then, though the killer had wanted it to look as if Albert Grenier had done it.

'And with the most recent killing?' asked St-Cyr. 'Was the lifting on the haft of the knife simply due to jealousy?'

Laloux removed his glasses, for Madame la Maréchale's jealousy had been implied. 'Or hatred, or both, but desperation, I think, Jean-Louis.'

'Male or female?'

Blanche had turned away, was fighting for composure, thought Inès, as Coroner Laloux said, 'I've puzzled over this and wish I could be more precise but there is no clear evidence. The same person may have killed all of them, but then, each could also have been killed by a different assailant.'

'Surely the garrotting of Camille Lefèbvre took strength?'

'But that of a man – is this what you mean? Really, Jean-Louis, are women not as strong as men? Many of them most certainly are.'

A man, said Inès sadly to herself and wept inwardly for Céline who had trusted him as she had. That Opinel, Inspectors. Monsieur Olivier has one. I've seen it, for my valise had a rope tied round it when I left the train and this he cut while we were in the café, a place where only those he was certain of would be present.

Two of them had looked her over as she'd shown him the portrait mask of Pétain. Two of them.

The Clinique du Dr Raoul Normand was on the rue Hubert Colombier in the old part of town. St-Cyr knew this well enough but with no lights, street names would be impossible and he had used, Inès surmised, the silhouette of the nearby Église Saint-Blaise against the night sky for guidance. 'Part fifteenth century, part 1930s, Hermann,' he had said, no doubt peering out his side windscreen. 'The latter with magnificent art deco mosaics and stained glass.'

And a black Virgin, Inès said to herself. The Notre-Dame-des-Malades to which I have, during my brief visit, already prayed. The Madonna is surrounded by the commemorative plaques of the faithful, each of which attested to her having answered their prayers and cured them of their afflictions, but could the Virgin ever cure Vichy of what ailed it?

Monsieur Olivier had told her to meet him there after the Maréchal's viewing of the wax portrait. 'But I don't yet know when that will be,' she had said and he . . . he had answered, 'Don't worry, I'll know.'

As he had known everything? she wondered. When Céline would go to Pétain, when Lucie would leave for Clermont-Ferrand or Paris . . . Paris. And the portrait mask? Tomorrow, monsieur? At 9.50 a.m. and just after the Maréchal's breakfast briefing? How, please, could he have known of this so far ahead of time? And *why* was she to meet him? More messages to deliver in Paris, but now ... now with Lucie dead, there could no longer be a way for him to get them to her, unless ... unless he was counting on her to take them across the Demarcation Line.

Two knives: the Laguiole of the wife who had killed herself in despair on 18 November 1925, at the age of thirty-four, and the cold and worn Opinel of his own pocket.

Had he killed Céline? Had he killed them all?

The clinic, a manor house, was not of the new-Gothic, Flemish style, nor was it neo-Venetian or neoclassical as some buildings in Vichy were, thought St-Cyr, but was, in itself too, superbly of the *fin de siècle*, of art nouveau and of old money. Lots of it.

Lustrous curves and flowing lines were in the mahogany panelling, banisters and mouldings. Tall corridors opened upwards to floral, stained-glass lights which gave the sense of being in a verdant, year-round garden. Kentias, in cylindrical jardinières, glazed white and blue, lined the walls at intervals. Stylish red, morocco-covered, cushioned benches allowed for rest and patient reflection. Water played musically in the distance. A mosaic of soft blue lilies, submerged in the white of the tiles, was underfoot, each flower revealing a yellow-dusted stamen that opened into a gorgeous naked nymph whose arms were thrown wide in rapture. Youth, health and beauty were everywhere, especially in the painting of nereids *au bain* above the doorway at the far end of the corridor, where limpid-eyed girls stood in foam-flecked shallows splashing a buck-naked Nereus, as dolphins swam and seashells basked.

The grey-skirted, trimly aproned little maid of twenty with the clear complexion, brown eyes and chestnut hair, paused. 'Messieurs et mesdames,' she announced hesitantly. 'It is this way, please. The doctor awaits.'

'And is expecting us?' asked Kohler from behind the ladies.

'As he expects all who come here, monsieur.'

347

'*Foie, diabète et estomac,* Hermann,' grunted St-Cyr. Liver, diabetes and stomach problems. 'Gout, too, and obesity. It's all in the mind. You need the cure, you want the cure and *voilà,* you take it and feel better.'

'Having paid a fortune! Louis!'

Vénus et Diane stood on either side of the doorway in their gilded birthday suits, life-sized and all the rest. The lighting became softer, the corridor turning as the playful sound of water increased and one saw, as if looking down through a leafy tunnel between full-frontal nudes of a teenaged boy and girl whose arms were languidly raised to pick dream-fruit perhaps, others bathing in a secluded forest pond. Some were half-undressed, most were naked, some were submerged right up to their pretty necks. The farthest bather wore a gossamer sheath that clung to her in the most favourable of places.

'I like it, Louis. Maybe my knee would too.'

'And that aching shoulder you forgot to tell me about?'

'Quit worrying so much. I'll be there when you need me.'

'It's the needing I'm worrying about.'

They were moving quickly now. A spacious lounge held a bar, billiard and card tables, armchairs and kaftan-clad, felt-slippered *curistes,* among them the greying local Kommandant and others of the Occupier. Too many of the others . . .

'Ignore them!' hissed Kohler as men, women, young boys and girls watched their progress, the conversation falling off. No sign of Pétain, though. None of Ménétrel either.

The room, the examining office-cum-dispensary, was a clutter. Weighing scales for the patients to step on, others for preparing their prescriptions. Pharmaceutical jars of herbs, bottles of the various Vichy waters, the Célestins, Hôpital, Dôme and Boussange among them. The bank of wooden filing drawers must hold each patient's card and record of progress; carved models of hands and feet would be used for arthritic enlightenment, gout too. Even an array of the regulation, measured glasses stood sentinel with a graduated cylinder.

A wall mirror, astutely positioned on the left of the desk,

would reflect each *curiste's* towel- or sheath-draped figure for lessons in obesity that permitted few secrets.

A little man, grey, balding and sharply goateed, with necktie, shirt, waistcoat and suit under a white smock, Dr Raoul Normand was pushing seventy. He scribbled hard, the gold-rimmed pince-nez balanced on the bridge of a slender nose. Another prescription. Thirty cubic centimetres of the Chomel ... *le gymnase, la hydrothérapie et les inhalations de gaz* ...

'Doctor, some visitors,' whispered the maid, having timidly approached the desk.

'A moment, my child. Will you see that Herr Schröder follows my orders strictly? Positively no alcohol for five days. We must convince him of this.' He fretted. '*Zaunerstollen* ... what is this, please?' he asked, consulting the request sheet he'd been given by his latest *curiste*.

'A nougat,' offered Kohler, the others standing aside. 'Ground hazelnuts and almonds, with grated chocolate, butter, cream and crumbled bits of *Oblaten*.'

'*And what is that?*' snapped the doctor, irritably fussing with the sheet of notepaper.

'Round wafers filled with buttered, ground almonds and sugar.'

'*Merde*, how in heaven's name is his liver to possibly continue? Twenty-five cubic centimetres of the Chomel, Babette, three times the half-day. The tisanes of rose-hip, elderflower and lime at all other times. Absolutely no pâté, pork, goose or anything but the fish steamed and the vegetables unbuttered. No coffee or tea. I must insist. Fifteen cubic centimetres of the Grande Grille first thing on waking and another fifteen on retiring, but to be gently sipped so as not to shock the system. If he complains, don't listen; if he threatens, please tell him that though I dislike admitting failure, I will have to ask the Kommandant to consider sending him to Baden-Baden where they do have these ... these ...'

'*Zaunerstollen*,' said Kohler.

'*Merci*.'

'Bad Homburg might be better. It's just outside of Frankfurt am Main.'

'Hermann, please!'

Louis knew that the SS had taken over the Rothschild spa there and had coupled it with one of their *Lebensborn*, their life fountains, where blonde, blue-eyed, voluptuous *Rheinmädchen* were brought in to couple with the elite and produce pure Aryan cannon fodder.

'And the Frau Schröder, Docteur?' interjected the maid.

The little man looked up and removed his pince-nez. 'Is to understand that our latest synthetic-rubber baron's liver is in a state of crisis. The hot and cold baths for her, seven minutes at a time and alternating for the full hour. The steam afterwards, and after that, the full body scrape and message *complet*, to be followed by the warm effervescent bath with the rose petals and the *cure de silence* for at least another hour. A little wine with her dinner – one glass ... Ah! perhaps two, but positively no sugar, fat or starch. If she accuses us of being concentration camp warders, apologize but make sure you emphasize that we've never heard of such places. Now ... Ah! Madame la Maréchale, *excusez-moi*. Messieurs, Mesdames Richard et de Fleury, what a pleasant surprise. Mademoiselles,' he acknowledged Blanche and Inès. 'Please forgive the small delay. We are, I'm afraid, short-staffed and totally overloaded. What can I do for you?'

If not a cure, thought Kohler, then at least the negatives of certain photographs.

'Madame Deschambeault,' said Louis. 'A few small questions. Nothing difficult and don't say it's impossible.'

Communication between the two detectives had been by a look so slight that none but herself could have noticed it, felt Inès. They were ushered out of the doctor's office and the door was then locked behind them. St-Cyr, Madame Pétain and the other two ladies had gone off with a disgruntled Dr Normand to visit Madame Deschambeault.

Herr Kohler had stayed behind and had told Blanche and herself to find a bench in the corridor nearby.

Blanche sat silently beside her, a Kentia to her right, the girl's reflection clear in the mirror opposite, Blanche pale and withdrawn and terribly worried. Everything would now be decided on the outcome of this murder investigation. Her brother's future, her own, their claim to what they felt was rightfully theirs. Herr Kohler could hardly wait to get rid of them. No sooner had they turned their backs on him than he'd have been at that lock.

He would be in the consulting room now, hurriedly going through the files, and would find that Marie-Jacqueline Mailloux had assisted in the treatment of Madame Deschambeault until that one had learned of who she was: the mistress of Alain André Richard, the husband of a dear, dear friend.

He would find that, as Céline had written in one of her letters, Marie-Jacqueline had also attended to Albert Grenier's sore back and shoulder – his 'spine' – at his house or in the groundskeeper's little 'nest', out of the goodness of her heart, and that Albert had loved her for it as he had loved the others.

He would soon know, if he and St-Cyr didn't already know, that Dr Ménétrel received regular reports from Dr Normand on the progress of Madame Deschambeault and that everything that poor woman had said while under treatment had not only been written down, but repeated. He would see that Sandrine Richard hadn't just threatened to kill Marie-Jacqueline at the château, but that she had also done so here, early last summer, on 12 June, the day after Marie-Jacqueline had, on leaving the Hôtel Ruhl, noticed in a café across the street two very well-dressed ladies who were, she had concluded, watching that entrance for just such a departure as her own.

Madame Richard and Madame de Fleury. But would Herr Kohler realize that Marie-Jacqueline had also looked at that file?

Kohler couldn't believe what he was reading. Here, line by line, were the exact details, barring the rats, of how they had found Lucie Trudel.

Speaks of smothering her husband's lover in the girl's bed, Normand had written well before any of the murders.

Wants her corpse naked so that he can see what she's really like with that riding crop in her hand. Patient is severely paranoid and terrified of losing her own sizeable fortune, her status also, and husband. Claims the girl will use pregnancy as a means of trapping Gaëtan-Baptiste into marriage. Claims he's fool enough to think such a thing possible but will ensure it by demanding that the courts declare her insane and grant the divorce.

Continues to view the *hydrothérapie sauvage froid* as a punishment for her failure as a wife. While under this treatment, often tears the sheath from herself and begs the attendant to use more force. The breasts, the mons and buttocks, she defiantly standing to face the hose until driven to cower, shivering, in a corner on her hands and knees.

Is, frankly, a very sexually repressed and mentally disturbed woman. A danger to herself let alone Mlle Trudel, the husband's mistress and personal shorthand typist.

There was more, lots more ... Pages of it.

10 November 1942: Has confided that Mme Richard will definitely 'take care' of Mlle Marie-Jacqueline Mailloux; that 'someone' will do the same with Camille Lefèbvre on payment of a large sum by Mme Richard, but that Mlles Trudel and Dupuis will be taken care of by Sandrine Richard and herself, Élisabeth de Fleury knowing of it and having agreed, but lacking the courage to 'participate'.

The woman had, apparently, been absent from the clinic on

Thursday, 28 January, and hadn't returned until 3 February, the day after the most recent murder.

She'd also been absent at the times of the first two killings but was it all hogwash? Had Ménétrel told the doctor what to write?

The paper was crisp, the penmanship precise but there were no faded places over the almost two years the bugger had been treating Julienne Deschambeault.

Fountain pens always run dry and have to be refilled or dipped, and each time that happens, the likelihood of leaving a blot or at least a misplaced period spells it out.

Other files, chosen at random, verified that Normand had written the file at a sitting and not on different dates as it implied.

In the corner next to the wall mirror, and buried under clutter, there was a small, turn-of-the-century cast-iron safe. Frantically Kohler searched the desk but Normand wasn't the type to have written the combination down on the back of the wife's photo or tucked beneath a corner of the blotter. He'd have kept it safely in his waistcoat pocket or wallet, though if either were misplaced ... ? An overworked, understaffed practitioner of *la médecine thermale* with added sidelines in forgery and herbalism?

Jars and jars of rose petals, spruce needles, juniper berries, et cetera, were ranked on the shelves above, their Gothic-script labels bordered by gold leaf and each of them bearing the Latin name ... *Vitex agnus-castus L. Verbenaceae* ... Monk's pepper. *Zanthoxylum americanum Mill. Rutaceae* ... Toothache Tree. *Mein Gott,* the bark had been used by the Red Indians of the Americas!

Turning the jar, lifting the lid to first tentatively smell the contents and then shake out a little on to a sheet of paper for the sculptress, he saw the combination written in time-faded ink on the underside of the label.

2-27 *left,* 1-4 *right,* 17 *left,* 9 *right,* 3 *left.*

Julienne Deschambeault's file was there at the top of the heap. Like doctors the world over, Normand had thought it best to keep a little insurance.

*

Stark in a white-collared, beige house dress with crocheted shawl tight about thin shoulders, Julienne Deschambeault stood as if trapped before drawn blackout curtains, her expression that of a woman of fifty-five who was haunted by guilt and fear.

Clearly distraught, she'd been pacing endlessly back and forth in her room. The Thonet chaise longue and matching wicker armchair had been shoved aside. On the small, round wicker table with its lace cloth, the glass beside the measured bottle of the Chomel had fallen over to roll about as the table had been hurriedly lifted aside.

'*Eugénie, why have I been locked into my room? Why am I not allowed to leave if I so choose?*' she shrilled.

'It's for your own good,' said Dr Normand ingratiatingly. 'The Chief Inspector merely wishes . . .'

'A Sûreté?' she yelped, the ribbed and knitted gloves rolled down below the wrists, the hands clasped tightly and pressed hard against the bony chest and just beneath the angular chin.

'The negatives,' said St-Cyr.

Her hazel eyes were quick to register suspicion.

'*You can't have them. I haven't got them!*'

The shoulder-length, auburn hair was awry and framed the haggard countenance of one whose crisis was definitely of the nerves and whose lips were parted in despair.

'My dear,' interceded Madame Pétain, 'we have had to agree to turn them over.'

'*Gaëtan has forbidden me to do so!*'

'Gaëtan . . . ?' blurted Madame la Maréchale, throwing Sandrine Richard a glance of alarm.

'Madame, was he here?' demanded St-Cyr.

'Here?' the woman asked, tossing back her hair. 'He never comes here. He telephoned.'

'Inspector . . .' began Normand.

The room was rebounding with their voices. 'A moment, Doctor. Madame, when, exactly, did your husband call you?'

Had the Inspector discovered the truth? *Had he?* wondered Julienne. 'Late this afternoon. He said that if I would agree not to

354

give up the negatives but to turn them over to him, he would see that I received the very best of legal defences and would want for nothing.'

Ah *merde alors...*

'He accused you of killing Lucie Trudel, didn't he?' asked Élisabeth de Fleury, aghast at the implications of what must have happened. 'He told you in complete detail how it was done.'

'*I wanted her dead! I wanted her smothered!*'

'But you didn't do it, did you?' implored Madame Pétain.

Swiftly the woman looked to Sandrine Richard. 'The negatives, Julienne,' said that one firmly. 'Don't say anything. Just give them up.'

Beseechingly the gloved hands went out to her. 'She lost the child, Sandrine. She spilled her baby into the armoire.'

'*Please, it's best you do exactly as I've said!*' implored Sandrine.

'My dear ...' attempted Madame Pétain.

The woman tore her hair. '*It would have been a son, Eugénie! An heir. I couldn't have that happen, could I? She had to be stopped!*'

'Inspector, this isn't right,' seethed Madame Pétain. 'You can see the state she's in. That ... that husband of hers *would* call to accuse her!'

Élisabeth de Fleury had stepped from the group to comfort Madame Deschambeault, and hold the woman in a tight embrace.

'The courts will be lenient,' offered Raoul Normand blandly. 'The judges are always very understanding in such cases.'

Madame Pétain and Sandrine Richard exchanged glances of alarm.

'Madame Deschambeault,' said St-Cyr, 'who told your husband that you would have the negatives?'

Again glances were exchanged. Madame de Fleury released Madame Deschambeault who, looking to Madame Richard, said, 'Sandrine, forgive me, but he said that it was Alain André who had told him. They met and they talked. An urgent conference.

Honoré was with them, Élisabeth, and . . . and Secrétaire Général Bousquet.'

The four of them. 'Then tell us, please,' sighed St-Cyr, 'what was on Lucie Trudel's night-table?'

Once more the woman looked to Sandrine Richard for advice, then flicked an apologetic glance at Élisabeth de Fleury. 'The Chomel, as I have it here on my own table.'

'And the rats?' he asked.

'Rats?' she bleated, throwing questioning looks at each of the other three. 'What rats?'

Something would have to be said, thought Eugénie Pétain. 'Inspector, Julienne *did* want to smother Lucie Trudel. Sandrine *was* determined to drown Marie-Jacqueline Mailloux and to pay Henri-Claude Ferbrave to garrotte Camille Lefèbvre, since Monsieur Bousquet's wife was not among us.'

'And God forgive me,' said Élisabeth de Fleury, 'I wanted desperately to stab Céline Dupuis in the heart.'

'We spoke of it often, Inspector,' confessed Madame Pétain, 'both here when visiting Julienne, and at our committee meetings in my flat, when Julienne was free to join us and when she has not, but I swear to you none of these ladies would have done as they'd said. It was all talk, but didn't it help them to cope with what was happening to them? Didn't I know exactly how each of them felt? How hurt and utterly betrayed, how insanely jealous, how totally exposed to the ridicule of others and to financial ruin?'

'We also talked on the telephone when in need,' said Élisabeth de Fleury. 'No matter what hour of night or day, Madame la Maréchale was always there to patiently listen and stand by each of us, but as to our carrying out such threats . . . Would that we had had the courage.'

'Inspector, let the courts decide,' advised Dr Normand. 'Your task is simply to take down their *procès-verbaux* and then to leave it all up to the examining magistrate.'

'It's good of you to remind me, Doctor, but . . .'

'Good *Gott im Himmel*, Louis, haven't I told you time and again it's the paperwork that counts?' stormed Kohler as he

barged into the room, a file folder in each hand. 'Papers ...
papers, Chief. Always get the record down straight, even if you
have to write it out twice, eh, Doc, and even if at one of those
times it is dictated to you by another doctor?'

'My safe ... You ...' blurted Normand.

'Had no right?' shot Kohler, towering over him. 'A member of
the Geheime Stattspolizei, *mein lieber Doktor*? You're the one
who has no rights.'

Kripo bracelets came out to be clapped round Normand's
wrists, the doctor slumping into the wicker chair.

'A glass of the Chomel for this one, ladies, and then the
hydrothérapie sauvage and a few shots of the *électrothérapie*. Book
him, Louis. Complicity to murder, and forgery. This son of a
bitch must have known those girls were to be killed. He tried to
lay the blame on these ladies.'

'For Ménétrel?'

'And the husbands, this one's in particular!'

Gaëtan-Baptiste Deschambeault. 'Perhaps, Hermann, or
Charles-Frédéric Hébert, but ...'

'No buts, Louis.'

'The Hôtel Ruhl, Inspectors. Room 3-17,' said Inès faintly from
the doorway, sickened by the prospect of what was to come.
'Then you will have seen everything, I think.'

They sat a moment in the car, these two detectives, outside the
Hôtel Ruhl. The boulevard de l'Hôtel de Ville, the town, the river
and the hills would be in darkness, Inès knew, though she
couldn't see a thing. St-Cyr had withdrawn into his thoughts,
Kohler too. Both knew that word would get out of what had
happened at the clinic. Ménétrel would be bound to hear of it
and soon, too soon. Ménétrel.

St-Cyr had taken the negatives that Madame Deschambeault
and the others had hidden in one of the tubular posts of her bed.
Kohler had entrusted Dr Normand to Madame Pétain and had
given her the key to his handcuffs. And Blanche? Inès asked
herself. Blanche had been so distressed at not being allowed to

accompany them that tears had wet her pale cheeks. 'Paul couldn't have taken that knife from Mother's room,' she had sworn. 'He'd not have done something like that without telling me!'

'Not even to buy his freedom from the STO?' St-Cyr had demanded, not sparing her.

'Edith,' she had blurted. 'Edith did it. She despises the Maréchal and blames him for everything. She hates women who betray their soldier husbands and their country, as Camille did, those who get pregnant like Lucie did, and Mother, too. Céline . . . Céline played the cabaret, Mother also. Albert . . . Albert can and does do anything Edith wants.'

'Such as trying to kill this one?' Herr Kohler had asked, indicating Inès.

'Such as putting things in Céline's room for you to find. Things only Edith could have given him.'

'And the attempt on Mademoiselle Charpentier?' he had asked.

Blanche had hesitated. 'Yes, but . . . but Albert is also impulsive and often can't see the consequences of what he does.'

'Like walking Céline to the Hall des Sources and then holding its doors shut on her?' Herr Kohler had said.

'A game,' Blanche had wept. 'Albert would have thought it a game!'

They had demanded to know how Mademoiselle Pascal could possibly have known Céline was to have gone to Pétain's room and at what time, but Blanche had had no answer for this. 'Her brother took the knife, Hermann,' St Cyr had flatly said, 'but what I want to know are her thoughts on Charles-Frédéric Hébert. Isn't he the one you're really so afraid of, Mademoiselle Blanche?'

'Yes. Yes, he is.'

'St-Cyr's a patriot,' Monsieur Olivier had confided when he'd met her at that café near the railway station, Inès told herself. 'Kohler's a conscientious doubter of Nazi invincibility, but you must never forget that he's one of them, one of *les autres*.' The others.

Sickened by what she knew of the rats that had been left in Lucie's bed, Inès asked herself again if she should tell St-Cyr and Kohler of it. Could she break the vow she'd made to herself?

A match was struck, she taking in a sharp breath as the flame burst before her, causing her to blink hard in panic only to realize the two detectives were sharing a cigarette.

'Hermann, Mademoiselle Charpentier had best be left with the concierge.'

The words were out before she could stop herself. 'Please don't! Please take me up to that room. My eyes will be fine if there are lights on in there.'

'Your eyes ... What is this, please?' asked St-Cyr. Had he turned to look at her?

'Night blindness,' she confessed.

They didn't say a thing. The cigarette was passed over, looks exchanged most probably, but still she couldn't see them and they must now know of this.

'Louis, leave her with me, then,' sighed Kohler.

'And Monsieur Olivier, mademoiselle?' asked St-Cyr. 'Does he, too, suffer from this little affliction of yours?'

'Monsieur Olivier .. ?' What was this he was saying? 'I ... I wouldn't know, Inspector. How could I possibly?'

It was his turn to sigh and he did so deeply and with evident regret. 'Then why, please, has he claimed it and why have you kept it from us?'

Olivier, she said to herself. Olivier lied about it! 'Shame ... Fear. Have you never walked the streets of Paris after dark and not been able to see, Inspector? One is jostled, one constantly bumps into people and is shoved away or sworn at, handled, too, once the person realizes you're a woman, and not just by the men! My handbag, my papers, I ...' Ah *Sainte Mère, Sainte Mère*!

St-Cyr must have leaned over the back of the front seat to get closer to her, for she felt a breeze as if he'd waved a hand before her eyes.

'And once again, mademoiselle, you have a ready answer,' he

said, 'but if you know anything at all that is useful, now is long past the time to have divulged it.'

When she said nothing, he turned back. 'Hermann, see that she leaves that valise of hers with the concierge. Then it'll be one less thing to get in the way.'

I will never leave it now, Inspector, she silently vowed. They checked their weapons, and she could hear St-Cyr flick open the cylinder of his Lebel, Kohler removing the clip from his pistol and jammed it back in with the heel of a hand to then retract and release the slide.

Both weapons would be left at half-cock.

'Ménétrel wanted them dead, Louis. He told the boys to do it or else.'

'Or Charles-Frédéric Hébert, but then . . . Ah *mais alors, alors,* Hermann, our killer or killers knew everything that would happen and were ahead of us at every step of the way. Ahead of Ménétrel, ahead of Bousquet and even Laval – they'd have had to have been, *n'est-ce pas?*'

The telex to Boemelburg, the identity card, the dress and the *billets doux,* that copy of *L'Humanité* that had been left on the stairs for Louis to find, the Résistance graffiti also.

'Surely for all those things to have happened, every scrap of information would have had to have been funnelled into one location, collated, plotted and used,' said St-Cyr.

Herr Kohler started the car and they drove the short distance around the corner to pause outside the old PTT, to gaze at it through the frost-covered windows, to get out and stand in the cold street and to stare at its darkened silhouette.

'The room, Hermann, and then the source, I think,' said St-Cyr.

'I warned you, Louis. I told you, you shouldn't have let him go.'

And me? wondered Inès. Am I to be victim number five? Betrayed just as Céline was; killed just as she and Lucie and the others? Removed to silence; left secure?

*

360

At a glance, Kohler took in the dimly lit foyer that was such a sugar cake of dusty ornament, and had once been the watering place and campground of kings, counts and visiting courtesans. Gilded putti clamoured for seashells or shot arrows from above draperies and columns of variegated marble. Bathing sirens soared to a well-muscled Neptune who stood with trident upheld and a dolphin curled about bare toes, atop a tiered heap of drained Vicenza stone, where buxom mermaids cradled once-spouting cornucopia. The vault of the ceiling rose through several storeys of railed galleries to cavorting bathers among still more horns of plenty.

'It is, and must once have been, stupendous, Hermann,' exclaimed St-Cyr in awe of what they found themselves in, for the wives and Madame Pétain had given no such indication. 'Magnificent, *mon vieux*. Neo-baroque, 1870 at least, and a national treasure.'

As if that were all they had to worry about! snorted Kohler inwardly. Everywhere there were bas-reliefs of bathers, of amphorae, fruit, helmets, horns, shields, masks and lutes; everywhere the health-giving powers of taking the waters, but all gone dry. 'Just where the hell is the *réceptionniste*, Louis? The concierge, if it's another dosshouse!'

'Mademoiselle, wait by the desk.'

'*Don't leave me!*' shrilled Inès.

'Louis, stay with her. I'll find him.'

It didn't take long. 'The *salaud* was on the telephone to Ménétrel,' shouted Kohler. 'We've trouble, Louis, but this one has lost his tongue!'

Dragged from the switchboard's little room, thrust up against the Carrara marble desk where half-sized copies of Carrier Belleuse's *La Source* emptied *amorini* from the shoulder while supporting the rest of the structure, the concierge threw a terrified glance at each of them, then apprehensively wet his lips and let his faded grey eyes settle doubtfully on herself, Inès noted. He was hoping for sympathy no doubt.

'*Verfluchte Franzosen!*' shrieked Kohler. '*Ein* Gestapo Detektiv

Aufsichtsbeamter, *Dummkopf. Schnell! Schnell!'* Hurry! Hurry! 'Open up that can of worms of yours and spill out everything the doctor said!'

The echoes came. The echoes rebounded. Hermann was really very good at this play-acting of his when necessary, but something would have to be said. 'Herr Hauptmann der Geheime Stattspolizist, please go easy on him. He's too old to be shoved around like that and can't understand a word you're saying.'

'Comfort from a Sûreté, eh? Then you shoot him and we'll claim he tried to escape and died of a heart attack!'

Herzlähmung – would they really do so? panicked Inès. Cardiac arrest was a favourite excuse of the Gestapo of the rue des Saussaies, the SS of the avenue Foch, and the French Gestapo of the rue Lauriston. 'Monsieur, these two ... ' she blurted. 'They're in a terrible hurry.'

The doctor hadn't mentioned a valise-carrying girl. 'I'll lose my job. I'll not be able to find work, not at my age!'

'Fuck your age!' railed Herr Kohler, jamming the muzzle of his pistol into him.

'Ménétrel ... The doctor, he has telephoned in great urgency to ... Ah *sacré nom de nom,* must you force me to say what I've been forbidden? You ... you had no right to arrest Dr Normand and steal his file on Madame Deschambeault. You have now initiated a national crisis that Dr Ménétrel will be forced to deal with.'

'Angry was he?' breathed Kohler.

'Furious.'

'And demanding that we return the file and stop everything immediately?' he asked.

'Most certainly.'

'Gut!'

Herr Kohler snatched the key from among a scattering of others and headed for the stairs, bypassing the bronze birdcage of a dubious lift. Out of the shadows, a life-sized Cupid and Psyche adorned the first landing, a copy of the Louvre's shy and lovely *Bather,* by Falconet, the second, the figure caught gracefully looking down at the water while timidly dipping an exploratory toe.

A copy of Paju's *Psyche* decorated the third landing; a superb *Vénus* stood beside a mural of voluptuous women taking the cure. One suckled a child, another raised her measured glass in salute, a third gazed raptly into a Cupid-held mirror as satyrs picked fruit and hair was combed, but all were as if removed, as if suppressed by the faded light the Occupation demanded.

'Room 3-17 must be at the far end of the gallery, Louis.'

How haunting the sculptures were, but could she remember their locations? wondered Inès. Could she find her way in the dark if necessary?

'Ménétrel will call out the troops, Louis. If not the Garde Mobile and Henri-Claude Ferbrave, then the local Milice!'

The formation of France's newest militia had been announced by Pétain not long ago right here in Vichy but already they were old acquaintances. 'Stay close, mademoiselle. It seems that we've ruffled more than the feathers of a few stuffed birds.'

Caught in a large cheval mirror, the sculptress appeared pale and shaken at the sight of the room, which was, of course, nothing like the wives and Madame Pétain had indicated.

Instead of a bed that squeaked when used and stank of stale piss, one could see at a glance, St-Cyr told himself, that this canopied masterpiece was simply unmade, its sheets, blankets and spread thrown back but of excellent quality, if of that other time and a touch worn.

There was no second-hand water pitcher, but an unblemished Sèvres jug; a copper bath that gleamed even in the faded electric light; a large, handsome marble sink with gilded bronze and porcelain taps, the hot and the cold; even the luxury of a bar of soap that could be left lying around; and plenty of towels, most certainly not thin, for one could hardly have worn them out.

Cold ashes lay in the grate, ample charcoal and wood indicating that a welcome fire could always be lit. The regulation notice as to safe and unsafe sex had, of course, had to be posted just inside the door, he noted, but here violets, dried long ago, had been woven round it, probably by Mademoiselle Marie-Jacqueline.

The carpet was an Aubusson. The armoires, desk and chairs were Marjorelle and nothing to be sneezed at, even if not neo-baroque but most certainly of the turn of the century.

'Louis, I'd best check the street.'

'You won't see anything,' yelped Inès. 'They'll not let you.'

'It's what I'll hear that counts.'

Herr Kohler left them, left the door wide open. Again Inès took in the bed, again she told herself Céline couldn't have had time to make it, for that had been the rule. After each visit, each of them had tidied up.

Tuesday ... last Tuesday afternoon, she said, 2 February, lying naked there in the arms of Honoré de Fleury. Céline whose laughter had been so gentle and yet full of warmth and excitement. Céline whose smile had always been so encompassing.

'There's ... there's a ballet shoe under that chair, Inspector,' she heard herself saying. 'A practice slipper.'

And we are alone at last, mademoiselle, but you haven't yet decided if you should tell me all you know. 'It's the other shoe that puzzles me,' said St-Cyr. 'Don't ballet teachers who have to rush off early in the morning throw their things into a bag of some sort? Her handbag hasn't turned up, yet her ID has.'

'The bag, it ... it was of a soft brown suede, a rucksack I bought her before the Defeat.'

'Before the death of her husband?'

And attempted suicide? 'Yes. Well before that. She was so happy, so full of life. Annette had just been born. On my way to see them at the Hôpital Cochin, I came across it in the window of a second-hand shop on the rue Mouffetard and knew she'd have the baby to carry and everything else, so would need something easy to handle.'

'You were still living at the home of your aunt and uncle then?'

'They ... they had passed away. I ...'

364

'Had you the studio then, the job at the Musée Grévin?'

'Yes! The ... the student who had owned the rucksack had been on holiday in Switzerland but had run out of money. Please ... please don't look at me like that in the mirror, Inspector. I ... I *can't* tell you. I mustn't!'

Sconces on either side of the mirror held candles whose soft light would have bathed Céline's reflection ...

The Chief Inspector went straight to the chair and bent to pick up the shoe. He would come to her now, this Sûreté, and would place it in her hand – she knew this, knew, too, that the tears couldn't be stopped.

'I loved her as one does a sister. I had no one else. No one, damn you!'

'On arrival here in Vichy, mademoiselle, you met with Auguste-Alphonse Olivier. You'd been couriering messages for him in Paris. Perhaps he'd a snapshot of you that Mademoiselle Dupuis had given him, but she felt the perfume necessary as well – a little password, *n'est-ce pas*, and had asked you to wear it.'

Her head was bowed; the faded pink satin slipper, with its tightly wound ties, was in both hands; the finely curving lashes were wet.

'He discovered you couldn't see when going from a lighted room into darkness. He warned you not to tell us of your night blindness so that he could use it. You were to watch what you said to us and what you did, but you began to look for things yourself. Why was this, please?'

The Inspector was still looking at her reflection in the mirror, a glass in front of which Céline would have stood to be admired, made love to, fucked! 'He ... he was upset with me for not having told him of my night blindness. When ... when I asked where Céline was, for she, not him, was to have met me at the train, he ... he said he didn't know.'

Yet he must have. 'You then found out and threw up before seeing her for yourself.'

Ever so slightly she nodded.

'He didn't want you coming to this hotel, did he?'

'It ... it was not even mentioned.'

The delicately boned chin and lower jaw were still determined. The sea-green eyes avoided him. 'Then can you think why Monsieur Olivier would have warned me to stay away from it and threatened me if I didn't?'

'Monsieur Laval's clairvoyant ... You asked him about her?' 'I did.'

'Then perhaps it is that you should ask her yourself, Inspector?'

'Shall I leave you here, then, while I do?' he said angrily.

'Céline was silenced; Lucie also, Inspector.'

'And the others?'

'Most probably.'

'But she tried to protect him? She tried to hide the earrings?'

Was it that this Sûreté did not want to believe the truth? 'Monsieur Olivier took her from the Hôtel du Parc and she went willingly with him, Inspector. She tried to remove and hide the earrings both to protect Blanche and Paul – she must have known they'd taken them – and to let you and Herr Kohler know who had betrayed her.'

'He'd have taken them, then, would he?'

'Yes. Yes, I tell myself that must have been so.'

'But he didn't, mademoiselle. Had Monsieur Olivier seen even one of his wife's earrings, he'd have removed it and left us to find the other, or come back himself to search it out.'

'Then why didn't her killer take it?'

'Because, I think, the assailant wanted us to find it. That is certainly why the cigar band was left, but to point us towards Albert Grenier and the past.'

An earring had been loosened ... 'And Edith Pascal?'

'Would not have left any of it, for she would not have wanted to implicate in any way the man she loved.'

'A *résistant*.'

A *grâce à Dieu*, the girl had broken at last. 'You *were* his courier in Paris. Please, mademoiselle, you can trust both Hermann and myself. Monsieur Olivier told me he was district leader of the FTP. Hermann knows of this also.'

366

'Then you will know, as I do, that Monsieur Olivier has people at his command. The slogans we saw on those walls, the warning Monsieur Bousquet was given . . .'

Mademoiselle Dupuis's *carte d'identité*. 'The civil war the boys speak of.'

'Has started.'

As he listened to the street, listened to the town, Kohler hoped Louis could prise what was needed from the sculptress before it was too late. At the very edges of the pollarded, tree-lined boulevard de l'Hôtel de Ville, the shadows were deeper, the darkness complete in places, thinner where the stumpy, naked branches reached out to the snow-covered road. Two *vélo-taxis* struggled towards him. A few pedestrians were about but none of the town's *autobuses aux gazogène*, for those would have stopped running at 7 p.m. as they had done even before the Defeat. Like towns and villages all over France, Vichy shut down hard and early for most people, even with the presence of the Government.

Far in the distance, a Wehrmacht motorcycle patrol let the world know it was busy. Out of the darkness urgent voices came.

'*Chéri*, I forgot the blankets.'

'*Merde*, Heloïse, you know how cold it is in that flat of theirs. Now we'll have to keep our overcoats on and play cards in mittens!'

Parsimoniously the light from the blue-blinkered torch was rationed. Now on, now off, the husband smoking an American cigarette, the tobacco mild, totally foreign, raising hackles only to have them die as the couple hurried past, not even realizing he was standing in the shadows. Shivering. Not wanting, at the moment, to think about Giselle and Oona and Paris, for people there said exactly the same things, and if one stayed out beyond the curfew, one stayed put until 5 a.m. or else!

Giselle, he knew, often went round the corner to see her friends and former colleagues at the house of Madame Chabot on the rue Danton. Hadn't he leased the flat on the rue Suger just so that she could do that and not feel lonely when he was away?

Oona would have gone after her by now. Oona never said a thing about Giselle's little visits. Close ... those two had become really close.

'But their living with me can't go on,' he said aloud and to himself but softly. 'Louis and I've crossed too many. One of these days we'll all be taking a train east to nowhere unless I can get them out of France and to safety. Louis, too, and Gabrielle.'

As if to mock him *and* the night and Vichy, *and* the Occupier, some son of a bitch put his wireless set next to an open window and cranked the volume up.

'*Ici londres ... ici londres ... des français parlent des français ...*'

'*Jésus merde alors, idiot,* have some sense!'

'*Radio-paris ment.*' Radio-Paris lies ...

Kohler fired two shots harmlessly into the night sky above him. Kids ... it was probably just that couple's kids!

Immediately the waveband was switched to 'Lily Marlene'* and he heard the voice of Louis's chanteuse reaching out to the boys on both sides of this lousy war.

'Gabi ...' he said, swallowing with difficulty at the thought. Some stopped on their way to listen. Others hesitated. One even began to hum along with her.

A last glance up the street revealed that a van – perhaps an armoured one – had drawn to a stop some distance away.

When he looked back down the boulevard towards the rue du Pont, he thought he could detect another one but they made no sound; he hadn't even heard them. Like soldiers everywhere in this bitter winter, he'd been sucked right in by that voice.

Madame Ribot occupied a suite on the same floor as Room 3-17, but much closer to the lift, noted St-Cyr, the brass nameplate giving: PALMS READ, FORTUNES TOLD. ALL WHO ENTER LEAVE ENLIGHTENED.

Readings were at twenty francs, the Tarot at forty, and

* This is the title of the French version; the one translated into English for the British troops is 'Lilli Marlene'; the German, the original, 'Lili Marleen'.

under a loosened strip of sticking plaster whose inked UN-
AVAILABLE had smudged, TEA LEAVES FIFTY FRANCS INCLUD-
ING THE PRICE OF THE TEA.

The hours were from 4 p.m. until 7 p.m., THE TUESDAY, THE
THURSDAY, AND THE SATURDAY ONLY. AT ALL OTHER TIMES
CONSULTATIONS ARE AS WHEN NECESSARY, THE RATE BEING
TWO HUNDRED FRANCS, NOT NEGOTIABLE.

A Louis XV sofa wore its original, ribbed green velvet up-
holstery; the dented cushions their rescued remnants of tapestry,
frayed and with pinfeathers protruding. No two pieces of
furniture matched. The sconces were neither art nouveau nor neo-
baroque but a mixture of art deco and the fourteenth *siècle*, he
felt. Everything looked as if it had been left by others in payment
or as legacies too bulky to be moved in haste from rooms that
had had to be vacated, or simply forgotten. Yet, in total, there
was the atmosphere, if musty, of something grand and worldly, of
ages and lives past, of refinement and fortune, good or bad.

A scratchy gramophone recording gave a lusty chorus from an
operetta. The Apollo in Paris, 1912, he thought. *Le Soldat de
Chocolat*, by Oscar Straus. A favourite of Pétain's? he wondered.
The green-shaded, Empire desk lamp in the consulting room-
cum-study, with its zodiacal charts and those of the palm, was of
the thirties, the desk itself utilitarian but of an indeterminate
origin, for it could hardly be seen under the clutter.

Like the half-filled, two-litre, hand-blown wine bottle at her
left elbow, Madame Ribot was an ample woman whose watery
blue eyes matched the tint of the bottle above the deep red of its
Chanturgue and her rouged cheeks. The frizzy mop of grey hair
was thick and wiry, the neck of the bottle not straight but
suffering from arthritis, too, and bent towards the woman, its
distractedly replaced cork loose and tilted the opposite way.

Her glass had been drained some time ago.

'Madame Ribot . . .' hesitated the petite *bonne à tout faire*.

'Fingerprints,' muttered the woman irritably. 'Why does
Monsieur le Premier insist on emphasizing their importance
when it is the hands that can tell us so much more?'

The shoulders were rounded under the tartan blanket that some Scot must have left behind at some hotel...

'Love, lust, jealousy and murder, even assassination,' she said, still not looking up. 'Lisette, *ma chère*, you're such a delightfully dutiful creature, a treasure to a stubborn old woman such as myself, but I am conscious of the presence of these visitors. Now you must ask them to wait a little longer. Please stop the music. I thought it would help, but it has not done so at all. Indeed, it is a frightful racket to a woman who dotes on Debussy, Saint-Saëns, Brahms and Chopin!'

'Monsieur ... Mademoiselle ...' blurted the girl to Inès and St-Cyr. 'Madame, she is working on an urgent matter for Monsieur le Premier.'

'The fingerprints?' shot St-Cyr, but no answer was given. Inked palm prints – done by rolling the hand with black ink and then gently pressing it flat on tracing paper, after which the hand and paper were held up to work the ink in carefully and the paper then slowly peeled off – had been positioned on a makeshift light-table of frosted white glass. Bent over this table, the woman used a hand-held magnifier, instead of the spectacles that dangled against the tartan folds.

'Monsieur Laval has again telephoned to ask if an assassination is in the offing. Four times today, no less,' said Madame Ribot, still studying the prints. 'Progress reports, of course, were given.'

'And the fingerprints he was concerned about?' asked St-Cyr.

'The police photographer's efforts have yielded nothing so far. Not from the envelope in which press clippings were slid under the door, not from the Hall des Sources either, nor from the Hôtel d'Allier and the rooms of these two.'

She lifted away the handprints she'd been studying and replaced them with two sets. 'These, Inspector, are Lucie Trudel's, and these, Céline Dupuis's.'

Ghost-like – as if the dead, in terror, were pressing their hands to the underside of a window, with them trapped inside and drowning, thought Inès – the prints cried out to them.

'Céline was an Aries; Lucie a Virgo,' said Madame Ribot,

conscious of the sculptress's pallor and wondering if she could convince the girl to allow prints of her own hands to be taken. 'Camille Lefèbvre was an Aquarian, Marie-Jacqueline a . . .'

Firmness would be best. 'But you weren't examining any of those when we came in here,' said St-Cyr. 'Please replace the ones you were studying.'

This was the Chief Inspector of the Sûreté whom Monsieur Laval had requested from Paris. 'Very well, as you wish.'

A suitcase, set to one side on the day of the Defeat, its brass studs and corners scoured by years of travel, bore once-colourful, now tattered and long-faded labels: The Peter's-Bad Hotel um Hirsch, at Baden-Baden . . . The Splendide, at Evian-les-Bains . . . The Nassauer Hof, at Wiesbaden . . . The Hôtel les Bains, at Spa, in Belgium . . . The Grand, at the Montecatini Terme in Tuscany . . .

Not for a moment would this one have entertained the thought of taking less expensive lodgings and surreptitiously acquiring the stickers. She had gone from one to the other during each season for years and had stayed at nothing but the finest hotels.

'Two prints, the left hands first, Inspector. Monsieur le Maréchal would most certainly not have allowed me to take one had Noëlle Olivier not begged him to join her for a reading on my return in the early autumn of 1924. I saw suicide even then, but could not bring myself to warn her and have chastised myself ever since.'

'And the other print?'

'Is Monsieur le Premier's, whose excellent wine, so generously given, and whose wood and coal keep these old bones warm because he is genuinely concerned with my well-being.' There, that ought to stop him from questioning her about having them! 'A Taurus,' she said of Pétain, 'and a Cancer; the one ruled by Vénus, the other by the Moon. The one an Earth Hand, the other, a Water Hand, but there are many complexities with both and I cannot convince myself that the analysis is wrong. Regrettably I must disagree with what Herr Kohler and yourself have told the Premier, Inspector, for I feel assassination is a very distinct possibility. Though I seldom use Belot, I have consulted his sixteenth-century work on palmistry and its relationship to the signs of the zodiac. Between the line of Life and that of Fate, and just near the latter's juncture with the Line of Head, there is a region where, if the fine lines criss-cross many times and the Line of Life is broken, one can, after consulting the zodiac, deduce assassination. The analysis is not much used, if at all today, and has been widely discredited, but it does reinforce the others I've made, and when one seeks answers for such a man as the Premier, at a time of such crisis, one leaves no stone unturned.'

Hermann should have heard her but where was he? Why hadn't he rejoined them? Trouble . . . ? Had there been trouble?

'I have, of course, also used Belot's analysis of the first joint of the middle finger and have found there *morte en prison* both for Monsieur le Premier and le Maréchal. Contradictions . . . There are always those. In life one tries. Isn't that all one can do?'

She was genuinely upset. Part Gypsy, part Jewish, part Russian or Hungarian – the possibilities were limitless, the roots deep – she had probably not left the hotel in all the years of the Occupation. 'Madame, the fingerprints?' he said gently, having suppressed the impatience he felt.

Must the police always be so stubborn? wondered Madame Ribot. 'As I have told Monsieur le Premier many times, Inspector, both here and over the telephone, each of those girls came to me. After their little moments in Room 3-17, they would often feel the need, the one believing herself deliciously wicked and triumphantly so, another guilty for having betrayed her husband and wanting to know if he would discover what she'd been up to, the third simply naive enough to have hoped marriage possible. And the fourth, you ask?' She would pause now, she told herself. 'A *réaliste* who came to believe her life and that of Lucie Trudel were in grave danger.'

'You saw her on Tuesday, between five and seven in the afternoon,' said Inès, finding the words hard. 'You warned her to be careful.'

'My dear, I told her death was imminent. Here . . . There it is.

Mon Dieu, mademoiselle, see for yourself. Your hand, a forefinger, *s'il vous plaît*! Press it to the glass, to this area, to just beyond the Mount of the Moon and nearest the break in the Line of Fate. Death by one's enemies!'

Céline would have had to have bared the scars of her attempted suicide in order for Madame Ribot to have made the prints . . .

The Inspector was going through those prints that had been set aside. 'No names,' he grumbled. 'How, please, do you identify them'

'By memory,' breathed the woman, watching him closely. There must have been thousands and thousands of such prints, thought Inès, and surely no human being could ever have remembered them all?

'Come, come, Madame, you always make two sets,' he said. 'The one, when dry, goes into the file with the name written below each hand; the other you use when writing up or giving your analysis. Then those, too, are kept. A truly professional clairvoyant such as yourself would not do otherwise.'

This was no ordinary Sûreté. 'That is correct. An attic room holds the legacy of the years, this office the most recent, but it is not from among any of those cabinets that you will find the ones you seek.'

'Monsieur Laval wouldn't have telephoned you so many times today, Madame, unless he was worried, and not simply about himself and his Government. The iron man's fingerprint sweeps haven't yielded anything useful because the *commissariat de police* hasn't anything on file with which to compare them!'

'Only the thumbprints each of us must leave in order to obtain our *cartes d'identité*, and those prints were, alas, not clear.'

'When did he last telephone?'

'Not two hours ago.'

'While we were at the clinic . . .' managed Inès.

'Four murders, Inspector, and in the autumn of 1925, one woman and three of her lovers juxtaposed here on this glass.

Noëlle Olivier was a Gemini and possessed of an Air Hand, which is usual for such a one; August-Alphonse a Capricorn and . . .'

'And Charles-Frédéric Hébert?' he demanded.

'Noëlle brought each of them to me for a reading, yes.'

'What about Edith Pascal and Albert Grenier?' bleated Inès, sickened by what was happening and wondering why Herr Kohler hadn't rejoined them.

It was St-Cyr who snapped, 'The files on Olivier and Hébert, Madame. All prints. You have no choice and must shout it out to anyone who comes for them that I have taken them.' Hermann . . . Where the hell was Hermann?

Madame Ribot did as asked. Two files . . . only two, Inès told herself, giving a last glance at the light-table, at Céline's prints and those of Lucie.

Olivier, she said silently. It was Olivier and he'll have Edith Pascal with him and she'll have Albert, who has already tried to kill me, not because I'm a threat to the Maréchal or ever was, though Mademoiselle Pascal must have convinced him of this, but because I know too much.

The letter boxes of the FTP in Paris . . . the messages I had to deliver for him but worst of all, who he, himself, is, their Vichy leader.

Auguste-Alphonse Olivier.

11

Louis wasn't in Room 3-17 and neither was the sculptress. Frantic now, Kohler rang downstairs to the front desk to beg that son of a bitch of a *réceptionniste* to ignore the Gestapo rough stuff and stop the two from leaving the hotel.

There was no answer. None at all. The unmade bed looked lonely; the bevelled mirror threw back his reflection and he saw himself grey and dissipated, the shabby greatcoat undone, his scarf dangling as if to slip away, fedora pulled down hard and gun in hand.

'Louis ...' he said, feeling caught, trapped, the moments ticking by too fast.

'The fire alarm,' he told himself and, rushing out on to the gallery, threw a look along it both ways beneath gilded plaster grapes, seashells and putti blowing horns before shattering the glass with his pistol butt and yanking on the little bronze lever.

'Nothing ...? *Scheisse!* No fire inspectors?'

Again he yanked on the wretched thing and again, cutting himself, the blood pouring from a forefinger to race down his hand. '*Verdammt!*'

Back in Room 3-17, he ripped a pillowcase apart, wound and tied the bandage tightly; saw a clutch of hairpins; remembered Céline Dupuis's bed, that other room and the depression she'd left there in her mattress at the Hôtel d'Allier on waking; knew that here, too, on that last day of her life she'd had to hurry, that she must have fallen asleep after the lovemaking.

Picking up the Walther P38, he headed for the door again, the mirror throwing back a glimpse of him that popped, blinded –

seared its image on memory as the lights went out and the sound of the lift ... the Christly lift ... ground to a mid-floor halt!

'*Merde*,' came Louis's muffled curse from out of the pitch darkness of the shaft. How many times had he been warned by his partner never to trust the lifts of France?

Other voices were heard both from above and below, some old, some middle-aged, some male, some female; complaints were muttered. The door to one of the rooms opened. A head and shoulders were stuck out. Neighbour began to question neighbour even from gallery to gallery. 'An air raid?' 'I heard no siren.' '*Les Allemands?*' 'As a punishment for what, please?' 'They often do this in Paris. *Arrondissement* by *arrondissement* if necessary, *quartier* by *quartier* if during a *rafle*.'

A house-to-house round-up with searchlights ready on the streets below to nail those on the roofs above.

Steps sounded – boot cleats on the marble floor of the foyer, rushing cleats ...

The voices ceased, the doors were silently closed. Like hotels the world over, news of trouble travelled quickly and silence was often the best and only defence. Lock bolts were gently eased in place.

The bars of the lift-well were criss-crossed, their bronze cold. 'Louis ... Louis, it's me. Stay where you are,' he whispered. 'Ferbrave and the Garde Mobile are here. I'll find the hand crank in the cellars and try to ease you down.'

'Madame Ribot, Hermann. The clairvoyant may be their first target, though I've already taken what they want. Her suite is to your left.'

'Three doors and then the one just after you get to a life-sized terracotta wood nymph with garland, by Frémin,' said Inès faintly. 'I know because I ... I have always now to memorize such things. Both breasts are exposed; the left arm is missing at the shoulder, and she is stepping forward with that foot.'

The furniture was old, the suite musty, but what Kohler couldn't understand was why the door had been left off the latch and ajar because Louis wouldn't have done that. Had the clairvoyant managed to slip away in the short time he'd been at the lift, or had it been left that way for a cat who liked to stray?

Ferbrave and the others had gone into Room 3-17 but had soon left it. He'd have to let them find the door of Madame Ribot's flat just as he had, would have to let them enter and notice, as he now did, that a faint light shone out into the darkness of a distant corridor.

Maybe that would draw the moths and he could come up behind them . . .

The pungency of burning black tobacco came to him. A Gitane – one of Laval's? he wondered as the door was swung softly open and a single torch beam penetrated the frayed carpet first, with its floral patterns in dark blues and red, then a small round table, carved at its edge and with a lamp and photos in silver frames, then a chaise, a *fauteuil*, a landscape on the opposite wall and, finally, the distant corridor.

'Henri, is she alone?' whispered one, only to be silenced.

'Messieurs,' she called out. '*Entrez, s'il vous plaît.* I have, I think, what you've come for, since Monsieur le Premier has telephoned to ask that I get them from the files.'

There were three others, with Ferbrave in the lead, and all were wearing black, hobnailed boots, white gaiters, black trousers, black three-quarter-length leather jackets and black berets.

Schmeissers, Bergmanns, Lugers with drum clips, and stick grenades – the much-coveted weapons of the Occupier – were carried, yet still they were careful, still they touched nothing, knocked nothing over, smashed nothing. Were careful, considering they could well have instantly wrecked the place and should have done. A puzzle.

'Ah, *Dieu merci*, it's you, Capitaine Ferbrave, and your men,' said Violette Ribot as they gathered in front of her desk. *Durs*, she swore silently, pointing those guns of theirs at her. *Gars* whose mothers hadn't suckled them enough! 'These are the palm prints of Monsieur Auguste-Alphonse Olivier, and these, of Charles-Frédéric Hébert.'

'She's lying, Henri. The phone's been left off the hook.'

'But ... but he has only just telephoned, monsieur,' she exclaimed, not touching the thing, not replacing it.

A half-empty wine bottle was to the woman's left, her glass brimful. The cigarette clinging to her lower lip, she stood facing them, a tartan blanket draped over her shoulders, but would they kill her? wondered Kohler. Would he have to jab his pistol against Ferbrave's head to stop it from happening?

Round and outwardly bowed, the vase on the desk before her was of sapphire-blue glass on which, as if from the health-giving depths of a sunlit pool, voluptuous *sirènes* playfully grappled, some hugging the knees of others as they rose to the surface.

Ferbrave and the rest looked at the girls. They had to, and she'd damned well known they would!

Two sets of palm prints on tracing paper lay on either side of the Lalique vase turned crystal ball whose flame gave the lie of motion to the bathers and flickering shadows to its time-ravaged owner.

'Here are the names,' she said. 'Always I must write them in at the bottom of each print.'

If she had noticed that he, too, was in the room and now close behind them and armed, thought Kohler, she wasn't about to let on.

'Are there others?' hazarded Henri-Claude, indicating the prints with a nudge from his Luger.

'Ah *oui*, here in these file folders I have taken from the cabinets. Two sets, always I make two, Captain. Both are identified. See for yourself. The folders are dated, the one from before the Great War and the other during it, the exact times of the visits ... You must excuse the memory. Always now I have to check, but is it that you require both sets, or only the one?'

Ménétrel must have warned them to go easy with her.

'Both,' grunted Ferbrave.

'Then it is as Monsieur le Premier has said. Uncertainty still exists. And the *détectives*, messieurs? Monsieur Laval did say that they, too, would pay me the little visit, but the wiring in this old place ... The electricity has gone off again and they have not yet arrived, so I have purposely left the door off the latch.'

Some of the boys were beginning to look up at the charts on the wall behind her.

'Your maid, where is she?' demanded Ferbrave.

'Lisette Aubin? Gone to her mother's. A bad cold I did not wish to catch, not at my age. The chest, never good, has got worse.'

She coughed deeply and did so again, swallowing phlegm. 'The flu ... *Merde*,' she swore, 'I can feel it coming on!'

Even so, one of them thought to down her glass of the red, but she was swift to respond and laid a hand on his. 'Would you deny an old woman what the Premier has so kindly given?'

'Leave it,' said Ferbrave. 'We're here to help the two from Paris.'

'And the terrorists?' she asked, releasing the hand. 'Is it true that they might invade the hotel, messieurs? Monsieur Laval, he was most concerned and has said there might be the threat of this. You will be careful? Please put the lock on when you leave. Ah! the receipt. I have forgotten. Please sign here, Captain. Read it first, if you wish.'

Silently Inès continued to count off the seconds and minutes. By now here eyes should have adjusted, but still she couldn't make out a thing. St-Cyr, she knew, would be looking up to the floor above, listening hard, each sound coming to them, some faint, others but slightly louder. It wouldn't take Henri-Claude Ferbrave long to discover they were trapped in the lift. He'd want the palm prints St-Cyr had, would want the negatives and the files on Julienne Deschambeault, but did Herr Kohler still have the latter?

They did not know, were forced to wait, to agonize, herself especially, since she knew things she should have revealed.

'Inspec—'

St-Cyr put a finger to her lips, then pointed to the floor above by simultaneously touching both her chin and the tip of her nose.

As always now, the smell of bitter almonds permeated the air about them and why, please, had Albert had to go into her valise to spill that oil and all but drain its little bottle?

Why, dear God? The smell would now give her away.

No sound was heard, no light from a torch passed over the shaft above – St-Cyr would have seen it, wouldn't he? she wondered.

His overcoat collar was up. Her forehead touched his fedora. At last her lips found his right ear. 'Olivier,' she whispered. 'He butchered those rats. He has a pocket knife like that.'

An Opinel.

He gave no response. He remained so still, she wanted to shriek, *Inspector, believe me, I know who killed them!*

Cold against the hand that clutched her bag and valise, she felt the metal of St-Cyr's revolver. Three short, quick taps were given, three longer ones, and then, again, the first three.

An SOS. A warning.

Kohler knew he didn't have much time, but *Gott sei Dank*, Madame Ribot had yet to toss off her wine.

Unaware of his presence, Ferbrave and the others had left the suite, even putting the lock on and closing its outer door. The woman reached to replace the telephone receiver only to find that this Kripo had slipped back into the room.

Beneath the palm prints and files she'd given them, she had earlier placed two photos, ready for a last glimpse. 'The one is of myself,' she said, 'taken in the autumn of 1900, here in Vichy, when I was thirty-two and had been left with but a few sous and a two-year-old daughter; the other is of that daughter in the summer of 1922, at Royan. Last year I sent her to America, and every week since then she has both telephoned and written me two letters, though now they no longer reach me and she can no longer telephone.'

As of 11 November 1942. 'And the girl who's with her?'

The photo had been taken of them standing under the canvas tarpaulin of a rustic porch overlooking the Atlantic. Middy blouses, pleated skirts, bobbed hair, cloches and smiles. A homeward-bound *sardinier* was in the near distance, the sloop close in to the wind.

'I think you know that is Noëlle Olivier, Inspector. She begged me to let my Marianne accompany her and the twins, who were then nine years old, and I agreed, though I had my doubts. Noëlle's objective was not only to get away from Vichy and its vicious gossip, but to settle her mind and search out the meaningful in life. The children loved that holiday and grew even closer to her, and to my Marianne.'

'And Monsieur Olivier, who disowned them three years later?'

'Has never for a moment forgotten my daughter nor myself. It was he who arranged to get Marianne and her little family safely out of France. As for the twins and his disowning them, is it not now better for them that he continue to do so?'

A wise woman. Royan was at the mouth of the Gironde, about equidistant between the U-boat pens at La Pallice, near La Rochelle, and those at Bordeaux. Lovely in the summer of 1922, no doubt, but a far cry from what was to come.

The photo of Madame Ribot showed her in a wide-brimmed, tailored-suit hat, round whose crown was wrapped a matching ostrich plume. From under that brim, two dusky eyes gazed steadfastly to one side of the lens, the nose fine and long and a regular ski jump, the face a soft, clear oval whose lips, unpainted and unparted, were perfect.

A white silk neckerchief, pinned with a single stick-pearl, stylishly set off the hat and the plain black, seersucker dress. No earrings were worn – those had probably already been pawned. The auburn hair was pinned up under that hat. An extremely genteel and handsome woman who had just spent her last sou on a portrait to launch her career.

Magnificent, but he couldn't let it influence him. Louis would only be fussed if he didn't indicate the telephone. 'That's one of his pipelines, isn't it? Keyed through the switchboard downstairs but elsewhere also – the old Poste, Télégraphe et Téléphone building next door, eh? That's why that little thumb-switch is on the base of the transmitter. When Laval comes for advice, the switch is thrown and the receiver left off the hook if possible; if not, you simply relay to Olivier later on what was said.'

A Gestapo would have dragged her from the room. This one hadn't. 'In 1900 I knew I faced an uncertain and difficult future, Inspector. In 1940 it could only be more so, but as for my being a conduit for anyone but my clients, I could not possibly say.' She would replace the receiver now, Violette told herself, and then raise her glass in salute.

Ah damn the French and not just Louis. Must they constantly force him into choosing? 'Don't. Please don't, madame. Prussic acid's reaction isn't pleasant to watch, and we're on your side. Just keep it handy. Maybe it won't be needed.'

The hand with the receiver gestured. 'Then is it, Inspector, that you do not suspect Monsieur Olivier of having killed those girls, but have decided it was Charles-Frédéric Hébert?'

Persistent. *Mein Gott*, but must she insist? 'Since you've let the one know I'm still here, perhaps you'd ask him where he is.'

'And give away the treasure of treasures?'

'Just do it!'

'I can't. I hang up and take the acid!'

Kohler moved. The glass shattered as it hit one of the filing cabinets, the receiver was replaced, the line having gone dead.

'Please, you must not lead them to Monsieur Olivier, Inspector. He has no one but himself, having warned the others to stay away and go to ground.'

The darkness was total, the hotel as silent as a tomb. No one entered because the Garde Mobile had men at the front door and all other doors; no one dared to leave. *Merde*, what the hell was he to do? demanded Kohler. Let Ferbrave use the ratchet to lower the lift to the next floor?

Of course they thought all three of them had taken the lift and found themselves trapped. Of course they hadn't yet realized this wasn't so.

Two of the Garde had been left up here on the third floor in case anybody should attempt to climb out. Though neither of them had moved in some time, their leather coats hadn't relayed the fact that they'd been touched by him. One man was leaning against the gallery railing, next to an upright and sucking on a dead fag end for comfort; the second stood mid-corridor, feet widely planted in front of the lift, his submachine-gun no doubt trained on its gate. Both would have torches when needed, and orders to get the files on Julienne Deschambeault that were in his overcoat pockets, but would they have been told to shoot if necessary? Two detectives from Paris caught in the crossfire as they hunted down the killer, a terrorist, eh?

What terrorist? They couldn't know Olivier was of the FTP, couldn't even suspect this, and neither could Ménétrel, or had they finally realized it?

Traces of smoke began to filter into the lift cage through the pitch darkness. Alarmed, St Cyr waited. Had the Garde set the hotel on fire?

Sickened by the thought, he felt the sculptress urgently place her free hand questioningly on his shoulder. Still there were no voices, still no torch beams.

When he peered down through the criss-crossed mesh of the gate, flames were seen. Little flames.

The lift rose a fraction as the ratchet was engaged, then it settled back and down, only to rise again before settling further.

'*Dieu le père*, forgive my sins,' whispered the sculptress. As he reached out to her in comfort, tears wet his fingers but her lips continued silently to form the words. Had she decided on doing this long ago if captured? Prayers . . . focus on them and only on them. Don't scream. Don't give the Gestapo what they want.

The smoke came from burning paper, he was certain. *L'Humanité?* wondered St-Cyr. Did they now know who had drawn up that death notice?

Again he looked down through the gate. This time he'd have to press his face against the bars and stand on tiptoe. They'd opened the gate below, so silently.

Flames . . . the heat was carrying the smoke upwards. Charred bits of tracing paper crumbled, pages caught fire one by one.

'They're burning some of Madame Ribot's files?' the Inspector whispered, but could not understand why this should be since he had what they wanted.

Again the lift rose a fraction only to descend a notch, and again and again, and where was Herr Kohler, why hadn't he tried to stop them?

'Go to the far corner, mademoiselle. Stand with your back to it and your valise and bag clutched in both hands. Leave me to face them from this side.'

'It was Monsieur Olivier,' she blurted, her voice a little louder than a breath.

'He had no reason to kill any of them and every reason to make certain your friend remained alive. Indeed, I think he may well have tried to stop her murder from happening.'

'Then why the rats?'

'He didn't butcher them.'

'*But he has such a knife!*'

'And our killer knew of this, knew of him, his past, his wife, his life as a recluse whom people endlessly found tragic but of interest.'

'A bitter man who must hate all such girls and the Maréchal most of all.'

'It's a cover-up, mademoiselle. The Garde won't kill you. That would only cause too much trouble with Pétain whom Ménétrel wants kept totally in the dark on this.'

'And Monsieur Hébert?' she asked.

'Holds the papers that are being set alight.'

Scorched bits of paper drifted down into torchlight. There were two of the Garde at the ratchet, and as they looked up the lift well in puzzlement, Kohler moved.

They'd laid their torches and weapons on the cellar floor close by and had jumped down into the lift well, hadn't seen him yet had been bent over the thing, one with a hammer to seat the pawl

384

properly between each tooth of the wheel, the other cranking down hard on the lever to lower the lift cage.

But now they paused. 'Jacquot, is it the end of the world and they're not able to piss anything but ashes? *Jésus putain de bordel,* what is going on up there? Don't they know how difficult this is?' swore the one with the hammer, the *argot* not of the Auvergne but of Paris, La Villette and the Marché aux Bestiaux, the stockyards. Well, what was left of them.

'It's nothing, Marcel. Only a little cremation. *Merde,* your eyes. Are they really that bad?'

'Specs? Do you think I need specs at my age?'

'Easy. Go easy, eh? I wasn't insulting you.'

'Then watch what you . . .'

The guns had been gathered, the torches too. Kohler put a finger to his lips, pointed up the shaft and whispered, 'One word and it's your last. Now climb out. You first,' he indicated the older one with the scar, the squint and the three days of growth, a drinker. 'Untidy,' he said, 'and you in uniform. Look, there's grease on your jacket.'

Hit and hit hard with the butt of a Bergmann, scar-face's eyes flew open, blood burst, teeth broke, but the *salaud* didn't go down. *Sacré,* he'd pulled a slaughterhouse knife!

Again the Bergmann was swung, but now the barrel was grabbed, yanked, the feet slipping. *Verdammt!* Grease on the hand that clutched his overcoat. Grease on his own hand but none on the one that held the knife close in and as delicately as a feather.

Round and round they circled in the shattered light of both torches which had rolled or been kicked to the sides.

'Marcel, take him. It's Kohler.'

'*Do you think I don't know who it is?*'

Short, squat, bull-headed, the iron-grey hair cut so close it was a bootbrush, the 'old' man with the scar and the 'weak' eyes never gave him a chance. Always the lunge, always the feint, a drop down to the left or right, the hobnailed boots giving better purchase than wet, leather-soled Gestapo shoes and a left knee that shrieked pain every time it was moved!

Two fingers of a free hand came up to motion him in, the forefinger missing all but its second joint, the other only its first.

'*Jacquot, is it stuck?*' came a yell from above.

The hand with the knife went in and up, the arm went back and broke.

'Now you,' managed Kohler, his foot jammed down hard against the old one's neck, his right shoulder shrieking, 'or is it that I'm simply to shoot you?'

The lift hadn't moved in some time. No longer was there the smell of smoke, the sight of Charles-Frédéric Hébert or anyone else, no longer words that had echoed as they'd been called down to the cellars. *Merde*, what was he to do? wondered St-Cyr. Hermann *would* leave their torches in the car! Too impatient, too worried and distracted . . .

The cables would be old and frayed, but surely there'd be an iron ladder bolted to one side of the shaft in case of just such emergencies. Then what if Ferbrave and the others suddenly decided to lower the lift, what if the electricity was switched on?

It didn't bear thinking about. These old lifts, so many competing designs . . . roof hoists, cellar hoists, counterbalances, trips and locks to catch a falling cage if all else should fail. 'Mademoiselle,' he whispered, 'stay exactly where you are even if the lift should tilt a little. I'm going up to the floor above. A short climb, difficult perhaps, but possible, I think.'

'And hope?'

'Let's not argue. Hermann must be in trouble and will expect this of me. The others have, I believe, taken him.'

'And if they haven't?'

'You'll be certain to hear us.'

There was no difficulty in locating the hatch above and climbing out through it. Once on the roof, the Inspector seized hold of the cables. He had planted his feet firmly, Inès knew. Chunks of broken plaster must have littered the little roof. Some of these could not help but be disturbed and when they fell, she listened hard for them to hit someone in the cellars, but they did not hit anyone.

'There is no ladder,' she heard him say under his breath. 'My gloves,' he muttered. Had he left them in the lift? she wondered. Crouching down on hands and knees, and setting her case and bag aside, she began to search the floor.

'*Mademoiselle, what are you doing?*' he whispered urgently.

'The gloves,' she said. 'I can give you mine.'

'It's not necessary. I was only fussing about ruining them. Replacements are impossible.'

The sculptress moved back to her corner, the cage tilting that way a little, its guide rails worn.

'Now stay there, please,' he said. 'Everything is fine.'

Inès tried to remember lifts she'd taken in Paris. Many had gone up through the wells of spiralling staircases. Between the ages of ten and twelve, Céline and she had been fascinated by them and had often played a game of racing each other, the one taking the lift, the other the stairs, until caught, sent down by the concierge and banished for a time to walk the streets arm in arm and window-shop. Then they'd dare each other to venture in, not only to gush over the most insignificant and appallingly tasteless items, but to ask their price and try to bargain. Then they would decide to leave and, in full view of the shopkeeper, give the money to the first beggar who came along.

Céline . . .

The little light above her came on. There was a loud, metallic click, a clunk, and the pulleys began to strain, to turn as she blinked.

Terrified, Inès groped for the buttons. Must stop the lift. *I must!* she cried out to herself and began to press and then hit them with the palm of her right hand. The lift went down and down, only to suddenly stop.

Timidly she put an exploratory hand through the gate to touch the cold wall of the shaft. Again she pressed a button. Now the lift started up, only to stop. Now she pushed the button hard, and again the lift started up, only to descend and quickly come to another abrupt stop.

She hesitated, waited – pushed another of the buttons.

Down and down the lift went until at last its cage door was opened and then closed.

'Albert . . .' she said, her voice not loud or shrill, but flat and toneless as she backed away until she could no longer move.

He did not answer. He drew in a breath as he studied her. Was he puzzled? Had he been pushing the buttons too? Surely he must want to know where St-Cyr had gone?

Another breath was taken, then he gave a little sigh and the smell of him came to her.

Kohler was moving fast. He had to draw the Garde off, had to help Louis out, couldn't let them have the trumped-up, pseudo-medical file on Julienne Deschambeault either, would have to hide it and the other one some place, but where?

He had propelled the two from the lift-well partway up the main staircase and into the rest of the Garde, had run from these as they'd come thundering down into the cellars. He had gone to ground himself, but every time he entered a corridor, the lights would be thrown on and they would catch a sight of him.

Merde, if only he could find Olivier, if only Madame Ribot could have told him where that one was hiding. The old PTT? he wondered again, as he and Louis had . . . An ear constantly to the telephone lines not just from this hotel, but from the Hôtel du Parc, the Majestic and all the others. Olivier and that bank of his had financed the building and the move to a bigger, modern exchange, but was there a corridor to it, a tunnel of some kind? Old cables . . . had those been what he'd seen running along the ceiling of this corridor?

A treasure, Madame Ribot had said. A treasure.

'The baths,' he muttered, coming upon an arched, oaken door with mounted placard, as yet another light switch was found and thrown on well behind him.

The door's lock was flimsy. *Jésus, merde alors*, would it hold long enough for him to hide the files?

There was a notice on its back: *Établissement Thermal – Service Médical* ... The names of Vichy's 'medical' consultants, Raoul Normand among them ...

The towel room? he wondered.

TARIFS DES BAINS, DOUCHES ET AUTRES SERVICES ... BAIN DE CÉSAR ... Caesar's bath, 2 francs ... GRANDE DOUCHE CHAUDE ... the hot shower, 1 franc 50, PETITE DOUCHE LOCALE, 1 franc 25 ... BUVETTES ... a season's pass to all of them, the Hall des Sources, the Chomel, the Parc and Célestins, et cetera. Ten francs.

Where ... where the hell could he hide the files and not be caught with them?

Gossamer-clad maidens combed their hair or bathed in the buff as coy little half-submerged virgins beckoned to a young lad from among a mural of dark green lily pads. Blue and gold tilework paved the floor. Mustn't slip, he warned himself. Must keep going in spite of that knee of mine.

From the half-shell of a giant scallop, a life-sized marble statue of a naked girl stood on tiptoes with slender arms upraised and entwined as a bearded, ancient Neptune summoned her by blowing on a conch.

Water fell over marble bas-reliefs of romping, life-sized nymphs. Sumptuous things, gorgeous things, pure and innocent in their nakedness and completely at ease with one another among tall reeds at the bank of a river, the Nile ... Was it the Nile?

The sculptor Girardon, Louis would have said, as he had when they'd visited Versailles in the autumn of 1940, Occupier and Occupied getting to know one another. The original had been cast in lead, in 1670 or thereabouts.

'Kohler, that's enough!' cried Henri-Claude Ferbrave. 'Be reasonable. All we want are the files. We've burned the rest.'

The rest ... The rest, came the echoes. What rest? he wondered, frantically tossing his head as he looked for a way out and muttered, 'The handprints they took from Madame Ribot.' Four, five ... no, seven of the bastards were heading for him. Hard, no-nonsense sons of bitches, tough ... *mein Gott* they were tough. Charles-Frédéric Hébert was the last of them and the only one without a weapon.

The baths, separated by reclining mermaids, were surrounded on three sides by the bas-reliefs, and it was among these that the mildly effervescent water fell over pleasing thighs and breasts and gorgeous backsides to stream on to the head of a laughing nymph who playfully splashed another but seemed to mock this Kripo.

His Gestapo shoes, broken at the seams, were soaked through, his feet warm. His left sock protruded. There was a hole in its toe.

Verdammt! He was standing on the walkway between the bas-reliefs and the baths. Coursing around and over his shoes, the water gave up the smell of its sulphur, and he heard, as if in the distance, the trickling music of it and finally the gentleness of its fizzing.

Vapour rose up from the baths and for an instant he thought, Please just let me lie in one of the them, but ...

Louis ... he said silently. Louis, I tried.

The lift had descended to the cellars, its gate opening and closing, but no words had been spoken, or not that he had heard, thought St-Cyr. And as for Hermann, the Garde seemed to have vanished with him.

There were none of them in the foyer when he chanced a look over the third-floor gallery railing; none, apparently, on the staircases, rushing to overtake him; yet surely by now they must know he was no longer in the lift with the sculptress? Surely they'd want her out of the hotel and safely tucked away in her boarding house, if for no other reason than to finish things here in private? Surely Ménétrel would have insisted on that?

A cover-up, a frame-up, too, and if not the wives, as Dr Normand's file on Julienne Deschambeault had indicated and Charles-Frédéric Hébert had stated, then Blanche and Paul Varollier or Albert. And if not Albert, then Edith Pascal, and if not Edith, then Auguste-Alphonse Olivier, recluse, ex-banker, old enemy and cuckold. But had Olivier really tried to stop the murder of Céline Dupuis? Had he been right in this? She would have constituted a distinct threat to the FTP had she been taken and questioned by the Gestapo.

Hermann had found no evidence of anyone having tried to intervene. There had been no signs of Céline's having tried to get away until she had reached the Hall des Sources. Why hadn't she tried to escape beforehand, why hadn't she run?

Merde, this investigation, he swore. No time to think things through; Hermann needing him now. Hermann . . .

Albert was to have delivered a hamper to Chez Crusoe early on Tuesday evening. Some caviar, a little pâté . . . a bottle of the Bollinger Cuvée Spéciale, one also of the Rémy-Martin Louis XIII, but that hamper hadn't turned up and neither had Céline Dupuis's rucksack and handbag, only her ID, which had been left in her room for Bousquet to find.

Hébert's pocket knife – the Laguiole he had had since a boy – had been in that hamper, or so he'd stated, a reminder to the Maréchal of better days and other conquests: that of Noëlle Olivier.

Albert had left that knife in the sacristy of the château's chapel, thinking Hermann wouldn't notice the difference. He had then tried to kill the sculptress with Madame Olivier's knife, having perceived her a threat to his hero, but what threat, please? he asked himself. Herr Gessler and Herr Jännicke had vetted the girl's valise and, having satisfied themselves, had then asked her to make certain nothing had been taken.

Albert had emptied a phial, causing the case to reek of bitter almonds. The girl had been certain he had known who had killed her friend, but she couldn't be a threat to Pétain, could she? Certainly she'd been a courier, had received and delivered messages for Olivier and was, yes, like Céline had been, a distinct threat to the FTP should the Gestapo get their hands on her. A threat Olivier had naturally made no mention of, even though Edith Pascal had called him a fool for having divulged he was their leader, a man who had known beforehand everything that would happen.

Had that hamper and Albert been intercepted en route to Chez Crusoe? Had Lucie Trudel been stopped on her way back to the Hôtel d'Allier after Albert had helped her to get a bottle of the Chomel for her father?

Had Olivier, knowing full well what must happen to those girls, not intervened but waited instead, and then used the killings, particularly the two most recent, to let Bousquet and the others know their every action was being watched and that they would be called to account?

If so, then the civil war they feared had, as the sculptress had said, already begun. Cruelty would be matched by cruelty, the innocent caught between the two sides. Henri-Claude Ferbrave and the Garde, the Milice and all the others on the one hand; the Résistance on the other.

Still St-Cyr heard nothing. Timidly a door opened and a head darted out only to be withdrawn at the sight of him. Again he looked over the railing, this time letting his gaze sweep round the galleries until it came to rest on the fountain below. If the water were turned on, the dust blown away, the chandeliers lit and there were couples about, arm in arm to laughter, music and whispered tête-à-têtes, it would be so like the Vichy he had experienced as a boy. *Grand-mère* and he hadn't stayed in anything so opulent. 'A *pension* will serve us just as well, Jean-Louis,' she had said, 'but we will take our meals in nothing but the finest restaurants, if they have such establishments in this place.'

This Vichy. This tourist trap, she had finally come to call it. Aurore Irène Molinet, he reminded himself. She'd favoured Balzac, Victor Hugo and Dumas for the sheer pleasure they had brought her as a girl who'd been forbidden to read them.

'Stay close. I will awaken your eyes,' she had confided, rejoicing in the sight of so many obviously unmarried couples whose men had been old enough to have known better than to consort with girls, who certainly had known better and were often far less than half their ages.

She had introduced him to tobacco and had known full well he had taken three of her Turkish cigarettes, yet had said nothing of the theft.

She had introduced him to gambling and the Grand Casino, where the Chambre des Députés, under Laval's conniving and cajoling, had met in July 1940 to vote themselves out of office by a margin of 569 to 80, thus putting an end to the Third Republic and initiating what some had called the 'Casino Government'. She had introduced him to crime as well, for she had loved nothing better than a juicy scandal, and had avidly read the news reports of such to him, commenting at length on what had lain between the lines and the sheets. She would have had much to say about the current scandal and the murder of those girls.

And, yes, he said as he started cautiously down a far staircase, she would have agreed with Pétain's return to the soil, especially as one-third of all of France's agricultural workers were in POW camps in the Reich. But she would not have agreed with Marcel Déat, that France was and should be 'Germany's vegetable garden'. 'The Boche are savage, Jean-Louis,' she had said, referring to the Franco-Prussian War of 1870–1. 'I am going to send you to a farm near Saarbrücken to stay with distant relatives so that you will not only learn their language but how they think.'

Aurore Irène Molinet . . . Had she known then that the Boche would be back?

He hadn't thought of her since their last investigation. Once he had innocently asked her here in Vichy if her side of the family had descended from the poet and chronicler Jean Molinet, who'd been in the service of the dukes of Burgundy in the late 1400s and early 1500s.

She had answered as only she would, 'I have no patience with poets,' and that had been it. A woman – a lady – of great contrasts. One who had introduced him to absinthe and, if truth were told, had no use for the convention that had seen her strapped into a whalebone corset under widow's black.

393

But was it at moments like this that the legacy of one's past became clear, or was her ghost simply trying to tell him he must have missed something?

Louis wasn't with him. Louis hadn't backed him up. *Verdammt!* swore Kohler silently, what the hell had happened to him? Killed? he asked himself and answered, I heard no shots. Shots would have echoed down here in the cellars.

Two of the Garde were stationed at each of the far corners of the baths. Bergmanns there and no chance of a way out. Sour, still in a lot of pain and just itching to pull the trigger, the one with the broken arm now cradled it and a long-barrelled Luger with drum clip – thirty-two shots. *Merde!*

Burning sheets of paper – the files he'd taken from Dr Normand's safe – were being held up, page by page, to be released only at the last by Charles-Frédéric Hébert, their charred remains drifting slowly down until extinguished by the water that coursed around hobnailed boots. And why must that God of Louis's allow things like this to happen to honest, hard-working detectives?

Henri-Claude Ferbrave, that little gangster from the roof of the Jockey Club and the foyer of the Hôtel du Parc, now had a Schmeisser tucked under his right arm. As he lit each page, he handed it to Hébert. Disarmed, Kohler knew he could only wait it out and hope. But when the sculptress and Albert Grenier were hustled in to stand with him on the walkway between the bas-reliefs and the baths, the girl, still clutching her valise and bag, shrilled, 'The lift, monsieur. The Inspector had climbed out and was standing on it when Albert and I punched the buttons and caused it to go up and down.'

The lift . . . Ah Christ, had Louis fallen? Was he caught in the cables, torn, mangled, bleeding?

'Not there,' said one of the two who had brought the girl and Albert. 'We looked, Henri-Claude. He must have reached the third floor.'

Afraid of Ferbrave, Albert clung to the sculptress, which only made her cringe all the more. His woollen hat was pulled down, the scarf loose, the jacket of the *bleus de travail* open.

The burlap sack he held, he now released, letting it fall into the water at his feet.

'Ah *bon*, it's done,' sighed Hébert as the last of the pages was torched. 'Now there is no proof.'

'And Ménétrel will be happy, eh?' yelled Kohler.

The bushy eyebrows arched as the faded blue eyes sought him out. 'I did not kill them, Inspector. August-Alphonse Olivier did.'

'Th— That's right,' said Albert. 'Monsieur Olivier took the knife you promised you'd give me. He . . . He dropped it in the shit. I saw him.'

Saw him . . . Saw him . . .

Water coursed over naked stone thighs, releasing bubbles and catching the light as it ran to swirl around their boots.

'I took Mademoiselle Dupuis to the Hall just like I was told to,' said Albert, dragging off the hat his mother had knitted. 'I closed the doors on her and held them tight so she couldn't get out. She screamed.'

'Albert . . . Albert, she was your friend,' wept Inès.

'Not friend. *Enemy!* Pay . . . I was paid!'

Glances of alarm flew between Ferbrave and the grand-uncle. 'Albert . . .' began Hébert only to find that the string which had held the sack tightly closed had loosened. Kohler moved, yanked – dumped the bag.

Dead rats and bundles of share certificates, some of which had broken loose of their rubber bands, spilled out. Sodden, the certificates headed for the baths. Lithographed borders bore coloured scenes of Vichy and its spas, of well-dressed *curistes* strolling under parasols, the pictures of health.

'La Banque du Pays Bourbonnais-Limagne et Crédit Industriel, Commercial de Vichy,' sighed Kohler, having plucked one of the certificates out of the water. 'Bearer bonds to the tune of ten thousand francs each. Total capitalization: ten millions, dated Paris, June 1907 and worthless. Albert, tell us again how you got these.'

No one moved. The boy, the man, his tricoloured scarf trailing in the water, ducked his head towards his grand-uncle. 'I help him,' he gushed. 'I'm the best rat catcher Vichy ever had. He lets me use his chapel. I built a shrine there.'

A nest, too. 'And did you give him the rats he put in Lucie Trudel's bed?'

Albert blinked hard, grimaced and frowned deeply. 'Rats?' he blurted. 'Bed? Uncle Charles didn't *steal* my rats, did he?'

'You fool!' swore Hébert. 'Henri-Claude, shoot them. You must!'

'Messieurs ... Messieurs, a moment,' sang out a voice.

Louis ... was it really Louis?

'A few small questions. Nothing difficult.' St-Cyr held up the Lebel. 'I will leave it here on this lovely old stone bench. Excuse me,' he said to the two at that end of the bas-reliefs, and, elbowing his way past one of them, walked on. 'Charles-Frédéric Hébert,' he said, and Kohler knew that Sûreté voice, 'the pocket knife, please, that you are now forced to carry.'

The water found the Chief Inspector's shoes and rapidly soaked into them, Inès noted. He and Hébert were of about the same height, St-Cyr's shabby overcoat open, the battered fedora tilted back a little; Albert's grand-uncle still in Auvergnat black trousers, black cable-knit cardigan and boots. The hands rough, the fingers strong.

'That old pocket knife ... ?' he blurted. 'Henri-Claude, what is this? You allow him to question me when I know enough to put you in prison for life?'

'It's in your pocket, Uncle,' said Albert, wanting to be helpful.

'An Opinel, mademoiselle,' said Louis, opening the thing. 'You butchered those rats, monsieur, but first you smothered that girl and finished her off in her armoire.'

Frantic now, Hébert threw the others a look of alarm only to be met with the mask of indifference. His black felt fedora was swept off. '*Salaud! Imbécile!*' he cried. Albert cringed as the hat repeatedly swatted him. 'Auguste, you idiot. Auguste did it!'

The hat was snatched away, a wrist grabbed, the arm bent

behind Hébert's back. Water coursed and fizzed, and where it poured into the baths, it swirled the share certificates round and round.

'The foyer, I think, Hermann. Unless I'm mistaken, there will be visitors who are most anxious to hear what we have to say, since I've managed to telephone them.'

Laval hadn't just brought Ménétrel, he had insisted on Bousquet and the others being present. Honoré de Fleury, uncomfortable at being summoned and wondering what the future held, was there, as were Deschambeault and Richard. A full house, snorted Kohler silently, but *grâce à Dieu*, Madame la Maréchale and the wives hadn't been invited.

Bousquet, handsome and well dressed as always, remained a little detached from the others. Deschambeault stood near the desk; Richard and de Fleury sat on the lip of the fountain. The Garde, still armed, stood to one side with the prisoner.

Alone, Laval sat in an armchair the concierge had dragged out for him, the Premier still in his overcoat, gloves and fedora. Those black patent leather shoes of his with their grey-cloth and buttoned uppers were all too evident, as was the white necktie and, certainly, the soggy butt of the Gitane that clung to his lower lip.

The dark eyes took in everything swiftly, even to noting that among the hotel's residents, a few had timidly approached the gallery railings and were now in attendance.

'Messieurs . . .' began Louis, drawing on his pipe and then exhaling to gesture with it as he always did at such times, 'these killings, the deaths of these "flies" as you called them, Premier, occurred at a particular point in time. There was, of course, the party at the Château des Oiseaux Splendides on 24 October last, but then, suddenly, everything was lost with total Occupation on 11 November, the killings starting on 9 December with that of Mademoiselle Marie-Jacqueline Mailloux.'

He would take a moment now, thought Inès. He would let them all think about it.

'With the drowning, since quite obviously the victim was a little drunk, there could be little question among the investigating police. Death by misadventure. Later, however, my partner and I discovered what they'd failed to note: that Sandrine Richard had threatened to do just that to Mademoiselle Mailloux, and the evidence is that she and the other wives not only knew exactly where her husband's lover would be but when.'

'Get on with it!' muttered Hébert.

Laval had brought along a bottle of his own wine and a glass, but had yet to light another cigarette or take a sip.

'Ah *bon*, Monsieur Hébert,' said Louis, unruffled. 'With the second killing, that of Camille Lefèbvre, there could be no such question: she was killed with a wire, similar to that which your grand-nephew uses for his snares. Monsieur le Secrétaire Général thought himself the target and so was born the myth of a Résistance threat, one that you, Doctor, wanted sown and encouraged.'

'You'll never prove it,' snapped Ménétrel.

'I will if pressed,' countered Louis. 'Monsieur Bousquet fired two or three shots at the intruder or intruders, and then beat a hasty retreat to Paris, notifying no one of the killing.'

'I really did think the terrorists were after me,' grunted Bousquet. 'Bernard, why couldn't you have taken us into your confidence?'

'Because, Secrétaire, confidence is not the way of an *éminence grise* when plotting revenge.'

'How dare you! Pierre, how can you sit there and let him ...'

'Bernard, be quiet,' said Laval, lighting a cigarette and inhaling deeply.

'A Résistance or terrorist plot to bump off the boys,' said Louis. 'Little for my partner and me to go on in the police reports and primary autopsies. Information withheld also by each of you, damning information, but ...'

He'd let them think about that, too, thought Inès. She had chosen to sit on the edge of the fountain as far to one side as possible, but unfortunately Albert had again cosied up to her, and the Chief Inspector, though he was aware of this, had let it be.

'But,' he said, gesturing with the hand that held that pipe of his, 'certainly the killer knew where Monsieur le Secrétaire Général and his mistress would spend the night. A cabin downriver, perfect isolation, and perfect for eliminating yet another of the flies.'

'Informants. Why not call them that?' demanded Ménétrel.

Ignored . . . he'd be ignored, thought Kohler, squeezing the water out of his socks and draining each shoe. Examining the burns their last case had given him between the toes of his right foot. The Milice had done that with molten metal.

'This killer,' said Louis, 'had his or her ear so close to the ground that he or she knew of everything you'd do well before it happened.'

'Olivier,' snapped Hébert.

'We'll come to him, monsieur. But . . . but what we failed to realize is that although others might or might not know everything in each case, someone other than the killer most definitely did, and so began a tug of wills we did not see until very recently. The killer determined to kill, while this other person hesitated to intervene for fear of revealing the very ear he used.'

'You said he or she, and now use only he,' interjected Ménétrel.

'Auguste-Alphonse Olivier,' said Louis. 'With the third killing, that of Lucie Trudel, there was the possibility that someone might have stopped the girl on her way home to the Hôtel d'Allier at just after 5 a.m. I mention it only as a suggestion. We know the details of the killing, how savage it was, but had this other person, this shadow of yours, Monsieur Hébert, really tried to stop you?'

He turned away from them, began to lose himself in thought, tried this and that, arguing always. Then he said, 'I want to think he must have, but of this I am far from sure. The girl either didn't believe him or he thought it best to let her be, and allow

399

her to escape to Paris. Tragically she invited her killer to enter her room.'

'And with the fourth killing, Louis?' said Kohler. 'That of Céline Dupuis at about 10 p.m. on Tuesday, 2 February.'

'Premier, you telexed and then telephoned Gestapo Boemelburg after you had viewed the body.'

'I have it here, Louis,' said Hermann. ' "Flykiller slays mistress of high-ranking Government employee in Hall des Sources. Imperative you immediately send experienced detectives who are not from this district. Repeat, not from this district." '

'The whole business threatened to blow up in our faces,' said Laval tersely. 'A scandal – vans from the Bank of France, the girlfriends . . .'

'Informants, Pierre!' seethed Ménétrel.

'You said it, Bernard, not I who knew nothing of such a serious breach of security.'

'Messieurs, a moment more,' interjected Louis convivially. 'Had you not also telephoned Gestapo Boemelburg, Premier, we might never have realized the ear this other person had, but you did.'

'And *L'Humanité* published your name at the top of their latest list!' shouted Hébert.

'And you saw fully then, didn't you, monsieur, just how in tune that ear was? You suggested to the Doctor that the earrings and the perfume would remind the Maréchal of Noëlle Olivier; you had him tell Paul Varollier in no uncertain terms that her knife was needed. Blanche and Paul would have told you of it, *n'est-ce pas*? You then sent Albert Grenier to deliver a hamper to the dressing room at Chez Crusoe, a hamper Céline Dupuis was to have taken with her.'

'But . . . but it never got there,' muttered Albert, ''cause Edith took it from me.'

'But gave you as a little reward your uncle's pocket knife, the Laguiole he'd had since a boy.'

'Edith and Olivier let the other side know they were on to what would happen, Louis,' said Hermann sadly. 'Albert waited on that balcony for Céline, and she went with him willingly enough, since you told her, didn't you, Albert, that Monsieur Olivier wanted her to go to the Hall?'

'And would ... would take her to safety,' said Inès.

'They did not intervene,' said Louis. 'You see, by then Edith had told Auguste-Alphonse that Charles-Frédéric must have realized where this ear was hidden.'

'Where?' asked Laval.

'A moment, Monsieur le Premier. You were not the only person able to duck into the Hall to view the corpse. Monsieur Olivier also did, but the beam of his torch gave him away as he tried to unscrew the second earring and ...'

'He removed the knife, Louis, and then dropped it into the outhouse for Albert to find, because Albert had seen him.'

'But not leaving the matchstick V for Victory, Hermann. If it had been present at 5 a.m. or thereabouts on Wednesday, he'd have taken it.'

'Then that one left it. The doctor, Louis, when he pronounced her dead and saw an end to the four informants.'

'Just as our killer left the cigar band on the counter of the Buvette du Parc, knowing his grand-nephew would be sure to find and wear it and that we'd notice this.'

'Giving us suspects and suspects so that we would have to sort through them to find the one they wanted us to arrest,' said Kohler.

'The identity card is left for you to find, Secrétaire, and later, the dress, the sapphires and letters for Hermann and myself – Edith Pascal perhaps, or Olivier himself. Both sides were desperately working against each other, the one to hide who the real killer was, the other to lead us to him.'

'And the location of this "ear"?' asked Laval.

'The old PTT next door,' said St-Cyr. 'Switchboard lines to the Hôtel du Parc and other hotels and places have been reconnected. That is why I telephoned you, Premier. To test the theory.'

'And warn him!' shouted Ferbrave, as he and the Garde swept

out, leaving them in a cold draught that blew in through the front entrance.

'They'll find nothing,' spat Hébert, 'because you let him go.'

'Not at all, monsieur. I had no choice but to telephone Monsieur le Premier and Dr Ménétrel, and it was only as I did so that I realized there were two of you who knew everything beforehand and that I might well have let the other side know. You had your information from the doctor; Olivier, from yours and his telephone conversations, and those of others, including the wives and Madame la Maréchale.'

'Auguste always was a hands-on administrator. When he pushed through the new PTT, he took an active interest in everything, even to forming a separate company of his own to acquire the old building.'

'Which, due to the Depression of the 1930s, has, perhaps, remained vacant.'

'Not at all, but the old cables still run through its cellars.'

'And he tapped into them?'

'Yes!'

'Inspectors, is there anything else we need to know?' asked Laval, filling his glass and testing the wine's bouquet, before raising the glass not to them, but to Madame Ribot, who leaned on the gallery railing so far above them.

'She predicted I would find my answer in two visitors from Paris,' said Laval grinning appreciatively, 'and as with so many things, her advice was good. Bernard, enough said. We all know you wouldn't have asked anyone to kill them, but would merely have voiced your intense displeasure at the horrendous breach of security they represented. Please don't forget we've a briefing with his lordship tomorrow morning. Gentlemen, this affair is over. No reports are necessary, and everything you have learned is to be kept in absolute secrecy.'

Even though the gallery audience must have heard it and would be certain to spread the word!

'And me?' demanded Hébert. 'What is to become of me?'

402

'That,' said Laval, flinging his cigarette away, 'I leave entirely to your mentor in the fond hope that he won't screw up again.'

At the sound of the Premier's armoured car starting up, Ferbrave returned with Céline Dupuis's rucksack and bag, and a pencilled note: *Station closed until spring.*

'Until the invasion comes and the Occupier is kicked out, Louis.'

Everyone knew the saying, but would it ever come? Olivier and Edith would have left town, gone underground, whatever. With total occupation and a Government of zero influence, the listening post had served its usefulness. For it to have operated from the autumn of 1940, no doubt, seemed enough.

Everything had been done to let the other side know Monsieur Olivier was aware of what they were up to, but had he tried to intervene or had he let it all happen to shield himself and his source? wondered Inès, but couldn't bring herself to ask.

When a burst of gunfire came to them from the street, she knew that Henri-Claude Ferbrave and Dr Ménétrel had not let the killer survive but had told him to run.

The baths at the Hôtel Ruhl were heaven. Drained, cleaned and replenished, the warm and mildly effervescent water soothed an aching right shoulder and left knee, but was it salve to Louis's troubled conscience? wondered Kohler.

'Shot while attempting to escape,' he said. 'We'll have to leave it at that, Louis. If we object, Ménétrel will only accuse you of warning Olivier to get clear.'

The doctor would do it, too, but still ... Pétain would be taking his breakfast behind that screen of his in the Majestic's Chante Clair Restaurant, the Government's ministers, their wives and families, et cetera, sipping their *café au lait ou noir* and picking at their hot buttered croissants ...

'A meeting,' muttered St-Cyr, lying flat out in the bath.

'Admit it, we've done what we had to. Relax.'

The sculptress had been taken to her boarding house where she would have spent the rest of the night. She'd have caught an early bus, would be sitting in the foyer, waiting for the great one to eat and get his briefing over.

'Nine-fifty,' murmured Hermann dreamily. 'My bones feel like rubber, Louis. No pain, no aches, every joint in my body loose and relaxed.'

They'd been left alone in their little stew. It was now 9.30 a.m. Saturday, 6 February. The midday train to Paris didn't leave until 1 p.m., if they were lucky and it was on time.

Would the sculptress book another sleeper, a girl who had no money to spare?

'Did Olivier really let the killings happen, Hermann? Am I right in this? I have to feel he did. I tell myself that the Résistance, because of circumstance, can't be free of such implications, that there is still unfinished business also, and that Albert Grenier was right about our sculptress, and that Inès Charpentier feels she has been betrayed.'

'The smell of bitter almonds,' hazarded Kohler. 'Gessler did vet the thing.'

'*Plastic* ... could it have been from that?'

Cyclonite did smell almondy but Nobel 808 reeked of bitter almonds so much one inevitably got a hell of a headache when using it. 'A timer ... A pocket watch and battery. It would have to have been a watch, Louis. Those time-pencils the British are dropping to the Résistance freeze up in the cold.'

'And are delayed by hours. Their acid does not work as quickly when the bulb is squeezed and broken to release it on to the wire that holds the spring back, until that is freed and the pin strikes the detonator.'

'A watch, then,' said Kohler. 'And blocks of 808 embedded in a sculptress's beeswax. Accessed while left in the elder Grenier's care and updated last night at her boarding house, the kid not knowing a thing about it. Surely Olivier wouldn't do that to one of his own?'

Who knew too much and was the only person who could, in all innocence, carry a valise into a meeting to show the Maréchal the portrait mask she had completed?

404

'They'll all be at that briefing, Hermann. Laval, Bousquet, Richard, Deschambeault, the others, too, and Ménétrel. People will say she had good reason, that Pétain had given the order to have her father shot.'

'Hurry, Louis. We've got to hurry!'

Trousers wouldn't pull on easily over wet legs. Shirts refused to be buttoned; shoes were complicated, wet and troublesome, especially if their laces were broken and had been knotted too many times.

The goddamned car wouldn't start! Ten degrees of frost was in the air, the sun still struggling to rise as they ran, came to the rue du Casino, cut into the Parc des Sources through the snow, found the covered iron promenade and tried . . . tried to reach the Hôtel du Parc before it happened . . . it happened.

They skidded into the Majestic and among the tables, knocking diners aside, raising their voices to drown complaints. '*Out! Get out! Explosives! A bomb!*'

Coffee cups shattered, plates shattered. A few people screamed, the screen went over; the kid, startled, looked up from that mask of hers, of Pétain, the blush of health on its cheeks, china-blue eyes . . . surgical glass eyes. Ferbrave intruding . . . trying to stop them.

'The valise. Here, take it!' cried Kohler, shoving it into the bastard's hands. 'Run! For God's sake run!'

'Messieurs . . .' began the sculptress, only to be told, 'You left your valise unattended in the cellars of the Hôtel du Parc yesterday, mademoiselle. You couldn't have known the Résistance got at it. Even Gestapo Gessler didn't find the bomb!'

The windows shattered. Glass rained inwards, pieces and pieces of coloured glass, the stench of cordite and plaster, of stone dust too.

Kohler caught and dragged her down as Louis fell. Blood spattered the tablecloth and the Maréchal's brow. '*Merde!*' exclaimed Pétain. 'It's exactly as it was at Verdun!' And hadn't Madame Ribot predicted just such a thing?

The shrieks, the accusations, denials, threats and counterthreats were now over.

Subdued, still very much in terror of being arrested, Inès stood on the platform a little to one side of the detectives. The train, though agonizingly late, had finally arrived but it could not and would not be allowed to leave until Laval had spoken to them. A fag end glued to his lower lip, the Premier hurried towards them.

'Ah *bon*,' he said, 'and in the nick of time, eh?' Meaning their arrival at the Chante Clair.

'Premier . . .' began Louis, only to be silenced by an upraised hand.

'Mademoiselle,' he said to Inès, 'you make a mask of the Maréchal, and it blows up nearly killing all of us. Herr Gessler continues to have serious doubts about you, but is forced to admit that he and Herr Jännicke examined that valise of yours, while I . . .'

'Premier, she could not have known of the bomb,' insisted Louis.

'She was cheated, had mistakenly bought a phial of bitter almond instead of one of cloves. For . . . for the toothache, you understand.'

'But Albert had a look, Premier,' said Kohler.

'He spilled almost all of it,' muttered Inès hesitantly.

'Olivier also had ample opportunity to get at that case,' said Louis.

'My valise . . .' wept Inès. She had let Monsieur Olivier open it, had shown him the portrait mask but . . . but dare not say anything of this. 'Céline . . . Céline and others knew I always carried my first-aid kit in it.'

'But by the time the bomb was planted in blocks of beeswax to replace your own, mademoiselle,' said Louis, 'it would not have mattered, since Albert had, by spilling that phial, done the necessary to divert us all from the smell of the Nobel 808.'

Had he been told to do so? wondered Inès. Had he?

'*Peut-être*,' muttered Laval. Should he have this girl arrested?

406

One whose life was still ahead of her? 'Go then. Take her with you. Ah! I almost forgot.'

Digging into his overcoat pocket, he pulled out the telegram he had received from Gestapo Boemelburg in Paris, and handed it over.

'"*Karneval*," Hermann. "*Kolmar*. Contact Kommandant Rasche. Hangings, Stalag III *Elsass*. Heil Hitler."'

Alsace and what was now the Reich. Louis would have to cross the frontier. He'd have no authority there, would ...

'A POW camp, Louis. A little warning of Boemelburg's for us to keep quiet about things here or else.'

But what kind of *Carnival*? wondered St-Cyr, looking up to that God of his. What kind of a warning? Paris ... they'd both wanted desperately to get back to Paris.

Rasche ... Hadn't he heard that name before? wondered Kohler, not liking the thought but conscious of Louis. 'Maybe this Kommandant won't keep us too long, *mon vieux*,' he said, the memories flooding over him like ice-cold spa water, for not only did he damned well know who Rasche was, he'd spent nearly two years in such camps, had learned to speak and write French while there, hadn't known how useful it would become.

The Premier handed the chief inspector a packet of Gitanes and, tipping his hat, grunted, *À bon chat, bon rat, mes amis*. Tit for tat. One good turn deserves another. *Au revoir*, mademoiselle. A safe journey.'*

Through the soot-streaked windows of their compartment, Inès watched as Monsieur le Premier shouldered his way along the platform, to finally disappear from view. St-Cyr had lighted a cigarette – one only – and sensing, she surmised, that it was a moment he and his partner must share, had passed it to Herr Kohler.

Two men from opposite sides of this war, thrown together by chance and common crime, Inès told herself, and taking a pencil and paper from her handbag, sketched the two of them as they were. No smiles, each so different, yet both grave with concern for the other and this new task, their respective loved ones also, and for what would happen to them and to France when spring finally came.

Tue-mouches – Flykiller – was the *nom codé*, the code name, of the *résistant* Jean Schellnenberger, who was captured, interrogated and then shot in Dijon in 1942.